THE
BISLEY
WOOD
MURDERS

An absolutely gripping mystery and suspense thriller

BIBA PEARCE

Detective Rob Miller Mysteries Book 3

Originally published as
Righteous Anger

JOFFE
BOOKS

Revised edition 2021
Joffe Books, London
www.joffebooks.com

First published in Great Britain in 2020
as *Righteous Anger*

Cover art by Nebojsa Zorić

ISBN: 978-1-78931-863-0

PROLOGUE

The Shepherd carried the body of the young girl into the clearing.

It was a beautiful afternoon. The sun-dappled leaves cast flickering shadows on the ground, tall trees stretched up into the clear blue sky as if standing to attention, and as he walked, he inhaled the heady scent of wildflowers, underscored by the earthy smell of decomposing leaves.

The only sounds breaking the idyllic silence were his own boots crunching on broken twigs and pine needles, and the odd squirrel rustling in the branches above.

It was a perfect day for the burial.

He laid his young victim down on the leaf-strewn ground, her dark hair haloing out around her like an avenging angel. Standing up, he admired her for a moment. Her skin was so pale, almost alabaster in the muted sunlight. The faint blush that had once stained her cheeks was long gone, but so was the pain and fear that had scarred her eyes. She was at peace now. No one would ever harm her again.

A surge of something close to happiness rose in his chest and he gasped with the sudden intensity of it. It was the feeling he'd got when he'd helped his dear friend find peace, so many years ago. He'd forgotten how good it felt, like he'd done something noble, something righteous — he'd righted a wrong and ended someone's suffering.

Shaking with adrenalin, he picked up the spade and began to dig. He'd found the perfect spot to lay her to rest. Under an ancient oak tree, surrounded by nature, rimmed by cornflowers and meadowsweet that would soon cover the grave, their pretty flowers her only marker.

It was hard, back-breaking work. He hadn't done anything so strenuous in a long time. Still, it was worth it. For her.

An hour later, he stopped and wiped the sweat from his brow. Was it deep enough? He didn't want the foxes to get at her. She would decompose naturally, become one with the earth, as God intended.

He dug on, just a little more, to make sure. Then he smoothed over the bottom, patting it down with his hands. He gathered some leaves and spread them over the flattened earth, creating a verdant mattress on which she would lie.

Then, ever so gently, he lowered her into the grave.

"Sleep well, my love," he whispered, placing her hands onto her chest as if in prayer. A leaf swept down from an overhead branch and landed across her just-parted lips. The woods were already claiming her as their own.

He removed it, then took a fold-up comb out of his trouser pocket and arranged her hair over her shoulders, brushing it to a high gloss. Then he secured it at her temples with two sparkling blue clips. They had glitter on them, just like *she'd* had. Leaning forward, he kissed her cool forehead for the last time, then climbed out of the grave.

He removed a linen sheet from his backpack. He shook it out and watched it billow above her, before lowering it over the body. He blinked at the sudden loss of her image, then bent down and tucked it around her.

Covering her up again didn't take long. As the first crumbs of dirt fell on the sheet, he began to pray.

"*The Lord is my shepherd; I shall not want. He makes me lie down in green pastures; he leads me beside quiet waters. He restores my soul. He guides me in paths of righteousness for his name's sake. Even though I walk through the valley of the shadow of death, I will fear no evil, for you are with me; your rod and your staff, they comfort me."*

He finished reciting the psalm as he filled in the grave. He tried to make it look natural, even throwing some more leaves and twigs on top. It wouldn't fool anyone looking, but then no one knew she'd be buried here, less than a mile from where she'd been taken a fortnight ago.

He'd waited until the furore had quietened down, keeping her safe in the shed on his allotment. No one had thought to ask him. Why would they? He was nobody. Most people walked past him on the street without batting an eyelid. He was the grey man.

But inside, he was a seething, red-hot mass of righteous anger. A saviour. The Shepherd. That's what he called himself when the darkness threatened to overwhelm him. He led the little children into the light. Delivered them at the right hand of the Lord.

He packed up his backpack and swung it onto his back, carrying the shovel in his hand. His car wasn't far away. Glancing back, he made sure he hadn't left anything behind, nothing that would point the authorities to the burial place.

It was clear. Whistling a tune, he strolled back to the car.

There was one more thing he needed to do. He drove the two miles into Bisley, the closest village to where she was buried, and pulled over outside the parish church. The sun had begun its descent, but it was still very warm, and he was sticky from the hard work. It would have been preferable to have gone home first and changed, but this couldn't wait.

He entered the tranquil confines of the proud stone church. A recent refurb had seen the scratched wooden floors replaced with shiny fresh beams, and new lighting installations meant it wasn't as dark as it used to be. He preferred it the old way.

He made his way quickly down to the pews at the front. Here he veered to the right and knelt in the front row. He prayed feverishly for about ten minutes, then feeling rather lightheaded, stood up and moved, unnoticed, to the side aisle, where he lit a candle in remembrance.

There.

He watched it flicker for a moment, then turned away, walked quietly up the aisle to the front door and exited the church.

CHAPTER 1

Lisa Wells slumped down at the kitchen table and stared into her cup of tea. Was it only Tuesday? She'd overslept and it had been a mad rush to get Katie off for school. The poor lass had just had time to scoff down a slice of toast before Lisa had kissed her on the forehead, handed her her pink rucksack and shoved her out the door. Her friend Candy would have been waiting at the corner to walk to school together.

Her neighbour, Margo, said Katie was too young to walk to school without supervision. Was eleven too young? In her day, she'd caught the local bus to school from age ten. Besides, Katie had a friend with her. The two girls were besties and hung out together all the time. That reminded her, she must phone Candy's mother and invite them round for an early supper on Friday. The girls could watch a movie while she and Nelly had a glass of wine and a natter in the kitchen.

She wrapped her hands around the mug and forced her brain into gear. She was still groggy from the sleeping pill she'd taken last night. Bloody Brian. How could one man cause her so much anxiety? Imagine calling her a bad mother, just because she'd moved on and he hadn't. Prick. It wasn't her fault he didn't have a life.

A rush of sadness swept over her. *They* had been his whole life — her and Katie. He'd told her that once, soon after their daughter was born. Now they were at loggerheads, screaming at each other whenever they met. They hadn't had a civil conversation in months. How had it all gone so terribly wrong?

She shook her head and gulped down her tea. Twenty minutes until she had to leave for work. God, she was tired.

She put the cup in the sink and went upstairs to get changed. Luckily, her job was nearby in Barnes Village. She enjoyed the walk, especially on days like today, with the sun already up and the blue sky joyfully promising a warm June day.

She pulled on her skirt and blouse, freshly pressed the night before, and ran a brush through her hair. It was still luscious and thick, although grey strands were starting to show. That was Brian's fault. They'd only popped up in the last year since he'd moved out.

She sprayed a touch of perfume on her wrists and checked her appearance. Not great, but it would do. The old-age charity where she worked didn't require her to be immaculate. She wasn't client-facing, after all. Her jurisdiction was the office at the back, where she did the accounts.

It wasn't where she'd seen herself five years ago, but it was a decent, steady job and the hours suited her. She worked from nine thirty to three, which meant she was able to pick Katie up after school. Not many working parents could say the same. And it was close by.

She was about to leave the house when the telephone rang. She frowned. Hardly anyone called her on the home phone these days. Only the doctor, the electric company and the school. They always tried her landline first, then reverted to mobile if there was no answer. She put the keys back down on the side cabinet and slid her handbag over her shoulder. "Hello?"

"Mrs Wells? This is Bianca, the receptionist at Barnes Prep. I'm just phoning to find out if Katie is sick today."

6

"What?"

There was a moment when time stopped. All she could hear was her heart pounding in her ears. "No, she's not. She left for school over half an hour ago."

A pause. "Oh, I see. Well, she hasn't arrived."

"There must be some mistake. I saw her off myself. Is Candy there?" She held her breath.

"Yes, Candice is here."

Thank God. "Well, Katie must be there. They always walk together."

"I know they usually do, but Candy arrived by herself this morning. I know because the teacher at the gate was surprised to see her by herself."

The pounding grew louder.

"She arrived alone?"

"Yes."

There was an awkward pause. Lisa dropped her handbag to the floor and leaned against the wall. She felt sick.

"Mrs Wells, might I suggest you inform the police. I don't want to alarm you, but she's definitely not here. She may have got lost, but the police should be informed."

"Oh, God," Lisa whispered. "I've got to go."

She hung up and immediately dialled Brian's number. It rang for ages before he eventually picked up. "Brian, is she with you?"

"What? Who?"

"Katie. Is she with you?"

"No, why would she be with me? Isn't it a school day?"

A sob escaped her. "She isn't there."

"Lisa, what do you mean 'she isn't there'?" But Lisa couldn't speak. Great gasps wracked her body as she tried not to panic. It didn't work.

Oh, God. Oh, God. Please, let her be okay.

"Lisa, what's going on?" he demanded, his voice rising.

"She's missing," Lisa croaked out. "She left here but didn't arrive at school. They've just rung me."

"What?" He was shouting now. It was too much. Lisa burst into tears and slid down the wall, all the energy draining out of her.

"Where is she, Brian? If she's not at school and she's not with you . . . where is she?"

"I'm coming over."

The line went dead.

CHAPTER 2

When Acting Detective Chief Inspector Rob Miller arrived at the house in Barnes, West London, he was confronted by a scene of utter chaos. Lisa Wells, the child's mother, was inconsolable. Her cheeks were bright red, and she was panting like she'd run a marathon, while simultaneously screaming at a man he assumed was her husband.

He grimaced. Only a husband and wife could fight like that.

"It's not my fault," she cried. "She always walks to school with Candy."

"You should have checked." He had his hands on his hips, his shoulders forward in a classic intimidation stance. "You let her leave the house alone. She's eleven, for Christ's sake. What were you thinking?"

Lisa shook her head. "You're not listening to me. She was *meeting* Candy."

"Up late with the construction worker, were you? Is that why you couldn't be bothered to take your own daughter to school?"

"Fuck you, Brian. I didn't see Sergio last night."

"Liar." His face twisted with rage. "I know he was here. I saw his car."

"Oh, so you're spying on me now?"

"Someone's got to make sure Katie is safe, because it isn't going to be you, clearly."

Lisa's hands balled into fists.

Rob glanced at Mallory, who gave a brief nod. They had to find out who Candy and Sergio were, and dissolve this situation before these two went for each other.

"Good morning. I'm DCI Miller and this is DI Mallory. You reported your daughter missing?"

His presence acted like a bucket of cold water, and the feuding parents recoiled from each other and turned to face him. Lisa's eyes were glazed and zombie-like, while her husband's were hot and accusatory.

The two coppers who'd responded to the call from dispatch had walked the route Katie would have taken to school, accompanied by the frantic Mrs Wells, just to check she hadn't got lost or distracted — there was a small park on the way — but there was no sign of her. Concerned, they'd called in the Major Investigation Team. It was starting to look like an abduction.

Mallory took the father aside, while Rob led the distraught mother into the house. "Let's sit down and you can tell me what happened."

She sniffed and rubbed her hands on her skirt. Dirt smudged across the material. Her blouse was damp under the armpits and she smelled of sweat and fear.

"Right, let's start at the beginning." He moved a pile of charcoal sketches aside and placed his phone on the table. "Do you mind if I record this conversation? I don't want to miss anything." Unlike Mallory, he couldn't remember every little detail.

She nodded, her hands clenched together. Her whole body was taut with strain and she kept gnawing on her lower lip. This woman was barely holding it together.

"Okay, what time did Katie leave for school?"

"Eight forty," she replied immediately. "I remember because we were running late."

"Does she have a mobile phone?"

"Y—yes, but it's switched off. I've tried ringing her several times."

Rob took the number down and immediately texted it to DS Will Freemont, a member of his team. He'd triangulate it and see if he could pick up her signal.

He said as much to Lisa, who nodded but kept biting her lip.

"You said you were running late," Rob continued. "Was there any particular reason?"

Her gaze dropped to the floor. "I overslept — I haven't been sleeping well lately — and had to rush her. I sent her off without a proper goodbye." Tears filled her eyes.

That was tough. Rob felt her guilt from across the table. She blamed herself for her daughter going missing. "Why aren't you sleeping well?" he enquired.

"What?" She seemed confused. "Why is that important?"

"Please, if you could just answer the question."

Her shoulders sank in a defeated sigh. "My husband, Brian, and I are having problems. We're getting divorced. He wants custody of Katie."

Rob studied her for a long moment. She wasn't an unattractive woman, although right now she looked awful. Eyes puffy and glazed, face pasty-white, with the make-up she'd applied this morning smeared all over it.

Under normal circumstances, he imagined she'd be rather striking. Her hair was rich and glossy, despite its current wild state, her eyes a soft, cornflower blue, and it was obvious she took care of herself. He glanced at her expertly manicured fingernails with their little white tips, showing up against her dirty hands.

Barnes was a small village situated in the borough of Richmond upon Thames and positioned snugly in a bend of the river. The "Barnes Trail", a circular walk taking in the riverside and local woodland, was popular with locals and visitors alike, and Rob remembered jogging along it when he'd first arrived in the area. That was back in the days when he still had the time and inclination to exercise. Now, most of his free time was spent poring over case notes in his armchair at home, his Labrador, Trigger, at his feet, or with Jo.

"And you want Katie to live with you?"

Her gaze rose to meet him. "Of course. She's my baby girl. I'd be lost without her."

They could delve into the court proceedings at a later stage. Right now, time was of the essence, so he pushed on. "Then what happened? You saw her off and she walked down the street to meet her friend. Is that right?"

A sob. "That's what I thought, but Candy must have gone on ahead. Katie was ten minutes later than usual. They normally meet on the corner at eight thirty."

"Does Candy live nearby?"

She nodded. "In the next street."

"And you've confirmed Candy is at school today?"

"Yes, she arrived by herself." She took a shuddering breath. "Shouldn't you be out looking for my daughter rather than sitting here questioning me? I don't know what else I can tell you."

"We have people out looking for her," he assured her.

"I thought she might have gone down to the river," she stammered. "She likes it there. The gate to the nature reserve is on the way to school."

"Do they often go there before school?"

She shook her head, her eyes glistening with new tears. "No, not normally. They've been told not to. But I take her after school sometimes. She loves to walk along the water at the old reservoir." A sob caught in her throat and she stopped talking.

Rob could only imagine what she was going through. He didn't have children, but there couldn't be anything worse than not knowing what had happened, or was happening, to them. *He* didn't even want to think about it.

"Mrs Wells." His voice softened. "Is there anyone who would want to hurt Katie?"

Her eyes grew wide. He could see the panic in them.

"I'm sorry, I have to cover all bases." Some questions were hard to hear.

She stiffened. "No, why would anyone want to hurt Katie?"

"To get back at you, perhaps?"

"You mean Brian?" Her voice dropped to a whisper. "No, Brian loves Katie. He would never hurt her. Not even to get back at me."

Rob nodded. "Okay, and what about Sergio?"

She stared at him. "Sergio has nothing to do with this."

"Are you in a relationship with him?"

She went very still. "Yes, but it's nothing serious. It's more of a physical thing than anything else."

"How long has it been going on?" he asked evenly. No judgement, just the facts.

She fingered the corners of the charcoal sketches. "About four months."

"And how was he around your daughter?"

"Fine."

She traced her finger over one of the drawings. It was of a woman standing in front of an open window, smoking a cigarette. She wore suspenders and high heels and nothing else. The lines were smooth, and the elegant curves of the woman's body drew the eye. The artist had skill, even he could see that. He wondered if they were hers.

She glanced up. "He adores Katie. Sergio is a decent man. I wouldn't bring just anyone home."

"Of course. Well, we still need to talk to him," Rob insisted. "If you could give us his contact details."

Her lip quivered. "I was lonely. It's hard being a single parent, you know?"

Rob didn't know, but he nodded anyway.

"Brian left a year ago," she continued, "when Katie was ten. He — *we* argued all the time. It was better that he go."

"What did you argue about?" asked Rob.

"Money, mostly. And about me going back to work. Brian thought I should stay at home and look after Katie."

She gulped. "Maybe he was right. If I'd been in less of a rush, I might have walked with her to school. Maybe this would never have happened." Her voice cracked and her knuckles grew white as she tried to control her emotions.

"You can't blame yourself," he said soothingly, not that she was listening. "If only" was a game they all played. He'd seen it many times with grieving relatives. *If only I'd come home sooner, if only I hadn't left her alone, if only . . .* "Let's try and focus on where she might have gone, okay?"

"She wouldn't have gone anywhere. She was on her way to school."

"You mentioned the nature reserve. What about the park? Or a shop?"

"Not if she was running late," Lisa insisted. "She'd have gone straight there. The school is only down the road."

"Is that Barnes Prep?"

"Yes."

They were just finishing up when a door slammed and Brian Wells could be heard shouting, "What the hell are you doing here?"

CHAPTER 3

"That's Sergio," Lisa whispered, stricken. "Oh, God. I hope Brian doesn't hurt him."

Rob got to his feet. That was handy. He wanted to meet the new lover and gauge the interaction between him and the soon-to-be ex-husband. He hadn't ruled anyone out yet. Both men would have had time to grab Katie and hide her somewhere before coming to the house. Or worse. One of them could even be a killer. When kids went missing, it was usually someone they knew, most likely a relative or a friend of the family.

Mallory had positioned himself between the two men, but he wasn't happy about it. His usually serious face was etched with worry. Mallory, recently promoted to detective inspector, wasn't the most physical of men, and if they went for each other, he'd have a hard time pulling them apart.

"What's going on here?" asked Rob, entering the lounge. He put on his booming policeman voice, a trick he'd learned from Detective Chief Superintendent Sam Lawrence. An intimidating presence was a useful tool for a police detective, particularly in these situations.

Lisa flew into Sergio's arms.

Nothing serious, eh? Rob checked him out. A construction worker, Brian had said. He certainly looked the part. Stocky, with a rugged, outdoor complexion and brawny arms capable of carrying large blocks of concrete up ladders. He could see why Lisa might find him attractive. Paint-stained denim jeans and a white T-shirt completed the look.

"*That* man is not welcome in my house," snapped Brian.

"It's not your house," Lisa retorted.

"I still own it," he retaliated.

"Are you all right?" Sergio ignored Brian and wrapped a beefy arm around Lisa's shoulders. He sounded Eastern European, Polish maybe.

"Mr . . . ?"

"Wójcik," replied Sergio, holding out a grubby hand. "I am a friend of Lisa's."

Brian snorted.

Rob caught Mallory's eye and gestured to the door. It was time for the husband to leave. They had his details and would talk to him again, along with possibly searching his premises. But right now, they needed to diffuse this pressure cooker of a situation. A girl was missing and every second counted.

Rob shook the man's extended hand. "How did you know to come here?"

"Lisa texted me."

Lisa was still clutching his other arm like it was the only thing holding her up. She bit her lip and nodded.

"Okay. Well, since you're here, maybe you can answer a few questions."

"Sure."

Nothing in his demeanour aroused Rob's immediate suspicions, but that didn't mean squat. Some of the worst killers were the best liars.

"When did you last see Katie?"

"Katie?" He seemed surprised by the question. "I saw Lisa last night, but Katie was already asleep when I came round."

"When was that?"

"I arrived at nine."

"And how long did you stay?" He met the man's gaze head on.

There wasn't a flicker of hesitation. "A few hours."

Lisa nodded. "That's right, he left just before midnight."

"And did you check on Katie before you went to bed?" This was directed at Lisa.

"Of course. I always check on her before I go to sleep."

Something in her manner gave Rob pause. It was guilt. Had she been too tired to check on her daughter? After all, her lover had been here. But that wasn't a crime.

It struck him that they only had her word for it that her daughter had left for school that morning. As awful as it sounded, the two lovers could have got rid of Katie the night before, then concocted this plan to avoid suspicion falling on themselves.

While he wanted to believe her, he knew from experience that the most impassioned plea could be fabricated. He glanced around the kitchen, looking for clues. There was an empty mug of tea on the table, but no cereal bowls and nothing in the sink. If she'd been in a rush like she'd claimed, she wouldn't have had time to wash the dishes before leaving for work. Was there any proof that Katie had actually been in the house this morning?

"Where do you live, Mr Wójcik?"

"Mortlake."

Not far from Barnes, also in the Richmond borough. "Can anyone confirm you were at home this morning?"

Sergio looked stunned for a second, then recovered himself. "Um, yeah. My neighbour, Bill, saw me leaving to come here. And I called work to tell them I'd be late."

There were no outward signs that he was lying, but Rob never took anyone at face value. Useful habit or occupational hazard? He wasn't sure.

Right, it was time to kick this investigation up a notch. He glanced at his phone, just to be sure. No messages. Shit. That meant they hadn't found anything.

Leaving Sergio and Lisa in the house, he walked outside. Mallory was talking to an officer holding a large clipboard. His job was to record everyone who entered or left the premises.

"What did the husband say?" Rob asked.

Mallory turned to face him. "He hadn't seen his daughter since the weekend. They spend every second one together."

"Did you believe him?"

Mallory shrugged. "Hard to say. He's pretty angry, which could mask his guilt. I've sent a team round to his house to do a spot search."

In situations like this, when a child's life was on the line, a warrant wasn't strictly necessary. It was the lead detective's call, and Rob had the utmost faith in his DS. It was yet another indication that the rapidly promoted detective was ready to lead his own investigation.

"Good move," Rob said. "We should do the same here, and at the boyfriend's place. It's been less than an hour since she went missing — there's still time."

Mallory gave a succinct nod. He knew, as Rob did, that the first few hours were crucial if they hoped to find Katie Wells alive.

"Let's get eyes in the sky," he continued. "I'm launching a full-scale alert."

Mallory got on the phone while Rob called the control centre and asked for an update. As expected, they'd found nothing during the preliminary search.

It was time to get serious. He rang DCS Lawrence and told him they had a kidnapped girl and needed to act fast. There was no doubt in his mind that she was at risk.

"Christ, Rob. Really?" After the highly publicised Surrey Stalker case, followed by the equally macabre revenge killings earlier in the year, the chief super did not need another media shitstorm. Especially since he was retiring at the end of the year.

"'Fraid so, sir. I've ordered a helicopter and the K-9 unit is on its way. Maybe we can pick up her trail. I've also authorised searches on the primary residence and that of the ex-husband and boyfriend."

"No ransom demand?"

"Nothing yet."

"Okay. Keep me posted."

"Will do."

He hung up. It was full steam ahead. Rob mentally checked off his to-do list: Katie's phone. Search the premises. CCTV. Speak to the best friend.

"Let's head back to the station," he barked. First, he had to brief the team and get the ball rolling.

Mallory fell into step beside him. "Helicopter's ETA is twelve minutes."

Rob updated the sergeant with the clipboard. "A search team will be here soon. And for God's sake, don't let Brian Wells back inside. Point him in my direction if he has any questions concerning the investigation." The husband had struck him as a hothead and all that pent-up aggression he harboured towards his soon-to-be ex-wife and her lover would only complicate matters. They didn't need to add an assault charge to the mix.

As they drove away, Rob stared at the dense vegetation in the Barnes nature reserve and at the River Thames as it wound lazily towards Richmond.

"Hang in there, Katie," he muttered. "We're coming for you."

CHAPTER 4

DCI Rob Miller strode into the office at the Major Investigation Team's headquarters in Putney. "Can I have everyone's attention, please?"

Computer keyboards fell silent, heads glanced up and the general office murmur quietened down. Even the printer spewed out one last page then ceased its output.

His voice carried over the heads of his colleagues. "We have a missing person and we're going to need all hands on deck with this one."

The Major Crime Team, as they were informally known, consisted of twenty-one detectives, two constables and four police staff, all overseen by DCS Sam Lawrence, a beast of a man in his fifties with a booming voice that could lead troops into battle.

They had one DCI, a burly Scot named Galbraith, who was currently sunning it up in Tenerife with his wife. For that reason, Rob had been temporarily promoted to acting DCI. Galbraith's team was present, however, and Rob planned to put them to good use.

Mallory had already darted into the briefing room and wheeled out the whiteboard that they used for presentations. The glass-enclosed briefing rooms might have looked impressive, but they didn't allow for more than a dozen officers at a time.

DCS Lawrence emerged from his fishbowl and stood at the back, his hulking, silent presence a stark reminder of how grave the situation was.

Rob filled them in on the details. "Eleven-year-old Katie Wells went missing on her way to school in Barnes this morning. Her mother, Lisa Wells, saw her off at 8.40 a.m., but the school called at 9.20 a.m. to find out if Katie was unwell. The friend who she usually walks to school with arrived alone. From what I understand, Katie was later than usual this morning and the friend, Candy, didn't wait."

Nobody moved. They were hanging on to his every word. The trusty office clock that usually ticked its way through charged silences such as this one had been replaced by a digital upgrade that screamed out the silent passing of time in neon blue.

"We're assuming she was abducted, in which case the abduction would have occurred between 8.40 and 9.20 this morning. That's a little over three hours ago."

Several eyes flew to the glaring blue digits.

"Jeff and Harry, can you get onto the council for any CCTV footage in the area during that window? There's a council estate around the corner as well as a newsagent further down the road — they might have security cameras."

The rookies always did the CCTV work, although more and more they were outsourcing it to civilian operators trained to pick up the slightest clues in body language.

Jeff nodded. He'd been on CCTV duty before and knew what they were in for, but Harry, a rookie DC with exotic, movie-star good looks, gave an enthusiastic, "Yes, sir." Rumour was he'd had a bit part in *EastEnders* and supplemented his income by appearing in the odd commercial.

Mallory wrote Katie Wells's address on the whiteboard. In a short while, he'd pin a map of the area beside it, highlighting her street and the route she usually took to school.

"What school does she go to?" asked an American voice from Galbraith's team. Evan, Rob thought his name was. He didn't know the soft-spoken DC that well, since he was fairly new to the department, but he seemed competent and his desk was always immaculately tidy.

"Barnes Prep. We'll put up the details shortly."

Mallory wrote the school name underneath Katie's home address. Below that, he wrote "Candice Dalling" and a question mark.

That led Rob on to his next point. "DI Mallory and I will talk to the school friend, but I don't expect she'll know much, since she didn't see Katie this morning." He moved on. "Will, you've got Katie's mobile number. We need to see if we can get a read on her. Her mother says it's going straight to voicemail."

Will, a competent DS who used to work in the vice squad prior to transferring to CID, said, "It's switched off, so we can't trace it. It may have been damaged or destroyed. But I'm looking into her last known position."

Rob gave him a terse nod and pushed on. "We've scrambled a helicopter and the dog unit is on their way. When you study the map, you'll see there's a wooded area next to the river — that's a Barnes nature reserve, and we think she might have been taken there. It provides the most coverage and would have been the quickest way of getting her off the road and out of sight."

"Wouldn't Lonsdale Road have been busy at that time of day?" asked Jenny Bird. "It was rush hour." An up-and-coming DS, Rob respected Jenny's perspective. She'd been instrumental in bringing the Revenge Killer — *bloody journalists and their nicknames* — to justice last year.

"Yeah, but don't forget Hammersmith Bridge is still closed, so not many cars use that route anymore, unless they're travelling locally. The only way across the river is via Putney or Chiswick Bridge. Still, there is bike and pedestrian traffic. We'll put out a public alert, someone may have seen something." He snapped his fingers. "Get Vicky Bainbridge up here. She needs to hear this."

Vicky, a stylish, cool-as-a-cucumber woman was the Homicide and Serious Crime Command's press liaison officer. She controlled the flow of information from the department to the public and helped them issue any appeals for information. She also trained the officers who gave statements to the press, making sure they maintained a confident, capable air on television, and didn't divulge too much or get flustered under the often-aggressive media onslaught. Even now, Rob hated doing press statements, but with Vicky's guidance, he'd become a lot better at them.

Jenny fired off a text message. Her phone buzzed in response. "She's on her way up."

Rob gazed over the heads turned towards him until it settled on a dark, curly-haired DC with a smiling, round face. "Celeste, I need you to organise a door-to-door. We have to canvass everybody who lives on Katie's street, as well as on her route to school. It's only a short walk, but we need to do it ASAP."

Celeste turned bright pink at being singled out, but her face broke into a wide grin. She was one of the youngest members of the team but learning fast. She'd handle the uptick in responsibility. "Yes, sir!"

Rob addressed the entire room. "We have to move fast, people. I don't have to tell you that every second counts. The helicopter and K-9 unit will feed info back to this department. Any leads, call me directly."

His team nodded.

"The rest of you, we've got search teams at Katie's house and at her father's, Brian Wells, as well as the mother's boyfriend, an Eastern European by the name of Sergio Wójcik."

Mallory had written their full names and addresses on the board.

"Find out all you can about these three persons of interest. Any criminal records, domestics, mental health issues, you know the drill. Also, check the CCTV footage in their areas, see if their alibis hold up. Both men claim they hadn't left home by the time they got the message from Lisa saying

Katie had disappeared. I also want all ANPR data for vehicles leaving that area in the given time frame. Every car, van and lorry must be documented and traced."

Heads bobbed. Nobody questioned the orders. A missing child was as serious as it got.

Vicky Bainbridge sashayed in. As usual, she was immaculately attired in a navy skirt suit with a white blouse, open at the neck, displaying a sleek gold necklace that glittered against her tanned skin. She'd just got back from one of the Greek islands, but Rob couldn't remember which one.

"I've heard. The disappearance is all over social media. There seems to be some sort of local search and rescue going on."

"Christ." Rob ran a hand through his hair, which was becoming increasingly wayward as the day wore on.

"Get over there, Rob." Lawrence's belting voice from the back made several unsuspecting officers jump. "We can't have community helpers contaminating a potential crime scene, no matter how well-meaning they are. Have we cordoned off the nature reserve?"

They hadn't. Not yet, anyway. "I'm on it."

"Are we issuing a Child Rescue Alert?" Vicky turned to Lawrence. This was the UK equivalent to the US Amber Alert system upon which it had been based. "If we are, might I suggest doing it sooner rather than later, before the trail goes cold."

She knew her stuff. Prior to the police service, Vicky had been a news presenter on a local talk radio station until a caller had begun leaving threatening messages. After what had happened to Jill Dando, the BBC *Crimewatch* presenter who'd been gunned down outside her house in West London, she hadn't wanted to take any chances. "No career is worth my life," she'd told Rob once, after drinks at the local pub.

DCS Lawrence nodded. "I'll take care of it. Rob, you get going."

Rob raised his eyebrows. It wasn't often the chief super issued a press release these days. But he was right, Rob was better utilised elsewhere right now, and since DI Mallory would be with him, the chief super was the highest-ranked officer on site.

Vicky pursed her lips, also surprised. "Okay, Sam. I'll mobilise the powers that be. Shall we say half an hour out front?"

He nodded and disappeared back into his glass office. He didn't need a pre-release briefing. His thirty years' experience was more than enough.

CHAPTER 5

Rob and Mallory listened to the child abduction alert on the radio on the way to Katie Wells's house. It interrupted the local programme, and it would be broadcast to television stations across the UK, followed by the social media channels.

Lawrence pitched the perfect blend of sombre and urgent as he urged the public to keep their eyes and ears open, and if they saw anyone resembling eleven-year-old Katie Wells — dark hair, blue eyes, wearing a school uniform and carrying a pink rucksack — to contact the police straight away by dialling 999.

"Let's hope someone saw something," Mallory murmured as they drove alongside the Thames. The rowers were out in full force this morning, their streamlined eight-man boats flying along with effortless grace, hardly creating a ripple on the glittering surface.

Rob grunted in reply. It was unlikely, but you never knew. Sometimes they got lucky.

The street in which Katie lived was now cordoned off with uniformed officers stationed at each end. Police vehicles were parked along both sides of the road, their unapologetic blue lights sending an ominous message. *Back off. Something terrible happened here.*

Uniformed officers were conducting house-to-house enquiries. Residents were out on the pavement answering questions and straining their necks to see if they could spot Lisa, the hapless, ill-fated mother of the missing child. Every parent's worst nightmare.

A small crowd had gathered outside a neighbour's property. It was a well-maintained terraced house with overzealous pot plants positioned on either side of the glossy black front door. A Porsche four-by-four stood in the driveway. It made the Wellses' house look dingy by comparison, even though theirs was in keeping with the general middle-class standard of the neighbourhood.

A tall, middle-aged man stood on the steps outside, addressing the group. He had a commanding presence. Rob was familiar with the kind. Successful businessman. Married. Moved to the area for the schools but worked in the City.

Several people had their phones out and were capturing the moment.

"What's going on here?" Rob marched up, closely followed by Mallory, who scanned the faces of everyone in the gathering. Rob knew he would commit them to memory and, while not as effective as a photograph, he'd still be able to recognise a face if it popped up later. Perpetrators often involved themselves in an investigation by joining the search. They'd take names and contact details too, just in case.

Rob walked right up to the speaker and held up his warrant card. "DCI Miller from the Putney Major Investigation Team. We're leading this investigation. Could you tell me what's going on here?"

"We want to help find Katie," the homeowner said.

Nods all round.

"And you are?"

"Ed Maplin. I head up the neighbourhood watch."

Aah. "Okay, Mr Maplin. While we appreciate what you're doing here, we have officers conducting a thorough search of the area, including the nature reserve."

As if to emphasise the point, the police helicopter flew overhead, its propellers throbbing. Everyone glanced up.

"That you?" Maplin asked.

Rob nodded, then addressed the group. "Please could everyone here give their names to my DI." Mallory raised his hand. "If we need any additional assistance, we'll let you know. In the meantime, if everyone could keep their eyes peeled for sightings of Katie in and around the neighbourhood while they go about their normal business, that would be great. Thank you."

Maplin hesitated. He wasn't used to being upstaged or taking orders. Rob lowered his voice so only Maplin could hear. "You understand the importance of not contaminating a potential crime scene."

He gave a grunt. Thankfully, he was a sensible man.

"Guys, we're going to postpone the search and let the police do their thing. Can I ask that you all stay vigilant? If you see anything suspicious, let the police know."

Rob gave a curt nod. "Thank you for your assistance."

Mallory took down everyone's name. The yellow and black National Police Air Service helicopter circled above, preparing to do another flyby over the area. Rob beckoned to a uniformed officer standing nearby. "Can you take a video of this gathering before it breaks up?" he asked. "I want a frontal shot of everyone here. Don't make it obvious."

The policeman nodded and pulled out his phone as he walked across the street. He positioned himself behind a police vehicle and began filming.

Rob turned back to Maplin, who was talking to a leathery, grey-haired woman in oversized jeans and a loose T-shirt with a vintage-style Kew Gardens logo on the front. She had dirt under her fingernails and stains on her knees. "Are you sure there's nothing we can do?" she was saying.

Rob cleared his throat.

"This is Tessa Parvin," Maplin said. "She's a local resident and a member of the neighbourhood watch."

"I can't believe what's happened," she said to Rob. "And right here, in Barnes. It's unthinkable. This is supposed to be a safe area."

"We're doing all we can to find her," Rob stated.

Up close, Tessa Parvin was much younger than she looked. Probably mid-forties. It was the grey hair and ruddy complexion that made her appear older.

"Did you know Katie?" he asked.

"Yes. I mean, I've seen her around. Her mother, Lisa, was friendly to me when I first moved into the neighbourhood. We met at the village fête the first summer I was here."

"When was that?"

"Three years ago. I came here because it was so safe. I never imagined . . ." Her voice faded out.

It's not the area, he wanted to say. *It's the actions of one delusional kidnapper.* Abducting a child wasn't done on a whim. It was planned. The perpetrator would have been waiting for the opportunity to get Katie alone. They'd probably been watching the house for some time, knew her routine. When she was late for school, unattended, they'd pounced.

His throat constricted. God only knew what they were doing to her now. He blinked and squeezed the thought from his mind. He had to stay focused. There was still time.

His phone buzzed. It was an urgent alert from the team searching the nature reserve. He called the number. "DCI Miller. Any update?"

"This is PC Winters, sir. We're in the nature reserve near Leg o' Mutton Reservoir. We've found a rucksack partially submerged in the water."

A shiver shot down his spine. He wanted it to be hers, but at the same time, he didn't. Because he knew what it meant.

"Colour?"

"Pink, sir. It's got 'Katie Wells' written down the side."

Shit. "Okay, cordon off the entire area and call SOCO. I'm on my way." He beckoned to Mallory. "Let's go. We've got our crime scene."

CHAPTER 6

The crime scene investigators were already there when Rob drove up the pavement in front of the Swedish School on Lonsdale Road and cut the engine. The forensic van was open at the back and two crime scene officers were getting kitted up.

"Morning." Rob climbed out of the car.

They nodded back at him. There was no pathologist present as they didn't have a body. Yet. Rob prayed it stayed that way.

Etched through the nature reserve from road to river was a dirt track. On the right was the school and on the left, hidden in thick woodland, the disused reservoir, which in reality was more of a large pond. He remembered coming here years ago and being surprised at the sudden reveal. It was completely invisible from the road and the river path. One moment he was on a nature hike, and the next, the woods had opened up and he was staring at a glittering lake flanked by magnificent beech and poplar trees, many over a hundred years old.

Rob nudged Mallory and pointed towards the right. Positioned on top of a stark metal pole in the schoolyard was the dark, bulbous eye of a private security camera.

"I'll get on it as soon as we get back," his DI said. "If she came this way, it had to have picked her up."

They veered to the left, through a rickety gate overgrown with prickly hawthorn bushes. Up ahead, a narrow dirt path wound through the tall trees into obscurity. A pair of pastel-blue butterflies flickered past, chasing each other in a haphazard air-dance. Already, the sound of traffic from the road had dwindled to nothing as the warm air rustled branches and creatures scurried in the undergrowth.

"Beautiful spot," Mallory murmured.

"Wait till you see the reservoir."

They trudged along, past a dog walker and a fit elderly couple with trekking poles hurrying the other way. They'd obviously been told to evacuate the area, judging by the concerned expressions on their faces.

Suddenly, the trees parted, and the secluded lake shimmered in front of them. It really did look like a leg of mutton, wider at their end and narrowing on the far side. Birds waded around the edges, while dragonflies swooped over the surface. The heavy perfume of meadowsweet mixed with the damp twang of reeds and rushes.

"Wow," Mallory breathed. "I had no idea this was here."

"Not many people do," Rob acknowledged. "It's a well-kept secret."

On the far side, uniformed police officers wound a roll of no-nonsense yellow tape around the trees, securing the area where the rucksack had been found. Rob squinted, sunlight stabbing at his eyes. Was that a smudge of pink against the muddy bank of the reservoir?

Mallory surveyed the body of water. "It's bigger than I expected."

"Yeah, that surprised me the first time I came here too. Come on, let's get over there."

Footsteps caused them to turn around. The white-clad masked-up crime scene officers looked absurdly out of place in the natural environment, like astronauts navigating a strange planet.

"Where is it?" one asked.

Rob pointed to the far side. "Follow us. We're heading that way."

They followed the path around the lake to the far side and came to a stop outside the cordoned-off area. Rob and Mallory flashed their ID cards, as did the forensic officers. A policeman lifted the cordon and waved them through.

Plastic tiles had been placed on the ground to avoid contaminating the scene. The forensic officers walked down them, then squelched into the wet grass and mud at the edge of the water. They surveyed the area, looking for larger, more obvious clues. Finding nothing, they moved closer.

"How many of you have been on site?" asked the lead forensic officer.

A deep-voiced policeman replied, "Only three of us, sir, and only one got within a metre of the rucksack."

"We'll need your boot prints," he said. "For elimination purposes."

The policeman glanced at the muddy ground. "How?"

"You can give them to us at the van, afterwards."

The forensic officer turned back to the rucksack. They studied it up close for a long time, then carefully lifted it from its muddy resting place and placed it into a large, clear evidence bag.

"Can we look inside?" Rob took out a pair of latex gloves.

The officer nodded, but he wasn't happy about it. They were potentially compromising evidence. But this wasn't a homicide investigation. Yet. That backpack could contain something that would lead them to the missing girl.

They laid the evidence bag on one of the plastic tiles, then Rob gingerly took out the backpack. It was heavier than he expected. Katie's name was sprawled in permanent marker down the side. Lisa's handwriting, no doubt.

The bag was wet and stained by the water, but inside it was merely damp. The plastic lining had protected it from too much damage. He took out a pink jumper and swallowed.

This wasn't good. There was a whiff of talcum powder and something else, something sweet. And a glittery rose-gold pencil case — new, by the looks of things. Opening it, he saw it had the obligatory pencils, rubber and sharpener inside.

A lunch box with a transparent lid. A blurry image of a sandwich and what looked like carrots and cucumber slices. Lisa was a competent parent. A packet of crisps and a bottle of water had also been stuffed in the backpack.

Nestled at the bottom was a large stone. That would explain the weight. Rob glanced up at Mallory. "Look here." He lifted out the stone and placed it beside the backpack.

"Weighted down," remarked Mallory.

"We'll analyse it for fingerprints and DNA," the forensic officer said.

Rob put it back into the evidence bag. Would the kidnapper have been stupid enough to leave prints on the rock? They could only hope.

"No phone?" asked Mallory.

He had another rummage. "Nope." Another bad sign.

Mallory peered into the murky water. "Maybe he threw it in separately. To destroy it."

Rob scrutinised the water around the rushes, but it was too muddy to see clearly. "Will is tracing her last known position."

Mallory nodded, but his expression was grim.

Rob looked around. "Why here? You'd think the kidnapper would want to get her out of sight as fast as possible. Not waste time at the reservoir."

"He wanted to get rid of the backpack?" Mallory suggested.

"Yeah, of course. But he could have thrown it in the river, or into a bush or something. He didn't need to come into the reservoir to do it."

"You don't think . . . ?" muttered one of the police officers. He'd gone pale.

The sparkling surface of the lake took on a more sinister glint.

Mallory caught Rob's eye. "We'd better call in the divers."

Rob clenched his jaw. This was a pretty deserted spot. It had been nearly — he checked his watch — four hours since Katie disappeared. Plenty of time for the kidnapper to do his dastardly deed and dump the body. A midge dive-bombed his face and he swatted it away. "Yeah, do it."

"Jesus," murmured the other copper. Nobody wanted to consider that Katie Wells might be at the bottom of the lake.

"It's just a precaution," stated Rob. "We have to explore every avenue."

Mallory got on the phone.

"This isn't a very well-known spot," Rob pointed out. "The kidnapper had to have been a local or, at the very least, familiar with the neighbourhood."

"They're on the way." Mallory hung up.

Rob glanced once more into the water. Was she in there? "Let's go," he said. "There's nothing more we can do here, and we need to talk to Katie's friend Candy."

They walked back towards the path. A feeling of dread hung over them.

"There's only one reason to get rid of the backpack," Rob said. "Because Katie wouldn't be needing it."

Mallory didn't reply.

"He wasn't planning on holding on to her," Rob continued. "He knew she wouldn't be needing her jumper or her packed lunch."

Mallory swallowed. "Let's wait to see what the divers find before we jump to conclusions."

His DI was right, but it didn't look good for Katie. The sense of dread intensified.

CHAPTER 7

Candy Dalling was a confident, blonde cherub with wide eyes and a ready smile.

"I waited for five minutes," she told Rob and Mallory in the school canteen, "but then I had to go. Miss Smith doesn't like it if we're late."

"Miss Smith is Candy's and Katie's class teacher," explained the red-faced head teacher sitting in on the interview. "She realised Katie was missing when she took the morning register."

Rob leaned forward in his chair. "While you were waiting," he asked, "you didn't see anyone else on the street, did you?"

Candy shook her head.

"Not a man or a woman walking by, or anyone waiting near you?" Rob pressed.

"Well, it *was* rush hour," said the girl precociously.

Mallory hid a smile behind the bad styrofoam cup of coffee they'd been given from the staffroom.

"So, yes, there were other people walking by, but I didn't notice anyone just hanging around."

"Okay, thank you, Candy."

"I hope you find Katie," she said. "It's not like her to go off by herself."

Rob hesitated. He didn't know what she'd been told, and the last thing he wanted to do was alarm her.

"What makes you think she went off by herself?" He ignored a warning glance from the head.

"Oh, I don't. Katie's shy, she wouldn't go anywhere by herself. I had to go into the shop with her the other day to buy Maoams."

Rob looked at the head teacher. "It's a sweet," she said.

He had never heard of Maoams. "Would she have talked to a stranger?" he asked Candy.

"No, definitely not. We know all about stranger danger." The child's eyes were sombre now.

Rob nodded. "That's good. Don't worry, we're doing our very best to find Katie."

Candy gave a firm nod, her lips pressed together in a satisfied smile. Rob wished everyone had as much faith in the police.

* * *

Mallory drove them back to the station while Rob fielded one call after the next.

"The police helicopter didn't pick up anything and is going back to base," Jenny told him. "I've sent the dog unit to the nature reserve, as requested."

"Thanks, Jenny." *Please let them pick up her scent. Anything to indicate she isn't lying at the bottom of that reservoir.*

"Rob, the press has set up camp outside the front entrance. You might want to come around the back." Vicky Bainbridge's voice was filled with suppressed excitement. She loved it when they had a big case on and the journalists came sniffing.

"How'd the press release go?"

"Short and sweet. You know Sam."

He did. The chief superintendent didn't mince his words. "I heard the alert go out on the radio."

36

She sniffed. "He did what needed to be done. We've roped in Twickenham to help man the hotline. Hundreds of people are calling in with sightings of Katie."

It was always the case. It would be up to the officers to filter the information and report back anything that warranted further investigation.

Frustration burned in his gut. If they weren't paying attention, things got missed, but then he couldn't micromanage everything. He should be back at the station overseeing the case, not out interviewing witnesses, but there was something about this case. He wanted to be in on it. It was important. A little girl's life depended on him.

"Thanks, Vicky, keep me posted."

"Did you find anything?" she asked.

He paused. "We found the child's rucksack in the reservoir."

"Christ," she croaked. "Poor little thing."

"I've got to go, see you later."

He knocked his fist against the car window. "We need a fucking lead."

Six hours.

Time was running out.

* * *

"Fucking hell," snapped Rob as they turned off Putney High Street and came to a standstill. The traffic had backed up to the intersection thanks to the crowd that had gathered outside the Putney MIT headquarters.

There was an impatient honking of horns as motorists tried to get past. A motorcyclist weaved through the backlog, nearly swiping his side mirror.

"Where's traffic control when you need 'em?" muttered Rob.

As they drove past the front of the building, they saw a uniformed police officer frantically waving cars by and ushering the indifferent reporters onto the pavement. It wasn't doing much good.

Around the corner, it got even worse. Press vans were ramped up the pavement and camera crews were setting up, oblivious to the "no parking" signs and the yellow line running down both sides of the road.

"Don't the rules apply to the media?" Mallory shook his head.

"It's a goddamn circus." Rob put on the siren and forced his way through the mayhem to the underground car park entrance around the back. They entered the building via the internal elevator, bypassing the furore outside.

Instead of going up to the top floor, where the major crime teams were located, he pressed the button for the ground floor. Mallory raised an eyebrow but didn't comment.

"Get rid of those reporters," Rob barked to the sweating duty sergeant, who'd disabled the revolving door. "This is a police HQ, for God's sake. Get some officers out there."

The man grabbed the telephone. "Yes, sir."

"Unbelievable," Rob muttered, shaking his head.

They took the elevator to the top floor.

"Rob! My office!"

The chief superintendent's voice rebounded around the squad room the moment they walked through the doors.

"Here we go," he murmured, as Mallory fled to his desk. "Sir?"

"What the fuck are you doing waltzing around Barnes? I need you running things from here. You're not a DS anymore."

"I was visiting the crime scene," he said.

"Well, make sure you're here from now on. Someone's got to keep this show on the road."

"Yes, sir."

"What have you got? The police commissioner is breathing down my neck and there's a riot in the street outside."

Rob didn't dare sit down. "We found the kid's rucksack in the reservoir. The dog unit's there now trying to pick up her trail. There's CCTV in the area, so we're hoping to find something on that."

"Jesus Christ." Lawrence also recognised the relevance of the discarded backpack. "What about the school friend?"

"She didn't know anything."

"Shit, Rob. We have to find this girl, and soon. Nobody wants to see news of Katie Wells's dead body in the papers tomorrow."

"I know, sir." Tension clawed at his insides.

Lawrence sat down, his seat groaning in protest. "What about the parents?"

"We're searching each of their premises, as well as the boyfriend's," he told him. "I'll follow up now." *In other words, let me get back to work.*

The DCS glanced at the framed photograph on his desk. A younger, fuller-haired version of himself with his wife and their two daughters. They were older now, in their twenties. That photo had been on his desk ever since Rob joined the department.

"We'll find her, sir," he said quietly.

Lawrence nodded but didn't meet his gaze. "Keep me posted, Rob."

CHAPTER 8

"Where are we on the CCTV?"

Rob directed his question to Jeff, who looked up from his laptop.

"Not good news, I'm afraid, guv. The camera at the Swedish School is broken, and they're waiting until the autumn term to fix it. Seems they don't have the budget this year."

Rob rolled his eyes. *Damn.* He'd been counting on getting something from that. A murky figure or a shadowy shot of the girl. Anything that would give them a lead. "What about the council estate up the road?"

"We're going through the feeds now, but nothing so far."

"Okay, keep on it."

He turned to Mike Manner, a black South London copper who'd transferred to the department last year. He was a big bloke with a gym-built body and a rough scar along his jawline. Rob still hadn't asked him how he'd got it. "Any luck with the ANPR?"

Mike raised his head, his scar catching the light. "There are five Automatic Number Plate Recognition cameras in and around Barnes. I'm going through the data now, but I can't find anything that jumps out. Sorry, guv. I'm looking at the speed cameras too, just in case."

Rob sighed. "Thanks, Mike." So, nothing visual. "Where's Celeste?"

The DC he'd put in charge of the door-to-door enquiries came in holding a cup of coffee. He was about to shoot her a disapproving look, then remembered this wasn't a detention centre and she was entitled to a hot beverage. In fact, he could bloody use one too.

"Any good?" He eyed the murky brown liquid in the takeaway cup. The canteen had recently changed suppliers, which had made everyone nervous. The coffee hadn't been all that bad before.

"It's okay."

That meant it was crap. Perhaps he'd wait and grab one from across the road. "Any news on the doorstepping?"

She sat at her desk and tapped the space bar. Her laptop lit up. "Not as such. We have a lot of very concerned citizens. Most of the neighbours knew Katie, or had seen her and her mother in the street or at the local summer fête last weekend on Barnes Common. It seems to be quite a close-knit community."

Fantastic. Rob didn't give a monkey's how close-knit they were, unless one of them had seen something and could give him a lead. "Nothing of interest?"

She shook her head. "Not yet, sorry."

Shit. Everyone was sorry. *He* was sorry. He rubbed his eyes. "What about the mother, the father or the Polish boyfriend? Do we have anything on them?" *Please, give me something.*

Evan, the soft-spoken American, lifted his hand. Rob felt like a schoolteacher. "Yeah, what you got, Evan?"

"The mother is completely clean. She hasn't even had a parking ticket in the last five years. However, her husband, Brian Wells, worked in the City as a finance manager until last year when he got fired for gross incompetence. He now runs his own business from home. Some sort of consultancy, by the looks of things."

"That might be worth looking into. Find out why he was sacked."

"Yes, boss."

He'd never been called "boss" before, but it sounded right in Evan's soft, American drawl.

"What about the Polish construction worker?"

"Nothing on him, but I haven't looked outside the UK yet."

"Okay, keep me posted."

Evan nodded.

Gross misconduct. Now that was interesting. Rob glanced at Mallory, who was typing rapidly on his computer. "Let's go and have a word with Brian Wells," he said. "We'll check how the property searches are going while we're there."

Mallory slid his chair back and got to his feet.

"And let's get a decent cup of coffee on the way. I'm gasping."

* * *

Belgrave Road, the street Katie Wells lived in, was still closed to traffic, an unrepentant police vehicle parked horizontally at each end.

"That didn't take long." Rob eyed the press vans parked outside the cordons. They weren't allowed in but had set up their cameras for sweeping shots of the street the little girl had been abducted from.

"The school just rang. They've got reporters outside too."

Rob spread his hands. You had to pick your battles.

He flashed his warrant card to the officer on duty and drove through. Lisa Wells's windows were all shut with the blinds drawn, despite the balmy summer's day. Rob didn't blame her. It was only going to get worse. Once they took down the cordons, the media would be free to camp outside the property and lie in wait.

As they climbed out of the car, the front door opened and two police officers emerged. They were wearing gloves and shoe protectors, but unlike forensic officers, they didn't have full protective suits. They were conducting a house search, not examining a crime scene.

"Find anything?" Rob asked.

The woman shook her head. "No, sir. We even had the cadaver dogs in. Nothing."

Thank fuck for that. "Okay, and you checked the basement and the attic?"

The man nodded. "The house is clean, sir. Katie isn't there."

It was Katie now. You knew the press were winning when everyone began calling the missing girl by her first name. It wasn't necessarily a bad thing. Humanising her might make the kidnapper think twice before hurting her. That was supposed to help, although he'd yet to see any evidence of it. A sane, rational kidnapper, perhaps, but most of the sick, deranged psychopaths he dealt with would have committed their crime no matter how human their victims were made out to be.

They found Lisa crying in the kitchen.

"Mrs Wells, may we have a word?"

She nodded through her tears.

Rob sat down while Mallory took up a less obtrusive position by the door.

"Is there anyone we can call to be with you?" he asked. Her eyes showed the haunted, hollow look of desperation. And she was dressed in the same dirty, ragged clothing from that morning. "A sister or another family member, perhaps?"

She gave a brief, shuddering gasp. "My brother and his wife are driving down from Yorkshire. They'll be here soon."

That was something. "Okay, good. Now, Mrs Wells, do you mind if I ask you some questions about your husband?"

She wiped her nose on her sleeve. "Brian? Why do you want to know about him?"

Rob ignored the question and ploughed on. "We heard he'd recently been fired from his job in the City. Is that true?"

Her voice was croaky as she brushed away her tears. "He went to pieces after we separated and started drinking heavily. He worked for a big import–export company and was responsible for millions of pounds' worth of payments, so when he started dropping the ball and people weren't getting paid, they dismissed him."

She knew a lot about the intricacies of her husband's job. He said as much, but she shrugged. "Brian used to talk to me about his work, back when we could still communicate without having a row." She hung her head in her hands. Tears hovered, threatening to fall, but somehow didn't, making her eyes gleam. "It wasn't always like this, you know?"

He did. He *really* did.

"I didn't think it was right, them sacking him like that," she continued. "Especially since they didn't give him any notice. They paid him a month's salary instead, so there was nothing he could do."

Rob frowned. That was a bit weird. They wanted rid of him so urgently that they didn't give him the official notice period, preferring to pay him off instead. He must have seriously screwed up. "When was this?"

"Some time ago now. When we first split up."

"A year ago?" He cast his mind back to their first conversation. Mallory nodded in silent confirmation.

"Yes."

"How's he been earning a living since then?"

"He consults, advises people on their finances, that sort of thing." She pursed her lips. "As far as I know, anyway."

Rob had seen how strained things were between them. Whatever communication had existed had shut down as soon as she'd begun sleeping with Sergio.

"Do you mind if we have a quick look at Katie's room?"

He hadn't been up there yet, and even though the house had been thoroughly searched, he wanted to take a peek, just in case anything jumped out at him.

Lisa looked up. "Oh, sure. Although the police have been up there all morning."

"I know. It's just so I can get a feel for what Katie is like." He nearly said *was*. Christ, that wouldn't have gone down well.

Seven hours.

Lisa showed them to Katie's room. It was a typical tween girl's room. Pink floral bedspread, matching curtains, a tasselled lampshade and posters of Ariana Grande on the wall.

"She loves her." Lisa nodded to the poster. "We considered going to that concert up in Manchester, but in the end, Brian said she was too young. Thank God we didn't."

Rob nodded sagely. Thank God, indeed.

Her lip quivered. "Turns out he was right about that too." Mallory gave her a sympathetic grimace.

There was a photograph of Katie and her parents in a gold frame on the dressing table. They looked happy. Brian had his arm around Lisa, Katie stood in front of them, beaming into the camera. They were on a beach somewhere, with straw umbrellas and the sea twinkling in the background. Happier times.

"Where are you in the divorce proceedings?" he asked.

Lisa's face clouded over.

"I'm sorry, but I have to ask."

"That has nothing to do with Katie's disappearance," she insisted. She adjusted the angle of the photograph, remembering. "Brian is a good man. He'd never hurt his own daughter."

Stranger things had happened.

Mallory drew back the curtain and peered out of the window. "Direct view onto the street below," he said.

Rob turned to Lisa. "Still, you said he wanted custody of Katie."

The quivering lip again. "Yes, but I think it's just because he's angry at me for moving on. You know, with Sergio."

"But that's nothing serious?" Her words.

She gave a weak nod. "Brian doesn't like the thought of a strange man in the house."

Perhaps he had a right to be cautious. Then again, divorce brought out the worst in people. Rob knew that first-hand. His own had yet to be finalised, even though they'd completed the negotiations. Luckily, Yvette, being an ex-lingerie model, had her own money and hadn't wanted anything from him. She'd turned her nose up at his small, one-bed semi in Richmond, even though it was in a sought-after area.

To be fair, she hadn't been in the best frame of mind during the proceedings. Her mind clouded by panic attacks and agoraphobia, she'd just wanted the whole thing over with as soon as possible.

He'd offered to wait, to give her some time to consider her options, but she wasn't interested. Every minute married to him, she'd said, was a stark reminder of the trauma from which she was trying to recover. He'd never felt more of a pariah in his life.

Maybe this whole custody battle was just a spiteful attack on Lisa and had nothing to do with Katie herself. Hopefully, the courts would decide in the child's best interests, whatever that was.

There was nothing in the bedroom that aroused his suspicion, and the more he spoke to Lisa, the more convinced he was that she had nothing to do with her daughter's abduction. She talked about Katie as if she were still alive, in the present tense. She couldn't stop crying, even when no one else was around. She was still clinging on to hope.

"Ready to leave?" Rob asked Mallory. The DI was leafing through a book on Katie's bedside table. A piece of paper fell out.

Mallory took out a latex glove and carefully picked it up. "*We'll be together soon. Love Dad,*" he read.

Lisa stared at the note. "What's that?"

Mallory held it up. "Have you seen this before?"

"No." She squinted at it. "Brian must have given it to Katie. He sometimes comes round to read her a bedtime story."

Rob studied the note. "Is it his handwriting?"

She nodded. The note was handwritten on a small, rectangular piece of paper, the sort you'd write a shopping list on.

"Do you know what he meant?"

46

"No, I . . ." Her voice faded, and she shook her head. Then she paled, and her hand flew to her mouth. "You don't think . . . ?"

She swayed alarmingly.

"Sit down." Mallory led her to the bed, where she collapsed. She'd gone whiter than the walls of her daughter's bedroom.

"I think we'd better get over to Brian Wells's house." Rob held out an evidence bag he'd pulled from his inside jacket pocket. Mallory slipped the note inside.

There was a moment before they left when Lisa clutched Rob's hand and begged him to bring her Katie home. He assured her he would, even though he left with a massive lump in his throat. He prayed he wouldn't have to break that promise.

They were on their way to Katie's father's house when Rob's mobile phone rang. "DCI Miller," he barked.

It was one of the officers searching Brian Wells's house. "Sir, we've found something. You'd better get over here."

Rob flicked on the siren. "We're coming as quick as we can."

CHAPTER 9

Brian Wells was fast becoming their prime suspect.

He lived in an apartment in East Sheen, not far from Barnes, above a fishing tackle shop. The sound of afternoon traffic on Upper Richmond Road swept into the living room through the open sash window, as did the faintly acrid smell of exhaust fumes. His flat was a shambles, but whether it was from the police officers searching it or Brian himself, Rob wasn't sure.

"Are you renting?" Rob asked.

The disgraced financier sat on the sofa staring straight ahead, oblivious to the goings-on around him. If Rob didn't know better, he'd say he was in shock.

"Yes."

"How long is your lease for?"

Brian blinked. "Six months."

"That's not very long." Rob circled the room, clocking the workstation in front of the window, the television set balancing precariously on a bookcase that was too small for it and the well-worn leather sofa. For someone who'd been a finance manager in the City, his apartment was surprisingly barren.

"I was hoping to resolve things with my wife." He made eye contact with Rob for the first time. "Then she shacked up with that Polish builder." He shook his head.

Rob nodded. The officers searching the flat had found two one-way Eurostar tickets on the printer, dated two weeks from today.

He sat down next to Brian. "Were you planning on taking Katie on a trip?"

The man didn't respond.

"Brian, this doesn't look good. Your daughter has gone missing and you have two one-way tickets to France in your names booked for the Friday after next."

Still no response. Brian stared blankly at the television screen. He was in marginally better shape than his wife. His hair was dishevelled, his face was sallow and he hadn't shaved for a good twenty-four hours. He *looked* like an innocent man whose kid had gone missing. That didn't mean he was.

"Look, we're trying to be objective here, but unless you can explain these train tickets, we're going to have to take you down to the station."

He burped, then leaned forward. "I'm going to be sick."

Shit. Rob hopped up and took a few steps back, out of the line of fire. "Okay, Brian. Take a moment."

"I gotta go to the bathroom." He pushed past Mallory. The house was swarming with coppers. There was nowhere to run. The bathroom door banged shut.

"There's no sign of Katie here," Mallory filled the gap. They could hear Brian retching in the toilet. "He has some of her clothes in a drawer, along with a sketch pad and art materials plus a few other bits and pieces, but that's not unusual since she stays with him every second Saturday." Lisa had told them that.

"He doesn't have a second bedroom?" Rob remarked.

"Apparently, she sleeps in his room and he takes the couch."

The toilet flushed.

"He could have hidden her somewhere else," Rob said.

Mallory nodded. "Yeah, that's the most likely scenario. He'd know we'd search his flat."

"Let's get him back to the station and find out. I'm sick of waiting. God knows where she is, but if he had anything to do with it, we'll get it out of him."

Rob banged on the bathroom door. "Mr Wells? Can you come out, please?"

There was no answer.

He sighed. "Mr Wells? Brian? If you don't come out, we're going to come in and get you."

Nothing. Great, this was all they needed.

Mallory beckoned to a uniformed officer standing just inside the front door. He came over and kicked it down. It didn't give straight away, but took two more sturdy boot kicks before it flung open.

The bathroom was empty.

Fuck. "Outside!" yelled Rob.

The officer was already running out the door. Brian had made the one-storey drop and was sprinting up the busy high street.

Two policemen raced after him.

"The bugger jumped." Rob shook his head. Already, the officers in pursuit had radioed in the suspect's location. Before long, sirens came screaming down the road.

Rob's phone buzzed. He glanced at the screen. "They've got him. Stupid bastard. Let's get down to the station and find out what he's got to say."

* * *

Mallory pressed the record button and introduced everyone present. He was leading the interview, and beside him sat DS Jenny Bird. Brian Wells sulked on the other side of the table.

He'd requested legal representation after his arrest. He didn't have a solicitor — not many people did, to be honest — so one had been assigned to him.

50

The solicitor, a confident Asian woman with sincere eyes magnified by thick glasses, sat beside him, an open notepad in front of her.

* * *

Rob watched from the viewing room. As SIO, his job was to study and analyse. Lawrence would go mental if he was the one conducting the interview.

There were two screens in front of him. One monitored the suspect head on, the other afforded a side view. The interrogation room was small and functional. It contained a table and four chairs, nothing else, and the suspect's chair was nailed to the floor.

"Brian . . . Can I call you Brian?" Mallory asked.

The suspect shrugged.

"Could you explain why you bought these tickets? For the record, I'm showing the suspect two one-way Eurostar tickets in the names of Brian Wells and Katie Wells for Friday the nineteenth of June."

"We were going on a trip."

His solicitor had obviously primed him. Being seen to cooperate with the police was the best strategy in this case. Guilty people tend to clam up or take the "No comment" approach, but that often harmed their defence when they got to court.

Brian hadn't got off to a great start by jumping out of the window and high-tailing it up the road, though. The evidence was also pretty damning, but Rob would reserve judgement on that one.

"Was Katie's mother, Lisa, aware of this proposed trip?" asked Mallory.

Brian hung his head. His solicitor nudged him.

"No." His voice was barely a whisper.

"Were you planning on informing her?"

He shook his head.

"For the record, Brian Wells is shaking his head to indicate no," Jenny clarified.

"Why not?"

"She wouldn't have let us go. I only get to see my little girl once every two weeks. It's not enough."

His voice cracked. From behind the screen, Rob narrowed his gaze.

"Where were you taking her?" asked Mallory.

"To the seaside, for a holiday."

"Your tickets were to Paris."

"I was going to hire a car and drive to the coast."

"Did you have anywhere booked?"

He shook his head. "Not yet."

"Why the one-way ticket? Was it because you weren't planning on coming back?"

His head popped up. "No. I swear, we were coming back. I just wanted to spend some time with her, that's all."

Rob wasn't convinced. No return ticket, no definite plan. Everything pointed to a desperate Brian Wells running away with his daughter.

"Brian, do you acknowledge writing this note?" Mallory slid the piece of paper they'd found in the book across the table. It was in a plastic sheath, and the harsh, fluorescent light bounced off it with an accusatory gleam. "For the record, I'm showing the suspect a handwritten note that was found in his daughter's bedroom."

Brian stared at it for a long time.

"Brian?"

He nodded. Jenny stated that he'd responded with a nod. "What did you mean by it?"

"Nothing." His gaze flickered and then he glanced away, back at his lap.

Rob leaned back in his chair. There was something he wasn't saying.

"I think you meant that you'd be taking her away soon, without her mother knowing." Mallory's tone changed. Harsher.

"No."

"Where is she, Brian?"

A pause.

"The suspect has failed to respond," said Jenny.

Brian shifted position. Beads of perspiration appeared on his brow. Mallory pushed on with the line of questioning, applying pressure.

"Did you take her, Brian? Did you lure her into the nature reserve, dump her backpack in the pond and hide her somewhere, to make it look like she'd been kidnapped?"

"No."

"Are you sure? Because I think you planned to keep her hidden away for a few weeks until things had settled down, and then you'd quietly leave and take her to France, where it would be just the two of you."

"No!"

"Detective, do you have any actual evidence that my client kidnapped his daughter?" This from the smooth-talking solicitor.

Rob shook his head. They didn't. That was the problem. The note and the tickets were circumstantial at best.

"We know he was thinking about taking her to France." Mallory didn't take his eyes off Brian Wells.

"Thinking isn't doing, Detective, as well you know."

Still, they could hold Brian in custody for twenty-four hours and have another crack at him later, once he'd had time to ponder his predicament. Or they could let him go and hope he led them to Katie.

Mallory tried one more time. "If you know where she is, Brian, tell us now. She's probably alone and frightened. You don't want her to suffer, do you?"

Brian's gaze darkened. "I don't know where she is. If I did, I'd tell you."

Mallory sighed. "I'm going to speak to the custody sergeant and recommend we hold you for the full twenty-four hours. I urge you to think very strongly about telling us where your daughter is, because you won't be seeing her for a while."

Brian swallowed, but didn't reply.

"Is there anything you want to add?" Mallory asked.

"The suspect hasn't responded," noted Jenny.

"My client has already stated he did not kidnap his daughter."

Rob watched as a surly-faced Brian was led from the interrogation room. He'd be put in a holding cell overnight.

* * *

"Let's leave him to sweat." Rob paced up and down the squad room. "Perhaps then he'll tell us where he's hidden her."

"*If* he's hidden her," pointed out Mallory. "I'm not sure about him."

Rob acknowledged the truth of that statement with an annoyed nod. "It won't do him any harm to sit in the holding cells for a few hours. If he hasn't said anything by midnight, we'll release him. But let's put a tail on him, make sure we know where he is at all times."

Mallory nodded. He knew the drill.

"Hell of a coincidence that he has those tickets booked for two weeks after Katie disappears."

Mallory grunted. "Doesn't mean he did it, though. Could just be lousy timing."

Rob shot him a look that said, *Really?* Mallory shrugged and sauntered off to his desk.

Rob's phone beeped as a text came in. A surge of adrenalin shot through him. "The dog unit have picked up Katie's scent."

A pause hung over the squad room. Rob called the officer in charge. The team hung on to his every word.

"Yeah, great. Okay, thanks. I'm on my way."

Finally, some good news. "They tracked her to the towpath." He grinned. "She wasn't in the pond, after all."

A collective sigh of relief.

"What about the divers?" asked Jenny. "Did they find anything?"

"Only her mobile phone," said Rob. "She's definitely not there."

The chief superintendent had left for the day, so Rob had a quiet word with Mallory. "I'll pay Sergio Wójcik a visit on my way back."

Mallory nodded. "See you later."

They both knew no one was getting any rest tonight. Not while she was still out there.

The bloody press were still camped outside. As he drove out of the underground parking lot, they swarmed him, but Rob put his foot down and screeched up Church Road, not even bothering to look in his rear-view mirror.

He was almost at the nature reserve when his phone rang. He converted it to hands-free.

"Jenny. What's up?"

DS Bird's voice was breathy with excitement. "Sir, it turns out Sergio Wójcik has a criminal record in Poland. He served six months for burglary back in 2006."

CHAPTER 10

Rob slammed his foot on the brake, just stopping himself from careening into the delivery van in front of him.

"Burglary, did you say?"

"Yes, apparently he robbed his girlfriend's house."

Hmm . . . Rob turned down the radio. "His girlfriend?"

"Well, his ex. She laid a charge against him and got a restraining order."

That was interesting. Burglary was a very different crime from kidnapping and required a different mindset. "Were there any cases of domestic abuse?"

"Not that I can find, guv."

"So why'd she take out a restraining order?"

"The order states that he wouldn't stop pestering her."

"But he never assaulted her?"

"It doesn't look like it."

"Jenny, contact the ex and get the full story. In the meantime, I'll be sure to ask him about it when I see him."

* * *

The Thames was grey and foreboding. It was a river of extremes, Rob reflected, as he marched along the darkening path towards the officers assembled further down, changing moods on a daily basis.

The overcast sky added its shadowy tinge while white crests danced on the surface on account of the surging current. There were no rowers this evening. They preferred still water. The Thames on a pushing tide was not something to be fought against. But it was still hot and humid, made worse by the oppressive cloud cover, and sweat dripped down his back between his shoulder blades. He took off his jacket and swung it over his shoulder.

"Thanks for waiting," he said to the dog handler, who nodded in response. "What you got?"

"The trail was pretty strong from the reservoir down to the river path," he told Rob. "But we lost her round about here."

The German Shepherd on the lead barked in confirmation. His handler patted his head. "Harley tried his best, but there are just too many people on the path. The smell was diluted."

"At least we know she came this way," said Rob. "Lonsdale Road is a hundred metres away. That gives us something to go on."

The dog handler nodded.

Rob was about to walk away when his colleague said, "Glad she wasn't at the bottom of that reservoir, sir. That's a relief."

Rob patted him on the shoulder. "Thanks, guys, great job."

A relief was an understatement. Katie Wells might still be alive.

* * *

Sergio Wójcik lived in a brown-brick multistorey housing estate on Mortlake High Street opposite the old brewery, a sad, derelict building scheduled for redevelopment. It was also one road back from the river, which meant if you followed the towpath from Barnes, you'd eventually get here. It was a solid two-mile walk, doable for an eleven-year-old.

The Polish builder's apartment was on the third floor, at the back of the block. He didn't have a river view. Instead, he looked out onto a small, concrete play area and a narrow alleyway that ran between two blocks of houses.

Not bad, thought Rob as he walked along the external corridor to flat number thirty-two. The playground was clean, the alleyway free of graffiti, and in the distance he could hear church bells ringing. He rang the buzzer. It was after eight o'clock in the evening, so Sergio should be home from work.

Eleven hours. The beginnings of a headache throbbed at his temples, but that was probably due to lack of caffeine as much as the strain of the investigation. Every minute that passed, the chances of finding Katie alive diminished.

The door swung open.

"Hello?" The stocky Pole stood there in tracksuit bottoms and a sleeveless vest, holding a cigarette between his thumb and forefinger.

Was that Pink Floyd playing in the background? Rob recognised the laid-back melancholic music and was hit by a wave of nostalgia — no, not nostalgia, but something. His father used to play it while he worked on his motorbike in the garage and ignored his wife and son.

"DCI Miller. I need to ask you a few questions. Can I come in?"

"I remember." Sergio stood back to allow the detective entry.

Rob stepped into a cloud of smoke, but instead of swatting it away, he inhaled. Old habits die hard. As the smoke filled his lungs, he felt the niggles of a craving. How long had it been?

Since Yvette left. He'd thrown away his last pack the day she'd walked out the door. A fresh start in more ways than one. He eyed the burning fag between Sergio's fingers and longed for the relaxation a good drag afforded him.

"You want one?" Sergio pulled the tattered Stuyvesant box out of his tracksuit pocket and held it out.

Was he *that* obvious? He shook his head. "No, thank you."

They went into the living room, a decent-sized area with an adjoining kitchen. The flat was frugally decorated with a corner sofa, standard-issue carpeting and gauze curtains over the Juliet-style balcony windows, which let in ample sunlight. The air was heavy with smoke.

Rob took a seat on the sofa while Sergio turned down the music and sat opposite him on a well-used armchair. The television was positioned in front of the chair on a purpose-built cabinet. Rob admired the craftsmanship. It was the perfect height, with two lower shelves and smooth wooden surfaces polished a dark mahogany. He bet that was Sergio's handiwork.

"How is the search coming on?" the construction worker asked between drags. The ashtray on the side table was overflowing.

"We're pursuing several lines of enquiry," Rob replied.

Sergio nodded, as if this was to be expected. "What can I do to help you, Detective?"

Apart from the cigarette smoke, the flat was surprisingly clean. The carpet was crumb-free, which was more than he could say for his own, and the kitchen countertops were clear. There wasn't so much as a beer can in sight. He couldn't see any evidence of a young girl having been here.

"I wanted to talk to you about your misdemeanour charge in Poland back in 2006."

Sergio's gaze hardened. He didn't reply for a long moment, just took a deep drag of his cigarette and exhaled. A wispy plume stretched towards the ceiling. Eventually, he said, "That was a long time ago."

"What happened?" asked Rob. Everyone made mistakes, he knew that. He sat back, prepared to listen to Sergio's side of the story.

"I was twenty-one," Sergio began in his deep, accented voice. The cigarette between his fingers had burned down almost to the filter. "I had this girlfriend. Aggie, her name was. She was beautiful, but what a pain. She used to make me crazy, you know. But I loved her, so I put up with it."

This was sounding creepily familiar. Rob tensed, but nodded for him to continue.

"One day we had an argument. We were always arguing about something, I don't even know what." He shrugged and looked perplexed. "She threw all my clothes out of the window onto the street below."

Rob raised an eyebrow. At least Yvette had never done that to him.

"She told me if I ever came back, she'd destroy my CD collection." He scowled at the memory.

"CD collection?"

Sergio nodded. "I have a large rock collection. You like rock 'n' roll?"

Rob nodded. "Yes, I like it." When he got round to listening to it. Suddenly, Pink Floyd made sense.

"So, when she was at work, I broke into her flat to get it. She knew I wanted it back, that's why she kept it."

Rob sighed. Relationships. "That's when you were caught?"

"Yeah. A neighbour saw me and called the police. I spent six months in jail." He inhaled viciously. "For trying to get something back that was mine to start with."

There was nothing left to smoke, so he stabbed the butt out on the corner of the ashtray and dropped it in.

Rob believed him. Sergio didn't strike him as the kidnapping type. He wasn't even a burglar. Not really. The man wore his heart on his sleeve. He wasn't sophisticated or secretive enough to pull off an abduction. His house had been searched too, and they hadn't found anything relating to Katie.

Rob stood up. This was a dead end. "Thanks for talking with me."

Sergio seemed surprised the interview was over so quickly, but he didn't question it. He got to his feet and saw Rob out.

"When can I see Lisa?" Sergio asked.

"Whenever she's ready," he replied. "Give her a call." Lisa could use her lover's support right now, especially since she wouldn't be able to leave her house without being swamped by reporters.

Sergio nodded.

As he walked away, Rob heard the rustle of the cigarette box, followed by the inciting hiss of a lighter, before the door shut.

CHAPTER 11

Rob stared into his double espresso and tried to make sense of what they knew. He'd go back to the squad room in a minute, but right now, he needed to think.

The *Evening Standard* lay beside him on the table, Katie's serious face staring back at him. She was front-page news, and on every radio and television station in the country. Rob was listed at the end of the article as the senior investigating officer, along with a reminder that it was his team who'd apprehended the notorious Surrey Stalker last year and the Revenge Killer earlier this year.

So much for managing expectations. The press were baying for a culprit already.

Rob considered what he had learned about Brian Wells. He had been planning to take Katie on holiday to France. In light of the custody battle, he was getting ready to run. And he could easily have convinced his daughter to go with him to the nature reserve. She loved it there. But so far, there was no actual evidence that he'd abducted his daughter. He'd arrived at Lisa's house as soon as she'd called him at nine thirty this morning, which meant he couldn't have been far away. If he had hidden Katie, it had to have been close by.

Brian had been escorted home from Lisa's house, then his apartment had been searched, and the Eurostar tickets found. He hadn't had time to move his victim. Rob scratched his head. Where the hell could he have hidden her? All the evidence, circumstantial though it may be, pointed to Katie's father, and yet they had nothing on him.

Rob glanced at his wristwatch. Nearly nine. Should they have another crack at him, or let him go and see where he went? If he had secreted Katie away somewhere, the little girl would be hungry and thirsty by now.

Unless he'd had help.

He rang Mallory. "Was Brian Wells seeing anyone?"

The DI's tired voice replied. "I don't think so. He didn't mention a girlfriend."

"Have we checked his call records?"

"Got them from the service provider an hour ago. Will's going through them now."

"Look for anyone he may have contacted this morning around the time of Katie's disappearance, as well as anyone he was in contact with regularly."

"You think he had an accomplice?" Mallory asked.

Rob nodded at Katie's photograph. "Maybe. I don't see how he could have hidden Katie otherwise. There wasn't enough time. He must have dropped her off somewhere and raced back to Lisa's house after she called him."

"I'll ring you back." Mallory hung up.

As the caffeine hit his blood stream, Rob began to perk up. There was still a lot to do, leads to chase up on. It was going to be a long night.

He texted Jo, the woman he was seeing. Sort of. She worked for the National Crime Agency and they'd met on a previous case and become friends. It was only recently that they'd got together.

Where Yvette had been clingy and demanding, Jo was independent and non-committal, which suited him fine. He couldn't deny he had feelings for Jo, but after the mess he'd made of his marriage, he wasn't ready to jump into another long-term relationship.

Working late on the Katie Wells case. Talk tomorrow.

He hadn't reached the point where he put kisses after his text messages yet. His phone buzzed almost immediately.

Okay. Good luck!

Neither had she.

He downed the rest of his coffee, bought a sandwich to go and crossed the road, back to the station. The press vans were still outside. Didn't they have homes to go to? He put his head down and tried to dodge around them to the back entrance, but a wily-eyed journalist spotted him. In an instant, he was besieged.

"DCI Miller, do you have any idea where Katie is?"

"Do you have any suspects?"

"What leads are you following up?"

"Are you any closer to finding her?"

"Do you have someone in custody?"

Microphones and recording devices were shoved in his face. He ignored them and fought his way through the pack to the front entrance. They didn't know Brian Wells had been arrested yet.

The duty sergeant saw him coming and unlocked the revolving door. He slipped through the glass panel and heaved a sigh of relief.

"Can't we do anything about them?" he muttered.

The officer shrugged. "Not really, sir."

He checked on Brian before going upstairs, but their main suspect was lying on the bench in the holding cell, staring up at the ceiling. He wasn't agitated or anxious, like Rob would have expected if he needed to get back to a young girl he'd stashed away somewhere.

Perhaps they'd got it wrong.

He entered the squad room. "Will, where are we on those phone records?" he barked.

The tech whizz glanced up. "Nothing stands out, guv. Mr Wells called his solicitor several times yesterday, but not this morning."

That tied in with his statement. *Shit. Back at square bloody one.*

He marched over to Mallory's desk. "Let's hold him until midnight, then release him. See where he goes."

Mallory gave a curt nod. "Lawrence wants to issue a *Crimewatch* appeal."

Rob stared at Mallory. "Seriously? So soon?"

"He's got the commissioner breathing down his neck."

Didn't they all? "Okay, I suppose it can't hurt."

"They want to do a reconstruction," Mallory told him.

"That's a new one for us." While they'd used the media in the past, he'd never experienced a reconstruction shoot before.

"Vicky said to contact her first thing."

"Okay, although someone else can brief them. Put Harry on it — with his looks, he was made for television." Rob wasn't in it for the limelight and he had better things to do than pander to the press.

Harry raised his head. "Sir?"

"Brush up on the specifics, Harry. You've got an appointment with the *Crimewatch* team tomorrow."

The young constable blinked, then grinned. "If you say so, guv."

Mallory masked a smile, then his phone rang. He answered it, listened for a moment, and the smile vanished from his lips. "Can you bring it in?" he barked.

Must be serious, Rob thought. Mallory never snapped at anyone.

"What?" he mouthed. "Yep, now would be good," he said to the caller.

Rob stared at him. It was very late to be asking someone to come into the station. "You got something?"

Mallory hung up. "That was Candice Dalling's mother. She's just listened to her daughter's mobile phone messages and found one from Katie Wells. The timestamp is 8.43 this morning."

CHAPTER 12

Rob, Mallory and Will stared at Candy's iPhone in its sparkly pink plastic case. "Play it again," said Rob.

There was no direct message — it must have been a false dial — but there was the sound of cars going by, a dog barking and a woman's voice.

A woman's voice.

They couldn't hear what was being said, but by the cadence, it sounded like a question.

"I'm waiting for my friend," came Katie's reply.

The woman spoke again, indeterminate, and then there was rustling until the phone cut off.

All three men stared at one another, then back at the phone. Eventually Mallory said, "We can rule out Brian Wells, then."

Rob wasn't so sure. "It could be an accomplice," he said.

"Who?" Will gestured to the phone records scattered over his desk. "He doesn't have any close female friends."

That they knew about. Rob sighed. They were probably right. It looked like Brian Wells may be totally innocent.

"Let's get this recording analysed," he said. "Maybe they can work out what the woman is saying."

"If she's the kidnapper," Will added. "It might be a random person asking Katie if she's okay. She was waiting on a street corner by herself."

"It's possible, although it's more likely to be the kidnapper, given that it's in the time frame of her disappearance."

Will acknowledged his cynicism with a grimace.

"So, are we looking for a woman?" asked Mallory. They'd all been thrown by the latest turn of events.

"Seems so," said Will.

"It's bound to be someone who knows the family." Tiredness prickled at his vision. "We need to speak to Lisa Wells. Tell uniform to bring her in."

Mallory made the call as he walked back to his desk. "Yes, now. Thank you."

Things were happening. This was the first solid lead they'd had. Normally, he'd update the chief superintendent, but Lawrence had left long ago.

Rob sank into his chair and swivelled around so he faced the window. The sky was a dark smudge, the sun having set over two hours ago. Across the road, the gothic silhouette of the church spire reached upwards, its reverent stillness strangely comforting.

A woman perpetrator put a different spin on things. Serial offenders were hardly ever female, and it likely ruled out a sexual motive — thank God — which left one question.

Why?

Was it trafficking? Suburban West London was a strange hunting ground. Too middle-class. Too settled.

As he ate his sandwich, he pictured Katie's serious little face, and wondered where she was now. And if she was still alive.

* * *

They invited Lisa Wells into the briefing room. She wasn't under caution, just helping with their enquiries. Right now, she stared at him across the boardroom table.

Instead of the creased skirt and blouse she'd been wearing earlier, she was wearing jeans and a simple T-shirt, her hair tied back in a ponytail. Practicality over vanity.

"Have you found anything?"

Rob cringed at the hope in her voice. "Lisa, Candy had a missed call from Katie this morning . . ."

Her eyes lit up.

"She didn't leave a message, but there was a woman's voice in the background."

"A woman?" Lisa frowned. "You think a woman took her?"

"It's possible." Rob leaned forward. "Lisa, I need a list of anyone you've had contact with in the last few weeks, anyone who's shown an interest in Katie, any friends of the family, even visitors to the house. Can you do that for me?"

"Okay."

"Now, please. If you don't mind." He placed a piece of paper and a biro on the table in front of her.

"I'll have to rack my brains," she said.

"Take as much time as you need."

She nodded and picked up the pen.

In the interim, Rob checked on Jeff and Harry, who were ploughing through the CCTV footage in the vicinity of Brian Wells's and Sergio Wójcik's flats.

"The entrance to Brian's flat is around the back, so the camera on Upper Richmond doesn't pick him up," said Jeff. "But I've got him on the ANPR at 9.32 heading to Katie's house. It ties in with his story."

It did. "Okay, good. What about Sergio?"

"He's safe too. He leaves shortly after nine thirty, when he gets Lisa's call. It matches his phone records. He then passes the ANPR camera on Lonsdale Road a few minutes after Brian Wells."

"He did arrive a few minutes after him," acknowledged Rob.

It seemed the two men were in the clear.

"Okay, thanks, guys. Good work."

He told Mallory to release Brian Wells, and went to see how Lisa was getting on.

"Making progress?"

Lisa had written half a page of names. She was chewing on the end of the pen. "I can't think of anyone else." She slid the list over to him.

He studied it. There were several names he didn't recognise. "Let's start at the top."

They went through them all.

First was the neighbour, Ed Maplin's wife, Julia, who popped in to ask for help with the annual street party. Every year they closed off the road and put stalls out so the residents could mingle and get to know one another. Like Jenny had said, they were a close-knit community. Theoretically, every resident in the street was a potential suspect. But the door-to-door enquiries hadn't picked up anything suspicious, and he had to trust they'd done their jobs correctly.

He suppressed a shiver. What if Katie was only a few houses away, hidden in someone's attic or basement?

Next was the cleaner who came in once a week. "She lives in Surbiton and always uses public transport," Lisa said. Rob took her details, but it was unlikely she was involved. She hadn't been working the day of the abduction and she had no obvious motive to kidnap Katie, and no vehicle with which to do it. Still, they'd ping her mobile phone and check where she was on her day off.

Candy's mother was on the list, but they'd already discounted her, along with Katie's teacher, who'd been at school when Katie was abducted.

"Who is Mrs Patel?" Rob asked.

"Oh, she's the lady who works in the newsagent around the corner. We often stop there for a cold drink on the way home. She knows Katie." Lisa shrugged.

"Okay, good." They'd check her out too.

"Karen Prior is a work colleague. She came back to mine for a drink after work last Friday. We sat in the garden and had G&Ts."

"Does she drive?"

"Yes, it's a red car — a Honda, I think, but I can't be sure. I don't pay that much attention to cars."

It would be easy enough to check with the DVLA.

"Is Brian still in custody?" she asked, her voice quavering.

"We're releasing him tonight. He's no longer a person of interest."

She heaved a sigh of relief. "I knew it. I knew he had nothing to do with this."

"He *was* planning on taking Katie out of the country," Rob reminded her.

The haggard look was back. "This divorce has been very hard on him. He misses being with Katy."

"Why don't you let him see her more often?" Rob asked, not that it was any of his business.

She sighed. "He went off the rails after we split up, lost his job, started drinking heavily. And he looked terrible. I didn't feel comfortable leaving Katie with him."

Rob could understand that. "Maybe you guys need to have a talk," he said, then shut his mouth. Not his problem.

Lisa nodded. "Yes, we do."

Rob showed Lisa out. Suddenly, they'd gone from having no leads to having a whole street to follow up on, as well as the cleaner, the newsagent and the work colleague.

He fought off the encroaching weariness and wondered if he ought to attempt a coffee from the new machine before heading back upstairs.

Bugger it. How bad could it be? He needed to stay awake. Katie's life depended on it.

CHAPTER 13

The coffee *was* really bad.

They had the recent bout of budget cuts to thank for that. Rob grimaced and threw it away, grabbing a coke from the vending machine instead.

Back upstairs, his extended team was hard at it. No one was even considering leaving while Katie was still missing.

He got everyone's attention. It was time for a pep talk. Weary faces turned towards him, fingers stopped typing and the neon blue digital clock flicked to 23:24.

"It's been fourteen hours since Katie disappeared," Rob began. "There's been no ransom demand, which quite frankly isn't good news, so we have to assume the kidnapper never planned to release her."

Heads drooped as the reality of what he was saying penetrated. *If* we *don't get her back, she's not coming back.*

"As you know, the voice on Candy's phone was female. We've sent it off to be analysed, but we won't get anything back until tomorrow afternoon at the earliest. In the meantime, I need you to look into all the possible suspects on the list Lisa Wells made this evening. You've all been emailed a copy. Mallory and I are going to visit the residents in the street tomorrow, just in case the door-to-door missed something."

At Celeste's worried frown, he added, "We're running out of options." He wasn't criticising her work. "There's no CCTV in Belgrave Road, but there is on Lonsdale Road and at the roundabout by the Waterman's Arms, so let's see if any of the residents' vehicles were picked up on that during the window of Katie's abduction."

Heads nodded.

"Thanks for staying, everyone. I know it's late. Let's push through and get as much information as we can, and then call it a night. Try and get a few hours' sleep before you come back in tomorrow. You're no use to me if you're a bunch of zombies."

A few smiles.

"Oh, and we have the *Crimewatch* team coming in tomorrow. Harry will be their point of contact, so refer them to him if they try to speak to you directly. We can't have them getting in the way of this investigation."

Harry grinned good-naturedly at the few joking murmurs passed his way. He was extraordinarily good looking. Being mixed-race with Indian heritage, he had almond-shaped brown eyes, criminally long lashes and a model bone structure.

"Right, thanks again, everyone. We'll have an update at eight o'clock tomorrow morning."

By four a.m. Rob was falling asleep at his desk. The squad room was eerily quiet, the neon clock casting its blue light over the sleeping computers. There was a camp bed in one of the back offices, if he was desperate, but he only lived down the road.

He scanned out and said goodbye to the duty sergeant. Weariness tugged at his body and he stumbled rather than walked the short distance home. Anyone watching would think he was drunk. It was a balmy night. Tomorrow was going to be hot.

"Christ, Trigger, I'm sorry." The golden Labrador launched itself at him. He'd completely forgotten to dash home and feed the dog. Since Yvette had left, he'd taken to leaving the sliding patio door open so Trigger could get into the back garden, and he had plenty of water, but he no doubt was starving.

Rob fed him, then collapsed on the ancient, worn sofa in the lounge. He'd spent many a night on it when Yvette had been having one of her sulks. Now *that* was something he didn't miss.

He closed his eyes and tried not to think of Katie. It was impossible. Her small, serious face with her clear blue eyes flickered behind his vision. He was dimly aware of Trigger coming into the lounge and curling up on the floor next to him. Katie's face morphed into Lisa's, her eyes glistening with tears.

You will find her? she begged. *Please, get my Katie back.*

And finally, the images faded to black.

* * *

Rob woke groggy, unsure of where he was.

Aah, the lounge. Already Trigger was prancing around him. *Feed me*, he seemed to be saying, his pink tongue lolling to the side.

Crap, what time is it?

His phone, on its last bar, read 07.30. *The briefing.* Spurring into action, he fed Trigger, showered, dressed and left the house, all in twenty minutes.

"I promise I'll take you for a long walk later," he told a panting Trigger as he closed the door. These long hours were thankfully few and far between, only when he had a big case on. Normally, it wasn't like this.

Trigger whined pitifully as he closed the door. Yvette had refused to take him when she'd left, even though he'd bought the dog for her. A clean break, she'd said. Nothing to remind her of *him*.

It was crazy to think he'd had such a detrimental effect on someone else's well-being. And how much she hated him for it. But that was on him. It wasn't Trigger's fault.

At least Jo was also in law enforcement, so she understood. Her own hours were unpredictable, her own caseload erratic and inconsistent. There were times when he hardly saw her, and others when she'd stay for days and he was almost happy. But then she'd leave again, before they got too comfortable. It was perfect.

* * *

Everyone was in by eight, including the chief superintendent. No surprises there. He always arrived before everyone else. Rob could tell by his loaded gaze that he wanted to have a word, but there wasn't time. He'd promised a briefing.

Almost twenty-four hours.

He updated his team on their tasks for the day. Chasing up forensics, analysing camera footage, and digging into their new pool of potential suspects. The tail they'd put on Brian Wells hadn't resulted in anything. He'd gone straight home after his stint in the nick and hadn't left.

"That rules him out, then," stated Mallory.

It really did look like it, but Rob left the tail on him, just in case.

He eventually succumbed to DCS Sam Lawrence's silent summons and entered the fishbowl. The normally stalwart chief superintendent's pinched expression said it all.

"I don't mind telling you, Rob, I'm under a huge amount of pressure on this one. Is there anything definite on the girl?"

"Only the woman's voice on the phone, but we don't know if she's the kidnapper. We're assuming she is, for now."

Because it's all we have.

"What do the tech guys say?"

"Will's chasing it up, but they need more time." The magical techies who conjured the truth from voice recordings and the twisted bowels of laptops and mobile phones were good, but they couldn't work miracles.

The chief superintendent sighed. His hand shook slightly as he raked it through his hair. "Time is something we don't have. Have you released the father?"

"Yeah, it doesn't look like he had anything to do with it. The only thing he's guilty of is wanting to spend more time with his kid."

Lawrence shook his head. "Damn shame." Once again, his eyes flickered to the family photo on his desk. "What a way to go out," he muttered.

"Sir?"

"We have to find this girl, Rob. I don't want to retire with this hanging over my head."

It was the first time Rob had heard Lawrence admit he was packing it in. Everyone knew he was, but he'd never come out and said it. Because that would make it real.

"You'll be missed, sir."

"Thank you, Rob." He seemed to pull himself together. "I'll update the commissioner — he's coming in later this morning. When are the *Crimewatch* crew turning up?"

Fuck, he'd forgotten about them. "I'm not a hundred-per-cent sure, but I've put Harry — I mean, DC Malhotra — in charge. He's had some experience with the industry."

"Very good." Lawrence nodded. "And let me know the moment you find something. We could all do with some good news."

"I'll do my best, sir."

* * *

It was mid-morning when the film crew arrived. Vicky strode in followed by the chic female *Crimewatch* presenter. Behind them were the entourage — sound engineer, cameraman, gaffers and an assortment of equipment.

"That's our cue to leave," Rob murmured to Mallory.

Too late. Vicky made a beeline for him.

"Morning, Rob. Do you have a moment?"

75

He pointed to his phone. "Sorry, Vicky. Can't stop. DC Malhotra's ready for you. He'll brief you and help you get set up." Harry came forward, a smile on his perfect face.

The *Crimewatch* presenter smiled back.

"But . . ." Vicky's reply was lost as he dashed out, followed closely by Mallory.

* * *

The south-east of England was gripped by a rare heatwave with average temperatures soaring into the mid-thirties. Red-faced pedestrians walked around in strappy tops and shorts, fanning themselves, while inside the police vehicle they were blasting the air con.

Belgrave Road, where Katie lived, was no longer cordoned off, and they drove right up to the house.

"This heat is crazy." Mallory stepped out onto the shimmering tarmac. He'd replaced his normal long-sleeved shirt with a short-sleeved one, displaying pale, skinny arms.

Rob noticed Ed watering the pot plants either side of his glossy front door. Obviously not at work today, then. "Morning," Rob called.

Ed glanced up. "Morning, Detective. Any news on Katie?"

"We're following several promising leads," he lied.

"I heard you had Brian Wells in custody."

"We let him go. He wasn't charged."

Ed nodded. "Glad to hear it. Terrible to think that the kid's own father . . ." His voice petered off. Rob knew what he meant.

"We'll be by later to have a chat," Rob told him. He turned to Mallory. "Let's start at the far end. I'll take the houses on this side — you do that side." Mallory gave a curt nod and marched towards the first house at the far end.

A lot of what they were doing was pure gut work, as Rob liked to think of it. They weren't just searching for signs of Katie, like items of clothing or supplies, but also for anyone acting abnormally, trying too hard, being subversive or just giving off suspicious vibes. Rob trusted Mallory implicitly. If there was something fishy going on with any of the residents, no matter how small, Mallory would flag it.

He watched as Mallory rapped on the door. They made a great team. It would be a shame when Mallory moved on, but move on he must. He deserved to run his own murder squad. Rob made a mental note to talk to the chief super about it.

Rob worked his way down his side. It was basic policing, usually left to the uniformed division, but surprise was key. If any of the residents were hiding Katie on their premises, they wouldn't be expecting a second visit.

It didn't take longer than half an hour to get through the entire left side of the street. He saved the Maplins' house until last, so they could have a chat.

This time it was Mrs Maplin who answered the door.

"Please, call me Julia," she said, as she showed him into the living room, an eye-watering floral extravaganza that proved money couldn't buy good taste. "Is this about poor Katie?"

"Yes." Rob sat down on a daffodil-yellow loveseat that hurt to look at. "We're recanvassing the area in case anyone remembers seeing anything unusual the morning of her disappearance."

"Would you like some tea or a cold refreshment?"

"No, I'm good. Thanks." Rob could have done with a cold drink, but he didn't want to impose, and he was in a hurry. They'd wasted enough time. This was fast turning into a useless endeavour. He needed to get back to the station to corroborate any evidence that had come in this morning. They were still waiting on the DNA samples from Katie's backpack.

She nodded and sat down. "Well, I'm not sure how I can help you, DCI Miller."

"Could you take me through your movements yesterday morning?"

Her eyes widened. "Yes, of course. As soon as we heard that Katie had gone missing, we rallied everyone together. The idea was to form a search party and look for her."

"How did you hear?"

"It was hard not to. Lisa was running up and down the road screaming her name." She shook her head. "My heart broke for her. I went to see if I could help. Then you lot arrived, and the street was cordoned off . . ."

He knew the rest.

"And your husband didn't go to work yesterday?"

She chuckled. "No, he works from home most days now, although he still goes in for the odd meeting."

"What does he do?"

"He's a financial consultant." She emphasised the job title like it was a revered position.

It must be nice to work from home, Rob thought. It wasn't a luxury he'd ever be afforded in the police service. You couldn't catch criminals from your spare room.

Julia uncrossed her legs, smoothing down her skirt. He noticed the sizeable diamond on her ring finger, flanked by a thick gold band.

"Do you work?" he asked her.

"Only part-time." She smiled. "I volunteer for the local charity shop three days a week."

"What did you do before that?"

"I was in property." She wrinkled her nose like it was something nasty, something she wanted to forget. "I found this house for Ed. That's how we met, actually." A secretive smile.

"How long ago was that?"

"Hmm . . . About fifteen years ago, now."

"Do you have any children?"

"I don't, but Ed has two from his previous marriage. They're at university now. Makes one feel old." She grinned. "I was very fond of Becca and Peter. The house felt strange after they'd gone."

Appearances were deceiving. Here, he'd thought they were the perfect suburban family — husband, wife, two kids at the local school — when in fact, she was his second wife and the kids had already flown the nest.

"Ed's first wife died," she told him. "He moved here because of the schools. I remember when we first met. It was pouring with rain and we hid inside this house until it had eased up. That's how we got talking."

Rob nodded encouragingly, willing her to go on.

"He was really torn up over his wife's death. So were the children. They were . . ." She paused, searching for the right word. "Lost."

He raised an eyebrow.

"I know," she hastened. "It's hard to believe a man like Edward could be in that position, but he was. Newly widowed with two kids to raise." She shook her head. "So very tragic. We always said it was fate that brought us together."

Fate, indeed.

Edward chose that moment to walk into the room. "Hello again, Detective. I'm about to have an espresso. Would you like one?"

Rob hesitated.

"It's no bother, really. I have a little machine that does it all for me."

How could he refuse? "Thanks."

"You know," Edward continued, "I was thinking about this whole ghastly business and I recall something a couple of years back, something similar happening. Do you remember, Jules? One of our neighbours was talking about it."

Rob perked up. "Really?"

Julia's brow furrowed. "Yes, now that you mention it, I do recall something like that. Hang on, let me have a think."

"I'll be back with the coffee." Ed walked out, but he didn't beckon to Rob to follow, so he sat where he was and waited for Julia to remember.

Come on.

"That's it!" She snapped her fingers. "Gosh, if Ed hadn't mentioned it, I'm not sure I would have ever thought about that again."

"About what?" He struggled to keep the impatience out of his voice.

"It was Sylvia — at number twenty-seven — who mentioned it during dinner one night. I was astounded because *she'd* never said a word."

"Who hadn't?" Rob said.

"Tessa Parvin."

"Who?" The name was vaguely familiar. He racked his brains. Where had he heard it before? Mallory would know.

"Tessa, she lives around the corner. Her daughter was taken."

Rob's heart skipped a beat. "Taken? As in kidnapped?"

"Yes, just like Katie. It was a while ago now, but I'm quite sure that's what it was."

Ed returned with the coffee. It smelled great, but Rob hardly noticed. His mind was flying. A woman in the immediate area had also had a child go missing. Coincidence? Maybe. *Maybe not.*

He accepted the coffee from Ed. It was in a proper glass espresso cup with just the right amount of *crema* on top. "Thanks." He fixed his eyes on Julia. "What happened to the child? Did they ever find her?"

She shook her head. "As far as I know, she's still missing."

CHAPTER 14

This was arguably the best espresso Rob had ever had, but unfortunately, he wasn't in a position to enjoy it.

Katie. Tessa. Sylvia. A second missing child. Never found.

It must have been before his time. It was surprising the chief superintendent hadn't mentioned it. He'd been around for decades. The thoughts flew through his head, mingling and merging in an array of disjointed information.

"Can you tell me anything more?" he asked. "Like when her daughter was abducted?"

Ed sat in a vacant chair. "It didn't happen around here, I don't think." He looked at his wife for confirmation.

Julia shook her head. "No, Tessa only moved into the area three or four years ago. I think that's why she relocated."

Rob exhaled. That's why they hadn't heard about it. It was outside their jurisdiction.

"Wasn't it something to do with Tessa's ex-husband?" Ed asked.

Julia sat up straight. "Yes, that's right. Sylvia said Tessa's ex had taken the girl back to Syria, or wherever he was from. It's such a male-dominated society over there. The wife has no rights."

"How did she know the father took her?" Not that he was disputing what she said, but if the father had kidnapped her, it was unlikely to be connected to the Katie Wells case.

"I'm not sure. I think that's the conclusion the police came to." She looked at Rob like he ought to know. She had a point.

"We'll look into it," he said gruffly. "Could you give me Tessa's address?"

"Of course." Julia fished in her handbag and scrolled through her phone contacts. "Here it is." Reaching for a small notepad and pen, she wrote down the address, then handed it to him.

It was literally around the corner. Not in the road they'd just canvassed, but less than 500 metres away. "And Sylvia is number twenty-seven?"

She nodded. Mallory's side of the road. Just then his phone buzzed. Mallory was outside waiting for him. He finished the last sip of his coffee and passed the cup to Ed. "Thanks, I needed that."

He grinned. "Any time. Good luck, Detective. We're counting on you to bring Katie home."

* * *

"Did you speak to a Sylvia Grey?" Rob asked his partner as soon as he got to the car.

Mallory nodded. "Yes, she's in number twenty-seven. Nice lady. Very knowledgeable about plants."

Rob couldn't care less about her plants. "Did she mention anything about Tessa Parvin's missing daughter?"

Mallory frowned. "No. Did I miss something?"

"It's something the Maplins said. Apparently, Tessa's daughter went missing a couple of years back. The police thought the husband had taken her back to the Middle East."

"Sylvia didn't mention it." He ran a hand through his thinning hair, clearly agitated with himself.

"Not your fault," Rob said. "It's probably not relevant. Is she there now?"

"Yep."

"Let's have a quick word and get her take before we go and see Tessa Parvin."

They walked back up the lavender-scented street and knocked on Sylvia's door. It was a dove grey, like her name.

She opened the door with a warm smile. "You're back, DI Mallory. Did you forget to ask me something?"

She was younger than Rob had expected, late thirties with a heart-shaped face and chocolate-brown eyes, which were fixed on his partner.

Mallory smiled back. "Yes, sorry to disturb you, Miss Grey."

"Please, I asked you to call me Sylvia."

Was Mallory blushing? Rob cleared his throat. "Excuse us for interrupting, Miss Grey." The first-name basis did not apply to him. She shifted her melting gaze onto him. "We want to ask you about Tessa Parvin. I believe you know her?"

"Oh, Tessa, yes. Do you want to come in?"

They followed her into a tastefully decorated hallway consisting of a narrow bureau with a lamp, a basket for her keys and a wrought-iron coat stand. It was pleasantly bright and uncluttered, a total contrast to the kitsch design of the Maplins' place.

"Please, sit down." The living room was equally cheery, with sheer curtains lifting in the breeze from the open window. The furnishings were all light-coloured and minimalist, but of good quality. Rob sat on a stylish upholstered armchair, leaving Mallory to sit beside Sylvia on the L-shaped sofa.

"Could you tell us what you know about her daughter's disappearance?"

The smile fell from Sylvia's face. "Oh, that. I'm not sure I should mention it. Tessa doesn't like people to know."

"It would really help our investigation," Mallory said.

Her gaze flickered back to him and softened. "Okay, well, if you think it will help."

Mallory gave her an encouraging smile. "What do you know?"

The interplay between the two of them was interesting. Did Rob detect a spark there?

"It was shortly after Tessa moved into the neighbourhood." Sylvia clutched her hands in front of her. She had thin, elegant fingers. No wedding band. "I met her at the nursery, she was buying some petunias for her garden and we got talking. She used to be a botanist. Did you know that?"

"No." Rob resisted the urge to roll his eyes.

"Anyway, I went to hers for a cup of tea and commented on the photograph of her daughter. A pretty little girl. Mixed-race — that was a surprise. That's when she told me."

"Yes?" Rob leaned forward in his chair.

"Well, she fell apart. She said her daughter lived with her ex-husband in Iran, and she couldn't see her. It was very sad. I felt so sorry for her."

"Did the father abduct the child or was it an agreed arrangement?" Mallory asked. Rob was content for him to take over the questioning. Sylvia responded better to him, anyway.

"Just between you and me, I think he took her without permission. Tessa was distraught, it was still very raw. She admitted she'd moved because she couldn't stay in that house anymore, not without her daughter."

"Do you know where she used to live?" Mallory enquired.

Sylvia scrunched up her forehead, then gave a soft sigh. "No, sorry. I can't remember. I think it was the same county, though."

"Okay, that's fine." Mallory smiled. "Thanks, Sylvia, you've been amazing."

Amazing? That was a strong word.

She beamed. "I'm happy to help." Then, she gasped. "You don't think that's got anything to do with Katie's disappearance, do you?"

"Oh, no," Mallory assured her. "It just came up in our enquiries, and we're obliged to check it out."

She nodded, the smile firmly back in place. "Okay, well, if you're ever in the neighbourhood, do pop in for a cup of tea."

Rob masked a grin as his partner blushed. "I will. Thank you again, Sylvia."

They left the neat house with its grey front door. "She's nice," Rob remarked.

"Don't." Mallory held up his hand.

Rob laughed. "Okay. Come on, it's time we paid Tessa Parvin a visit. She's only round the corner."

Mallory raised his eyebrows. "Wasn't she the one at the volunteer search party? I remember taking down her name."

Rob nodded. It had come back to him too. "That's the one."

He didn't need to say it. He knew Mallory was thinking the same thing that he was.

* * *

Tessa Parvin lived in mock-Tudor turmoil. The house seemed slightly off-kilter, like it was listing to the side. Faded wooden beams gasped out for varnish, while the paint on the exterior walls had disintegrated in exhausted chunks.

The garden was wild and chaotic. Nettles drooped in the heat, while out-of-control lavender collapsed forward, unable to hold their purple heads upright. Rob and Mallory navigated the overgrown path, careful not to sting themselves, and rang the doorbell. It chimed a low melody, then footsteps sounded on the floorboards and the chain rattled.

"Hello?" Tessa Parvin's aquiline nose poked through the gap.

"Mrs Parvin? It's the police, could we have a word?"

There was a pause. The door closed again while the chain was removed. A bolt slid back, and the door opened. A stale, musty smell assaulted them, as though the house had been closed up for months.

"DCI Miller and DI Mallory from the Putney Major Investigation Team. May we come in?"

"What's this about?"

She didn't move, didn't invite them in. She had planted her body firmly in front of the door. Behind her was a dark hallway. So dark, Rob had to strain to see anything beyond a few metres.

"Katie Wells." Rob held up his warrant card. If he'd hoped it would intimidate her into letting him in. He was wrong.

Her back straightened and her shoulders squared for battle. "Why do you want to talk to me?"

"We understand you know the family?" He phrased it as a question, hoping it would encourage her to answer, but she merely nodded. He tried again. "You were part of the informal search party that was disbanded, weren't you? We met briefly yesterday."

Another nod. Her eyes narrowed as she glanced from him to Mallory and back again.

Rob was losing patience. "Look, Mrs Parvin, you can either let us in and answer some questions or we can take you down to the police station and answer them there."

"On what grounds?" she asked.

"On the grounds that this is an active investigation and you may know something that could help us."

"I don't know anything about Katie's disappearance. If I did, I would have told you."

That was his entry point. "Because you know what it's like to have a daughter taken from you, don't you?"

She stared at him, lost for words. When she'd found her tongue, she scowled. "*That* has nothing to do with this. If you want to come in, get a warrant. I know my rights." She shut the door in their faces.

Rob looked at Mallory. "By the time we get a warrant she may have moved Katie to another location, assuming she's there now."

Mallory frowned. "She was acting rather suspiciously. What should we do?"

Rob ground his teeth together, working his lower jaw. "Fuck it, let's caution her and bring her in for questioning.

We'll have to do this the hard way. And get a warrant to search her premises."

He banged on the door again. No answer.

"Mrs Parvin, if you don't open this door, we're going to break it down and arrest you. Please come out."

The silence dragged on.

"Get uniform out here with a battering ram," Rob snapped. "I'm going around the back. If she comes out, arrest her."

Mallory was already keying the numbers into his mobile.

Rob walked around the side. The house seemed to lean on him, casting a long shadow across the mangled garden. The upstairs windows were in darkness, curtains drawn. It didn't look like there was any movement. He considered the Tudor-style loft, but the small box window in the centre of the uneven triangular beams was closed. If Katie was in there, they'd never know from down here.

A battered blue Ford Escort sat in the narrow driveway to the side of the property. In front of it was a metal gate that led around the back. The hinges screeched as he pushed it open. Judging by the rust, it hadn't been used in quite some time.

The back garden was bigger than the front, yet equally chaotic. More sad lavender, unfriendly thistles, a tangled assortment of unidentifiable wilderness plants, even some sunflowers, their bobbing yellow heads hanging in shame. Rob recalled the stains on her knees and her dirty fingernails. An avid gardener, Sylvia had said. A botanist. You wouldn't know it by this mess. He fought his way through the foliage to the tiny porch. On it stood a worn wicker chair and a folded-up newspaper. At the foot was a bowl of water. But no dog.

Unlike his house, there wasn't a patio or sliding door. A wooden door led into what he assumed was the kitchen. The door was closed, and there was only one window on this side of the house. Second floor. No wonder it was so dark inside. He kept his eyes locked on the back door, until he heard sirens coming up the street. It wouldn't hurt to give the uncooperative Mrs Parvin a bit of a fright.

He heard Mallory instructing them to break the door down. He pounded on the back door. "Mrs Parvin, this is your last chance. Let us in or we're coming in to get you."

His request was answered with a stony silence. If he didn't know better, he'd assume the house was deserted.

He texted Mallory. *Go for it.*

There was a loud bash as the door was forced open. Shouting, as the uniformed police identified themselves and entered the property. They'd search every room until they located Tessa Parvin.

Mallory would arrest her for obstructing the investigation and when they had her under control . . .

His phone beeped. *Got her.*

CHAPTER 15

Tessa Parvin was led away in resentful silence.

"Let's have a look around," said Rob.

They pulled on their gloves, just in case. Rob hoped they wouldn't have to turn this into a crime scene.

They crept down the passage.

"Creepy," Mallory muttered. It felt like a ghost house. It was astonishing somebody was actually living there.

Rob tried the light switch. The bulb flickered, on its last legs, like it was too much of an effort to shine on this place. It cast a dull yellow over the clutter coating the dining room — boxes piled halfway up the walls, books balanced in precarious heaps on the sturdy eight-seater table, their spines worn and tattered. *Orchids of Kew*, he read to himself. *Rainforests of Brazil.*

The living room was marginally better, though *living* was too strong a word. This was where Tessa Parvin existed, in an armchair by the window. The rest of the room's sparse furnishings included a floor lamp, a pair of spectacles on the reading stand and a half-drunk cup of coffee. A television stood at the front on a second-hand cabinet. It looked relatively new. Everything else looked like it had seen decades of use.

Reading and television. Her two pursuits. It saddened him that she lived like this. "I don't know why she didn't just open the bloody door."

"Proving a point," said Mallory.

Rob shook his head. Some people.

The kitchen was equally bare, apart from the usual signs of human habitation. No fancy equipment, just a gas cooker, toaster, kettle and other basic necessities. Tessa Parvin lived a simple existence.

They creaked up the staircase.

"I'll take this room," Rob said. Mallory peeled off into the other.

The master bedroom overlooked the tangled back garden. That must be the window he had seen from below. He looked through the cupboards and under the bed. Nothing. No sign of Katie.

"Anything?" he called out.

"Nothing," said Mallory.

The bathroom was empty too. There was only one place left to look. They studied the square panel in the ceiling above the landing.

"How are we going to get up there?" Rob asked.

Mallory disappeared into the second bedroom and returned carrying a pole with a hook on the end. He pulled the loft hatch open. It folded outwards, revealing a metal ladder. Mallory dragged it down. "Do you want to do the honours?"

Anticipation fluttered in his stomach. What would he find up there? He mentally prepared for whatever it might be. Being caught unawares was when the shock set in.

He scaled the ladder and stuck his head into the pitch-black hole. He couldn't see a damn thing. Using the torch on his phone, he peered into the darkness and went further in. There were just more boxes — rectangular shadows with hard corners. Crates. A pungent odour hit his nose and made his skin crawl. "Ugh, what's that smell?"

"Can't smell anything from down here," came Mallory's reply.

He shone his torch around, looking for a light. *Aah, there.*

He pressed a switch and a hanging bulb sprung to life. Unlike the hall light, this one was blinding. *Look all you want*, it was saying. *You won't find anything.*

Mallory mounted the ladder behind him and shoved his head and shoulders through the hatch.

"There's not much space in here," Rob said. "Certainly nowhere to hide a body. Unless she's in the boxes."

Christ, what a thought.

"Where's that smell coming from?"

"Over here." Rob crouched down to inspect three or four enormous bags stacked in the corner. "Fertiliser," he said. "Enough for a small farm."

"Why would she keep that up here?"

"No idea. She ought to get a garden shed." He poked around a bit more. "Can't see any sign of Katie, can you?"

"No, thank God."

Rob seconded that. He'd hoped to find her alive and well. Then he could have slept easy tonight. Instead, they were still on the hunt.

"Let's get back to the station and talk to Tessa Parvin. She might be more amenable now she's facing an obstruction charge."

* * *

The sulky, tight-lipped woman glared at them from across the interrogation table. She was on the defensive, all right, her head held high, her body stiff, her features taut. Rob felt the animosity radiating off her.

He was the first to speak, after Mallory had presented their names for the recording. Tessa Parvin had refused her right to a solicitor.

"What for? I didn't do anything."

Rob shrugged, he wasn't going to argue with her. If she said anything incriminating, that was her problem. He was intrigued, however. All they wanted to do was talk to her, ask her a few questions about her daughter, and yet here she was acting like a suspect. Why bring that on yourself? Unless she was trying to mislead them — a double-bluff, if you like. Was he overthinking?

"Mrs Parvin, why don't you want to help us with our investigation?" he began.

He was expecting a "No comment", but she answered straight away. "Why should I help you? You weren't interested when my daughter disappeared," she hissed.

Rob stared at her, momentarily lost. "What do you mean?"

"You lot." She waved her arm around to indicate the entire police department. "My little girl vanished four years ago, and you did nothing."

Rob had looked up the case. Woking Police Station had handled the investigation. Arina Parvin had disappeared on her way home from school in Bisley, a small market town. The SIO, DI Purley, had come to the conclusion that Tessa's husband, Ramin, had smuggled Arina out of the country, back to his native Iran. He'd disappeared the same time she had, and no one had had any contact with them since. The Iranians had refused to confirm or deny whether Ramin Parvin and his daughter were in the country. Rob had left a message for DI Purley to contact him with regards to the investigation.

"Why don't you tell me about it?" he said softly.

Her eyes narrowed. "Why? So we can talk about how inept the police were? How they ignored everything I said and closed the case without ever finding out what happened to my Arina?"

"How old was your daughter when she disappeared?" asked Mallory. He knew very well how old she'd been, but Rob knew he was using the question to persuade Tessa Parvin into telling them her version of events.

"She was twelve."

Finally, they were getting somewhere.

"And where did it happen?" Mallory continued, working his advantage.

Tessa closed her eyes and gave her head a little shake.

The seconds ticked by.

She sighed and seemed to collapse as the fight sagged out of her. When she opened her eyes, they were muted and dull. "Arina was walking home from school through Bisley Common. That's the last place she was seen before she — she disappeared."

"Did she often walk through the common?" asked Rob.

Tessa nodded. "Yes, if she didn't catch the bus. It was a sunny day and she had two friends with her. They all lived on our side of the common."

"What did they say happened?" Rob had read their statements and knew they'd veered off the path before Arina.

"They said goodbye to her and took a different route home. That's the last they saw of her."

This was the tricky bit. "What made you think something had happened to her, that she wasn't with your husband?"

Her mouth clamped together, as she tensed.

"Ramin didn't care about Arina. She worshipped him, but he'd wanted a boy. No matter what she did, she couldn't change who she was."

Her hands balled into grubby fists on the table. "He wouldn't have taken her."

It was pretty convincing. Rob studied the woman opposite him. Dishevelled, with prematurely grey hair, baggy clothes. No make-up. This was a woman who didn't care what anyone thought of her. He wondered what she'd been like before her daughter disappeared, before her world had splintered. Maybe then she'd given a damn. But now there was nothing left to live for.

He glanced at Mallory and could see his partner was of the same opinion. "What did DI Purley say?"

Tessa frowned. "That man was only interested in closing the case. He didn't care about Arina, or about what I had to say. He palmed me off every time I rang the station, avoided my calls and eventually sent one of his deputies to tell me the case was closed and they'd called off the search. My Arina was still out there and nobody went to rescue her." A sob clutched at her throat.

Her anguish was palpable.

"I'm sorry for the way things were handled," he said. "It does sound like there were grounds to continue with the investigation."

She peered up at him. "Well, it's too late now. Four years. My Arina is dead, I know it."

It was the most likely conclusion. Unless the girl had been secreted out of the country. He'd have to ask DI Purley about that. Presumably, they'd checked with border control. Anyway, that wasn't his case, and this wasn't his fight. He brought them back to the current investigation. "Mrs Parvin, why did you move to Barnes?"

"I needed a change. Everything in that house reminded me of Arina. It was really just the two of us, you see. Ramin was away a lot."

"What do you think of the neighbourhood?"

"I used to think it was safe." She sniffed. "Before Katie went missing."

He tilted his head to the side. "Why were you at Edward Maplin's house the day Katie disappeared?"

"I wanted to join in the search for Katie. You see, I *know* what it feels like. I know what Lisa is going through. It's the worst feeling in the world." She wrapped her arms around herself.

Rob understood her need to help. "Why didn't you just tell us that to begin with? It could have saved us all this drama." She'd be released, but there was paperwork involved — processing, write-ups, reports. She could have saved everyone the time and effort by just cooperating from the beginning.

"I didn't feel like talking to the police." The stubborn sulk was back.

Rob stood up. Under the circumstances, even that was understandable, albeit inadvisable. "Thank you for talking to us, Mrs Parvin. DI Mallory will process your release forms. You're free to go."

She didn't move. "What about my daughter? What are you going to do about her?"

Rob froze. "It's been four years, Mrs Parvin. The case is closed. What do you want me to do?"

"Find her," she hissed. "Her body is out there somewhere. I want to bring her home. I want to bury my girl."

Rob sighed inwardly. But she deserved no less. "I'll talk to DI Purley," he promised. "But it's not my investigation, so there are limits to what I can do."

Her head dropped. "So, once again, Arina is swept under the carpet. No one cares that she's still out there, that her body was never found."

"It's not that we don't care, Mrs Parvin. It's complicated. Arina didn't disappear in our jurisdiction."

"Serial killers don't stick to jurisdictions," she spat.

Rob spun around. "What do you mean, serial killers?"

"Well, you don't think my Arina is the first little girl to disappear, do you? I looked into it. There are several girls who've gone missing in the greater Surrey area over the last few years. Most of them unsolved, of course."

She was accusing him, like it was his fault. Maybe it was — the police's, that is. But was it true? Had there been a spate of unsolved missing persons?

"Okay, I'll tell you what I'll do. I'll look into Arina's case. If it does mirror the other disappearances, we might have a shot at reopening the case."

Mallory gawked at him.

Tessa Parvin exhaled. "That's all I ask, Detective."

Rob was already regretting his words as he left the interrogation room.

CHAPTER 16

"What are you doing?" Mallory grilled him on the way back to the squad room. "You can't promise her you'll reopen her daughter's case. You have no control over that."

"I didn't promise I'd reopen it," he said. "I promised I'd look into it. Besides, it does sound like the SIO might have been too quick to call it a day. What she said about her husband's relationship with his daughter, or lack thereof, warrants further investigation."

"She could be making it up, grasping at straws. She was distraught, after all. People see what they want to see."

Rob knew that. "It doesn't hurt to check. Let's look into the other missing girls, if there are any. And find out if anyone on our team has any contacts in the Middle East. It would be useful to know if Ramin Parvin has his daughter with him. She'd be sixteen now. I'm going to pay DI Purley a visit. He's not returning my calls."

* * *

Woking was a forty-five-minute drive from Putney, but Rob made it in thirty. Blue lights had a way of making other motorists get out of your way.

He hadn't cleared Tessa Parvin from their investigation yet. Had she taken Katie as a replacement for her own daughter? Maybe she wanted revenge on the system? Who knew what she was really thinking? She appeared sane enough, but that didn't mean she was. He'd been surprised before.

DS Bird was looking into her background, into any properties she owned or connections she had. They hadn't managed to extend the warrant they'd got for Brian Wells and Sergio Wójcik's phone records to Tessa's, but if Jenny or Mallory came up with anything, he'd speak to the chief superintendent. Right now, his gut was telling him *not* to write her off as a suspect.

Rob didn't enquire whether DI Purley was available when he arrived at Woking Police Station. Instead, he flashed the duty sergeant his warrant card and walked past him like he knew where he was going. CID was on the first floor. A tip from Mallory, who'd been here before.

The door was shut, and he didn't have an access card. There was, however, a water dispenser outside in the hall, so he poured himself a cup while he waited for someone to come out.

A few minutes later, a female officer emerged and threw him a hesitant smile. He nodded a greeting, took his cup of water and went inside.

Like Putney, this was an open-plan squad room, but unlike his department, the ranking officers' offices weren't made of glass. He placed the cup of water on the first desk he came to, ignored the curious glances of the few people in the room and walked towards the back.

Detective Chief Superintendent Maxwell, read the name on the door. Next to it, *DCI Purley*.

DCI now, was it? A reward for closing the Arina Parvin case? Rob knocked and got a terse, "Come in."

He opened the door and walked in. Purley leaped to his feet. "Who the hell are you? How did you get in here?"

Rob held up his warrant card. "DCI Miller from the Putney Major Crime Team. I decided to save you the trouble of calling me back."

Purley mouthed like a guppy. Rob glanced at the chair. "May I? This won't take long."

Purley hesitated, then nodded. "Seriously, how did you get up here?"

"I walked up. Can we get down to business?"

Purley sat, the lines on his forehead deepening. "What is it you want, DCI Miller? I don't have much time, so I'd appreciate it if you could be brief."

Rob could see by the lack of light on the DCI's computer that it was in sleep mode or off, and his mobile phone was blinking on the desk in front of him.

"I can see you're a very busy man," he said, not without a touch of sarcasm. "I need to talk about Arina Parvin, a twelve-year-old girl who disappeared in Bisley four years ago."

Purley frowned. "What do you want to talk about her for? That was a long time ago. The case is closed."

"Mrs Parvin is a person of interest in a current investigation, and I'd appreciate your take on what happened. As a DCI."

Purley's chest puffed out. Pander to the man's ego and he'll tell you anything. "In that case . . . although, there's not much to tell."

Rob waited.

"Arina's father was a foreign national. He went back to Iran and took his daughter with him. That's all there is to it."

"Did you get confirmation that she'd left the country with him?" Rob asked.

The DCI gave a curt nod. "Mr Parvin was booked on a flight out of Heathrow the evening of his daughter's disappearance."

"Was he travelling alone?"

Purley reddened. "He was, but that doesn't mean his daughter wasn't on that plane. There were several other Middle Eastern passengers travelling with young girls Arina's age. He could have had a family member or friend assist him. It was an Emirates flight to Tehran."

"What about airport cameras? Did you check to see if any of the other passengers matched Arina's description?"

"Several did," he replied. "And with a headscarf and downcast eyes, it's very hard to tell which of them were Arina."

"It does leave quite a margin for error," Rob pointed out.

Purley shook his head. "Come on. The father disappeared the same evening as his daughter. What are the chances?"

Normally, Rob would have agreed, but in this case, the SIO could have been mistaken. He recalled Tessa Parvin's words. *She's out there somewhere.* "Did you know Ramin Parvin wanted nothing to do with his daughter?"

Purley didn't reply.

"He wanted a boy. He had no time for his daughter."

"Then why did he take off the same day as her? If he didn't have anything to do with her abduction, why run?"

Rob leaned forward, his senses prickling. "How do you know he ran?"

Purley sighed. "The wife was oblivious. She thought her husband was at work, until he didn't come home. When the daughter didn't come home either, she panicked and called us. Her first instinct was that her husband had taken her daughter. She even said as much in the 999 call."

That was news.

"Then, she suddenly changed her mind." He spread his hands and shrugged. "My superintendent agreed with me — she was trying to cover for her husband. Maybe he got to her, threatened her in some way. You know how they are. If she talked, he'd harm the kid. I don't know. But for whatever reason, she changed her story. A few days later, she appeared at the station harping on about a serial killer."

"She wasn't in her right mind," Rob said. "She was trying to make sense of what had happened. Maybe after she'd had time to think about it, she realised it was unlikely her husband had kidnapped Arina."

Purley frowned. "It didn't come across like that. The woman was irrational, grasping at anything and everything.

We recommended she see a therapist to help her cope with what had happened."

"How do you cope with losing a child?" Rob said.

Purley slammed his hands on the table. "The husband took her. That's it. I'm sorry it happened, but what the hell am I supposed to do about it? The Iranians wouldn't talk to us — they didn't want to know. There was no way of finding out whether she was there or not."

"So, you assumed she was and closed the case."

He gave a curt nod. "Any detective would have done the same thing."

Rob stood up. "Not every detective."

He left the office without saying goodbye.

* * *

Thirty-two hours.

Celeste had extended the house-to-house enquiries to the wider Barnes area. Police officers were searching Barnes Common and the Wetlands, as well as the river path. They even had a team in Richmond Park, assisted by the park rangers. Rob's team had moved to the second phase of the investigation. Intelligence. A sign they had no active leads to follow up on.

It was depressing. And behind the police were the press. Hounding, watching, applying pressure.

The chief superintendent had taken to pacing through the squad room, making everybody nervous. He'd halt at the whiteboard, stare at is as if wishing something new would appear, then ask Rob for the hundredth time if there were any developments.

"No sir. When there are, you'll be the first to know."

Lawrence would stride back to his office, his grizzly jaw taut with tension. Rob had never seen him so stressed. For his final case, this was turning out to be a doozy.

* * *

Rob pulled up Tessa Parvin's 999 call. As Purley had said, she'd initially thought her husband had abducted her daughter.

"Hello. My daughter hasn't come back from school and I'm worried about her. I think . . . I think my husband may have taken her."

"Who am I speaking to?" the operator asked.

"My name's Tessa Parvin. It's dark already and she's still not back. She should be back by now."

"Okay, Tessa. I understand. What makes you think your husband may have taken her?"

"He's . . . he's gone too. He packed a bag . . . I think he's left me." A sob. *"He may have taken Arina with him."*

"Okay, if that's the case, we'll find him for you. What is your husband's name?"

"Ramin Parvin. My daughter is Arina."

"Okay, ma'am. I'm going to send a police officer round to your house to get some details from you. Can you give me your address?"

"Oh, okay. It's——"

The rest was pretty standard. The operator had told her to keep calm and someone would be with her shortly.

To give the operator credit, she'd quickly dispatched an officer to the Parvin house. In the case of a missing child, it was imperative to act fast. Even if it turned out to be a false alarm, it was better to err on the side of caution.

Unfortunately, the police detective involved hadn't felt the same sense of urgency. He wondered who'd been dispatched. He looked it up and discovered it was a PC Brightman out of Woking. He'd been the nearest available officer and had arrived at Tessa's house half an hour later, at 10.47 p.m.

Tessa had waited until nearly quarter past ten before she'd raised the alarm and called the emergency services. Most likely, she'd been dialling around checking to see if her daughter had gone to a friend's house. That's what he would have done, if he'd had a daughter. He suppressed a shiver. Thank fuck he didn't. Not if *that* was the kind of worry it brought.

Yvette had made it quite clear she wasn't interested in having kids, so he'd gone along with it even though, at one point, he'd quite fancied the idea of being a dad. He grunted. That ship had sailed, and probably a good thing too. He couldn't remember to feed Trigger, let alone be responsible for another human being.

He closed the file and leaned back in his chair. Was Arina Parvin somehow linked to Katie Wells's disappearance?

"Hey, Evan." He approached the soft-spoken American sergeant who sat on the opposite side of the room.

"Yeah?" Evan glanced up.

"Would you do me a favour and look into this missing person case from four years back? It's Tessa Parvin's daughter." He handed Evan the file.

Evan's eyes widened. "The suspect you just interviewed?"

"She's not a suspect, just a person of interest at this stage, but yes. Her daughter disappeared four years ago, and the case was never solved. Not properly. The DCI in charge made the assumption that her father had taken her back to Iran, but it was never confirmed."

"You want me to confirm it?"

Rob hesitated long enough for Evan to raise an eyebrow.

He dropped his voice. "Actually, I'm interested in whether any other young girls went missing in the wider Surrey area around the same time as Arina. Mrs Parvin seemed to think there were some."

"You think it's part of a wider network?"

"I don't think anything yet. That's what I need you to find out."

"Got it." Evan gave him a confident grin.

Rob had heard from Galbraith what an asset DS Burns was to the team — now he hoped he could prove it.

CHAPTER 17

Harry knew a female officer at the Twickenham branch who had ties to Iran. "I think she mentioned her uncle worked in law enforcement in Tehran."

"It would be great if she could ask him to make some unofficial enquiries," Rob said. It was a long shot. "The chief superintendent has tried calling the Iranian embassy, but they're not responding." He wasn't holding his breath, either. Officially, there wasn't much they could do, but with no definite confirmation from the airport CCTV or the flight details, Rob was hesitant to put a lid on it. He didn't like loose ends.

"I've been looking for an opportunity to talk to her again," Harry grinned.

With his looks, it was a wonder he needed an excuse. Rob had seen how the women in this department responded to him. The handsome constable got more sideways glances and cups of tea than the chief superintendent himself.

The *Crimewatch* lady came up to him and asked yet another question. Harry put on a practised smile. "No, unfortunately you can't use the pink backpack — it's still in evidence. But I can give you a replica. Will that do?"

Rob backed away, but he wasn't fast enough. The reporter homed in, pinning him against Harry's desk.

"DCI Miller, could we get a few words from you as the senior investigating officer?"

"DS Malhotra is perfectly capable of speaking on behalf of the team." He turned to Harry and hissed, "We need to know if Arina is in Iran with her father."

"I'll do my best, guv," Harry replied. The grin was gone now. He understood the seriousness of the request.

Rob left him to it, much to the disappointment of the disgruntled *Crimewatch* anchor.

"Is he always so non-committal?" she huffed in his wake.

Rob sank into his chair. If Arina wasn't in Iran, DCI Purley was going to have to revisit the original investigation, and he wasn't going to like that, especially when it showed up his shortcomings. But that wasn't his problem. The DCI should have done the legwork the first time around.

DS Jenny Bird slid over. "I've looked into Tessa Parvin's properties like you asked, but the house in Barnes is the only one listed. There doesn't appear to be anything else. Could she have used a false name?"

Would Tessa Parvin have gone that far? If she had rented a property in a false name, she wouldn't be able to hide the money trail. "Let's look into her financials. If anything suspicious pops up, let me know."

It was a hell of a coincidence that Tessa's own daughter had gone missing. If it wasn't for that, Rob may have dismissed her entirely from the investigation. Rob sighed. Realistically, though, there hadn't been enough time for her to secrete Katie away. In a way, he was relieved. Tessa Parvin had had a tough time of it. He didn't like to think of her as the kidnapper.

"Also, the voice analysis is back from the tech guys," Jenny was saying. "They've emailed you a copy."

"Yes! Thanks, Jenny."

He spun around, logged on to his work laptop and opened his email. There, at the top of his inbox, marked "Urgent", was the voice-recording report. He couldn't open it fast enough.

The analyst had enhanced the audio and managed to isolate the woman's voice. Rob read the transcript first.

"Are you all right, dear? Are you lost?"

"No, I'm waiting for my friend."

That was it.

The analyst reported footsteps in the background, but she hadn't been able to isolate them enough to determine whether there were one or two sets. The dog bark was very clear in the enhanced file, and it was likely the lady who had stopped to ask Katie if she was lost was a dog walker.

Disappointment hovered. A dog walker concerned about a girl standing alone on a busy street corner was entirely plausible. It was a friendly neighbourhood, after all. The recording might have nothing to do with the abduction. Just a coincidence, a Good Samaritan. There was no way of knowing for sure.

Mallory, who'd been copied on the email, skulked over. By the expression on his face, Rob could see he was of the same opinion. He perched on the edge of Rob's desk. "Might not be our kidnapper."

"I hate bloody coincidences." Rob rubbed the strain out of his temples. "Would a dog walker kidnap a child?"

"She might have used the dog to lure Katie in," Mallory suggested, but his voice lacked enthusiasm. "Studies have shown kids are more likely to talk to strangers if they have a dog or puppy with them."

"I want to listen to the enhanced file." Rob scrolled down to the attachment. He pressed play and they both leaned in.

The woman's voice was louder than before, less obscured by traffic.

"Are you all right, dear? Are you lost?"

She sounded concerned.

Then the dog barked, making them both jump back. That was loud. It sounded like the dog was next to the phone, which would have been in the little girl's hand or pocket.

"That doesn't sound like a puppy to me," Rob stated. A year ago, he wouldn't have had a clue, but since he'd had Trigger, he was an expert on barks.

Mallory concurred. "It's close enough to be the woman's dog. It must have been sniffing around Katie at the time."

Rob sighed. "Shit, there goes another theory."

"We still don't know if we're looking for a man or a woman, then." Mallory stated the obvious. "It could be anyone."

"Back to the bloody drawing board," snapped Rob.

His mobile phone buzzed on the desk in front of him. Jo's name flashed across the screen. Mallory returned to his desk, giving him some privacy.

"Yeah?" he said, still thinking about the concerned citizen.

"Hello to you too," said Jo.

He cringed. "Sorry, I've just received some bad news. How are you?"

"Regarding the case?" She dispensed with the pleasantries.

"Yes, but it's not your problem. How are things? It's good to hear your voice." She was a breath of fresh air, dragging him out of the quagmire he was drowning in. "I miss you."

She laughed. "That's good to know. Hey, I'm in the area and I've got an hour free. Can you meet for a quick coffee?"

He hesitated. He shouldn't really leave the squad room, but after that last blow, he could really use a decent espresso, and Jo always made him feel better. "I'd love to. Text me when you're downstairs and I'll meet you across the road."

"I'm downstairs."

He grinned at his reflection in the laptop screen that had faded to black. A bit like this case. "Great, see you in five."

Being with Jo these last few months had made him realise what a train crash his previous relationship had been. It had disintegrated so slowly, he hadn't seen it coming. Before he knew it, he'd been dancing to Yvette's tune, pandering to her every whim, placating her increasingly paranoid demands, while trying to focus on his career at the same time. No wonder he'd been so stressed.

He used to hate going home. Now, he couldn't wait to rush downstairs and see Jo. He told Mallory to call him if anything came up and dashed out, taking the stairs two at a time.

"You have no idea how good it is to see you." He kissed her full on the lips outside the coffee shop.

She broke into a wide smile, the kind that reached her eyes and stayed there. "Ditto, DCI Miller." It had been a few days since they'd last been together.

The wind threw up a cloud of dust. It was a blustery day and people hurried past them to take cover inside.

"Let's go in." He held the door open, then followed her inside. Not even the smooth jazz playing in the background or the aroma of roasted coffee beans relaxed him.

"Bad day at the office?"

He rolled his eyes. "You have no idea. This case is driving me nuts. I keep thinking we're onto something, then it turns out to be another dead end. We've got to catch a break soon."

"I see the vultures are circling." She nodded across the road to the media vans lining the pavement.

"Oh, that's nothing. You should have seen it yesterday. It was absolute mayhem. We've got the *Crimewatch* crew in today. They're getting to grips with the case so they can do a reconstruction."

"Really? Wow. Sam's pulling out all the stops."

Jo knew the DCS from her work on the Surrey Stalker case, as well as the brief input she'd had into the revenge killings earlier in the year. She'd been an instant hit. Maybe it was her cheerful demeanour, or the way her intelligent blue eyes crinkled when she smiled. She was one of the most genuine people he knew.

"He's under a lot of pressure. This is his last case. He's retiring at the end of the year."

"That's a shame." She cocked her head to the side. "He's an institution around here."

"The murder squad's never been in better hands," Rob replied.

They ordered and took a table at the back, away from the door. Every time it opened, a blast of wind blew in a customer with dishevelled hair and grit in their eyes.

Jo, practical as ever, had tied hers back in a slick blonde ponytail. She studied him from across the table. "Why don't you give me an update? I heard the alerts and it's been in all the papers."

"You sure?" He didn't want to monopolise their coffee break.

"Yes, of course. Apart from my own professional curiosity, it often helps to soundboard with someone."

She was right. Talking about the case with her might unleash a fresh idea or line of enquiry. He could hope, anyway.

"Okay, thanks." He fetched the coffees and returned to his seat. "Where to begin?"

"How about where she went missing? It was Barnes, right?"

"Yeah, that's usually a pretty safe area. She was on her way to school, the friend she usually walks with had gone on ahead, so she was alone."

Jo tutted.

"She never made it. The school rang her mother, Lisa Wells, at nine twenty to ask if she was sick."

"Nightmare," murmured Jo.

They both paused as they considered what must have been going through Lisa's head at that point.

"Lisa called 999 pretty soon after that. By the time we got there, her soon-to-be ex-husband had arrived and was causing a stink with her lover, who turned up a short while later. She'd called him to help search for Katie."

"Sounds chaotic. And they're both in the clear?" She knew they'd have searched both their houses.

"Yep, a search turned up nothing, although Brian, Katie's father, had planned on secreting her to France for a holiday, against the mother's wishes."

"Hmm . . ."

"Yeah, that's what we thought, but it turns out he just missed his little girl. Lisa has full custody."

"What about the backpack? I read it was found in the old reservoir."

"The kidnapper must have taken Katie into the nature reserve and ditched the backpack. This hasn't been released to the public, so don't repeat it, but we found it weighed down with stones."

Jo gawked at him.

"Well, just one stone, actually. More like a small rock. Hey, are you okay? You've gone white."

She reached for her coffee cup but knocked it over. Luckily, she hadn't removed the plastic lid, and he managed to grab it before much had seeped through.

"Jo?" He touched her arm. "Was it something I said?"

A long moment passed.

"I'm sorry. I got a fright, that's all. You just reminded me of another case, a long time ago."

"Another case?"

"I don't know whether to tell you this or not." She flushed. "It sounds foolish after all this time."

"Don't be silly. Spill."

She took a deep breath. "When my sister disappeared, her backpack was found in a nearby lake, weighed down with a rock."

It took a moment to sink in. Rob knew about Jo's sister's disappearance, but that was twenty years ago. Her body had never been found. The mystery around what had happened had haunted Jo. It was the main reason she'd become a copper after finishing her psychology degree.

"It's probably a coincidence."

"Yeah, you're right." She nodded, more to convince herself than him. "It can't possibly be related. It was too long ago. And it was up in Manchester."

Whether naturally or by design, Jo had lost her Mancunian accent. Nobody who knew her now would have guessed where she was from.

"Nowhere near Barnes." There was a tremor in her voice. The similarity to the Katie Wells case had spooked her.

Rob released her arm. "Run me through what happened to your sister, again, just so I'm clear."

"It's not related, Rob. I'm sorry, I shouldn't have said anything, it just gave me a fright, that's all."

His eyes bore into hers. "Humour me."

"Okay." She wrapped her hands around her untouched Americano. "Rachel was out with a friend, a boy who lived in our street. I didn't know him very well — they were a few years older than me. Apparently, they said goodbye and the boy went home. The grocer reported seeing Rachel walk by a few minutes after that. She was alone. When she didn't come home, my mother and my uncle went looking for her. When they couldn't find her, they called the police."

Another nightmare scenario for the family.

"How does the backpack come into it?" he asked.

"She had this cute leather backpack, the kind with the long, thin straps. All the teenage girls were wearing them at the time. I wanted one too, but my mum wouldn't let me. They found it in a nearby lake, anchored down with a rock, just like Katie's."

Rob pursed his lips as he let this sink in.

"How old was Rachel when she disappeared?" he asked.

"Thirteen."

Another pause.

"It's a common enough thing to do," Jo pointed out. "If you want to prevent something from being found."

She had a point.

Serial killers don't care about jurisdiction.

A chill ran down his spine.

"Yeah, it's probably just a coincidence." There were far too many in this case already.

They lapsed into silence, each lost in their own thoughts. Eventually, Rob said, "Am I seeing you tonight?"

"Have you got time? This case sounds pretty full on."

It was, but he needed to see her, to hold her in his arms. He needed to feel something good, other than the sadness and frustration at work. Jo made him feel human again. But he didn't want to make promises he couldn't keep.

110

"Let's play it by ear. I'll call you later and give you an update."

She smiled, but it seemed forced. "Keep me posted."

Rob's phone buzzed as he received a text from Mallory. "*Crimewatch* has gone. The coast is clear."

"I'll leave you to it." Jo stood.

He also got to his feet. "Thanks for stopping by. Sorry I dredged up all that stuff about your sister."

She waved her hand dismissively. "Talk to you later."

Her haunted look told him she was still freaked out.

CHAPTER 18

Twenty years was a long time. Manchester was two hundred miles away. The cases *couldn't* be related.

Still, as soon as he got back to the squad room, Rob logged into the HOLMES database and pulled up the details on Jo's sister's disappearance.

Rachel Maguire. Thirteen years old. Reported missing by her mother, Valerie Maguire, at 7.20 p.m. on 5 June 1999.

A shiver snaked down his spine. Almost exactly twenty years ago.

A subsequent search by the authorities had turned up nothing. It was a local search team who'd discovered the backpack in the lake five days later.

Rob squinted at the low-resolution photograph of the backpack. It was black with long straps, just as Jo had described. The zipper was open, and the inside was glistening wet. There was the rock on the evidence table next to it. Roughly the same size as the one used to weigh down Katie's backpack.

Was he grasping at straws?

"A PC Brightman called for you." Mallory held up a finger with a yellow Post-it note stuck to it. Brightman's mobile number was printed across the top in Mallory's neat handwriting. "He asked if you'd call him back before five." He peered over Rob's shoulder at his screen. "What's that?"

"I'm not sure," mused Rob. "Probably nothing."

Mallory looked at him. Rob knew he wouldn't budge until he'd told him. The DI had a silent, stubborn streak that made him a good detective, but also a pain in the arse on occasion.

"It's to do with Jo's sister's disappearance." He kept his voice low, not wanting the rest of the department to think he'd gone off his rocker.

Mallory scrunched up his forehead, retrieving long-forgotten fragments of information. It was fascinating how his mind worked. "Rachel, right? Disappeared when Jo was young. They never found out what happened to her."

"Spot on." Rob nodded. "Anyway, it turns out Rachel's backpack was discovered in a nearby lake weighed down with a rock."

"You're kidding?"

"I'm serious. I thought I'd check the original case notes to see if anything else jumped out at me."

"And did it?"

"Well, it's almost twenty years to the day. The rock is a similar size. Rachel was thirteen, Katie is eleven." He glanced at Mallory. "Am I being ridiculous here?"

Mallory exhaled through pursed lips, making a soft hissing noise. "Could be a coincidence. Spooky, though."

"Yeah, that's what I thought. Jo's pretty freaked out too. Anyway, it's not worth mentioning at this stage." He closed his laptop. "How are we doing on the other angles?"

"Nothing on those women who knew Katie. Everybody on Lisa's list of suspects checks out."

"That was a long shot anyway, especially now we aren't even sure the perp is a woman."

"There's still nothing on the CCTV," Mallory said. "Katie's abductor must have parked in a blind spot. Stills from the ANPR camera at the roundabout aren't clear enough to make out who's in the vehicles."

"Damn."

The ANPR cameras weren't designed to show the individuals inside a car, only the licence plate, make and model. Without those details, the images were useless.

"So, we've got nothing."

Mallory shrugged. "We've looked at every car that passed through that camera an hour before and after Katie's disappearance. We'll cross-reference them with the vehicles of all the persons of interest in this case."

Rob nodded. "Good work."

"PC Brightman is waiting for your call," Mallory continued. "Do you want me to speak to him?"

Rob shook his head. "Nah, I'll do it. Thanks."

His DI nodded and went back to his desk, leaving the Post-it on the corner of Rob's screen. Rob picked up the phone. "PC Brightman, this is DCI Miller from the Putney Major Crime Team. Thanks for returning my call."

The police officer grunted. "What can I do for you, DCI Miller?"

Traffic roared in the background. Where was he? In the middle of a junction?

"I wanted to talk to you about Tessa Parvin," Rob began, shouting to be heard. A couple of heads in the squad room bobbed up.

"Who?"

"Tessa Parvin, Arina Parvin's mother. Remember the missing girl in Bisley four years ago?"

A pause. Rob thought he heard a sixteen-wheeler thunder by.

"I remember," came the response.

"Could you go somewhere a bit quieter?" Rob asked. "I'm struggling to hear you."

"Hang on." The traffic intensified momentarily, then faded to a muted hiss.

"Thanks," he breathed.

"What about Arina Parvin?" Brightman asked. "I didn't have anything to do with the case."

"You were the first responder, weren't you? You visited Arina's mother, Tessa, shortly after she called the emergency services."

"That's right." His voice was guarded. Rob wondered if DCI Purley had given him a heads up.

"What sort of state was she in?"

"She was distraught, as you can imagine. Her daughter had just vanished."

"Did she mention her husband at all?"

"Um, yeah, she did. She seemed to think he'd taken the child and done a runner."

"What gave you that impression?"

"He'd packed some of his belongings. She hadn't realised until we looked in his room and saw his suitcase was gone."

More new information. "What about Arina's room?" Rob asked. "Were any of her things gone?"

"Not that I can remember," he said.

"Doesn't that strike you as odd? That the father packed for himself but not his daughter?"

Brightman hesitated. "Maybe. Like I said, I only reported it as a missing person. I wasn't involved in . . ."

"I know," Rob interjected. "You weren't involved in the investigation. I'm just asking from an observer's point of view. So, you're sure nothing in Arina's room had been taken? No clothes, no suitcase, no personal items?"

"If there were, her mother didn't mention it."

He made a mental note to ask Tessa about that. "Is there anything else you can tell me about that visit?"

"Like what?"

"Like was anyone else at the house with her? Did she make any phone calls? Did anything strike you as strange?"

"There was nobody with her, but she received plenty of phone calls."

"From who? Do you remember?"

"From concerned friends and neighbours, I think, but it was a while ago. I can't remember every little detail. DCI

Purley interviewed all her daughter's friends later. Their statements should be in the file."

"Thank you, you've been very helpful."

"What's this about then?" Brightman asked, almost as an afterthought.

Rob talked over him. "That's all for now. Thanks again, Constable."

He cut the call. The digital clock blinked 20:30.

Thirty-six hours.

* * *

"Guv, I've got something." Will beckoned him over.

Rob pushed himself up from his desk. His limbs felt heavy like he was wading through mud, and weariness tugged at his eyelids. He stifled a yawn. "What is it?"

Please let it be a lead.

"I searched the sex offenders register and got a hit in Barnes. Sir, you may want to check this guy out."

It was standard procedure when a child went missing to look into local offenders, but according to statistics, eighty per cent of child abductions were committed by people known to the victim. Only twenty per cent by strangers. The chances of a complete stranger randomly selecting Katie Wells on her way to school was slim. Still, they had fuck-all else to go on. "Who is it?"

"A former art teacher called Anthony Payne. He works in a gallery in Church Road."

"What's he on for?"

"Possessing indecent images, voyeurism and sexually assaulting a minor."

"Christ."

"Yeah, the trifecta. He did six years at HMP Wakefield. Released five years ago."

"Any connection to Katie?"

Will shook his head. "Not that I can find, sir. I still thought it was worth mentioning."

116

"Okay, thanks, Will. Send me the details. I'll check him out first thing tomorrow." He stifled a yawn. Despite the espresso, his body was shutting down. The atmosphere in the squad room felt oppressive. He had a sudden urge to escape. A need for fresh air and normality. "Right now, I'm going home. I suggest you do the same."

Morale was low, they could all do with an evening off. Sitting here, drumming their heads against the wall wasn't going to make Katie Wells magically reappear.

He told everyone to call it a day, then rang Jo. She agreed to meet him at his place in an hour. Perfect. It would give him time to walk Trigger, and he desperately needed to clear his head. He didn't want to be on a downer when Jo got there.

* * *

When Jo arrived, she moved wordlessly into his arms and hugged him. He held her close, breathing in the warm, vanilla scent of her hair. Slowly, the tension of the last two days began to melt away.

"You're so good for me," he murmured.

She smiled, moving away. A moment of recognition. "I needed that too. Do you have anything to eat? I'm starving."

They went into the kitchen and made a comforting Napolitana pasta for supper, which they devoured with a loaf of chunky farmhouse bread that Rob had picked up on his way home. Fortified, they washed it down with a fruity Australian Sauvignon Blanc.

Jo put down her wine glass. "You looked into my sister's case, didn't you?"

They'd resisted talking about the case. Until now. He suppressed a grin. "How did you know?"

"I know you."

"Yes, but apart from the girls being roughly the same age and, of course, the rock weighing down the backpack, there aren't any other obvious similarities. It's unlikely they're related."

She gazed into her glass. "That's what I thought too."

"The funny thing is," he continued. "One of the Barnes residents who knew Katie also had her daughter taken four years ago. Talk about coincidences."

"Same age?"

"Twelve."

Jo stared at him. "Two missing girls, three if you count Rachel. I'd say that's more than a coincidence. Besides, I didn't think you believed in them."

"I never used to, but I have to admit, this case is full of them. There's the dog walker caught on voicemail who approached Katie in the street seconds before she was abducted, Katie's father who booked one-way tickets to France, Tessa Parvin and her missing daughter, the similarity with your sister." He ran a hand through his hair. "And none of them panned out."

"None that you know of," Jo revised. "Any one of them *could* be related, you just haven't found the link yet."

He sighed. "Do you really think there is one? I'm inclined to believe they're all dead ends. The woman was heard moving away from Katie with her dog, Brian Wells is a broken man who just wants to spend time with his daughter, Tessa Parvin wanted to help find Katie because she knew what Lisa was going through, and your sister was miles away in another county and another decade."

"What about alibis?" she asked.

"It mostly boils down to the timing. Brian arrived at Lisa's house within half an hour of Katie's disappearance, so he didn't have time to hide her anywhere, and the tail we've had on him hasn't turned up squat."

"Hmm . . ." Jo pursed her lips.

"Tessa Parvin is a similar story. She was part of the local search team run by Ed Maplin, head of the neighbourhood watch. I spoke to her myself. They wanted to go and search for Katie, but we shut them down. Again, she didn't have time to stash Katie anywhere."

"Unless she was hidden close by," Jo surmised.

"Yeah, but there was no sign of Katie found at either of their properties, and we checked the entire road. Twice."

Jo just shook her head.

Rob cradled his wine. "There's this paedophile in the area, a local guy called Payne. We got his name off the sex offenders register. But as far as we know, he didn't have any connection to Katie."

Jo frowned. "A paedophile? I can look into him, if you like. That's in our ballpark."

He nodded. "Thanks. Anything you can dig up would be useful."

He wasn't going to say no. The National Crime Agency had an entire department dedicated to child abuse and exploitation. It was one of their specialities. Any information they had on this Payne character would far outweigh anything Will could get his hands on — if there was anything to be found.

"It was awful," Jo whispered. "After Rachel disappeared."

Rob leaned back and watched her. He could see the grief hovering behind her clear blue eyes. "My mother fell to pieces. Rachel was her favourite. She was always so vibrant and girly. Popular too."

"What about you?"

"I was more of a tomboy. I spent most of my time playing football with my cousins up the road. I remember they had a big garden with a goalpost at one end. I didn't really get on with the girls at school. My mother never said as much, but I'm pretty certain she wished I'd been taken instead."

"You can't know that." Rob was shocked that she'd feel that way.

"We didn't have the best relationship," Jo said. "Mum was very feminine herself, Rachel was just like her. After she disappeared, Mum couldn't cope, so I moved in with my grandparents."

"I'm sorry." He pictured Jo as a lost little girl, reeling from her sister's disappearance, having no one to turn to.

"My nana was wonderful." Her face lit up. It was clear they'd been very close. "She became my surrogate mum. I spent the majority of the next few years at their house. I used to tinker with my grandfather in the garage, play for the local football club. I was happy." She shrugged.

"What about your father?" he asked.

"My father was at a loss at what to do. I remember him arguing with my mother in the weeks after Rachel's disappearance. It was terrible. That's one of the reasons my grandmother took me in. Their marriage broke up pretty soon after that. Dad moved to Scotland to be near the oil rigs. He wanted to get as far away as possible. Mum withdrew into herself. I remember her walking around like a zombie. She was there, but in her mind, she wasn't there, if you know what I mean?"

"Couldn't have been much fun for you," Rob remarked.

"No, but I was young, so I didn't really understand. I knew Rachel wasn't coming back, but I didn't know what had happened to her. I thought she'd run away." She paused, playing with the stem of her wine glass. "It was only when I was older that I began to understand the implications of her disappearance. My grandmother explained it to me when I was a teenager. My mother never mentioned Rachel again."

"That's tough," Rob commented.

She gave a dry little laugh. "You're the first person I've ever talked to about it."

"I'm honoured." He bowed his head. "I'm just sorry you had such an awful time of it. Do you see much of your parents?"

She shook her head. "Mum's in a home near Manchester. She never quite recovered. I haven't seen her in years. Like I said, we're not close."

"And your dad?"

"He died several years back. Heart attack."

"Shit, I'm sorry."

"That's okay. Everybody has their skeletons, right?"

She was right about that. He looked at her with new-found respect. Not only had she suffered parental neglect growing up, but she'd made her way through university into the police force and worked her way up to the rank of detective chief inspector for the National Crime Agency. Pride filled his chest, along with something he didn't care to put a label on.

She saw the way he was looking at her and whispered, "I'm tired of talking. Shall we go to bed?"

He nodded. Right now, there was nothing he wanted to do more.

CHAPTER 19

The gallery where Payne worked was situated in the centre of Barnes Village, a few shops down from the theatre. The glass frontage added a sheen to the contemporary works on display.

"I never did get modern art," Rob confessed to Mallory.

"It helps if you know the context," Mallory said.

Rob raised an eyebrow. "I didn't take you for an art lover."

"Not a lover, no. More of an aesthete."

Rob grinned. His partner was full of surprises.

Inside, it was freezing cold. Rob was always amazed at how, just because it was summer, people thought they ought to run the air conditioning at full blast. It wasn't even ten o'clock.

Pale floorboards stretched from one end of the gallery to the other. The walls were a muted white, and every painting had a light fixture above it, to illuminate the canvas in the most flattering manner.

A marble head stared blankly at them from a pedestal, while a predatory tiger made entirely from metal wire crouched in the corner, waiting to pounce.

"Can I help you?" a high-pitched nasal voice asked.

"Are you Anthony Payne?"

The man nodded warily. He was slim, well dressed, with a mousy-blonde comb-over.

"I'm DCI Miller and this is DI Mallory." They both held up their ID. "Do you mind if we ask you a few questions?"

He looked away. "This is about that little girl, isn't it?"

Rob raised an eyebrow. "How did you know?"

"Whenever something like that happens, the police inevitably come knocking on my door."

That's the price you pay for sexually assaulting a minor. "Is there somewhere we can talk?" asked Rob. The gallery was empty, but Rob didn't want anyone walking in and overhearing their conversation.

Payne gestured for them to follow him. "I have a back office."

They filed into the small musty space. Rob glanced around at the oil paintings against the wall, frames piled on a desk. The acrid smell of turpentine hung in the air.

"Take a seat."

They sat opposite Payne. Between them was an antique mahogany desk, on which was an open laptop. He closed it and gazed at them. "You want to know where I was the day that little girl went missing?"

It was clear he'd been down this road before.

"The morning, if you don't mind. Between eight and ten."

"Remind me which day it was?"

Very clever. Rob caught his eye and knew that he knew exactly which day the little girl had gone missing.

"Tuesday, the second of June." He kept his voice even.

"Ah, well I opened early on Tuesday. Monday is my Sunday, you see, and there are always deliveries and things to attend to on Tuesday morning."

"What time did you get to the gallery?"

"I was here by eight thirty. We usually open at nine thirty. Ten on weekends."

"Can anyone vouch for you?" Mallory asked.

The man ran his eyes over the DI, and Rob thought he saw an appreciative spark. If Mallory noticed, he didn't let on. "Indigo can."

"Indigo?" Rob frowned. "Who's that?"

"The barista at the Olympic Café. I get my morning coffee there before I open."

Rob glanced at Mallory, who got up and excused himself. The Olympic Café was right next door and there was no time like the present.

Rob saw Payne's eyes follow Mallory as he left the office. "How long did you do in Wakefield?" Rob asked.

"Six years." His eyes hardened. Not so amenable anymore.

"You assaulted a minor," Rob said. "You abused a position of trust."

He sighed, a bit overdramatically. "So I've been told. I served my time, okay, and I've kept to myself since then. I have no intention of going back inside."

They weren't too kind to nonces in prison. "Did you ever meet Katie Wells?" Rob watched for a reaction. The man would deny it, even if he did know her.

His eyes widened slightly. "No, I didn't."

The overriding expression was one of quiet defiance.

Rob sighed. "Okay, Mr Payne. Thanks for your time."

Payne saw him out and watched from the door as he joined Mallory at the café. Rob took a last look at the house. Payne waved. The smile on his face made the hairs on the back of his neck stand on end.

"Was he here?" Mallory had just finished talking to a tall, blonde woman in a floor-length sleeveless dress.

"The manager said Indigo only comes on shift at twelve. Do you want to wait?"

Rob glanced at his watch. It was ten fifteen.

"Nah, we've got too much to do. Send someone else to talk to him."

They walked back to the car. Payne had gone back inside his icy lair, but his shadowy figure could be seen lurking behind the glass frontage.

"That guy gives me the creeps," Rob said. "Let's check him out thoroughly and make sure he's not connected to the family in any way."

"You think he could be involved?" Mallory seemed surprised. He obviously hadn't picked up the same vibes Rob had.

He kept his eyes on the glass front until the shadow disappeared. "I'm not sure, but I don't trust him."

* * *

They stopped at Tessa Parvin's house on the way back. "There's something I want to ask her," said Rob.

It was another perfect day. Barnes pond was surrounded by mothers and toddlers feeding the ducks. Couples watched their kids play. Rob wondered, just for a moment, what it would be like to do that with Jo.

Tessa was pottering in her garden when they pulled up in front of her house. She raised her head and waved. A nice change from their last greeting. Her front door had been replaced.

"Good morning, detectives." She wiped her hands on a dirty tea cloth. "I was just pruning my lavender. It grows like wildfire this time of year. Lovely, though. Would you like some for the station? I have tonnes of the stuff."

"No, thank you," he said with a grin. "I've actually just popped in to ask you something."

She raised her eyebrows. "Is this to do with Arina's disappearance?"

"Yes. I spoke to PC Brightman, the constable who responded to your emergency call out the night Arina went missing. He mentioned your husband had packed some of his belongings, which is how you knew he'd left."

She nodded, shading her eyes from the sun. "That's right. He'd taken his suitcase."

"What about Arina's things?" Rob asked. "Had he packed any of her stuff? Was her suitcase missing too?"

Tessa tossed her secateurs onto the ground. "No. Arina's things hadn't been touched."

"You're sure about that?"

"Of course I'm sure. No one had been into her room. I told you, Ramin wasn't interested in Arina. There was no way he'd taken her with him."

That's what he'd thought. "Okay, thanks for clarifying."

"Does this mean you'll reopen the case?" Her voice was hopeful, desperate.

Mallory's eyes were fixed on his feet.

"We're still looking into it," Rob replied. Luckily, the glare prevented her from meeting his gaze. He didn't tell her she was still a potential suspect.

She nodded. "Thank you, Detective."

"We need to find out one way or another whether Arina Parvin is living in Iran," he said as they walked back to the car.

"I'll chase Harry up on that contact."

"That's the only way we'll know for sure whether she's a real missing person," he said. "It's unlikely we're going to get anywhere through official channels."

"Would the NCA be able to help?" Mallory asked.

He had a point. Jo's organisation would have contacts to non-profits and humanitarian groups in the country. They might be able to find out if Ramin Parvin had arrived with his daughter four years ago or where she was now.

"It's worth a shot," he said. "I'll speak to Jo when we get back."

* * *

Mallory got to work on Anthony Payne, digging into the sex offender's background. "Liaise with Jo," Rob had told him. "She was also going to look into him."

Rob went to find Harry. He got straight to the point. "Have you managed to talk to your friend with the uncle in Iran yet?"

Harry, who was on the phone, hung up. "Yes, I did. She's going to Skype him this evening and ask him to look into it for us. Apparently, he's not very high up in the police force, so she doesn't know how much use he'll be, but she said she'd ask anyway."

"Okay, good. Keep me posted."

Then he got hold of Jo. "Mallory's going to call you about Payne's background. We're trying to find out if he had any connection to Katie Wells."

"I've cleared it with my boss," she told him. "I'm going to look into him too. I'll give Mallory a call this evening if I haven't heard from him by then and we'll compare notes."

"Thanks, Jo." He hesitated. "There's something else I wanted to ask you."

"Yes." She dragged out the word, but he heard her smile.

"Arina Parvin, the girl who went missing four years ago, may be living in Iran. Do you or the agency have any contacts in that country who can find out for us?"

There was a pause.

"I think we may know some people. I'll see if I can get in touch."

Hope surged through him. It could be a better line of enquiry than Harry's friend's cop uncle. "That would be great. If she is there, we can rule out one of these coincidences."

And it would give Tessa Parvin closure.

* * *

The rest of the afternoon passed in a frustrating blur of false sightings, unhelpful forensic reports and useless CCTV footage. By five o'clock, Rob was ready to tear his hair out.

"There *must* be something." Even he could hear the desperation in his voice.

"I think there is," came Evan's quiet drawl.

Rob hadn't heard him approach his desk. "You got something?"

"I don't know what I've got. You'd better come and look."

Rob followed him back to his computer. The American DS glided rather than walked, in a smooth, efficient motion. It was the same when he eased himself back into his chair.

"I looked into the disappearances of other young girls in the area. There are several possibilities."

Rob lowered his voice. "Show me."

Evan clicked through to a digital map. On it, he'd pinpointed the locations of the missing girls.

"Cheam, Elstead, Dorking and Bagshot," read Rob. "All Surrey, except for Cheam, which is near Sutton, if I'm not mistaken."

"That's right. They're fairly spread out, which means they fall into the jurisdiction of different constabularies," said Evan. "That's one of the reasons nobody's connected the dots." Rob studied Evan's screen. "Ages?"

He glanced at his notepad. "Rosie Hutton was twelve, Elise Mitcham was eleven, Chrissy Macdonald was fourteen and Angie Nolan was ten."

"They fit the age range," he mused.

"They were all reported missing by their parents after failing to return from school or the park or the playground. Angie, the youngest, had been under the supervision of her grandmother. She didn't see who took her."

Rob gnawed on his lower lip. "If you add Arina Parvin to the list, and now Katie Wells, that's six girls that we know of who have gone missing in the last—" he glanced at Evan — "how many years?"

"I looked at the last five years, but it could go back further."

"Christ." Rob ran a shaky hand through his hair. Was this something? Or yet another coincidence?

"And get this," Evan said. "Rosie Hutton's school satchel was found weighted down in a nearby river."

It was *definitely* something.

He exhaled shakily. "I'm going to have to run this by the chief superintendent. I don't know what to make of it."

Evan stayed silent.

Sam Lawrence had been something of a mentor to Rob when he'd first arrived at the Putney MIT. He practised tough love, but it worked, and Rob had a soft spot for the feared DCS. He often ran ideas by him or bounced hypotheses off him. It was silly not to. The man had over thirty years' experience in the field.

He knocked on Lawrence's door. As usual, it was ajar, but that didn't mean you shouldn't knock. Many a DS had learned that the hard way.

"Come in, Rob." Lawrence beckoned to him. "I've been meaning to catch up with you. What's new?" He came around from behind his desk and gestured to the three armchairs positioned around a small circular table. "Let's sit here. I could do with some tea."

He picked up the phone and asked someone at the other end to bring them a pot and two cups. "Coffee's undrinkable."

They sat down. The chief superintendent leaned back and waited for him to start talking.

He swallowed. "Sir, there's something I need to run by you."

Lawrence frowned. "What's on your mind, son?"

The man was intuitive. He only ever called him "son" when he knew Rob was taking serious strain.

"It was something Tessa Parvin said," he began.

The chief super nodded. "Well, spit it out, then."

"She always believed her daughter was kidnapped, even though the official police report concluded the father had taken her to Iran."

"Bloody embassy never got back to me," Lawrence growled.

"Well, in our last interview, she mentioned other girls who'd gone missing in the county under similar circumstances to her daughter."

Lawrence's eyes narrowed. "She did, did she?"

Family members and friends of the victims were prone to overuse of Google and often got the wrong end of the stick. He was right to be suspicious.

"We proceeded with caution," Rob was quick to assure him. He hesitated. "DS Burns has discovered four other missing girls between the ages of ten and fourteen. All in the greater Surrey area."

Lawrence's eyes fixed on him.

"That's not all," said Rob. "A school satchel belonging to one of the victims was found near to where she disappeared, weighted down in a river. Like Katie's."

There was a long pause.

"You want to know what I think?"

Rob nodded. "To be honest, I don't know what to make of it, sir. If we add Arina Parvin and Katie Wells to that list, that's six kids in the last five years. And the satchel is a remarkable coincidence."

Lawrence didn't speak. There was a respectful knock and Celeste came in carrying a tea tray. Sensing the heavy atmosphere, she put it down and backed out of the room.

"Are you saying what I think you're saying?"

The chief super hated the S-word. The two most difficult cases of his career had been serial offenders.

"That's why I wanted to bounce it off you, sir. I don't want to jump to any conclusions, but we have to consider we may have a serial killer on our hands."

"For fuck's sake." His voice reverberated around the office. "Why can't it be a simple kidnapping? Why does it always have to be a fucking serial killer?"

Through the glass, heads dropped as colleagues concentrated extra hard on their tasks. *Hear anything? Of course not*, said the backs of their heads.

"Think about it, sir. Six missing girls. Same age. Same county. We have to consider that they could be related."

"They might be isolated events," he retaliated. "Young girls go missing all the time. They run away, become drug

130

addicts, try to escape abusive parents. What makes you think these six are related?"

"We don't. We haven't looked into them yet. It's just a line of enquiry that I thought we should pursue." The tea remained untouched.

Lawrence fell silent, his fingers drumming on the arms of the chair. Rob waited for him to say something. "Okay, Rob. I suppose you may have a point. But our focus is on Katie Wells, not these other girls. This could still be an isolated event. Fucking hell, it's more likely to be someone who knows the family than a deranged serial killer." He shook his head.

"Thank you, sir. I'll put DS Burns and DC Malhotra on it, while the rest of the team concentrate on Katie."

Lawrence glanced wistfully at the teapot but made no move to pour. "The *Crimewatch* report is going out tonight. I've seen the rough cut. Damn fine job your young sergeant did. He looks good on the box, doesn't he? We might have to get him to give the press statements from now on. Gives the department a good name."

How could Harry not have a positive effect on an audience? "I'll be sure to watch it," he said.

"They filmed on location too," he said. "Compelling stuff."

"Hopefully it'll generate some leads," Rob said, although his voice lacked enthusiasm.

"We're going to need some extra bodies to man the hotline," Lawrence said. "Hire civilians. The pros are too expensive."

"Yes, sir." He mentally added it to his to-do list.

There was a knock at the door. Rob was surprised to see DS Freemont standing there. That took balls, considering the chief superintendent's recent outburst.

"Enter," said Lawrence.

"What's up, Will?" asked Rob.

"Guv, you're not going to believe this. Lisa Wells knows Anthony Payne. She made two calls to his gallery back in March."

CHAPTER 20

Rob jumped up. "She *knows* him?"

"Yes, sir. They spoke twice, each time the call was longer than two minutes. They definitely know each other."

Holy shit.

He excused himself and followed Will back to his desk. Will pointed to the screen. "These are the call logs."

Rob could see for himself. She'd made two calls, one on 13 March and one on 15 March.

"Get her in here," he snapped.

* * *

This time, he met her in the interrogation room. Once again, he'd informed her she wasn't under arrest, that this was just routine questioning. To prove the point, he'd got them both a coffee on the way. It was the crap from the canteen, but it was the thought that counted.

"Do you mind if I record our chat, Mrs Wells?"

She shook her head. She seemed confused, frightened even. Like she was expecting bad news.

"How are you holding up?" he asked her.

"Okay, I suppose, given the circumstances." Her words didn't convince either of them.

"We're making progress with the case," he told her. "One line of enquiry we're following up on has to do with a man called Anthony Payne. Do you know him?"

She frowned, then her eyes widened. "Why, yes I do. Ant owns the gallery in the village."

Ant, eh? "That's right. Do you mind if I ask how you know him?"

"He acquired one of my paintings," she said.

He hadn't been expecting that. "I see."

"The gallery is across the road from where I work. I often pop in there on my lunch break. One day we got talking and I mentioned I do a bit of painting myself. He asked to see my work, so I showed him, and he agreed to display one of my pieces."

"Did you take them round to the gallery?"

"No, they're quite large. He came to the house."

Rob's breath quickened. "And this was back in March?"

"Yes, why? Is there a problem?"

Rob forced his voice to remain calm. "Lisa, did you know Payne is listed on the sex offenders register?"

Her mouth formed a perfect O. "I had no idea. I invited him into my house. He met Katie." She gasped. "You . . . You don't think he had anything to do with her disappearance?"

"We don't know at this point," he admitted. "But we're looking into it."

She shook her head. "I thought he was gay."

She had a point. Rob had got that impression too, but it didn't mean he hadn't abducted Katie.

Now they had confirmation that Payne knew the family, Rob leaped into action. It felt good to be moving forward again. The chief superintendent signed off on a warrant and Mallory organised a search of both Payne's house and the gallery.

"Get down there, Rob," Lawrence barked. "We can't risk anything going wrong. This has to be by the book."

The Olympic Café terrace was full to bursting point on account of the fine weather, and the diners gawked as the convoy of police vehicles pulled up outside the gallery. Another team had been dispatched to Payne's apartment in Putney.

Rob handed him the warrant. "We're here to conduct a search of the premises," he told the astonished gallery owner.

"But I haven't done anything," he retorted, going red in the face. He kept glancing at the diners next door, terrified everyone would find out about his record. "This could ruin me," he hissed to Rob.

"I'm sorry, sir, but you lied to us. You knew Katie's family and you denied it when asked."

"I don't know what you mean!" he fumed.

"Katie Wells? You have Lisa Wells's painting hanging in your gallery."

"That's Katie's mother?" he gasped.

Rob was impressed. If he was lying, he was damn good at it. "I had no idea Lisa was Katie's mother. I never made the connection."

"Uh-huh." Rob left him standing outside with a police officer and went to see how the search was progressing.

Gloved officers were systematically working their way through the back office. They confiscated Payne's laptop and mobile phone, much to his dismay.

Then a press van arrived and immediately began filming.

"Get rid of them," hissed Rob, as a man with a lens walked right into the gallery. Two uniformed officers escorted him out.

"I swear, I'm going to have to move again because of this," complained Payne. "Thanks very much!"

Rob ignored him. If he was innocent, it would hurt his reputation, but once again, he should have thought of that before he sexually assaulted a minor.

"Let's go to the apartment," Rob said to Mallory, once the forensic team had taken the electronics away.

Payne's apartment block was not much to look at. Constructed with ugly brown brick, typical of the council blocks in the seventies, it stretched sixteen storeys into the sky. His flat was somewhere in the middle.

It was much nicer inside. Payne had good taste — cream carpeting, classy off-white walls, a collection of impressive paintings by artists Rob had never heard of.

The master bedroom was a decent size for a council flat, even if it was dominated by a king-size bed. A landscape in a gilt frame hung on the wall in front of it. Cows grazed in a meadow with a series of hills in the background, but instead of the expected colours, it was painted in shocking pinks, vibrant yellows and luminous greens. The combined effect was a gauche explosion of colour.

Each to his own.

There was nothing to implicate Payne in Katie Wells's abduction. His flat appeared to be clean. They hadn't found so much as a packet of Haribo in the cupboard.

They were about to leave when an officer in the second bedroom gave a shout. It had been converted into a study.

"You got something?" The gloved officer was searching the desk.

He handed Rob up a sketch. It was pretty simplistic and looked like it had been drawn by a child. In the bottom left-hand corner was a signature.

Rob caught his breath.

Katie Wells, eleven years old.

CHAPTER 21

Anthony Payne was arrested on suspicion of the abduction of Katie Wells.

Rob let him stew while the team plundered his phone records, bank accounts and mobile data, looking for anything that put him in the vicinity of Belgrave Road on the morning of Katie's disappearance.

After that, they'd search for any co-conspirators he might have worked with, properties he might own or vehicles he might have leased.

Other than a storage facility on Lower Richmond Road, there was nothing suspicious.

Rob dispatched uniform to search the storage unit. It was in a secure building with constant CCTV coverage. No way could he have smuggled Katie in there without being seen.

"Look at that footage," he told the PC over the phone. "Make sure he wasn't there."

"I move around a lot," Payne said when the interrogation finally got under way. "I need somewhere to store my stuff."

"Why do you move around so much?" Mallory asked.

Payne raised an eyebrow. "You really have to ask?"

"We're searching it as we speak," Rob told him.

He shrugged. "Like I said, I've got nothing to hide. I don't know anything about Katie's disappearance."

"Where did you get the sketch?" Rob asked. "For the recording, I'm showing the suspect a pencil drawing by Katie Wells, found at his home."

He slid the paper across the table. Payne's eyes softened. "The kid drew that for me, okay? It's nothing sinister."

Rob frowned. "You expect us to believe that?"

"Believe what you want. It's true — ask her mum. While Lisa showed me her work, her daughter drew that. She was sitting at the kitchen table with us."

Mallory made a note to check with Lisa.

"Was that the first time you met Katie?" Rob studied him across the table. Payne was at ease, arms folded in front of him, brow unfurrowed, not a drop of perspiration under his arms or on his forehead. He didn't come across as a guilty man.

"Yes."

Beside him sat his solicitor, a chubby man with a goatee. He'd represented Payne during his trial and was well versed with his history.

"Is that when you decided to start spying on her?"

"What? Are you crazy?" Payne glanced at his solicitor. "Is he allowed to ask me that?"

"My client has denied he had anything to do with the disappearance of Katie Wells," the solicitor said.

"So you didn't watch her? Follow her around, learn her routine?"

"No!"

"And you weren't lying in wait on the morning of the second of June, when she walked to school?"

"Once again, my client has denied any knowledge of Katie Wells's disappearance."

Rob ignored him. "I think you liked what you saw that day you visited the Wellses' house, and it triggered a yearning inside of you. It's been over five years since you were released

137

from Wakefield. Five years of hiding your passion from other people, and when you saw Katie, you snapped. That's why you kept her picture."

Payne just shook his head, while his solicitor looked boot-faced.

Rob went on. "You planned your moment carefully, didn't you, Ant? When Katie was late for school, you struck."

"You've got nothing on me. You're grasping at straws."

Was he?

Rob scowled at Payne, who still hadn't broken a sweat. He was either a brilliant liar or a calculating psychopath — maybe both.

"Where were you the morning of the second of June?" asked Mallory.

"At the gallery. I already told you, I open at eight thirty on Tuesday mornings."

For the purposes of the recording they had to go over it again.

"And Indigo at the Olympic Café can vouch for you?"

"He served me an iced mocha frappé."

They hadn't checked up. Mallory fired off a text message to one of the officers still at the gallery and asked him to take a statement from the barista.

"You could have gone afterwards," Rob pointed out. "Katie was taken between eight forty and twenty past nine."

"Was she?" Payne looked straight at him.

Shit. He'd walked into that one.

"Yes, she was. Which means you could have got your iced whatever, then driven to Belgrave Road and waited for Katie to appear. Maybe you're there most mornings. Maybe you like to watch as she walks to school."

That touched a nerve. He shifted in his chair and for the first time Rob thought, *I'm getting somewhere.*

Unfortunately, there was no CCTV in Katie's street, but there was near the gallery. He met Mallory's eye, and his DI nodded and left the room. "For the recording, DI Mallory has left the room."

Once again, Rob saw Payne's gaze flicker over Mallory, but this time it was tinged with fear.

He finished up the interview and told Payne he was holding him while they cleared up a few things. Payne simply grunted in response. His previous cockiness had all but disappeared.

"I'd like to have a word with my client in private," the solicitor asked. He'd also sensed something was up.

"Sure, go ahead."

Rob left them to it and went to speak to the custody sergeant. It wasn't over yet. Payne had definitely flinched when he'd mentioned Katie's school. Were they on the right track? Did the sex offender have something to do with the missing child?

And was that a good or a bad thing?

* * *

"I've got Edward Maplin on the phone," Jenny told him as he entered the squad room. "He wants to talk to you."

"Put him through." Rob sat down at his desk, appreciating the air con. The interrogation room had been sweltering. "What can I do for you, Mr Maplin?"

He listened for a moment.

"We have covered those areas. But go ahead."

They could search them again if it made them happy. People liked to feel as if they were doing something proactive.

Jenny looked sheepishly at Rob as he put down the phone. "Sorry, guv. He was adamant, so I thought it best to put him through to you."

"It was nice of him to call," Rob admitted. "He didn't have to."

Three days. It was usually about now a body turned up.

* * *

Mallory had assigned two detective constables to look through the CCTV footage on Church Road. They'd isolated the camera nearest the gallery and were homing in on the footage taken on Tuesday morning.

Rob resisted the urge to peer over their shoulders. He'd been assigned that job when he'd first arrived at the Putney Major Crime Team, and he knew it required the utmost concentration. They didn't need a frustrated DI distracting them.

"Anything at the storage unit?" he asked Mallory.

"Nothing. Just a lot of sealed boxes that look like they've been there for years. They're going through them now."

"He probably put his stuff in there when he went inside," Rob remarked. He'd never thought about the logistics of going to prison before.

"Makes sense," Mallory muttered.

Half an hour later, a uniformed police officer sent through Indigo's statement confirming that Payne did indeed buy an iced mocha frappé on Tuesday morning at 8.17 a.m., according to the till slip.

"Bugger. Still, he got awfully edgy when I suggested he'd watched Katie."

Someone shouted from across the squad room. "Yes!"

Rob strode to where the two DCs were ploughing through reams of footage.

"We found something, guv." The young woman pointed to the screen. "That's the suspect. He's on foot, walking away from the gallery with his iced coffee at twenty past eight on Tuesday morning."

"He didn't go back to the gallery?"

"No, sir. Not until nine thirty."

Fuck me.

"That puts him in the frame for the abduction." He couldn't believe it.

"Yes, sir. Here's the clip of him coming back."

She ran the footage. Payne could be seen strolling back up the road towards the gallery. Relaxed, unrushed, the same loping gait as before, except the iced coffee was gone.

"Can you track him?"

"Only as far as the green. He disappears after that."

"But he'd have gone down the high street to get to Katie's road. There must be cameras on the high street."

"There are, sir, but he isn't on any of them. We've checked several times."

The young man next to her nodded.

Shit.

"What happened to him? He can't have disappeared?"

"He could have sat on the green and drank his coffee," the constable said.

"Or walked up Station Road." The female DC brought up an aerial view of the town. She pointed to a section of road. "There are no cameras until you get to Barnes station."

Rob stared at the map until his eyes watered. "Could he have cut through, taken another route?"

"It's possible," she said. "The area is riddled with pedestrian footpaths running between the houses."

Rob let out a long, slow breath. Payne could have gone anywhere in that hour, and they'd never know. "Thanks, guys. Keep on it. Let me know if you find anything else."

He turned to Mallory. "The guy disappears for the exact time frame of Katie's abduction. How can he not be involved?"

"He was on foot," Mallory pointed out. "Very difficult to pull off an abduction without transport."

"He could have parked a car by the towpath the day before. Then, all he'd have to do is lure her down to the river, walk along and get her into the car."

Mallory nodded. "That's possible. We'll go through CCTV again and see if any of the vehicles are registered to Anthony Payne."

Rob gave him a hard look. "He had her drawing, mate."

"I know."

"Anyway, it's enough to hold him overnight. We can have another crack at him later."

"You think there's a chance she's still alive?" It's what they were all wondering.

Rob met his gaze square on. "No, not if he took her."

In sexually motivated abductions, the victim was usually murdered within the first three hours of being taken. They both knew that.

* * *

Rob was about to go through his line of questioning for later that evening when his phone buzzed. He wanted to put the pressure on Payne, make him crack.

It was Jo.

"Hi." He answered before the third ring.

"Ah, I'm surprised you picked up," she said. "I know how busy you must be."

"Never too busy to talk to you," he said.

She laughed. "Listen, I got hold of our contact in Iran. She's going to look into Arina's whereabouts. She's got an address for the father."

"That's great news. How soon do you think she'll know something?"

"A day or two. I'll keep you in the loop."

"Thanks. Hey, we arrested Anthony Payne, the sex offender. He had a picture that Katie drew in his desk drawer, and he's got no alibi for the time of the abduction. He's looking good for it."

"Really? Wow, okay. I did a basic check on him, but nothing jumped out at me other than what you already know."

"Do you have a record of his whereabouts over the last five years?" he asked. "He moved around a lot."

"Yeah, we should have everything on file."

"There are others, Jo."

"Other missing girls, you mean?"

"Yes. Same age range."

There was a long pause.

"Are they related?" she asked.

"Can't tell at this stage."

"Do you think this guy is responsible?"

"Maybe."

"I'll get right on it," she said. "Check your email."

"Thanks, Jo."

* * *

True to her word, Jo emailed through a list of Payne's previous residences since his release. He'd got around.

"Look at this," he said to Mallory. "He lived in Croydon, then Guildford and now Barnes. Didn't one of the other missing girls live in Sutton? That's near Croydon, isn't it?"

"Fairly close," confirmed Mallory, who had all the locations committed to memory. "Elstead is near Guildford too. Do you have the dates he lived there?"

Rob forwarded him Jo's email. Was Payne responsible for the disappearances of the other girls too?

CHAPTER 22

"Where were you between eight thirty and nine thirty on Tuesday morning?" Rob spread the stills from the CCTV footage out over the table. "And don't tell me you were at work, because we know you weren't."

He watched as Payne's eyes dropped to the photographs. In the first, he was walking away from the Olympic Café, iced coffee in hand. In the second, he was further along Church Road, and in the third, he was walking past Barnes Green.

"What did you do after this?" Rob tapped the third photograph.

"You don't have to answer that," his solicitor said.

"It's advisable that you do," snapped Rob. "If you want us to believe you're innocent."

"I didn't do anything." His shoulders sagged. "I sat on the green and drank my coffee, I watched the kids feeding the ducks for a while, then I walked back to the gallery."

"You did that for an hour?" Rob narrowed his eyes.

Payne didn't react. "Yeah, what's wrong with that? It was a nice day."

"You like watching the kids feeding the ducks?" Rob goaded him.

The solicitor shot him a warning glance.

"Is that why you lured Katie down to the old reservoir at the nature reserve?"

"My client has already stated he was by the pond on Barnes Green," said Chubby. "Not at the nature reserve."

"Come on, Ant. I know you didn't want to hurt Katie, just like you didn't want to hurt the others, but you can't help yourself, can you?"

Mallory glanced at him.

"What others?" Chubby cut in.

"Oh, you don't know about those?" Rob raised an eyebrow. "Do you know about Katie, then?"

"Of course not. My client has already stated he had nothing to do with Katie Wells's disappearance."

"As you've repeatedly said," finished Rob.

Chubby leaned back in his chair. "Can we move on, then? Either charge my client or let him go."

"What others?" Payne growled.

"Don't indulge him," his solicitor warned.

"The other missing girls," Rob explained as if he were talking to a child. "You know, the ones who disappeared from the areas you used to live in. Croydon, Guildford . . ." He studied Payne's face, but it was a mask.

"Detective? Is there a charge?"

Rob had to let it go. "Not at this point, but I'm going to remand your client in custody for the maximum time allowed under the Police and Criminal Evidence Act."

The solicitor puckered his lips, then nodded. "Once again, I'd like a word with my client in private."

"By all means."

Rob and Mallory terminated the interview and left the room.

"What are you playing at?" blurted out Mallory.

"I wanted to see his reaction." Rob tucked the case folder under his arm. "If he knows we're on to him, he might crack."

"He might not be responsible for those other victims," pointed out his DI. "We don't even know if he's responsible for this one."

"I thought it was worth a shot," Rob said. "Although, I couldn't get a read on him. Could you?"

"I don't think he knew what you were talking about." Mallory swung open the squad room door and stood back to let Rob enter first. He didn't reply.

Payne had shut down faster than a steel security door. Something had been behind those blank eyes, but he didn't know what.

* * *

Six professional civilian telephone operators arrived a short while later and were shown into a designated control room. Their job was to monitor the hotline that would be buzzing once *Crimewatch* aired tonight at nine o'clock. They had strict instructions to vet the callers and were armed with a list of keywords to look out for and specific questions to ask.

For example, Katie's hair had been tied up in a ponytail, a fact that hadn't been released to the public. Anyone claiming to have seen a little girl with pigtails or hair that was loose could probably be discounted.

Katie had been lured into the nature reserve, but the sniffer dogs had followed her trail all the way along the towpath to a grassy patch near Nassau Road, a stretch of roughly 700 metres. Anyone sighting Katie in this vicinity, or on Lonsdale Road itself, warranted further investigation.

Rob didn't hold out much hope. He knew the kidnapper had been clever and had avoided crowds and CCTV. Besides, eyewitness testimonies were notoriously unreliable. The amber alert they'd put out the day Katie went missing hadn't resulted in many follow-ups, and those they had had turned out to be false alarms.

* * *

At nine o'clock they all gathered round the wall-mounted television in time for *Crimewatch*. The reconstruction was pretty authentic, apart from the few details that the press wasn't aware of, like Katie's ponytail, the meeting with the dog walker and her friend Candy's involvement.

Everybody cheered when Harry made his appearance. He did a great job of filling in the factual details of the case for the viewers. He was a natural on camera.

There was a plea by the distraught parents. How the *Crimewatch* team had managed to get them in the same room together, Rob had no idea. They were offering a £100,000 reward for her release! The Wellses didn't have that kind of money.

"Who's paying the reward?" Rob asked Jenny, who was sitting next to him.

"I'll find out."

The call lines opened, and the operators got to work. The room was soundproof, thank God, otherwise they'd have all been driven mad by the constant ringing of telephones.

They watched through the glass partition. Serious-faced operators furiously jotted down information on notepads.

"Just one reliable witness," prayed Mallory.

"How do you think he knew the camera at the Swedish School was out?" Rob muttered.

Mallory shrugged. "Just lucky, I guess."

"I'm not so sure. Payne used to be a teacher, right? He could have known someone at the school. Maybe he had inside information."

"Or he could have sabotaged it himself," suggested Mallory.

Rob grunted. That was a much more likely explanation.

"Do we know what's wrong with it?" he asked.

"No." Mallory gave him a look that said, *Really?*

Rob shrugged. "It wouldn't hurt to find out."

"Okay, I'll put someone on it." Mallory was learning to delegate. As a DS, he was used to doing most of the dog work himself, but lately Rob had noticed him passing on tasks to Will, Jenny and the other detectives on the team. It was a skill he still had trouble with.

After the broadcast, Harry came up to him. "Can I have a word, guv?"

"Yeah, what's on your mind?"

"I spoke to Fatima, who got in touch with her uncle in the police force, over in Iran."

"Yes?"

"He said he might be able to help, but it will take a few days. He's going to make some enquiries. I passed on Ramin Parvin's details, I hope that was okay?" He looked warily at Rob.

"That's great," Rob put him at ease. "Good work, Harry. And well done on how you handled the *Crimewatch* crew."

Harry glowed with pride. "Thank you, sir."

* * *

Rob picked up the case file and prepared to have another stab at Payne. There was no fresh evidence, but the man would be tired and nearing the end of his tether. If they left it any later, the guy wouldn't get his eight hours uninterrupted sleep before morning.

Rob was halfway down the stairs when Mallory called after him.

"Ed Maplin's on the phone. He says they've found something buried in the Wetlands."

148

CHAPTER 23

"Fucking hell." Rob jogged back up the stairs. "Are you serious?"

"Afraid so."

"What have they found?"

Mallory didn't meet his gaze.

"Please tell me it's not a body?"

"I'm not sure. Ed said it looked like a skeleton of some sort. Small, half-buried in the ground."

Rob squeezed his eyes shut. "Jesus."

"Even if Katie is dead, she wouldn't have decomposed so fast," Mallory pointed out rationally. "It's not likely to be her."

"Still, we don't know what he did to her. Have Forensics meet us down there. I want to be sure before we jump to any conclusions."

"What about Payne?"

"He'll keep. We've got twenty-four hours before we have to charge him or let him go."

* * *

By the time they got to Barnes Wetlands, it was well after midnight. The heat of the day hadn't let up and it was a balmy twenty-four degrees according to the temperature display in their vehicle.

It had been a quiet drive there. There wasn't much to say and no point in surmising. They had to wait until Forensics identified the bones. Then they'd know what they were dealing with.

They drove down Queen Elizabeth Walk towards the Barnes Elms Sports Centre and parked in the car park. The white SOCO van was already there, as well as two police vehicles, blue lights blinding in the darkness. There were no street lamps, the only source of light a grinning half-moon. Giant oaks cast black shadows onto the tarmac. They'd seen it all before.

Rob tripped on a pothole and nearly went flying. "Bloody hell—"

"Watch your step," the PC guarding the vehicles called out helpfully.

"Yeah, thanks. This way, is it?" He pointed down a gravel path that vanished into nothingness.

"That's it. Then across the rugby pitch and left along the river for about 200 yards. You'll see it from there."

Rob nodded and they set off, their torch beams jumping over the dry, pockmarked grass.

"You play rugby?" he asked Mallory. The white goalposts stretched for ever into the night sky. It seemed an inconsequential thing to say, but he was trying not to think about what they would find 200 yards downriver.

"No, I was more of a football player myself," Mallory replied. "How about you?"

It was clear he was having the same problem. "Nah, I didn't go to that sort of school, mate."

They trudged along the river path, towards the hazy glow from the forensic lights in the distance.

"What if it's her?" said Mallory.

"Don't. It can't be her, you said so yourself. It's too soon for that level of decomp."

He prayed they were right.

* * *

150

The remains weren't on the river path, but about twenty-five metres inland, in a heavily wooded area. A mound of freshly dug earth drew their attention and on a plastic sheet beside it lay a collection of tiny bones. A portable floodlight illuminated the find.

It couldn't be Katie. The bones looked far too old.

"What you got?"

The forensic pathologist, a slim woman with dark hair tied up in a bun, leaned over the bones. "We're still digging them out," she replied over her shoulder, "but from what I've seen, I'd say they were canine."

"Canine? You mean those are dog's bones?" Rob stared at the array of bones scarcely bigger than his finger. They could just have easily passed for a child's rib cage.

She looked up. "I think someone buried the family pooch here."

Mallory broke into a deep chuckle. "This was probably his favourite spot."

"Oh, for God's sake." Rob bent over and took a few deep breaths. When he stood up, he was shaking with the release of adrenalin. "So definitely not human?"

"No chance," the technician confirmed.

Rob shook his head. "Unbelievable. Is Ed Maplin around?"

The woman shrugged. "Who?"

"Never mind."

It turned out the neighbourhood watch group had been sent home once the emergency services arrived. "We didn't want them contaminating the scene," the officer said. "Didn't know it was Fido at that point, did we?"

They walked back to the car.

"For once I'm glad this was a false alarm," said Rob.

Mallory nodded, but didn't reply.

It hadn't been her this time, but next time it might well be.

* * *

"Coffee, anyone?" DS Bird breezed into the squad room the next morning carrying two takeaway trays filled with coffee. "Flat whites only, I'm afraid."

The team fell on them, but she reserved one for Rob. "Here you go, guv."

"Thanks, Jenny."

He'd been at the station since six reading the reports from Arina Parvin's case. He couldn't shake the feeling that it was related somehow, even though it appeared not to be.

She'd cut through Bisley Wood on her way home from school with two friends. They'd split up less than a hundred metres from the end of the path. The road would have been in sight. Both girls had given matching statements and Rob had no reason to doubt them.

Arina had been abducted on a hundred-metre stretch of woodland. Her school bag hadn't been found, nor was there any trace of her, although no official search had been authorised.

Because Tessa Parvin had initially said she'd feared her husband had abducted their daughter, they hadn't looked into any other possible lines of enquiry.

Instead, they'd set out to prove Arina had indeed been kidnapped by her Iranian father and smuggled out of the country. The evidence of this, in Rob's opinion, was heavily circumstantial. He'd never have signed off on it.

On a whim, he called Tessa Parvin. She answered straight away.

"Good morning, Mrs Parvin. Would you be able to meet me at the site where your daughter was kidnapped tomorrow morning? Yes, in Bisley. I'd like to see it for myself."

Tessa readily agreed.

"Okay, great. Shall we say eleven o'clock?"

Tomorrow was Saturday, and technically he was not working, but in investigations such as these, the days blurred into one another. He figured he'd take the morning off and check out the route Arina Parvin took home from school that fateful day four years ago.

Next, he texted Jo and asked if she'd like to come along. *Hell yes*, she responded, which made him smile.

* * *

"What is this?" DCS Lawrence burst through the door, newspaper in the air.

Everyone's heads whipped up.

"They know about Anthony Payne. How the hell did they find out about him?"

Their arrest outside the gallery hadn't exactly been low-key, but as far as Rob knew, no one had alerted the press as to who he was.

Lawrence smacked the newspaper down on Rob's desk. *Known Sex Offender Arrested*, screamed the headline.

Rob picked it up. "A confidential police source confirmed that known sex offender Anthony Payne has been arrested in connection with Katie Wells's abduction," he read aloud.

"Exactly!" fumed Lawrence. "Someone from *this* department leaked Payne's arrest to the press. Now it's all over the dailies. Christ, the man could sue us if he's innocent."

"I don't know how this happened, sir." Rob surveyed his team. Everybody appeared as shocked as he was. There were no guilty looks or shifty glances. "I don't think it's one of my team."

"Well, someone bloody leaked it." Lawrence stomped towards his office. "I want that person found and suspended until this investigation is over. We plan our press releases so things like this *don't* happen." He went inside and slammed the door.

A deathly silence fell over the squad room.

Rob stood up and addressed everyone in a low tone. "I don't for a minute think any one of you had anything to do with this," he began. "But if you do know something, now's the time to speak up. I'll do what I can to mitigate the consequences."

Nobody replied.

Mallory glanced at the room where the hotline operators were still busy taking down details from callers. The day shift had begun two hours ago. "Were all the civilian operators vetted?" he asked.

"Yes, sir," said Jenny, who'd been in charge of hiring them. "As much as we could on such short notice."

"Understood, Jenny," said Rob. "Ask Vicky Bainbridge to get hold of the *Daily Mail* and find out who their source is. Tell her to offer them an exclusive once we know who kidnapped Katie. That should do the trick. If not, we'll have to start questioning them, and we don't have time for that. I need all hands on deck. Katie's still missing, and until we have her safely back home or in a body bag, we're not giving up. Is that clear?"

"Yes, sir," chorused the team. Jenny scuttled out to talk to Vicky.

Payne's chubby solicitor was up in arms about the newspaper article. "This will ruin my client's reputation and his business," he shrieked.

"I'm sorry about that," said Rob through gritted teeth. "The leak is being dealt with."

"My client is going to claim compensation for this."

Rob nodded. "Unless he's guilty, in which case the only place he's going is prison."

Chubby didn't like that. Rob left him huffing and puffing and marched into the interrogation room, where Payne was waiting. Mallory walked in behind him, case file in hand. They had less than two hours in which to charge or release him.

"How did you sleep?" Rob sat down opposite the sex offender. Despite the uncomfortable holding cell, he seemed well rested and confident.

"You've got nothing on me," he sneered, ignoring the question.

Rob looked down at the list Jo had emailed containing the residences Payne had lived in over the last five years since his release from prison.

"Where did you live once you got paroled?" he asked the suspect.

Payne frowned, surprised by the question. "Um, Croydon. That's where I grew up, so that's where the council placed me."

"You know the area well?"

"Yeah, I guess so. What's this about?" He stared at Rob as if he were trying to work out the angle, but Rob gave nothing away.

"Did you know that while you were living in Croydon, a young girl called Rosie Hutton went missing?"

Payne swallowed. "No, I didn't know."

"Yes, she disappeared on her way home from school on the tenth of November 2016. She was twelve years old."

Payne didn't reply. He simply watched Rob with wary eyes.

"You moved to Guildford in 2017. Is that right?" Rob enquired.

Payne nodded.

"And while you were there, a young girl called Elise Mitcham disappeared on the way home from school."

Rob watched him for a reaction. He'd gone very pale.

"You can't pin those on me. I had nothing to do with those girls' disappearances."

"So you say," murmured Rob.

"You owned a white Ford Transit van," stated Mallory. "Registration LP03 8JR. Can you confirm that was your vehicle?"

He gave a small nod. "I worked as a delivery driver when I got out. What's wrong with that?"

"Would you say you knew the greater Surrey area fairly well?" Mallory asked.

"Yeah, so what?"

"It would be easy for you to kidnap unsuspecting school-girls with a van like that, and hide their bodies around the county," Rob cut in.

"What? No! I haven't kidnapped anyone!" He glanced at his solicitor, panic in his eyes.

"Detective, this is a fishing expedition and you know it. My client hasn't done anything wrong. You've kept him here for nearly twenty-three hours. I think it's time you made a decision. He's been through enough."

It killed him to admit it, but the solicitor was right. They had nothing linking Anthony Payne to Katie Wells's disappearance. He didn't own any property, his vehicle hadn't appeared on any of the ANPR cameras, and even though he'd disappeared off CCTV for an hour at the exact time she'd gone missing, they couldn't prove he was anywhere near her house or school.

The fact that he'd lived in the nearby vicinity of two other missing girls meant nothing. So did a million other people, a fact his defence team would not hesitate to point out.

"Okay, Mr Payne, you're free to go, but you're still a person of interest in this case, and we may need to talk to you again."

His solicitor thumped Payne on the back. "Come on, let's get you out of here."

Rob shot them both a dark look as they exited the room.

CHAPTER 24

Bisley Common was forty-six hectares of protected woodland, grassland and heath.

Rob and Jo met Tessa Parvin in a dirt lay-by on Stafford Lake Road, the pedestrian entry point where Arina and her friends would have begun their walk. The secondary school she'd attended was a couple of streets away. Arina's friends would be sixteen now and in their GCSE year.

Tessa Parvin climbed out of her car, flushed and jittery. The wind whipped her messy cloud of black hair around her face. She grasped Rob's hand. "Thank you, Detective. I can't believe someone is actually taking Arina's case seriously for once."

Rob nodded. He was operating purely on gut instinct here. There was nothing linking the two cases other than her, and the somewhat nebulous fact that Anthony Payne had lived in the general vicinity four years ago.

"This is my colleague, Jo Maguire," he said. Jo offered a bright smile.

He left out that she worked for the National Crime Agency and that she was less of a colleague and more of a girlfriend.

"How old was Arina when she went missing?" Jo fell into step beside Tessa. There was nothing awkward about Jo. People warmed to her, and Tessa Parvin was no different.

"She was twelve," she gulped.

"And this would have been her exact route home from school?" Jo confirmed. Rob had briefed her on the way over, and she'd had a quick look at the case files he'd printed out from the database so he could study them at home.

Tessa said that it was. She stared at the ground as they trudged along a well-worn footpath towards a wooded area up ahead. Tall grass and shrubs brushed their ankles, buckling in the wind. The heath changed from ochre to gold and back again as the gusts swept over its surface.

"It's beautiful out here," Jo mused. Rob picked up the scent of pine on the warm breeze. A small herd of deer huddled in a cluster, all facing the same way. He'd always wondered why they did that.

The footpath took them into the woods, weaving between pine trees, ancient oaks and holly. It was protected from the wind, although they could still hear the manic rustling of the branches above them.

"It's thicker than I thought," said Rob. From the map, the wooded area hadn't looked all that large, but it was surprisingly dense. It would be easy to lie in wait and not be seen.

Jo caught his eye. She must have been thinking the same thing.

They pressed on until they came to a fork in the road.

Tessa paused. "This is where they would have split up," she said. "The other girls live on that side of the common, so they would have gone that way around the lake. Arina would have walked on."

"Lake?" asked Jo.

"Yes, I think it used to be an old quarry. It's more of a deep pond, actually."

"Let's carry on then." Rob strode ahead, his head turning from side to side like a homing beacon. He could hear traffic and knew the road was close by, but on this section of the footpath, Arina would have been invisible. Anyone could have grabbed her and dragged her into the surrounding bushes.

A hundred metres later, they emerged onto a winding road. It was busy, cars rushing downwards through the green tunnel of trees. The woods didn't end here. The road had simply been carved through them.

"What's on the other side?" he asked.

"That's a school," Tessa told him. "A private boys' school. Arina used to go around the back to get home — she was too shy to walk past the front." Her eyes glazed over with memories.

Jo touched her arm. "Do you want to show us her route?"

They waited for a gap in the traffic. There was no hard shoulder, but there was a slim dirt verge where a vehicle could pull over if necessary. On the bend, it was a dangerous place to stop.

When there was a break, they darted across. A high wall flanked the pavement, behind which was the school.

They took the first right and walked around the building. Then they turned left, and 200 metres after that, Tessa came to a halt.

"This is it."

In front of them was a neat, red-brick terraced house. Tessa stared at it, unmoving.

"I'm sorry, this can't be easy for you," Jo said.

"I haven't been back here since . . ." Her words petered off.

"Thank you for showing us."

Rob glanced back the way they'd come. "Arina could have been snatched at any point from the fork in the footpath to here."

Tessa nodded. "That's right. But there are security cameras mounted on the wall surrounding the school, and the footpath is the most likely spot."

He'd seen one camera at the start of the road, but not any others. He'd make sure to pay more attention on the way back. The entire walk had taken them twenty-five minutes.

"Did Arina walk back home through the common every day?" Jo asked.

Tessa shook her head. "Not in winter, when it was dark. She took the bus then. It went around the common but dropped her at the bus stop outside the boys' school."

It was a pity she didn't take the bus that day. But it had been a warm, summer evening. Late July, if he remembered correctly. The temperature would have been similar to what it was now, in the first week of June. Warm, humid, with a light breeze, perhaps.

They walked back past the school. There was a second camera, but it was hidden from view by a tall Scots pine, which was why he hadn't noticed it earlier. "Did the police check the CCTV footage, do you know?"

Tessa shrugged. "If they did, they didn't tell me."

That wasn't unusual. The police didn't share their methods with the victim or the victim's family.

"They might not have, considering they assumed Arina had been kidnapped by her father," Jo pointed out.

His thoughts exactly. That was something he'd ask DCI Purley when he spoke to him next.

"Is this road always this busy?" Rob asked.

"Only in the morning and evening, and on Saturdays," Tessa said. "It's a shortcut to Woking and the A3."

Rob frowned. "When Arina was coming home from school, that would have been about . . . ?"

"Three thirty," supplied Tessa. "She didn't have anything on after school that day. She did computer club a couple of times a week, which ended at five, but not the day she went missing."

Three thirty. The traffic wouldn't have started building by then. The kidnapper could have parked on the dirt verge and hidden in the woods, waiting for Arina to walk past. Alone. Unguarded.

He suppressed a shiver. What kind of man lay in wait for a young girl like that? How twisted did he have to be?

"Did Arina mention anything suspicious in the months or weeks leading up to her disappearance?" Jo asked. It was a good question, and one he hadn't thought to ask himself. Most victims knew their attackers.

"No, I don't think so." Tessa wrinkled her forehead.

"No problems with friends or boyfriends? Any teachers giving her a hard time, or problems at school?"

"Nothing like that. She was a good, hard-working girl. She got good grades and didn't mix with boys. She was still too young for that."

Twelve *was* a bit young for boys.

"You mentioned she didn't have much of a relationship with her father," Rob said. "Was that something she found difficult?"

"What do you mean?" Her voice was sharp. Defensive. Rob met Jo's eye. It was a rather extreme reaction to a fairly simple question.

"It must have been difficult having a father who, in your own words, didn't care about her because he wanted a son."

She kept her eyes glued to the footpath. Dry twigs cracked underfoot, the echo making it sound like someone was following them.

"It wasn't ideal, but they were civil to each other. Ramin often worked late, so Arina would be up in her room or doing homework by the time he got back. They didn't speak much."

"Still, it couldn't have been easy for her," commented Jo. "Did she ever talk to you about it?"

Tessa shrugged. "Once, when she was little. I tried to explain, but what can you say that won't hurt their feelings? When she grew older, she understood."

That still didn't make it right.

They emerged from the woods out into the open heathland. Jo breathed a sigh of relief. The sun was high in the sky, the clouds wispy and fragmented, blown apart by the wind.

She turned her face upwards, absorbing some of the warmth and shaking off the gloom that had enveloped them.

Rob did the same. There was definitely something creepy about those woods.

* * *

"I think she was abducted in those woods." Rob turned onto the A3 back to London. "I want to check that camera footage from the school."

"If it's on file," added Jo. "They may not have requested it."

Rob grunted. That would have been a serious oversight, in his opinion.

"I wonder if they searched the woods for her school rucksack?" he said, thinking out loud.

"Even if they did, they may not have searched the lake." Jo glanced across at him.

He slowed down behind a lorry. "I can't authorise a search of the lake," he said. "This isn't my case. I shouldn't even be here."

"What if it's the same?" she said. "What if Katie, Arina, the others, they're all connected?"

"Unless I can prove that, I can't get Arina's case transferred. Besides, Lawrence would go apeshit. You know how he feels about serial murders. I'd never hear the end of it. For all we know, Arina could be safe and sound and living in Tehran."

"I'll get hold of my contact tomorrow," Jo said with a renewed sense of urgency. "One way or another, we have to find out whether that girl is still alive."

CHAPTER 25

On Sunday afternoon, Rob got a call from the duty sergeant informing him that Jo was in the lobby. He told the officer to let her up. She appeared at the top of the stairs, dressed casually in jeans and a white shirt.

He greeted her with a smile. "What brings you here?" She didn't usually arrive unannounced.

Evan and Harry were working silently on their laptops, along with two other members of Galbraith's team. The rest had the day off.

They were monitoring Anthony Payne's movements. According to the tail, he hadn't deviated from his usual routine. He'd worked on Friday, but after the press arrived at the gallery, he'd shut up shop and vanished out the back. The tail had picked him up again at his car and followed him home to his flat in Putney, where he'd been hunkering down ever since.

"I've heard from my contact in Tehran," she told him. "Is there somewhere we can talk?"

They went into one of the small, soundproof offices, used for meetings about things that were too sensitive to be said out in the open.

"What did you find out?" Rob asked.

"Ramin Parvin has remarried. He now has two sons from his second wife, aged one and three."

Rob's eyes widened. "He didn't waste any time."

"Indeed. Anyway, my contact managed to track him down. After making some discreet enquiries, she discovered that there is no sixteen-year-old girl living at that address. Only the two boys."

"So Arina isn't there?" Rob breathed.

"Not according to the neighbours, no. They've never seen a young girl with Ramin. They didn't even know he had a daughter."

He thought for a moment. "Do you think he's married her off already, or sent her to live with a relative?"

"It's possible," said Jo, "but that's not something my contact can uncover without compromising herself and the organisation."

Rob took a deep breath. "It doesn't look like Arina ever made it to Tehran."

"Which means she really is missing, probably dead."

He exhaled. "It might be time to reopen her case."

* * *

"I most certainly will *not* authorise a forensic search of a lake on Bisley Common," Lawrence bellowed the next morning in his office.

Rob calmly walked over and shut the door. He'd expected this reaction, even though it was his duty to inform the chief superintendent of his new line of enquiry.

"Sir, if you'll just give me a moment to explain."

"Don't 'sir' me, DCI Miller. I thought I'd made myself clear that we were not to focus on this serial killer theory."

"Actually, you said we could look into it, but not make it a priority. Well, we did, and I can't rule out the possibility that the cases are linked."

Lawrence sank into his chair. "This is why I'm retiring, Rob. Because one day, you're going to give me a bloody heart attack."

Lawrence was a good copper, with more experience than the rest of the department put together. He wouldn't let a potential lead go unfollowed, no matter how high the risk of cardiac arrest.

"What new evidence do you have? What is it that makes you think these other girls are connected to Katie Wells's disappearance?" he said.

Rob took a seat opposite him. "Anthony Payne has lived all over Surrey since his parole in 2014."

Lawrence raised his bushy eyebrows so they collided in the middle. "Tell me he wasn't living near to where these other girls disappeared?"

Rob nodded. "Two of them, sir. Three, counting Barnes. Not the same towns, but close enough."

"Jesus Christ." A long moment passed. The chief superintendent studied him. "What has this got to do with the lake?"

"You know Katie's backpack was disposed of in the old reservoir?"

He nodded.

"Well, we thought maybe Arina's was too. There's a deep pond, used to be a quarry, near where Arina disappeared. If it was Payne, who's to say he didn't do the same thing with her?"

Lawrence took a moment to gather his thoughts. Rob could see him trying to figure out how he was going to justify this to the Police Commissioner.

"What the hell," he said finally, throwing up his arms. "I'm retiring at the end of the year. May as well go out with a bang, eh?"

Rob grinned. "Yes, sir."

"I'll allow the search of the lake. If, and only if, they find something in there, will I speak to the Police Commissioner about getting Arina Parvin's case reopened. Until then, we don't tell anyone what we're doing. Understood?"

"Yes, sir. And thank you."

Lawrence gave him a hard look. "I mean it, Rob. If this gets out, we're all toast."

* * *

The divers went in first thing Tuesday morning.

The wait was excruciating. He couldn't concentrate. The reports swum before his eyes. Needing a distraction, he ambushed Harry, who had just arrived.

"Did your friend's uncle find out anything?" he asked before the sergeant had time to take his jacket off.

"Yes, sir. I was going to come and speak to you as soon as I got in."

He was a little flustered. Rob took a step back to give him some space. "And?"

"He looked into Ramin Parvin and found no reference to a daughter. Apparently, he has two sons, but no daughter."

"You're sure?" This was a second confirmation.

"Yes, if she's in Iran, sir, it isn't under her own name."

Right, that would have to do for now. It wasn't hard evidence, but it backed up what Jo's source had said, and justified the search of the lake.

* * *

The morning passed in a blur of impatience. The only highlight was when Jenny told him they'd found the mole who'd leaked the story about Payne's arrest to the press. The guilty party — a short, stocky bloke who looked more like a bouncer than a telephone operator — had been sacked on the spot. It turned out he had a gambling problem and thought he'd make some extra cash on the side.

"I don't know how we missed it," said Jenny. She was close to tears.

"Not your fault," he told her. At least they'd got to the bottom of that. If the search of the lake had got out, Lawrence would have sacked the lot of them.

Finally, just before lunch, he got the call he'd been waiting for. He pounced on it before the end of the first ring. "DCI Miller."

He listened, heart pounding. "You did. I see. Thank you."

He hung up, dazed. He couldn't believe it.

They'd fucking found it.

* * *

"You're kidding?" said the chief superintendent.

Rob had gone straight to him. Apart from Mallory, nobody else knew about the sanctioned dive.

"Yeah, and it was weighted down, just like Katie's."

And Rachel's.

* * *

"Everybody, briefing!"

Rob stood up as his team gathered around him. Evan and Harry, who were further away, rolled over on their chairs.

"We've had a new development."

He couldn't conceal his excitement.

Expectant faces stared back at him. They were desperate for a lead. Well, this was a cracker.

"As you know, we've been looking into the disappearances of several other girls of Katie's age in Surrey and correlating it with Anthony Payne's movements over the last five years."

Several nods.

"This morning we sent divers into a lake near to where Tessa Parvin's daughter Arina went missing four years ago. They found her school rucksack in the lake, weighed down by a stone."

A collective gasp spread around the room.

"According to Arina's case files, the SIO didn't feel the need to search the woods or look at any CCTV in the area, because he was convinced she'd been taken out of the country by her father. He did fly out on the same day. That was enough for them to close the case. We don't believe he had anything to do with his daughter's disappearance."

There was a pause as this sank in.

"What happens now?" asked Harry. "Do we reopen the case because it's linked to ours?"

"DCS Lawrence is going to speak to the powers that be and get it transferred," acknowledged Rob. "There'll be an investigation into Purley's actions, but that's not our concern."

"If there are four other missing girls, plus Arina and Katie, does this mean we have a serial killer on our hands?" The question came from Evan, who knew the details of the missing girls better than most.

"It's beginning to look that way."

The chief superintendent slammed his door shut, making everyone jump.

"He's not happy," said Rob. "He hates serial cases."

"Who's going to do what?" Mallory, as usual, was thinking like a DI.

Rob took a deep breath. "We'll break it up between us. These cases go back several years. Take Evan, Harry, DC Bartlett and DC Fagan and look into the four missing girls we know nothing about. Get their cases sent over, contact the detectives in charge, talk to their relatives and get up to speed. You can use Incident Room Two." This would give Mallory a chance to lead his own investigation, which was long overdue.

"The rest of you are with me," Rob said. "We'll look into Katie and Arina's disappearances, because there are obvious ties there. Katie is still our number-one priority. It's possible she might still be alive. We need to keep tabs on Payne — he's our main suspect. In fact, he *could* be responsible for all the missing girls. If we get him for these two, we might be able to get a confession out of him for the others."

It was a stretch, but serial offenders loved bragging about their victims. They liked people to know what they'd done. He'd learned that from his friend Tony Sanderson, a forensic psychologist and the UK's most sought-after criminal profiler. Actually, Tony might have a few insights into Payne. Perhaps he'd give him a call. They were due a catch-up.

As soon as the briefing was over, he headed outside. It was time to update Jo.

* * *

"Oh my God!" she whispered into the phone. "Do you know what this means?"

"I haven't told Lawrence about Rachel," he said. "He's having a hard enough time accepting there's a serial offender operating in his own backyard."

"It's got to be linked?" She sounded breathy, like she'd run a mile before answering the phone.

"Let's get together later and talk about this," Rob urged. "We need to decide how to handle it."

"Okay," she whispered. Her voice had a definite wobble in it.

"Jo, are you all right?"

"I don't know," she replied. "I'm still processing it all. With Katie's backpack, it could have been a coincidence, but now with Arina's . . ."

"I know. It does make it a lot more likely we're dealing with the same guy, or a copycat. Payne may not have been old enough to have been involved in Rachel's disappearance. He's only in his mid-thirties. Twenty years ago, he'd have been a teenager himself."

Jo sighed. "I know. I need some time to get my head around this. I'll speak to you later, okay?"

"Okay. I'll come to yours tonight, after I'm done here." They said goodbye.

Rob scowled at the cigarette butts scattered on the ground where he stood. He'd never felt more like having one. Big cases always brought on his craving. He doubted it would ever go away.

A gust of wind blew dust up into his face and he swiped it away, before striding across the road to grab a takeaway coffee.

Rachel was the anomaly. Her disappearance was too long ago to be related. From Payne's history, he'd been born and bred in Croydon. There was no mention of Manchester in his file. Besides, he'd have been too young to commit the murder, almost as young as the victim herself.

That meant they could be dealing with different killers — or Payne wasn't their man.

CHAPTER 26

Jo sat with a bulky file on her lap. They were in the Old Kings Head, a cosy pub near Jo's apartment in Borough.

"There's no mention of a father on Payne's birth certificate," Jo was saying, a pint of lager on the table in front of her. "But his mother remarried when he was two, so he had a stepfather. From what I can gather, they didn't get on. His psych report makes mention of sexual abuse at the hands of his stepfather when he was a boy and several attempts to run away."

"Christ." Rob took a swig of his beer. Obviously, that had had a major impact on the young Payne. "I almost feel sorry for the guy."

"Hold that thought," said Jo. "He left home when he was sixteen and began selling nude photographs of himself to make money. He stayed in youth hostels and squats in the area."

"I suppose it's better than selling yourself," Rob muttered.

Jo continued, "A few years later, he was cautioned for giving someone a blow job in a public park. He was let off with a fine."

Rob just raised his eyebrows.

"Then nothing until his sexual assault charge in 2009. He used to be a primary school teacher at a local prep in

South Croydon until a kid complained to a member of the support staff. He claimed Payne had fondled him during homework club. It appears this kid was special needs and required a bit more help with his schooling. Payne had offered to give him extra classes after school, and it was here the assaults took place."

She'd been reading from the file, but she paused and glanced up. "What a creep, taking advantage of a kid like that. He probably thought he wouldn't understand what was going on."

Rob frowned. Something had been playing on his mind ever since he'd first met Payne. "You know, there's something about all this that doesn't add up."

Jo leaned back with her drink. "What's that?"

"He's gay, right? The first time he was busted was with another guy, then the kid he assaulted was male too. There's no evidence that he's ever messed with girls."

Jo placed her drink carefully on the table. "I didn't even think about that. Are you saying that Payne might not be our man? That he might have nothing to do with Katie or the other girls' disappearances?"

Rob squeezed his eyes shut and gave his head a little shake. He was an idiot for not seeing it sooner. "I think I know where Payne was the morning Katie vanished."

"You do?" Jo leaned in. "Where?"

"I need to check something first." He pulled out his phone and dialled the squad room. DS Bird picked up. She was on late duty tonight.

"Jenny, I need you to do me a favour . . ."

After he'd told her what he wanted, Jo's eyes lit up with understanding. They finished their beers, talking in low voices, while they waited for Jenny to call them back.

Half an hour later, Rob's phone buzzed. He put it on speaker so Jo could hear.

"Sir, you were right. We picked him up on CCTV outside the boys' school on Station Road. Oakhurst Primary, it's called."

Rob exhaled low and long. He'd been right. "What was he doing?"

"Just watching, sir. He stood on the opposite side of the road. He didn't approach any of the boys."

Payne was a sexual predator, but he wasn't their kidnapper.

"Thanks, Jenny. You can document his alibi and we'll deal with what this means tomorrow."

"Okay, guv."

"Oh, and call off the tail."

"Will do. Goodnight, sir."

"Goodnight, Jenny."

He cut the call.

"I'm impressed." Jo smiled at him across the table.

He sighed. "It's a bugger really. The man's dangerous, for sure, but now he has an alibi for the time of Katie's disappearance." He dropped his head into his hands. "That means he's going to sue the hell out of us for wrongful arrest and destroying his professional reputation, and God knows what else."

Jo grimaced. "I'm sorry. That's tough."

"Yeah, Lawrence is going to have to handle the shitstorm."

"He's going to love that."

"It also means we've been chasing the wrong guy. There's someone else out there kidnapping little girls and we have no idea who."

She leaned forward. "It also means that it could be the same guy who took Rachel. *This* guy could have been active for twenty years."

They stared at each other as her words sank in.

"That's crazy," he said. "If it's true, then we're looking for a man in his forties or older, who moved to Surrey from Manchester over five years ago."

"It's a start."

Rob sighed. It was a start, but it meant throwing out everything they knew and starting fresh. Again.

"Where do you think he buried them?" Rob asked quietly when they were halfway through their second round.

Jo frowned. "I don't know."

"None of the bodies have been discovered. If the guy is as prolific as we suspect, he must have disposed of his victims somehow. They're not in the lakes or ponds with the backpacks, so where are they?"

"He could have buried them in the woods where the girls were taken," said Jo.

"That's one theory." He hesitated. "Perhaps they never left to begin with."

Jo shivered. "That's an awful thought."

"We'll have to search Bisley Common. It's not very big, only forty-six hectares. We'll get the dog squad out."

"Will they pick up anything after all this time?" Jo asked.

"They'll find a body," he said. "That's what they're trained to do."

"I want in," Jo stated.

Rob stared at her. "How?"

"I'll speak to my boss."

"Do you think he'd lend you to us for the duration of the investigation?"

"I don't know, but this could be my sister's killer, Rob. I need to be in on this case. Can you speak to Sam?"

"I can try, but I can't see him going for it. Not with you being so close to one of the victims."

"He knows I'm a professional. I can handle it." She took his hand. "Please, Rob."

"I'll see what I can do."

She squeezed. "Thanks, Rob. That's all I ask."

* * *

"I like Jo Maguire," Lawrence said, early the next morning. "But there's no fucking way the NCA's going to sanction her involvement. Firstly, it's not their case. It's got nothing to do with them. And secondly, if this killer is the same man

174

who took her sister, she has a personal connection. She could jeopardise the entire investigation. Hell, she might even be a witness or a person of interest."

Rob handed him a coffee he'd got from the expensive Italian café on the other side of town. He needed all the help he could get. "Look, I know she's a bright girl, but this is her *sister* we're talking about. I think she can handle it, sir. It was twenty years ago."

Lawrence accepted the coffee. "I'm sorry, Rob, it's not my call."

Jo would be gutted. "You know I'm compromised, sir, since we're . . . together."

Lawrence nodded. "I'm aware of that, and if you want to stay on this case, it's your duty as a senior police officer to act with discretion and be above reproach. You're not to talk to her about the investigation."

"Have you met Jo?" he blurted out.

Lawrence had the grace to grin.

"I can't see her backing down on this one." Rob said. "Besides, as an NCA agent, she could be a valuable asset to the team. She has access to things we don't, contacts we can only dream about. It would be a huge help if we could use the NCA's resources to help us solve this case."

Lawrence still wasn't buying.

Rob sighed. "Okay, here's another idea. What if she concentrated on the Manchester connection? We still aren't sure Rachel's disappearance has anything to do with our current investigation. There's a fifteen-year gap between the Maguire disappearance and Arina Parvin."

"Hmm . . ." Lawrence narrowed his eyes. "That might work. As long as it doesn't affect what we're doing here."

"No, sir. I'll make sure it doesn't."

"Okay, you win, Rob. I'll talk to Pearson over at the NCA, but that's all I can do. It'll be up to them whether they second her to us or not."

"Thank you, sir." Rob grinned.

* * *

As soon as Arina Parvin's case had been transferred from Woking to the Putney Major Crime Team, Rob organised a search of Bisley Common.

"Do you really think she's there?" asked Jenny, bringing him a cup of tea.

"I honestly don't know. I'm just doing what should have been done four years ago. I'm more concerned about Katie Wells at this stage. She's been missing for over a week now."

Thank goodness they had these other cases to distract them, because there were no new leads in Katie's disappearance. The situation was dismal. Even the papers had shifted her to page two. Reduced to a few lines of copy. In time, she'd be forgotten.

"I managed to get the CCTV footage of the school in Bisley," said Will. "They sent a copy over to Woking CID when it happened. It had been filed in their archives. I doubt they even looked at it."

Rob watched over his shoulder as Will opened the video and fast-forwarded Camera One to three thirty on the day Arina disappeared.

"School's out," said Will.

Boys poured out onto the pavement. Talking. Laughing. Jostling one another. Kids on bikes sped off in both directions. A bus pulled up at the bus stop and they piled on. It drove off. More kids gathered.

By four o'clock, the rush had ended. The street was once again quiet.

"Come on," Rob muttered.

At 16.02 a white vehicle pulled onto the narrow embankment beside the woods, blocking their view of the path.

"Get out of the way," hissed Will. "You're blocking the camera."

"Can you make out that vehicle?" Rob squinted at the screen. White paint. Sturdy wheelbase. Dirt-splattered tyres.

Will zoomed in. "Could be a delivery van."

"Can we send that shot to Peter Ansel on the second floor?" asked Rob. "He used to work as a road traffic collision investigator. He might be able to shed more light."

"You think it belongs to the kidnapper?" asked Will.

"The timing fits. If Arina left school at three thirty, she'd get there around four. It's a twenty-five-minute walk across the common and she was chatting with friends, which would have slowed her down. I'd say it's very likely to be the perpetrator's vehicle."

"Right." Will took a screen grab and sent it off to Peter Ansel's email address, all within a few seconds.

They watched for a while longer, but nothing happened. Arina didn't emerge from the woods, nor did they see anybody else. If anyone had got out of the vehicle, they'd done so on the side facing away from the camera.

"Forward it to when the vehicle drives off," said Rob.

Will sped up the footage until they saw the base of the vehicle shudder to life. It coughed a few times, then pulled out into the fast-moving traffic.

Rob checked the timestamp. 16:13. Eleven minutes. Enough time to grab Arina, subdue her and carry her to the van.

"I can't believe no one saw him load Arina into his van," said Rob. "It wasn't rush hour yet, but there was traffic on that road."

"Maybe she went with him willingly." Will glanced up at his boss.

Could Arina have known her attacker? "What car did her father drive?" he asked.

Jenny scrambled to look it up. "A navy-blue Honda Civic, sir."

"It wasn't him. Ask Tessa Parvin if Arina knew anyone with a white van. That includes extended family."

"Yes, sir." Jenny got on the phone.

"Pity we can't pick up the reg number when he drives away." Rob frowned at the screen. The camera had been

177

positioned towards the pavement, not the passing traffic. It didn't help that the entire road was under a canopy of trees, which made the images dark and grainy.

Will's computer pinged.

"It's a reply from Ansel," he said.

"That was quick." Peter must have been sitting at his desk and read the email almost immediately.

"He reckons it's a Vauxhall Vivaro or Movano, he can't be sure which."

"You get that, Jenny?" called Rob.

She gave him a silent thumbs up.

* * *

It was four thirty, and they were about to start their joint team update when Rob got an urgent call from a Sergeant Dixon, the police officer in charge of the search at Bisley Common.

"Is that DCI Miller?"

"Yes." His breath caught in his throat.

"We've found what looks to be human remains in a clearing in the woods on the west side of the common, sir. And from the size, I'd say it was a child."

CHAPTER 27

"They've found a body," said Rob, his chest heavy with emotion. Finally, something definite that the murder squad could focus on. An indication they were on the right track.

"Is it Arina?" asked Mallory.

"They don't know yet. But they think it's a child."

"Sweet Jesus," whispered Jenny.

"Forensics is on the way. We'd better get over there."

Mallory was already pulling on his jacket.

"Will, please update the DCS." The chief superintendent had left to go to a meeting and wasn't yet back. Will was the only one brave enough to face him.

"Sure thing, guv."

* * *

They sped across Surrey, wielding angry blue lights and an unapologetic siren. Cars parted like the Red Sea as motorists scrambled to get out of their way.

Sergeant Dixon had texted through the GPS coordinates. "It's in the western quadrant of the common," Mallory told him. "In a thick wooded area, by the looks of things."

Rob parked on Bagshot Road, the closest entry point to the burial site. There were skid marks where the police vehicles had ramped the pavement and driven across the heath to get as close to the crime scene as possible. He couldn't do that in his car.

A police constable directed them to the grave.

"Who would have thought it?" he puffed, as they strode across the heath. "The little lass buried right here on the common." It was clear he was a local.

The sun was still high in the sky and the common baked in a hazy blonde light. Midges darted out of the undergrowth at their faces.

The burial site was cordoned off. One small grave in the middle of a blazing yellow cordon. Onlookers craned their necks to see something, anything. But there was nothing to see. A white forensic tent had been erected over the remains. Stark and alien amid the soft golds and greens of the heath.

"Sergeant Dixon?"

A heavy-set man with sunken eyes and a thick jaw strode out to meet them. The man nodded and extended his hand.

"DCI Miller, and this is DI Mallory."

"Good to meet you. Come this way."

A PC handed them forensic overalls complete with shoe covers and masks. They kitted up.

Silver stepping plates led the way. Even though Rob had been at several crime scenes over the last few years, he never lost the sense of dread. He figured that was a good thing.

It was hot inside the tent, but the pathologist was working fast. She didn't look up as Rob and Mallory entered.

"Good afternoon, DCI Miller." She didn't take her eyes off the body.

"Liz."

Rob had worked with Liz Kramer several times before. She was a terse but highly intelligent woman who didn't suffer fools gladly. Nothing got past her. He was glad she'd been assigned the case. Beside her, holding a clipboard and recording all the evidence she was extracting, was an earnest young man. "What can you tell me?" he asked.

She didn't reply straight away, but rather removed a metal object from the soil close to the victim's head and carefully placed it into a plastic evidence bag. She glanced up. "Looks to be female, lower teens, maybe as young as eleven or twelve. I can't be sure until I get her back to the lab."

"But you're sure it's a girl?" His voice was raspy.

She raised an eyebrow. "I'd say so, judging by the pelvis, although it is hard to tell when they're so young and underdeveloped."

"Christ." It could be her.

"Is that what you wanted to hear?"

"Yes and no." He gave her a meaningful look.

She sighed. "I know what you mean."

There was a pause, then she added, "By the level of decomposition, I'd say she's been here for a couple of years. Again, I can't be sure until we've done all the tests. There is also some evidence of animal disturbance."

Rob forced himself to take a look. This was the part that got to him, for once seen, he couldn't unsee it. He carried a whole photo album of dead people in his brain.

If this was Arina, there was nothing left to identify her. Her skin was almost all gone, and what little was left was stretched tight across her skeletal face. Her hair was grey and dirty, impossible to determine what colour it once was. He recalled the photographs in the file. Arina had had glossy black hair reaching halfway down her back.

He swallowed to get rid of the foul taste in his mouth.

Her clothes had fared better than she had. "Is that a school uniform?" He peered at the threadbare fibres covering her torso.

"I don't think so," Liz replied. "It looks to me like some sort of covering. A sheet or a shroud. She is wearing a dress, but it's so discoloured, it's hard to say if it's a school uniform or not. I'll know more once I get it off her."

"She looks so peaceful." Mallory spoke for the first time. He, like Rob, was staring at the remains of what once had been a vital, healthy young girl.

"You're right, she does." Rob took a step back and studied her position. She lay on her back with her hands folded across her chest. "Do you think the killer positioned the body like this?"

Liz gave a grunt. "I'd say so. She had two blue metallic clips in her hair. One on each side." She nodded to two evidence bags the forensic technician had already recorded and placed in a plastic box.

"Could I have a quick look?"

The technician glanced at his boss, who gave a curt nod.

Rob emptied one of the bags into his gloved hand and inspected the contents. It was one of those hair clips that snapped shut when you bent them. Yvette's niece had some like it. He remembered Yvette doing her hair once when they went round for supper.

He turned it over, studying it under the portable crime scene lamp. This one was rusty and weathered, but beneath the dirt and corrosion, a cobalt blue colour was visible.

He handed it back. "I wonder if these were hers or if the killer put them in her hair," he mused.

Liz was once again focusing on the corpse. "All I can tell you, Rob, is that she appears to have been respectfully laid to rest, covered with a shroud, and then buried. The grave is fairly deep — whoever buried her was obviously afraid of wild animals getting to her."

"Or her body being found," pointed out Mallory.

Liz raised an eyebrow.

"Is there any indication of how she died?" asked Rob.

Lisa touched the child's head, gently moving a clump of course, grey hair to the side. "At first glance there doesn't appear to be any trauma to the skull and her bones are intact, but I can't confirm until I've had a chance to study her properly."

"What about sexual assault?" he asked.

She hesitated. "I can't say at this point, Rob."

He sighed. That was all he was going to get today. Still, it was more than most pathologists were willing to cough up on the spot. "Okay, thanks, Liz."

It was time to go. He gestured to Mallory and threw back the tent flaps. Outside, he tore off his mask and inhaled large lungfuls of fresh heath air. The oppressive melancholy that always befell him at crime scenes began to dissipate.

Mallory joined him. "It could be her."

They stripped off their suits and handed them back to the PC, who immediately put them into a box to be disposed of later.

"Yes, and if it is, it means she was buried in the same place she was abducted."

Mallory hesitated. "Does that mean Katie's buried somewhere in the nature reserve?"

Rob shook his head. "We searched the place. The sniffer dogs would have picked up her scent."

"Her backpack was found there," Mallory reasoned. "He may have taken her back there after we searched the place. If we're making parallels, we don't know when Arina was buried here. It may have been when she was taken, but it could have been days, even weeks later."

Rob stared at him. He was right. If Katie was dead, the killer could have gone back to the nature reserve to bury her body. What better place to hide her remains than somewhere the police had already searched?

"Organise it," he said.

CHAPTER 28

Rob and Mallory watched as the remains were lifted onto a stretcher. The waiting forensic van would transport them to the lab for further analysis.

"It's hard to believe they didn't investigate because they thought she was in Iran," Mallory mused.

Rob grunted. He'd keep his opinions on the incompetence of DCI Purley to himself. An enquiry into his incompetence would kick off anytime now.

A wail came from the woods behind them. They both span round.

"Tessa!" yelled Rob, recognising the dishevelled woman stumbling towards them.

"Is it her?" Her voice was a hysterical cry. "It's her, isn't it? I know it's her."

Rob caught her just before she reached the police cordon. She collapsed like a rag doll into his arms, sobbing. "Arina. My baby."

Mallory blocked her view so she wouldn't see the stretcher of bones being lifted into the SOCO van.

"We don't know it's her," Rob stressed. "Not until we've done a DNA test."

But Tessa was inconsolable. "It's my baby, I know it is. It was that paedophile. He killed my Arina."

Rob grimaced. A lawsuit looked unavoidable.

A female PC approached them. "Can I be of assistance?"

Rob smiled gratefully. She took the sobbing woman from Rob's arms and led her away from the crime scene, talking to her in a calm, reasonable voice.

Rob breathed a sigh of relief. Tessa's anguish only made the situation more distressing.

"She's going to go mental if it is Arina," Mallory said, his jaw set in a grim line.

Rob nodded. "At least she'll have some closure. Although, it won't be easy. She probably harboured some hope her daughter was still alive, even after all these years."

"Can't blame her." Mallory wiped his forehead. "It would have been better if she was in Iran with her father."

"We need to release a statement first thing tomorrow morning that Anthony Payne has been cleared from our investigations." Rob said as they walked back across the heath.

"I'll call Vicky and set it up," said Mallory.

"Get Harry to do it. Audiences will know him from *Crimewatch*."

Rob glanced back. The female police officer had led Tessa off towards where a park ranger's vehicle was stationed. They'd get her safely home, and a family liaison officer would be assigned to her, once they knew for certain it was Arina's remains they'd found.

* * *

Rob was already in bed when his phone rang.

"DCI Miller," he said, his voice groggy.

"Rob, it's Liz Kramer. Sorry to disturb you, but I thought you'd want to know the results of the DNA test on the remains."

Rob sat up so fast he got a head rush. "Tell me."

"It was Arina Parvin's body."

He stared in front of him at the bare wall as her words sank in. It suddenly struck him that Yvette had taken all their pictures and he hadn't got any of his own to put up in their place.

"You there?"

"Yes, I'm here." He cleared his throat. "Thanks, Liz. I appreciate the call."

"You're welcome. I'm off home. I won't be doing the post-mortem until Friday, but at least you know it's her. That should help you get the ball rolling."

"Thanks again."

Rob stared at the blank space for a long time as he tried to make sense of the discovery. Until this moment, there'd been a chance it wasn't Arina. That it was another little girl, from another time and place. Nothing to do with their investigation.

Now, his thoughts came fast and furious. Was this the act of the same person who'd abducted Katie? Did it mean Katie was dead too? Would they find her body when they searched the nature reserve? What about the other girls? What about the open spaces and commons near to where they were last seen?

Suddenly there was much to do.

He thought about Tessa Parvin and the abject terror on her face when she'd come flying out of the woods. She'd known. She'd always known.

* * *

The Shepherd watched as they pulled his little angel from the sacred ground and carried her to the van.

How dare they disturb her final resting place!

She'd been safe there, under the canopy of trees. Away from the people who'd hurt her. Sleeping peacefully for an eternity. Yet that eternity had been cut short.

Now she was just a pile of bones being taken to a lab to be analysed, probed and prodded.

Such ignorance.

His darling little angel. He recalled watching her pale face as her eyes had fluttered closed and she'd stopped breathing. At peace at last.

He remembered the smell of her hair, freshly washed. Thick and luxurious. And how it had felt as it had slipped through his fingers. He'd never known anything could be so soft.

"Darling Arina," he muttered. "What have they done to you?"

The shroud he'd used to cover her delicate, damaged body was gone, probably torn to shreds by now, her skin and flesh wasted away to nothing.

A high-pitched screech only metres away made him jump. Then a woman came hurtling out of the trees. Once his heart rate had returned to normal, he recognised her. She was the girl's mother.

Stupid bitch.

It was all her fault. She was just like the others — a neglectful, selfish parent. If she'd performed her maternal duty, her daughter wouldn't be dead. She wouldn't have had to die.

He blinked as a tall man in dark jeans and a casual shirt caught the hysterical, sobbing woman.

Who was he?

Was this the detective in charge? The senior investigating officer?

He strained his eyes. The man looked uncomfortable, unsure of himself. He didn't know how to handle the woman.

Fool.

Most men were useless when it came to emotion, but not him. He felt their pain. He felt it so acutely, it took his breath away.

So, this was the man who was going to try and track him down. The Shepherd knew how these things worked. He also knew how incompetent the police were.

If they did their job properly, he wouldn't have to do what he did.

He watched as Arina's remains were loaded into the van and driven away. Tears welled in his eyes, and it was a few moments before he could see clearly again.

He turned and melted into the shadows of the trees.

CHAPTER 29

Rob addressed the team. "DNA has confirmed it was Arina Parvin's body discovered at Bisley Common yesterday."

The news had filtered down, and even though it was early, everyone was amped and eager to get to work. The air in the squad room pulsed with energy.

Mallory stood beside him in a smart suit. He'd wheeled out the whiteboard from Incident Room Two, which contained photographs and essential information on the other four female victims.

"There's a hell of a lot to get through," said Rob. "So we're going to work in our designated teams. My team will dig into the people involved in Katie's life, particularly the men. I know we've looked at the list her mother provided, but we have to go deeper. I'm convinced this wasn't a random attack. The kidnapper must have met Katie at some point. He would have watched her, stalked her, waiting for the perfect moment to strike."

He turned to Jenny, who was hanging on to his every word. "Jenny, go and see Lisa Wells. Make a list of everyone who visited the house in the last few months, no matter how obscure. Take Celeste with you. We're missing something."

"Yes, guv."

"Jeff, you and Mike coordinate the second search of the nature reserve, Barnes Common and the Wetlands. Bring in the cadaver dogs. I think we have to consider that she could be buried somewhere in the local area."

Both constables nodded. They'd be only too pleased to be taken off the CCTV work.

This was going to be expensive, but they were working six different cases. Seven, if you counted Jo's sister.

"Will, I need you on the Arina Parvin investigation. Follow up on old witness statements, talk to her friends, and see if you can track down that white van. It could belong to our killer. There must be other footage of it in the area."

"I'm already searching the ANPR database," he said.

"Good. I have a feeling that's going to be key."

Rob nodded at Mallory to take over the briefing.

The DI cleared his throat. "My team looked into the disappearances of Rosie Hutton, Elise Mitcham, Chrissy Macdonald and Angie Nolan. We divided the victims between us and familiarised ourselves with their cases, all of which are still open."

"Talk us through them," said Rob. It was important they shared information in case there were any crossovers. It would all be marked on the database, but he was a firm believer in open channels of communication.

"Rosie Hutton was twelve years old and lived in Cheam, near Sutton. She was abducted on her way home from an ice cream parlour she and her friends had visited after school. Her mother alerted the police at seven o'clock that evening."

All eyes darted to the photograph of a mature-looking girl with blonde hair tied up in a messy bun. She was smiling into the camera, obviously laughing at something the taker had said. She had dimples and big brown eyes.

"Elise Mitcham was eleven, the same age as Katie. She vanished on her way to school. When she didn't arrive for class, her teacher raised the alarm. Her scooter was found abandoned in a ditch beside the road she used to take."

Elise was a serious, dark-haired little girl with a pale complexion and dark rings under her eyes.

"Chrissy Macdonald was the oldest of the missing girls at fourteen. She was last seen at a local newsagent with a friend. CCTV confirmed it. Her friend, however, said they parted ways outside in the street. Her school bag was never found."

The photograph of Chrissy was of a slim teenager in skinny jeans and a crop top.

"Finally, the last victim is Angie Nolan. She was only ten when she was kidnapped from a local park. Her grandmother, who was with her, didn't see anyone approach her. She said one minute she was there, the next she was gone. In a later statement, she admitted to not watching her as closely as she should have."

Angie was a cute little girl with olive skin, a dark bob and slanted eyes.

"The similarities with Katie and Arina's disappearances are striking," said Mallory, "but before we get the cases transferred, we need to prove a definite connection. We've logged their positions on a map and we're going to search local bodies of water for their backpacks or school bags. We can't sanction searches of the nearby open spaces yet, as there is too much ground to cover, and local searches were done at the time they went missing."

"Thanks, DI Mallory." Rob looked at the team. "I don't need to tell you to look for a connection with a man with a white van, or someone who they all might have been in contact with. A teacher, a priest, a tutor, a coach — anything that rings any bells."

Everybody nodded.

"Okay then, let's get back to work. We'll touch base this afternoon at four thirty."

Just then, Rob and Mallory's phone beeped simultaneously. Never a good sign.

"Shit, there's been an incident at the gallery," said Rob.

Mallory gasped. "A stabbing. You don't think . . . ?"

"Come on." Rob grabbed his jacket.

Mallory followed him out at a run.

* * *

The scene outside the gallery was one of utter carnage.

A local police officer was trying to keep the crowd back from two medics bent over a man lying at the side of the road. One was performing CPR, while the other measured his vitals.

"I've got a pulse," she called, her fingers pressed against his neck.

Another two police officers had apprehended a frizzy-haired woman who was screaming her head off. "He killed Arina. He killed my baby!"

"Christ, it's Tessa Parvin!" Rob jumped from the car. He flashed his warrant card to the flustered police officer and approached the man, who was bleeding all over the street. His eyes were shut and his face was paler than the white lines of the parking bay he had fallen across.

Rob's stomach lurched. It was Anthony Payne. "What happened?" he asked the medics.

"Stabbed multiple times in the chest and abdomen," replied the man who'd been administering CPR. He'd stopped thumping the man's chest and was now positioning an oxygen mask over his face. "He's lost a lot of blood."

"The ambulance should be here shortly," said the woman. The two medics had arrived in a first-response vehicle, which was great for arriving quickly, but not designed to cart someone away to hospital.

An ambulance blared up the road, its siren deafening. It pulled over beside Payne's prone body.

Rob got out of the way so they could work and joined Mallory, who'd gone to talk to the two officers holding a writhing Tessa Parvin. She was in handcuffs and her eyes had the semi-glazed look of someone in shock.

"Tessa, it's me, DCI Miller."

She gazed through him rather than at him.

"What are you doing, Tessa? This man is not responsible for your daughter's murder."

"How do you know?" she spat. "I saw the newspaper article. He lived in the same areas as those other missing girls. He's the serial killer I was telling you about."

Damn the papers. "No, he's not, Tessa. We eliminated him from our enquiries."

A flash of uncertainty crossed her face, then she started crying. "I wanted to punish him for taking my baby."

Rob shook his head. Tessa was in no state to be questioned. "Take her away," he told the police officers, "but be gentle with her. She's had a shock. She's going to need an FLO assigned to her."

They nodded and led a crying Tessa to the police car. Onlookers watched horrified as she was guided into the back seat and driven away.

"I saw it all," one man said as he walked past. "She went for him like a madwoman."

"One moment, sir."

Rob called the flustered police officer over. He read the man's name on his shirt badge. "PC Nelson, take this man's witness statement, along with anyone else who saw the altercation take place." He gave the officer his card. "Can you manage that?"

"Yes, sir." The man stood a little taller.

"Good. Thank you."

"What a shitshow," he growled as they got back into the car.

Anthony Payne had been stabilised and was being transferred to a stretcher. The medic held the oxygen mask over his face as he was carried to the ambulance.

"The press has a lot to answer for," said Mallory.

"How the hell did they connect the dots?" Rob frowned as he pulled out into the traffic. "We haven't announced the link between the other missing girls."

"Someone else must be leaking information," he said.

"Christ, the super's going to go apeshit. There'll be an enquiry into this."

"That's all we need." Rob turned into Rocks Lane and drove past the sports fields and up towards Barnes station.

"She's a loose cannon, that woman," murmured Mallory.

"She needs help." Rob turned into Upper Richmond and came to a standstill. Back-to-back traffic proceeded at a trickle. "It's all been too much for her."

An alert from the control room burst through the police radio. "All units, a young girl fitting Katie Wells's description has been found in Suffolk Road Recreational Ground."

Rob grabbed the receiver. "Is she alive?"

"Yes, sir. She was playing in the park. Over."

He and Mallory stared at each other.

"We're on our way."

CHAPTER 30

Rob switched on the siren and performed a U-turn in the middle of a busy intersection in Upper Richmond Road. Surprised motorists gaped through their windscreens as he expertly manoeuvred the vehicle through the heavy traffic.

He turned off as soon as possible and used the back streets to zigzag his way towards the park. Suffolk Road was a stone's throw from where Katie had been abducted and was on the same road as her school.

"Why there?"

He pressed his foot to the accelerator. Had she escaped? Had she been released? Was she injured? It didn't sound like it from the police broadcast, but until they got there, they wouldn't know for sure.

Mallory found out the particulars. Apparently, she'd been recognised by a mother who was at the park with her two children and their dog, and this woman was looking after her until the police arrived.

"We're closest to the location," Mallory said. "Other units are on the way."

Rob screeched to a halt outside the gated park. It was a small area with a child's play area in the middle, sporting a climbing frame, a slide and a roundabout.

Sitting on a bench watching the children play was a blonde woman, and beside her sat a dark-haired girl.

"Are we sure it's her?" hissed Mallory as they strode across the lawn.

"The woman seemed to think so."

They rounded the bench. The girl glanced up.

It was Katie. No doubt about it. Rob had seen those serious eyes look out at him from the posters for over a week. He'd know her anywhere.

"Katie Wells?" He bent down in front of her.

She nodded.

"I'm Detective Miller, and this is my partner, Detective Mallory. We've been looking for you."

She stood up. "Can I go home now?"

He smiled. "Yes. Yes, you can."

She appeared unharmed. Her hair was loose, but it looked clean. Her skin shone in the morning sun. She wasn't wearing the school uniform she'd disappeared in but a pale blue summer dress with daisies on it.

"My partner here will take you to the police car while I talk to this lady, then we'll take you home." He nodded to Mallory.

To his surprise, Mallory took Katie's hand and led her gently away. "That's a pretty dress," he remarked. "Where did you get it?"

They'd arrange for a forensic pathologist to meet them at Katie's house so they could take her clothing for analysis, then they'd question her in the presence of a responsible adult — in this case, her mother.

More police vehicles arrived as Rob introduced himself to the blonde woman who'd found her.

"I got here with my two, and there she was, playing on the climbing frame. There was no one else here, so I asked her who she was with. She said no one. That's when I recognised her from the news."

"There was no one here? You're sure?"

She nodded. "Absolutely. We usually come in the morning as it's quiet, and Bertie's always happy for a walk." Bertie was a fluffy cocker spaniel who was still prancing around the perimeter of the park, sniffing the grass and lifting his leg against as many oak trees as he could find.

"And you didn't notice anyone leaving as you arrived?"

"Not a soul."

Rob frowned. The sooner they questioned Katie the better.

"What state was she in when you found her? Was she upset? Frightened?"

"None of those things. She seemed happy. She was singing to herself when I got here." She shrugged. "It's amazing, really."

Rob was silent for a moment.

After a week of searching, Katie miraculously appears, singing to herself, apparently unhurt, just like nothing had happened. How was that possible?

* * *

Katie fidgeted in the back of their car, while Mallory spoke to the other police officers who'd arrived. They were full of questions.

"Yes, it's her," Mallory was saying. "No, not a scratch on her."

An ambulance pulled up.

He turned to Rob. "Shall we get her checked out?"

"Tell the ambulance to meet us at her house," he said. "I think it's important we get her home to her mother. We can do everything else there."

Mallory nodded and went to inform the ambulance driver.

Rob dialled Lisa Wells's number. She picked up on the first ring, her voice shaky, full of apprehension. "Hello, Detective?"

"Hi, Lisa. We've found your daughter. She's alive."

He smiled as she shrieked down the line.

He cut in on her barrage of questions. "We're bringing her back to you now. We can answer any questions you may have then."

She was crying as he hung up.

* * *

"Who gave you the pretty dress?" Mallory asked as they sat in Lisa Wells's kitchen, Rob and Mallory on one side of the wooden table, Katie and her mum on the other. Lisa's sister-in-law had made them a pot of tea and left them to talk in private.

"The lady did." Katie didn't seem remotely traumatised by her ordeal.

"Does this lady have a name?" Mallory asked. He seemed to have a way with kids, so Rob let him take the reins.

"She said to call her Rose."

"Rose?"

"Yes, she said that was her favourite flower."

"Oh, I see. And what did Rose look like?"

Katie shrugged. "She was normal."

"Did she have dark hair?" Mallory pointed at Lisa's hair.

Katie nodded, her eyes wandering. She was getting bored with the conversation.

"Could you draw her?" Rob asked.

She perked up. Lisa went to get some paper and pencils.

Rob made himself another cup of tea. A million questions were flying around his head, but he had to leave this to Mallory.

When Lisa returned, she set the paper in front of Katie and told her to draw the lady who'd kidnapped her. Rob grimaced at her choice of words.

Katie frowned. "She didn't kidnap me. She looked after me 'cos you were away."

"I didn't go away." Lisa stared at her.

"That's what she said."

"Is that what she told you?" Mallory kept his voice even. He didn't want to alarm her.

She nodded. "She said Mummy had gone away and I was to stay with her for a few days until she got back. She was nice. We drew pictures and played in the garden with Flash."

Rob glanced at Mallory. "Flash?"

"He's her dog."

It *was* the woman with the dog. That's how she'd got Katie to go willingly with her into the reserve. She'd concocted a story about her mother going away.

Katie was drawing a woman with dark, slightly wild hair, wearing jeans and sturdy hiking boots. Rob watched as she drew a cloudless blue sky.

"Did she meet you on the street corner while you were waiting for Candy?" asked Mallory, getting back on topic.

Katie nodded but carried on drawing. The woman stood on a green lawn, filled with flowers.

"Then where did you go?"

Katie looked up. "To the pond."

At the old reservoir.

"What happened to your backpack?" he asked.

She screwed up her face. "I don't know. I think I lost it."

Because the woman threw it into the reservoir when Katie wasn't looking, weighed down with a stone. Followed by her phone. Perhaps Katie had been looking after the dog.

"And then did you go for a walk or did she take you to a car?"

Katie thought for a moment. "We walked along the river with Flash, then got into her car."

"You drove to her house?"

Katie nodded. Rob realised it wasn't flowers in the garden, but strawberries.

"Did she grow strawberries in her garden?" he asked.

Katie smiled. "Yes, we picked them. They were delicious."

"Katie," said Mallory. She looked at him. "Did you know Rose from before?"

"I don't think so." Then she tilted her head to the side. "Maybe. I thought she was one of Mummy's friends."

"I don't know anyone called Rose," said Lisa.

"She may have used a different name." Rob kept his tone conversational so as not to spook Katie.

"Was it far?" asked Mallory.

"Huh?"

"When you drove to her house."

"Not really. We were singing along to the car radio."

"How many songs did you sing?" Mallory asked.

Katie shook her head. "Three or four, I can't remember exactly."

So, the woman's house must be within a ten-, fifteen-minute drive from here.

"And what did it look like, this house?" Mallory asked.

Katie sighed. "It was small, like a doll's house."

Rob frowned. "Like a shed in the garden?"

"Yes, like that, but it was a big one. It had a sofa and a TV and everything. I watched Cartoon Network." She cast a sly glance at her mother.

"I don't let her watch that channel," Lisa said. "I prefer more educational programmes."

"Did she leave you alone?" asked Mallory.

"Yes, I'm at an age where I can take more responsibility now." That sounded like something else the woman had told her.

"You weren't scared?" asked Rob. How could she not have been in a strange and unfamiliar place?

"I had Flash with me."

Still . . . "You're a brave girl, Katie," he said. "Very grown up."

She grinned.

"What about at night?" asked Mallory. "Were you alone at night too?"

"No, don't be silly. Rose was there," she said. "But Flash slept with me."

The shed was big enough for two beds at least, and presumably a kitchenette, or at the very least a place to eat.

Katie drew big red fruit hanging off a bush.

"Are those apples?" he asked.

"No, they're tomatoes." She gave him a *Seriously?* look.

"Oh, sorry. Silly me."

She giggled.

Before they'd begun the questioning, Katie had been given the all-clear by a paramedic. It appeared no harm had been done, thank God. Rob still couldn't believe it. He'd asked for a miracle and it seemed he'd got one. Here was their missing girl, hale and hearty and back with her mum.

Katie put her pencil down. "Can I go now?" She glanced at her mum. "I don't want to talk anymore."

Rob would have liked to question her some more, but he recognised the need for caution. He didn't want to wear her out. They could always come back later.

"Can I keep this picture?" he asked her.

She nodded and got off her chair. Lisa hugged her. "Well done, darling. I'll make you some lunch in a little while."

"Okay."

Katie slipped out of the kitchen and moments later they heard her footsteps going upstairs.

Lisa gazed at the doorway, remembering. "I can't believe she's back. I thought I'd lost her."

Rob couldn't either, to be honest. "I don't think the woman who abducted her planned to harm her," he said carefully.

"Why did she take her then?" asked Lisa, her brow furrowed. "Why take someone else's child if you're just going to let her go?"

Rob shook his head. "I don't know, Lisa. I've never had a case like this before. But Katie gave us some useful information, so we may be able to trace who took her from any DNA or fibres on the dress she was wearing." They'd also taken samples from her hair and fingernails in the hopes it would give them a clue as to where she had been taken.

"She could have had a change of heart," Mallory pointed out. "Or something happened to persuade her to let Katie go."

"Well, I just thank God for answering my prayers." She glanced upwards.

"Does her father know?" asked Rob.

Lisa nodded. "Brian's coming over this afternoon to see her. We're both so overjoyed she's safe."

"That's good."

Rob took the picture and studied it. A woman with wild dark hair and a dog, and who grew fruit and vegetables in her garden.

The strange thing was, they knew someone like that. And she was already in police custody.

CHAPTER 31

Rob watched the interrogation with Tessa Parvin on a monitor in the viewing room.

DI Mallory and DS Bird sat opposite the accused. She'd been charged with the attempted murder of Anthony Payne. The Crown prosecutor had had no problem approving that. She'd been caught red-handed by the police with at least five eyewitnesses.

Thankfully, Payne was recovering in hospital, otherwise she'd be standing trial for murder.

Her solicitor, a petite brunette who'd mastered the art of power dressing, sat beside her. Since she'd already been charged, they'd informed her she was being questioned on another matter.

DS Bird began by identifying them all for the recording, then she asked them to say their names. Tessa's voice was barely a whisper.

Mallory began with the basics. "Mrs Parvin, how do you know the Wells family?"

Confusion flashed across her face, and her solicitor frowned.

"Please answer the question," Mallory pressed.

"Um, well, I met Lisa Wells when I moved to the area three years ago. We're not good friends, but we see each other around, at garden centres and the summer fête, that sort of thing."

Rob felt the tension rise and forced himself to relax. Mallory had this.

"You like gardening, don't you?" Mallory asked, keeping his voice casual.

Rob nodded at the screen. He'd spotted the opening too.

"Yes, but what's that got to do with anything?"

"You used to be a botanist, is that right?"

"I did, but that was before . . . before Arina disappeared."

"What's your favourite flower?" he asked her.

"Excuse me, Detective, but what is the relevance here?" Her solicitor leaned forward, putting her hands on the table, breaking the flow.

This wasn't a court of law. Mallory was entitled to ask any question he thought fit. "If she could just answer the question," he replied.

Rob held his breath. The solicitor could prove difficult. But Tessa just shook her head. "I don't know. Daffodils, maybe."

"Are you sure it isn't a rose?" He fixed his gaze on her.

She shuffled lower in her chair as if hoping it would absorb her. "I'm sure." It was a mumble.

Mallory paused, then after a few reproachful seconds had passed, said, "Mrs Parvin, do you own an allotment in the area?"

Her eyes flickered towards his. "No, I have a garden at home."

If you can call that tangled mess a garden, Rob thought.

"Yes, I've seen your garden." Mallory offered a small smile. He was trying to throw her off guard. "But my question was, do you own an allotment?"

"My client has already stated she does not own an allotment," the solicitor confirmed.

Mallory kept his gaze on Tessa, who scowled at the table in front of her.

"I think you do." Mallory said. "When we searched your premises, we found several large bags of fertiliser in your attic. As far as I can recall, you weren't growing any fruit or vegetables in your garden, were you?"

Not intentionally, she wasn't. Rob recalled the overgrown lavender bushes, nettles and other unidentifiable plants. None of it had been fertilised.

"That was in storage," she said, without looking up.

Mallory changed tack, but he was rattling her, Rob could tell.

"Where were you the morning Katie Wells disappeared?"

"You know where I was," she retorted. "I was helping Lisa search for her daughter."

"That was around ten o'clock," Mallory pointed out. "Where were you between eight thirty and nine thirty?"

"I was at home," she said.

"Was anyone with you?" Mallory asked. "Can anyone confirm you were there?"

She shook her head.

"Mrs Parvin, do you own a dog?" He had changed tack again.

She looked up. "Yes, I do."

"What's its name?"

The solicitor shook her head. "Really, Detective?"

Mallory held up a hand. "Your dog's name, please, Mrs Parvin."

Tessa gnawed on her lower lip. "Asher."

"How often do you walk Asher?"

The solicitor gave a dramatic sigh.

Mallory raised an eyebrow. "Every day, would you say?"

Tessa nodded.

"And were you out walking Asher on the morning Katie disappeared? Say at around eight thirty?"

Tessa frowned. "No, I usually walk him later in the day."

"So this isn't your voice?" he said. "For the record, I'm going to play a phone message captured at eight forty-five on the morning of Katie Wells's disappearance."

They listened, silent.

Mallory looked at Tessa. "Is that your voice, Mrs Parvin?"

She shook her head.

"For the record, Mrs Parvin is indicating no," said DS Bird.

"Is that Asher barking in the background?" he asked.

Again, she shook her head, but she wouldn't look at him.

"For the record, Mrs Parvin is indicating no," repeated DS Bird.

Now for the crunch.

Mallory leaned forward. "You see, Mrs Parvin, we've done some clever voice analysis and discovered that it is indeed your voice in the recording."

She didn't respond.

"Would you like to revise your statement? Were you walking your dog the morning that Katie disappeared?"

"You don't have to answer that," her solicitor said.

"You don't have to answer," Mallory confirmed. "However, the evidence proves you met Katie on her way to school. If you had nothing to do with her disappearance, it would be in your best interests to come clean. It could harm your defence if you don't."

The solicitor pursed her lips, then leaned over and whispered something in Tessa's ear.

Tessa nodded.

"Is that a yes?"

"Yes, I saw Katie that morning."

"Why didn't you say anything?" asked Mallory.

"I knew how it would look. I left her there by herself and moments later she was abducted."

"It looks bad," Mallory acknowledged.

"After I heard, I immediately went to help. Don't you see? I had nothing to do with her disappearance."

"You had enough time to take her into the nature reserve, discard her belongings, bundle her into your car and take her to a shed on your allotment, then drive back home and go and help her frantic mother search for her."

Tessa shook her head. "No, that's not true."

"We've spoken to Katie." DS Bird spoke for the first time. "She reports being taken to a garden shed by a woman called Rose. You fit the description she gave. She also said Rose had a dog called Flash. That's quite similar to Ash, isn't it? If Katie had called 'Flash', a dog used to being called Ash would respond."

Tessa didn't say anything.

"Detectives, this is all circumstantial," said the solicitor. "You can't prove any of this. Just because Katie Wells's abductor looks like my client, doesn't mean it was her. And just because her dog has a similar name, doesn't mean it's the same dog. I think you're reaching here."

They were, but Rob was pretty sure they were on the right track. The rest of his team were looking into the ownership of allotments found within a five mile radius of the nature reserve, and he'd put through a rush order on the DNA samples from the clothing and samples they'd taken from Katie. But realistically, they wouldn't get those back for a day or two.

"If you're going to further charge my client with kidnapping, you'll have to come up with something better than this."

Rob took off the headphones and switched off the screen. Mallory would tie up the interview now, and they'd speak to her again once they had something more finite. But judging by that, Rob was more certain than ever it was Tessa who'd kidnapped Katie.

He just didn't know why.

CHAPTER 32

They walked back to the squad room.

"There's one way we can prove this," said Rob. "We find the dog. If Katie confirms it's Flash, then we're away."

"There wasn't a dog at her premises," said Mallory. "And I don't recall there being one when we searched the place last time."

"There was a dog's bowl," said Rob. "It was on the back porch. The dog itself was probably at the allotment with Katie by then, or wherever this mysterious garden shed is located. God knows who's looking after the poor thing."

"We've got a search warrant for her car," Jenny said. "Forensics are going over it now."

"If Katie was in that car, they should find something," said Rob.

Jenny nodded. "Let's hope she hasn't had it valeted."

"Guv, I've got something." Will shot up his hand like a schoolboy.

"What is it?" Rob marched over.

"I've picked up Tessa Parvin's car on the ANPR camera at the roundabout at Barnes Bridge station."

"Excellent!" Rob thumped him on the shoulder. "That proves she was in the vicinity. Well done, Will."

"It still doesn't prove she took Katie," pointed out Mallory.

"No, but it's one more nail in her coffin." Rob bounded back to his desk. They were on the right track, he *knew* it.

While Mallory went into a meeting with his team on the other missing girls, Rob briefed the chief superintendent.

"Why do you think she did it?" Lawrence leaned back in his chair and studied Rob. There were bags under his eyes and his salt-and-pepper hair was turning silver at the edges.

"I don't know," Rob said. "Maybe she missed her own daughter. Maybe she wanted to know what it was like to have a child again. Who knows?"

Lawrence sighed. "It's very sad. I take it we're pulling the plug on the other investigation, now that we know it isn't linked to Katie's disappearance?"

It wasn't really a question.

"We're the ones who found Arina's body," Rob said. "We can't abandon her."

Lawrence jutted out his lower lip. "The linkage has been disproved. We have no grounds to continue with the investigation."

"If we don't take it on," asked Rob, "who's going to find out what happened to her?"

"It'll revert back to Woking. It's in their jurisdiction."

Rob ground his teeth. He couldn't let this go. Not now, after all they'd discovered. "No offence, sir, but they didn't do a very good job the first time round."

"Agreed, but DCI Purley has been suspended pending a review. The case would fall to the DI, if there is one. If not, the DS will handle it."

Both would have to be fully briefed.

"My team is familiar with the original investigation," he said. "Anyone coming in would have to start from scratch. It makes more sense for us to keep it. Katie's been found. Tessa Parvin's been charged with attempted murder and possibly kidnapping. We have the time to dedicate to it."

Did he sound too desperate?

The DCS studied him for a long moment. "This is personal, isn't it?"

Rob shrugged, not altogether convincingly. "Arina deserves justice. Nobody knows the ins and outs of this case as well as we do. She was palmed off before. I think we should see it through."

Lawrence sighed. "What about the other missing girls? Have you found anything connecting them to the investigation, apart from them all being of similar age?"

He glanced at his hands. "Not yet, sir."

"Why not?"

"Budgetary constraints. We can't justify a full-scale search of every green area near where they disappeared." He gave the chief superintendent a sideways glance. "Can we?"

"No, we bloody can't. And before you ask, I'm not sending divers into every lake in the district either. You need something else linking the girls before we go any further. Failing that, let's cut back to Arina Parvin's case and concentrate on finding her killer — once we've put the Katie Wells case to bed."

"Yes, sir."

He breathed a sigh of relief. At least they were hanging on to Arina's case, albeit by the skin of their teeth.

Rob was about to leave when the chief superintendent spoke again. "Strange how Katie's backpack was weighed down just like Arina's. I guess there is such a thing as coincidence."

Rob blinked at him. A light had just gone on in his head.

"No, sir. There isn't."

"Pardon me?"

"I can't believe I didn't see it sooner. Of course it's linked. It's obvious when you think about it."

"Not to me," grunted Lawrence.

But Rob had thrown open the office door and was striding through the squad room.

"Where are you going?" Lawrence called after him.

Such was the power of his voice that everybody stopped what they were doing and looked up.

"I'm going to speak to Tessa Parvin," Rob replied. "I know why she did it. I know why she kidnapped Katie."

CHAPTER 33

Mallory, who'd seen him through the glass walls of Incident Room Two, swung open the door and ran after him.

"Hey, Rob," he called. "What's so important you can't wait?" He took the stairs two at a time after his DCI.

Rob stopped in the stairwell on the ground floor. "Come on, I'll explain on the way."

* * *

They had to wait for Tessa Parvin's solicitor to turn around on the A3 and come back to the station. By the time she arrived, Rob had filled in Mallory on his line of thought.

Now, as he sat opposite Tessa, his heart pounded in anticipation.

She looked like she'd been crying. Obviously, the last interview had got to her. Rob felt sorry for her. It was the police's shortcomings that had forced her to do what she did.

"I know why you did it, Tessa," he said, once Mallory had switched on the recording device and announced them all for the second time that afternoon. "I know why you kidnapped Katie."

She didn't respond, but her lip quivered.

"It was our fault, wasn't it?"

She glanced up. Her solicitor looked confused.

"We failed you when Arina went missing. We let you both down. I'm sorry about that."

She kept her eyes on him. Unblinking.

"That's why you kidnapped Katie, isn't it? You wanted to get our attention. You wanted us to reopen your case. And it worked." He studied her and saw a small blush creep into her cheeks. "You knew we'd look into her friends and family — you knew we'd discover your daughter went missing four years ago. That was what you wanted, wasn't it? You wanted us to make a connection between the two missing girls."

Tears welled up in Tessa's eyes. She nodded. "It was the only way I could get you to take Arina's disappearance seriously."

Yes!

She was talking. They had a confession.

Mallory stiffened beside him.

"You don't have to continue." Her solicitor lay a hand on her arm.

Tessa shrugged it off. "I want to."

The solicitor removed her hand.

"I never planned on hurting Katie," Tessa whispered. "I just wanted to find my girl, to know for sure whether she was dead. I couldn't stand not knowing."

It had eaten her up inside.

"I arranged Katie's disappearance to look like an old case I'd read about online. I knew there had been other girls that had gone missing in the county, so I looked into those disappearances, and I saw that one of their school satchels had been found in a nearby river. I thought if I did the same, you'd connect the cases and take Arina's disappearance more seriously. I didn't for a moment think . . ." She petered off.

Her solicitor sat stone-faced beside her. She was picturing the kidnapping charge on top of the one for attempted murder.

"That we'd find Arina's own school rucksack weighed down in a nearby lake?" Rob finished for her. *Or that it would lead to Jo making the connection with her sister.*

She shook her head. "I had hoped she was with Ramin in Iran, but deep down I knew she wasn't. I knew she was dead. I could sense it."

Tears flowed freely down her face, but she didn't care. She was beyond caring.

Rob's heart went out to her. Everything she'd done had been in search of the truth. If the original SIO had done his job in the first place, Tessa Parvin wouldn't be sitting here today. She wouldn't be spending the next ten or twenty years in prison.

They had what they needed for a conviction. He excused himself and left Mallory to finish the interview.

* * *

"Well done, Rob." DCS Lawrence pumped his hand when he told him they'd wrapped up the Katie Wells case. The CPS had given them the go-ahead to further charge Tessa Parvin with kidnapping.

"Let's issue a statement to the press ASAP. You do it. This is your moment."

But Rob shook his head. "I'll let DS Malhotra do it, sir. For consistency's sake."

Lawrence wagged his finger. "You'll never get ahead if you don't suck it up, Rob. If you want my job one day, you need to own your successes."

This didn't feel like a success. Tessa Parvin should never have had to resort to kidnapping to get the police to take her daughter's disappearance seriously. Besides, Arina's killer was still out there, and it was his job to hunt that person down. He wanted justice for the Parvin family.

* * *

213

With the case wrapped up, Rob decided to go home early and take Trigger to the park. He called Jo, but her phone diverted straight to voicemail, which meant she was busy. Had she managed to convince her superiors to second her to their team?

As he stepped outside the police station, he was besieged by a reporter. The young woman thrust a recorder under his nose. "How do you feel now that Katie's kidnapper is in custody?"

"I'm delighted." He pushed past her.

She ran alongside him. "Do you think Tessa Parvin will get a reduced sentence, seeing as it's the police's fault she was put in this position?"

"I can't comment on the outcome of the trial," he said.

"Are you in charge of her daughter's case?"

"Yes. Now, if you'll excuse me." He managed to get away from her and jump into a passing taxi, even though it was barely half a mile to his house.

He'd just paid the fare when Jo rang him back.

"Congratulations," she said. "I heard you made an arrest."

"Thanks." He still didn't feel great about it. "How are things there?"

She sighed. "I haven't spoken to Pearson. I think he's avoiding me. I'm going to stay late and try to catch him before he goes home."

"Good luck. So, I won't be seeing you tonight?" He didn't want to sound too hopeful. Now the insane rush of the last few days was over, it would have been nice to spend some time with her. But theirs wasn't the sort of relationship to beg. He couldn't have it both ways.

"No, sorry. I'm rushed off my feet trying to tie up my current projects so I can be with you tomorrow."

He knew she meant at HQ. "It'll be great having you back."

After the last few cases they'd worked on, she was almost an honorary member of the team anyway. He'd expected to resent her when she first turned up to oversee the Surrey Stalker case, but they'd worked well together and by the end of the case had been firm friends. That was two years ago now.

He smiled. Who would have thought they'd end up together?

"I can't wait. Chat later, Rob."

"Night, Jo."

* * *

Trigger launched himself at Rob as he walked through the door. He fondled the dog's ears. Unconditional love. No shame in it. "Let's go for a walk, yeah?"

It was a sultry night, the kind made for lovers. The moon sat high in the sky, suspended by an invisible string, flanked by knowing stars. Had they been shining the night Arina Parvin and the others had been abducted? Had they seen the horrors that had befallen them? Or had the rolling clouds blocked them out, blindfolded them — protected them?

Trigger tugged on the lead, eager to explore the bushes alongside the pavement, other people's gardens, other pet smells, until they got to Old Deer Park, when he let him off. The dog sprinted from one end of the park to the other, ears flattened against his face. Rob thought of Katie, safe in her bed. Free.

She still had no inkling of the drama her abduction had caused, her mother's anguish, her kidnapper's desperation. One day it would be explained to her, verified by a series of newspaper clippings. Her history, in print.

Back home, Rob had a beer while he made a sandwich. Then he had another. Tessa Parvin in custody. Her hell just beginning. Had it been worth it?

Four missing girls. Dead, of course. How long had it been? And a serial killer prowling the streets, perhaps using the clear night and unsuspecting stars to prey on his next victim. And they didn't have a clue who he was.

He sighed, and settled in his chair, Trigger at his feet. The television was on, but he wasn't watching. After processing things all evening, his mind was shutting down. The faces become a blur, voices like background music.

Eventually, he dozed off, into the deep, escapist sleep of a man who didn't want to know.

CHAPTER 34

Katie Found! screamed the headlines.

Rob bought a newspaper on his way to work, but instead of reading it, he folded it under his arm and headed straight to the coffee shop. He needed caffeine to stomach this.

DS Malhotra had given a press conference yesterday afternoon, and every journalist in London had been there. Good news stories like this one were few and far between.

Rob ordered a double espresso and sat down to read. Surprisingly, Tessa Parvin had been painted in a sympathetic light by the press. Rob had half-expected them to tear her to bits.

Even though the statement to the press had only covered the basics, they'd still managed to dig up Tessa's past, and Arina was mentioned almost as much as Katie. Four years too late.

Tessa Parvin, the woman charged with the kidnapping of Katie Wells, had herself lost a child four years earlier. Ignored by the police, she resorted to kidnapping Katie in order to get her daughter's case reopened.

Lawrence was not going to like that. The police commissioner, even less so. Stuff 'em. Lessons needed to be learned.

He read on. At the very end of the article it mentioned that the senior investigating officer, Acting DCI Rob Miller, was "delighted" with the outcome.

He was finishing up when his phone buzzed.

"Hi, Jo," he said. "You on your way in?"

"He didn't go for it." Her voice was heavy, accusatory. "We've got a new case and he needs me to run the team. If I can see this through there's a promotion in it for me."

Rob frowned. "I thought Sam was going to have a word."

"He did, but it's still a no-go. Pearson wants to make his quota, and this case will contribute multiple arrests. There's no way I can leave now."

Her voice edged with disappointment. They were dangling the promotion carrot in front of her. Forcing her to choose.

"I'm sorry, Jo. I know how much this meant to you."

"It's my sister, Rob."

"I know."

There was a pause. "I have some leave owed to me. I might ask Sam if I can work the Manchester angle on my own, as a consultant."

"What about your case and the promotion?"

"If this is my sister's killer, I don't care about any of that. Pearson can shove his promotion up his arse."

She was just letting off steam. She'd worked too hard to get to where she was to throw it all away over this. But then again, it could be her sister's killer. A lifelong quest.

"Look, don't do anything rash. Why don't you wait until we have something definite, then you can think about taking leave? At the moment, we have one body and four maybes. We don't even know for sure if they're connected."

Other than the satchel. The detail Tessa Parvin had picked up on, and mimicked in her own staging of the crime.

She made a strangled sound at the back of her throat. "I feel so useless."

"We're on this, Jo. My team is working around the clock to find a link. When we do, you'll be the first to know."

"Okay." She took a deep, regretful breath. "You're right. There's no sense in pissing off Pearson prematurely. But as soon as you have something, call me."

"You know I will." He smiled down the line.

"In the meantime, I'll go through the old case files. I've got them stashed away in a box in the attic."

"They gave them to you?" He was surprised, but then twenty years was a long time ago. Back then, they didn't have the same security protocols they had now.

"Copies," she clarified. "I haven't looked at them in years."

"Now would be a good time," agreed Rob.

* * *

"Meeting, guys!"

They had to tie up the loose ends in the Katie Wells case in order to prepare for Tessa Parvin's prosecution.

Everyone gathered around.

"First up, the allotment where she held Katie," said Rob. Tessa had given Mallory the location during her confession.

"Forensics went in first thing this morning," replied Jenny. "There's evidence of Katie having stayed there, including a box of old toys, presumably belonging to Arina, and Katie's old clothes were found in a tip out on the street."

"Great, that's good." Along with the signed confession, it should be a slam dunk. "Any sign of the dog?"

Jenny grinned. "Yes, that's the good part. Asher was found in the shed, and when the officer told Lisa Wells he would probably be put down, Katie asked if she could adopt him. So, Ash is now Flash and has a new home."

Rob chuckled. "I'm glad." At least something good had come out of all this. It wasn't the dog's fault, after all.

Next, Rob asked Will to update them on Arina Parvin's post-mortem.

"There was no obvious cause of death." He swiped at his tablet. "The pathologist couldn't find any evidence of strangulation or trauma to the body. Due to the level of decomposition, it's impossible to say whether she'd been sexually assaulted. She thinks not."

A small comfort. "But we don't know for sure?" said Rob. Will shook his head.

"Also, due to a process of elimination, the most likely cause of death is drug-related."

"You mean she was poisoned?"

Will shrugged. "Sedated. Drugged. Given a lethal cocktail. Although, it's little more than guesswork at this point. Her words. They've taken samples for a toxicology but with her having been in the ground for so long, they're not sure if they'll find anything."

"Understood."

They lamented the details of the post-mortem for a while longer, then Rob tied up the briefing. It had got to a point where they were just going round in circles.

"Keep looking into those other disappearances," he told them. "There must be a connection somewhere."

Several phones beeped at once. Mallory got to his first. "Shit."

"What?" said Rob.

"You're never going to believe this."

Rob waved his hand. "What is it?"

"The dog squad have located another body on Bisley Common, near to where Arina Parvin was found."

CHAPTER 35

Had he heard correctly? "*Another* body?"

But Mallory was reading another text.

They all waited. Nobody breathed.

He glanced up, grave-faced. "The K-9 team leader says the dogs were acting strangely when they left yesterday, so they thought they'd go back for another sweep this morning."

"Who's in charge?"

"A Sergeant Wilson."

"Give me his number."

The briefing clearly over, the team dispersed. Except Mallory.

It took six rings before Wilson answered. Judging by the wind echoing down the line, he was out in the open somewhere. Bisley Common, maybe?

Rob introduced himself and asked for particulars. He had to be sure. The second body could be part of some ancient burial site or another pet dog.

Wilson put paid to that. "It appears to be the corpse of a young girl. She's got long hair and looks to be wearing a school uniform of some sort. I can't tell much more than that, the bottom half is still underground."

His heart beat faster. "Is she covered by anything? A sheet, for example?"

"Yes, sir. It looks like a thin piece of material, but it's badly damaged and falling apart."

"Thank you, Wilson. Have you called SOCO yet?"

"They're on their way, sir."

He nodded to himself. Wilson seemed an astute and capable officer. Intuitive too, to take the dogs back to the crime scene. Rare, in his world. "Okay, and you've cordoned off the site, have you?"

"Yes, sir. We've called the local police, who've set up a perimeter."

"Good work, Sergeant. I'll be there as soon as I can."

"Er . . . sir, there's one more thing." The hollow wail of the wind down the line made Rob's hair stand on end.

"What's that?"

"The dogs are going berserk. I think there may be more graves."

Rob was shocked into silence.

"Judging by the dogs' behaviour," Wilson continued, "I suspect there are multiple bodies in this particular section of the common."

Holy shit. His voice was croaky when he replied. "Keep going, then. I'm leaving now."

* * *

Bisley Common was more sombre now the clouds had gathered. Rain threatened — Rob could smell the dampness in the air. Shadows flickered across the heath. He pulled his jacket tighter around him.

He marched towards the dense wood where Arina's body had been discovered. This next burial site was less than twenty metres from Arina, in a small clearing. Above, the murmuring leaves provided a restless and unnerving commentary.

The entire clearing had been cordoned off. A circle of police tape wound around the first line of trees. Rob was pleased to see the local cops were preventing walkers from stopping and were taking down the details of anyone who crossed the line.

Rob and Mallory showed their warrant cards and ducked under the cordon.

"What have we got?" he asked Liz, who was on her knees beside the freshly dug grave. A mound of dirt lay to one side. A crime scene technician was painstakingly taking samples of the soil around the body.

There were four other spots highlighted by police markers. At first glance, Rob wouldn't have known there was anything buried there. The ground coverage looked completely normal. Leaves, twigs, small weeds. Then, he noticed the texture. The soil was coarser, lumpier, and the weeds were thicker than elsewhere in the clearing.

"Young, early teens, no obvious cause of death," she barked. No hellos this time.

Rob walked around her and stared into the shallow pit. A weathered face with ghostly hair stared back at him. She could have been fourteen or forty, it was impossible to tell. Liz was still gently removing dirt from her face.

He averted his gaze. "Can you say how long she's been there?"

Liz sighed. "It would be a guess at best, but I'd say maybe two years. Not as long as the other one. This body is in better condition, her clothing more intact."

Rob nodded. So, up until two years ago, this guy was still active. *If* it was a guy. But he couldn't see a woman doing this. Female serial killers were rare.

"She was posed the same way as before. Hands over chest." She nodded to a plastic bag on the side of the grave. "Those were in her hair."

Rob picked up the packet and studied the two blue hair clips identical to the ones Arina was wearing. His breath quickened. "Same killer."

She nodded. "I'd say so."

Rob exhaled slowly. The investigation may have started with Katie Wells, but Arina and this child were certainly linked. Clear as day. He studied the other markers. "That where the other bodies are?" he asked Liz.

She inclined her head. "So I'm reliably informed. Those are the locations the dogs pointed out."

"Did you see them?" Rob looked around for Sergeant Wilson and the K-9 unit, but they were nowhere to be seen.

"Yep, when I got here there were four dogs lying on those exact spots, good as gold, waiting for their masters. So well trained. My Abigail would have been off like a shot at the first hint of a hare or a field mouse."

Trigger too. "Where is DS Wilson now?" Rob asked.

Liz raised her brows. "They decided to widen the search area. Didn't he tell you?"

Rob felt like he'd been punched in the gut.

"Not more bodies?" Mallory gasped.

She shrugged again. "Who knows. I guess we'll have to wait and see. Whoever this person is, this is the spot where he disposes of his bodies. This is his burial ground."

A chill passed over him, and he thought he saw Mallory shiver. Rob pointed to the other markers. "How are we going to get through all this? Are there more forensic teams available?"

"Just mine, I'm afraid." At his incredulous look, she added, "Resources outside of London are stretched thin. We don't often have so many corpses at one time. But my two lab assistants are on their way. They can do a lot of the preliminary work, uncovering the bodies and taking soil and tissue samples. This'll be a good learning exercise for them. Once we have all the victims back at the mortuary, I can perform the post-mortems and maybe we can get an idea who these lasses are."

They'd be here all day and almost certainly most of the night, if not into tomorrow as well.

"Right, let's set up shop." He turned to Mallory. "Get catering out here, and let's make sure there's enough grub to last twenty-four hours." As SIO he had the magical ability to summon coffee, sandwiches, portable toilets, anything the forensic team might require. "Does that sound about right?"

Liz nodded wearily. "That'd be great. Thanks, Rob."

"Anything else, you let me know."

He and Mallory walked to the edge of the clearing, out of earshot.

"It's going to be a long day," Mallory remarked. "We going to stick around?"

"No, we'll be of more use back at the station," he replied. "There's a lot of groundwork to cover. Besides, we'd just be in the way. Let's let them get on with it and we can come back later, once they've unearthed the other bodies."

Mallory glanced at the other police markers. "Four more, excluding this one. That's one more than we accounted for."

A beam of sunlight broke through the trees and illuminated the markers before they fell back into shadow. A crow cried disdainfully overhead. He was right. Apart from Arina, they had identified four other missing girls. There were five graves here. Potentially five additional victims of the same killer.

The hairs on his neck stood up. "Possibly more, if the dog squad finds anything else."

Mallory fell silent. The enormity of what they'd discovered was hitting home.

"We'd better go further back than five years." Rob said. "We stopped there because that's when Payne was released from prison. But he's no longer a suspect."

"Shit, the murders could go back years." Mallory stared at Rob. "Maybe even twenty years."

Serial killers don't stick to jurisdictions.

"Could be the tip of the iceberg." He thought of Jo's sister, Rachel. How many others? "The killer could have left a trail of buried victims across the country. We just haven't found them yet."

"Manchester?" Mallory whispered as if saying it any louder would make it more plausible.

Rob swallowed over the lump in his throat. "At this point, anything's possible."

225

CHAPTER 36

"How many?" bellowed the chief superintendent as Rob stood facing him in his office.

"At least five, sir. Maybe more. We don't know for sure yet. We're still waiting to hear back from the K-9 unit, and Dr Liz Kramer, who's on site with her team."

Before he'd come into this meeting, Liz had called to say they'd started work on one of the other graves and it appeared to be the same scenario. A young girl, early teens, posed, clips in her hair.

"Fucking hell." Lawrence sank down into one of the armchairs usually reserved for the police commissioner's visits. He stared at Rob with haunted eyes. "So we have a bona fide serial killer on our hands?"

"It looks that way, sir." Rob cringed inwardly, waiting for the explosion that never came.

Instead, Lawrence leaned back and closed his eyes. "All young girls, Rob. For fuck's sake, what kind of demented person does that?"

Rob knew he was thinking about his own daughters, all of whom were grown up now. "A very disturbed person, sir."

"Do we know who they are yet?"

Rob shook his head. "Not yet. We won't know until Liz does the post-mortems, provided the victims are on file."

Lawrence nodded. He knew how it worked. If the children hadn't been reported missing or there were no dental or medical records available, they wouldn't be able to identify them.

"Keep me posted. As soon as you know how many, I'll update the commissioner."

"It probably won't be before tomorrow," Rob said. "I'm heading back out there this evening to see how they're getting on."

Lawrence grunted. "I don't suppose we have any more resources to throw at it?"

"No, sir. We've already gone way over budget and Dr Kramer said her unit is stretched to capacity."

"Very well. We'll just have to wait, then," he huffed.

"Sir, I suggest we put together a task force to work on this. Once we know who the girls are, we can put together a pattern of his movements. We may even have to go back further. There's no saying how long this guy's been active."

"Jesus," groaned Lawrence.

"There might be more girls that we don't know about. Different counties. Spanning a number of years."

"You mean like Manchester?" His eyes narrowed shrewdly.

"It's not impossible, sir."

He scowled. "Wouldn't that make the killer very old?"

"Not especially. If Rachel — that's Jo's sister — was his first, or one of his first, victims and he was in his early twenties, that would put him in his mid-forties now."

"Yes, of course." He sighed heavily. "Okay, Rob. Pick your task force and let's get going on this. I can't believe it's happened — again — but now it has, we have to be beyond reproach. This is the biggest case this department has ever seen. All eyes will be on us, and the powers that be won't hesitate to send in the NCA if they think we can't handle it."

"Yes, sir."

"That means meticulous records. Everything documented. Any fuck-ups and it's both our heads on the block."

"Is this grounds to get Jo over here? We could use her insight, and she has the original case files on her sister's disappearance."

He shook his head. "I've already spoken to Pearson. He wants her there. I've got no sway over how he runs his people."

Rob gave a curt nod. Jo would find a way, she always did. There was no way she'd sit this one out.

He hadn't told her about the multiple graves yet. He'd call her tonight, when he knew more. At the moment, they had two definites and three more in the ground. Once they knew for sure they were all linked, all victims of the same child-killer, he'd fill her in.

Right now, there was work to do.

* * *

The official task force consisted of Rob as SIO and Mallory as his deputy. DS Bird and DS Freemont, the two most experienced sergeants in the department, would handle the main investigation into the missing girls, aided by DS Burns, the soft-spoken American who'd impressed Rob with his astuteness and attention to detail, as well as DS Malhotra, who had built a rapport with the public over the course of the Katie Wells disappearance.

DC Jeff Clarke and DC Mike Manner would provide assistance where needed, analysing CCTV footage and witness statements, and doing most of the groundwork.

"You've landed a big one, Rob," remarked DCI Galbraith, his ruddy complexion more beetroot than bronzed.

"How was Tenerife?" asked Rob.

"Magnificent. You should try it sometime. It's called a holiday."

The gregarious Scot had been in the police force for nearly twenty years and had worked his way up from a uniformed officer to the local CID and then to the Major Crime Team. He was ambitious and self-motivated, and a damn good detective.

Galbraith's return meant Rob was back to being a DI. He should have gone for a promotion after the Revenge Killer case, but Yvette's breakdown and the additional time he'd taken off work in the first half of the year meant he hadn't felt he deserved it. Maybe next year.

"Let us know if you need a hand," Galbraith said. "I've got additional resources you can borrow, if needs be."

"Thanks, Gav." Rob shook his hand. "I've already stolen a couple of your boys."

He gave a wide grin. "I noticed. They're good lads. Make sure you put them to good use."

Galbraith was an extremely competent SIO and ran his team by the book. He'd trained Evan and Harry well, and Rob could see the effects of that in his own investigation.

"Will do."

* * *

Rob moved his task force into Incident Room Three. It was more spacious than the other two, with a twelve-seater boardroom table in the middle. From now on, his unit would work here on their laptops, accumulating, analysing and documenting evidence as they progressed with the investigation.

Mallory was already wheeling in the whiteboard from Incident Room Two containing the background information on Rosie, Elise, Chrissy and Angie, the four girls who'd gone missing in the last five years.

As he waited for everyone to get set up — underneath the table was an alarming web of wires, power points and USB hubs — Rob removed the photographs and details pertaining to Katie from the board until it was only Arina's wide-eyed gaze that looked down at them.

"Right, everyone. We officially have two linked deaths and potentially three more, not counting Arina. That's six bodies found at Bisley Common. I suspect they'll all be posed in the same way, covered with a shroud and clips in their hair. Celeste . . ."

The young DC raised her brows.

"Keep in constant contact with Dr Liz Kramer at the crime scene. As soon as she has an update on the other bodies, let us know."

"Yes, guv."

"Also, I want you to attend the post-mortems and give us a full report as and when they're completed, in case there's anything else we need to know. That includes the identity of the victims, and any DNA or other evidence found on the bodies."

"Got it." She gave a firm nod, her cheeks flushed. This was her biggest role yet, but she was more than capable. Rob wanted to give her more responsibility. She'd make a good sergeant.

"Jenny and Will, look into our missing girls and see if you can find a link between them. We don't know for sure if they're the ones found at Bisley yet — Celeste will keep us updated — but until we have an ID for our bodies, keep digging. He's targeting them somehow, and we need to find out how. Jeff, Mike, talk to their friends and family, revisit witness statements, that sort of thing. Will and Jenny will advise you, so take your instruction from them."

All four team members nodded. Having worked with Rob on the revenge killings earlier in the year, they knew what was at stake. Finding that connection was vital. It was what would lead them to the killer. If they could decipher his pattern, locate his hunting ground, they'd be a lot closer to catching him.

"Evan and Harry, I think we need to go back further than five years. There might be more missing kids we don't know about. There's no telling how long this guy's been active. It could potentially be as far back as twenty years. Expand the search nationwide and look at those that have never been found as well as bodies that were discovered. Try to find similarities with our victims — posing, covered bodies, hair clips, that sort of thing. Flag anything that could possibly be related."

"Yes, boss," said Evan.

"Gotcha." Harry beamed. He was enjoying this.

Things were happening fast now that the bodies were being uncovered, and there was a sense of excitement in the incident room.

"Obviously, not a word about this to anyone. Not your better halves, not friends and definitely not the media. We need to keep this under wraps for as long as possible. It won't be long before the press discover the multiple graves, and then we're going to be issuing press releases and updates every few days. Harry, get ready for that."

The good-looking DS nodded and brushed an imaginary speck of dust from his shoulder. Celeste giggled, while Evan shook his head and grinned good-naturedly.

They were a great team. He was lucky to have them.

"Let's get to work."

* * *

"They've pulled up the third body," Celeste said, going to the whiteboard. She wrote, *Body 3 down the left-hand side underneath Body 1 and Body 2.*

As of yet, they had no idea who the victims were.

"Also posed?" Rob asked.

"Yes, just like the others."

"Clips?"

She nodded. "Two blue ones."

"Age?"

"It's also a teenage girl. Not sure yet when she was buried — Dr Kramer thinks possibly two or three years ago."

The muscles in his jaw tensed. "Okay, thanks, Celeste."

"Also, sir, Dr Kramer said to let you know the press has arrived."

"Shit." He ran a hand through his hair. "I knew they'd get wind of it soon." A cordoned-off area in the middle of

Bisley Woods was bound to attract attention. Not that there was anything to tell. Nobody knew who the victims were, and camping out beyond the cordon, they wouldn't have a clear line of sight.

On cue, the chief superintendent poked his nose into the incident room. "We need to issue a press release, Rob. My bloody phone is ringing off the hook. I've briefed the commissioner. Word is out."

"Yes, sir."

Rob glanced at Harry, who got to his feet.

"I'll go and speak to Vicky. How soon do you want it done?"

"How about in an hour?" Rob suggested. "Just the facts. Five bodies discovered, identities unknown, more information to follow."

The DCS gave a curt nod. "That should keep them off our backs for a while."

* * *

A frenzied silence fell over the incident room as fingers bashed away at keyboards and notes were scribbled on whiteboards. A soft murmur arose every now and then as a point was discussed or a lead developed.

Rob went outside with the aim of grabbing everyone a coffee, after he'd called Jo. She needed to hear it from him first.

"How many?" she croaked down the line.

"Three so far, but they've found five graves. Possibly more. We're still waiting to hear back from the K-9 unit."

"Christ, Rob. And they're all young girls?"

"Yeah, teens mostly. All female. The three that have been unearthed so far were dressed in their school uniform."

He heard her sigh. "I've got to get in on this. I can't sit here anymore while this is going on. These girls were just like Rachel. Innocents. What if it is related?"

"We don't know that yet," he cautioned her. "Just because Arina's and one of the other missing girls' rucksacks were found weighted down in water, it doesn't mean it's the same killer. Rachel died a long time ago. Weighting a bag down is a pretty common way of making sure something won't be found."

"I know . . ." She paused. "It's just . . . I feel it in my gut, you know? It's the same guy."

He did know. And he knew Jo. If her gut was telling her there might be a connection, he wasn't about to dismiss that.

"Is it worth losing a promotion over, though?" he asked. "At this point, it's still early days."

She sighed heavily. "God, I'm so frustrated. I haven't even had time to look at those Manchester files with this case going on. It's like Pearson's going out of his way to pile as much work on me as possible. Bastard."

"Give it until tomorrow," he told her. "We should have all five bodies up by then. I'm going to speak to Lawrence about searching nearby lakes and other bodies of water. Once we know who these girls are and where they disappeared from. If we find any more weighted school bags, then it might justify taking that leave you mentioned."

"Yeah, okay. Keep me posted, Rob."

"Will do."

CHAPTER 37

Rob met Tony Sanderson at Bisley Common after work. As they stared down into the fifth and final grave, the criminal profiler said, "Were they all posed like this?"

"Yeah."

Big, bulbous clouds hovered above them, threatening to burst at any moment. The forensic technicians worked quickly and grimly. One was scraping dirt from around the body while the other carefully brushed dust off her face, sampling anything that might be important as they went.

They were well practised by now. Novice to experts in one day.

A crime scene photographer took shots of the body in situ. He'd done so at every grave, from all angles. Later, in the comfort of the overly warm incident room, they'd analyse them. Compare them. Look for patterns.

It wasn't strictly necessary for Rob to be here. But he couldn't keep away.

Dr Liz Kramer stood beside the catering truck, her hands wrapped around a styrofoam cup. She stared into the distance, the vacant eyes of a woman who'd seen too much. She was done for the day. And done in, by the looks of things. He gave her a wave, but she didn't notice. Her mind was still in the dirt pit.

Tony stared long and hard at the emerging body.

"They were all buried with their hands over their chests and clips in their hair," Rob pointed out. "According to Liz, the pathologist, there's no evidence of sexual assault or any kind of physical trauma. The killer placed a shroud over them before he covered them up. The graves are fairly deep too. It would have been back-breaking work."

Tony nodded. "Probably too much for anyone over sixty. Unless they had help."

Rob muttered in agreement.

"But . . . I don't think that's the case," Tony continued. "These murders look personal. Private. I'll bet he took care of them, brushed their hair before clipping it back, making sure their hands and faces were clean before preparing them for burial."

"Why would he do that?" asked Rob.

"He cares," Tony replied. "These girls meant something to him."

"Then why kill them?"

None of it made any sense.

They watched as the final swabs were taken. The technicians meticulously documented every sample before storing it in a big evidence box. A crime scene officer checked every move they made. No mistakes. No mix-ups.

The female forensic technician beckoned to two men waiting at the catering van, who came over and began lifting the body onto a stretcher. They'd transport it to the local mortuary where it would join the others in cold storage overnight, ready for Dr Kramer to study with fresh eyes in the morning.

"Do you know for certain that he did?" Tony said.

Rob frowned. "What are you saying? That he *found* them and buried them?"

Tony shrugged. "It's a possibility. Or he felt he was justified in killing them."

"What could possibly justify killing a teenage girl?" Rob's voice soared across the clearing. Several heads turned in their direction.

"Nothing, obviously," Tony replied, giving him a look. "But to the killer, something."

Liz came over, jolted out of her reverie. "Hello, gentlemen."

Rob introduced them. "I don't think you've met. Liz, this is Tony Sanderson. Tony, meet forensic pathologist and the woman I couldn't do without, Liz."

"I know you by reputation." Liz held out her hand. "It's wonderful to finally meet you."

"Likewise." Tony shook it, smiling.

Rob could have sworn he saw the stalwart Dr Kramer flush, but she recovered quickly. She had no time for sentiment. "This last one's the most recent. Under a year — ten months, even. We're hoping to get some DNA off her. There appears to be decomposed flesh underneath her fingernails."

Rob's eyebrows shot up. "You mean she clawed her attacker?"

"Possibly."

Yes! Rob took a triumphant lungful of damp air. This could be the break they'd been waiting for. It could identify the killer.

"Find any marks on the victims?" Tony asked. "Any injuries of any sort?"

"Most of the bodies were too degraded to tell," she replied. "But the bones appeared to be intact, even the hyoid, so they weren't strangled. If you ask me, the killer took good care of them before he buried them."

"That seems to be the general theory," Rob murmured.

"It's a strange one, Rob." Liz stifled a yawn. "Excuse me, gentleman, I have to go. Believe it or not, I've got to go out tonight. After a day like today . . ." She flashed a wry smile. "I'll be in touch tomorrow, once we've had another look."

"Okay, thanks, Liz."

She bid them goodbye and trudged back to her car.

"I don't get it," said Rob. "What am I missing here? This guy abducts five girls — that we know of — over the course of the last few years, takes good care of them, then kills them and buries their bodies ritualistically in the woods."

"Is this sacred ground?" Tony looked around them. The clearing wasn't very large, but it was private. Hemmed in by trees. The police and forensic vehicles had parked as close to the clearing as they could get, yet they were still over 200 metres away.

At Rob's blank look, he expanded, "Is there any religious or other significance that would make this a good burial spot? Usually when a serial offender buries all of his victims in the same place, it's because it holds some special meaning for him, or for them."

That was a new angle.

"I'll look into it. I know the parish church borders on the south side, but I have no idea if that's relevant."

"The vicar would know," Tony pointed out.

Rob made a mental note to talk to him in the morning, or maybe he'd swing by the vicarage on his way home, if it wasn't too late.

"Also, your killer might not like violence. He prefers to drug his victims or smother them."

"Why wouldn't he like violence?" Rob could hazard a guess, but he let the expert explain.

Tony shrugged. "He might have been abused as a child, perhaps he witnessed a violent act or was subject to violence over a period of many years. There are any number of reasons why a person wouldn't want to use violence, particularly on children."

"He opted for a more humane method of killing them," Rob summed up.

Tony nodded. "It looks like it. Hopefully Dr Kramer will be able to shed some light once she's done the post-mortems, although after all these years . . ." He left the sentence hanging.

Rob knew the chances of them finding any useful evidence were slim. The peaty soil, bacteria, wild animals and the passing of time had seen to that.

* * *

Rob bribed Tony into going to the vicarage with him by offering to buy him a beer. They were in the area. Two birds and all that.

He parked on a grassy verge outside the ancient stone building. "St John the Baptist," he read. It was fairly isolated, being removed from the more developed part of the village.

"Looks fifteenth century." Tony admired the stonework and oak porch.

He didn't know. Old buildings weren't his thing. "Let's hope the vicar is around. It's gone six."

There was no sign of a vicarage or any cottages on the church property, so they pushed open the massive oak door and went inside.

"It's so modern," said Rob. By the state of the exterior, he'd expected dark wooden pews and dog-eared hymn books. Instead, it was light and airy. Warm pine floorboards and yellow lighting cast a welcoming glow, while modern seating filled the worship area. Up front, a tasteful wine-red carpet led to the altar, upon which stood several contemporary candlesticks and a divine flower arrangement.

"It's cold in here." Tony pulled his jacket closer around him.

"We're closing up for the night," a voice resonated from the wings.

They turned. A smiling middle-aged man in jeans and a leather jacket approached them. "How can I help you?"

"We're looking for the vicar," Rob said.

"You found him." He grinned again. "Reverend Edward Purvis, but you can call me Father Ed, everybody else does."

Rob blinked. "Sorry, you didn't look like . . . Never mind. I'm DCI Miller and this is Tony Sanderson. We were wondering if we could ask you some questions."

"Are you investigating the bodies found in the wood?" he asked.

Rob scowled. "How did you know about that?"

"Everybody is talking about it."

Great.

"Is it true they found several graves?"

"Yes, it's true." Rob walked further into the church. "Do you mind if we sit down?"

"Of course. Come this way."

He led them down the aisle. Rob hadn't taken this route since his wedding. He shivered involuntarily.

Halfway down, the vicar branched into one of the rows and took a seat. The chairs were comfortable, just the right height, with cushioned seats. If you were going to make people sit for hours, they might as well be comfortable.

"Now, what can I help you with?"

"We were wondering if the area in Bisley Common where the bodies were found had any religious significance?"

"The woods, you mean?"

Rob nodded.

The vicar thought for a moment. "I don't know about the land, but the well that the church was named after is supposed to have healing powers."

"The well?" Rob didn't recall seeing one. He glanced at Tony, who shrugged.

"Yes, the Holy Well of St John the Baptist. It's little more than a trickle now, and bricked up, but it's still there. It reportedly dates back over a thousand years."

"Where is it?" asked Rob.

"Along the footpath behind the church," he said. "Rumour has it that it has never dried up or frozen over. People still come to sample the water, although I wouldn't advise it." He chuckled. "At one point, though, it was the water supply for the whole village."

"Did you know a young girl called Arina Parvin?" Rob asked on a whim.

Father Ed thought for a moment. "I don't think so, but then I don't know all my parishioners. We get a good crowd in for Sunday service, but it's not what it was. And the youngsters don't come. Was she one of the people you found buried in the woods?"

Rob got to his feet. "Thank you so much, Father Ed. You've been very helpful."

"Glad I could help. Do you want to see the well?"

He raised an eyebrow at Tony.

"Why not?" the profiler said.

The vicar pointed them in the right direction. They followed the overgrown path until they came across a rectangular stone structure about a foot and a half high. It had a grate covering one side. A rusty pipe spat out a tiny trickle of water.

"So, this is the well of St John the Baptist," said Tony. A giant green sign to the side proclaimed the same. "I must say, there isn't much to see."

"Not anymore," Rob agreed. His eyes were elsewhere. "Isn't that the back of Bisley Wood?"

They peered into the deepening dusk. In the distance, they could see the hazy, purple treeline, and if Rob's bearings were correct, beyond the woods lay Bisley Common.

"Could be a factor," Tony mused.

"I don't know. Why bury them near a well? Even one with supposed healing properties?"

Tony shook his head. "You'll have to ask him that when you catch him."

CHAPTER 38

"I feel like we've been down this road before."

Rob sat across from Tony in the Cricketer, a local pub in Richmond. They'd chosen a table by the window so they could look out over the village green. A footpath sliced it diagonally in two, and white terraced houses stood like cardboard cutouts around it, their interiors burning softly. Families enjoying an evening meal, watching television, living their lives. It was comforting after the wild, windswept and, quite frankly, creepy heath where the bodies had been buried.

Tony grinned. He'd assisted Rob with a profile of the Surrey Stalker that had turned the case on its head. Tony was good at what he did, which was why he consulted for London's top law enforcement agencies.

"All killers have different signatures," he commented. "Yet, there are definite parallels. You're looking at someone who's been doing this a long time. Five bodies, possibly more?"

Rob nodded. The K-9 unit hadn't reported any more macabre finds — thank God — but that didn't mean there weren't others at different locations.

"It's taken time to hone his craft. Years, even. This pattern, the posing, the preparation, would have developed over time."

Rob reached for his pint.

"His first kills would be the most telling," Tony went on. "They're likely to be messier, more chance of being caught on camera or witnessed by a passer-by. The grave sites would be less thought-out. Easier to find. The bodies would be more dishevelled, less prepared."

"We don't know how far back to look," Rob remarked. Then he told Tony about Jo's sister.

"Twenty years!" Tony exhaled slowly.

Rob waited for him to assimilate the information, think about it, form a response.

"It's possible," he said eventually. "These killings were meticulous, well planned, the act of a sophisticated killer. He would've had to have started very young."

Rob pursed his lips. "Early twenties, maybe?"

"It could be even younger than that." Tony tapped the side of his glass with his index finger. "He takes care of his victims, doesn't use violence . . ."

Rob tried to work out where the profiler was going with this. He couldn't, so he sat back and sipped his beer, waiting for the gears to work.

"I'd hazard a guess — and this is purely an educated guess, mind you — that your murderer made his first kill as a teenager."

Rob spluttered. "What?"

"It stands to reason he witnessed extreme violence at a young age, was even a victim of it himself, and it's imprinted itself on his psyche. He's a killer, through and through, but he doesn't want to inflict pain on his victims. What does that tell us?"

Rob shook his head. This was way beyond his level of expertise.

"He's protecting them."

"From what?"

Tony shrugged. "We don't know. It could be anything. Pain, conflict, abuse, bullying. Perhaps he sees himself as a saviour of sorts."

This was feeling very tenuous now.

Rob frowned. "Are you sure we're not reaching? The victims didn't appear to be injured or abused." Although, the post-mortems would confirm that.

"Possibly," Tony concurred. "Like I said, it's educated guesswork, but given the way the bodies were posed, and the care taken with them, I'd say you're looking for someone with a traumatic childhood, socially awkward, perhaps quiet or introverted, and possibly a religious fanatic."

Rob rubbed his head. "Great. I suppose you're also going to tell me he's in his mid to late thirties, white and educated?"

His friend tilted his head to the side, an amused look on his face. "I thought that was a given."

Rob grimaced, but Tony's analysis had opened up a vast number of possibilities. If Rachel had been his first kill, she could turn out to be the most important victim of the investigation. Mistakes would have been made. Back then, he had been learning his craft.

If Jo couldn't join them, one of his team would have to look into Rachel's disappearance, and she wouldn't like that.

"If he's out there, we'll find him," Rob muttered, more to himself than to his friend.

"A serial killer will escalate as he progresses," Tony reminded him. "Always reaching for that elusive high that he gains from killing. One more is never enough."

"So, we can expect to find more bodies?" Rob surmised.

Tony nodded grimly. "He's probably hunting for his next victim as we speak."

CHAPTER 39

Rob couldn't sit still, but it had nothing to do with the two espressos he'd had that morning.

"Any news?" he asked Jenny for the umpteenth time.

"Not yet, guv." Her tone was becoming more clipped with each response.

He gave up. She'd inform him the minute Celeste reported back from the mortuary, where the first of the post-mortems were taking place.

DCS Lawrence had somehow managed to expedite them. No one wanted this case to drag on. The longer a child serial killer was out there, the more flack the police would get. As it was, the press statement this morning hadn't gone well.

Harry had returned flustered and agitated. "They didn't stop flinging questions at me," he'd said, pacing up and down the squad room. "I didn't know what to say. We don't have any more information to give them."

They were relentless, Rob knew. "You did well to keep your cool."

He'd seen it on the morning news. Despite Harry's movie-star looks and Vicky's suave corporate cool, they'd still taken a beating. He was just glad it hadn't been him.

The whiteboard was crammed with information. Last sightings, what the girls were wearing, schools, home addresses. Geographically, there was nothing linking them. They were all dotted around the county. No two victims lived in the same town.

"How the hell is he finding them?" Rob stood in front of the board. "What are we missing?"

"It can't have anything to do with their schools," Mallory pointed out. "None of them attended the same school and we've cross-checked all their teachers."

"What about caretakers, teaching assistants and support staff?" Rob asked.

Mallory shook his head. "Still waiting for that information, but what are the chances any of them worked at five different schools in the last five years?"

"Keep checking," barked Rob. Mallory was right, it wasn't likely, but they didn't have anything else to go on. "Any joy with that white van, Will?"

"No, sir. There are over 12,000 Vauxhall Vivaros and 7,000 Movanos registered in Surrey. I'm checking to see if any of them were picked up by the ANPR cameras in the areas the girls came from, but so far no hits. I'll let you know if anything pops up."

Rob sighed. They didn't even have confirmation it was that make of vehicle. They could be wasting their time.

"Okay, thanks. Let's leave that for now and concentrate on finding a link between these missing girls."

"Guv?" Mike raised his hand. The South Londoner might look tough, but he was actually quite shy. He didn't often put himself forward.

"Yeah?"

"I've found another victim who fits the profile," he said.

"Who?"

"Anna Dewbury from Hemel Hempstead. She was fourteen. Her body was found in a ditch next to a canal in 2011. She disappeared on her way to a friend's house one Saturday morning."

"That's eight years ago. She's the right age. What makes you think it's linked?"

"Her body was wrapped in a sheet. The crime scene photographs show her posed in a similar way to the others."

He spun his laptop around so Rob could see. The dead girl lay in a shallow grave, the sheet pulled back to expose her face. Soft blonde hair. A delicate, heart-shaped face. Porcelain pale.

He squinted across the table. "Are those clips in her hair?"

"Yes, sir."

He exhaled. "Add her to the list."

They had another victim. This one died eight years ago. The killer's time frame was lengthening.

"Good work, Mike. That makes it seven girls, that we know of."

There was a low murmur around the table. Mike sent the photographs to the printer. A short time later, it spat them out.

"Was anyone arrested for her murder?" Rob asked.

"No, but they questioned a young man in connection with her disappearance. A social worker named Alan Simpson. He wasn't charged."

"Get his details," Rob said. "Let's bring him in for questioning. In the meantime, find out everything you can about this girl. It looks like the body was in pretty good shape when it was found, so the post-mortem may have picked up something we can use."

He offered up a silent prayer. *Please.*

Mike was pinning Anna's photograph to the board when Jo walked into the squad room carrying two boxes of files. She glanced around, then dumped the boxes on the nearest desk.

Rob went to greet her. "Hey, what are you doing here?"

"I decided I was needed here more than at the National Crime Agency."

"And Pearson's okay with that?"

"Not really, but he'll get over it. Where do you want me?" She gave him a disarming grin and he felt like he'd been warmed by a ray of sunshine.

"We're in Incident Room Three." He nodded to the far end of the squad room where the glass-walled offices were located.

"I thought it looked a bit empty in here."

"Come on, follow me."

The team glanced up and smiles broke out on everyone's faces. Most of the crew knew Jo from when she'd worked with them earlier in the year. The sunshine had permeated their inner sanctum.

"Hi, everyone," she said, grinning back. "Great to see you again. Where shall I sit?"

Rob pointed to a vacant chair. Celeste was attending the post-mortems and would be gone for most of the day.

She put her handbag on the seat and a laptop case on the table, then said, "Let me grab my files."

Harry jumped up. "I'll help."

A moment later the two heavy boxes were stacked on the floor behind her. Rob had updated her on Tony's ideas the night before, so she knew the importance of Rachel potentially being his first case and was eager to get to work.

His phone rang. Everybody sat up. A Pavlovian response.

He grabbed it off the table. "Yeah?"

Celeste's voice. "Sir, we have an ID on the first girl. It's Rosie Hutton."

Rosie. One of the missing girls they'd already identified.

"Thank you, Celeste. That's excellent news. Do we know when she died?"

"Around three years ago. She also had an old fracture on her right forearm, but it didn't occur at the time of death. Dr Kramer says it's at least five years old."

Two years prior to her death. "Okay, keep us posted."

"Will do. The other DNA samples should be back any moment, so hopefully I'll have some more names for you then."

He turned to the waiting group. "Body one is Rosie Hutton."

"The twelve-year-old from Cheam." Mallory updated the board.

Rob told them about the broken arm. "It may be significant, although nothing to do with her death. We have to inform her next of kin. Jenny, are you okay to do it?"

DS Bird nodded.

"Take Becca or one of the other FLOs with you, and while you're there, ask how she broke her arm." He made a mental note to check the hospital records.

Something Tony had said was playing around in his brain.

He's protecting them from something.

* * *

By mid-afternoon three of the five unknown girls found in the clearing had been identified.

Rosie Hutton (12)

Chrissy Macdonald (14)

Angie Nolan (10)

"Elise Mitcham is still missing," Rob pointed out. "Her dental records are on file and they don't match either of the two remaining victims."

"That means there are two girls unaccounted for," said Jo.

"We need to look harder," said Evan. "We've missed a couple."

Rob glanced at Mike and Jeff, who'd been tasked with trawling the missing-persons notifications. "Anything?"

"There's one possibility," said Jeff. "Lucy Chang disappeared two years ago. She was fifteen years old, so older than the others. According to her mother's statement, she'd got in with a bad crowd. This wasn't the first time she'd disappeared. Which is why we didn't flag it before."

"Go talk to the mother," said Rob. "Take Mike with you. Find out whether she's heard from her daughter, and if not, ask her if we can use something of Lucy's for a DNA analysis."

"Yes, sir." Jeff leaped up, delighted to be let out.

"Find out why she ran away," Rob called after them.

His phone rang again.

"Celeste?"

"Dr Kramer is performing the post-mortem on one of the unknown victims, sir," she began, her voice hesitant.

"Yes?"

"Well, um . . ." There was an awkward pause. "It appears she wasn't a virgin."

"Seriously? You mean she was sexually assaulted?"

"At some point, yes, although Dr Kramer can't say whether it was at the time of death or before."

Rob closed his eyes.

"What?" asked Jo, who'd been watching.

He turned to her, holding his phone still at his ear. "One of the unidentified girls was sexually assaulted. It seems we've got another angle to look into."

CHAPTER 40

"Do you think the killer did it?" asked Jo, after Rob had hung up.

"Dr Kramer wasn't sure. It doesn't make sense, though. Why take so much care with the other girls, killing them humanely, without using violence, then raping this one? It's just not his style."

"It could have happened before she was taken," suggested Jo.

Rob frowned. "It's a pity we don't know who she was." He glanced at the other names on the list. "Rosie Hutton had a broken arm. I wonder . . ."

"If the others were being abused too?" finished Jo.

Rob nodded. "I know it's a long shot, but I think we should bring in the parents and ask them. Just in case."

"If that's what your gut's telling you." She smiled at him. It was.

"I'll get on it," said Mallory.

* * *

DS Evan Burns led the interviews, supported by DS Bird. Rob had read the American's file. He had an interest in forensic psychology and had trained in interview techniques. Good to know.

Rob listened in, yet another cup of disgusting canteen coffee in front of him.

Mrs Macdonald, a small, fragile woman with prematurely grey hair, was responding to Evan's soft American drawl. Her husband, not so much. He sat bolt upright in his chair, an annoyed expression on his face.

"I can't believe you've found our Chrissy after all these years," she gushed. "I never thought we'd get her back."

Evan smiled. "It's the least we could do."

"We're going to bury her close to us," she continued. "So we can visit every day."

Her husband's hard face didn't suggest he'd be visiting his daughter's grave every day.

Evan told them they were doing everything they could to catch her killer. "Do you mind if I ask you some questions about her disappearance?"

"Yes, of course. We're happy to help in any way we can. Aren't we, love?"

Mr Macdonald grunted.

Evan began by asking them to describe the last time they saw their daughter. Mrs Macdonald welled up, while her husband sat stoically beside her.

"Was she acting strangely before she disappeared?" Evan asked. "Acting out, or moody or depressed?"

"No, nothing like that," said Mrs Macdonald, but she didn't meet his gaze.

"How was her relationship with you?" he asked.

"What does that mean?" snapped Mr Macdonald.

Evan rephrased the question. "Was she an easy child? Did she get on with both of you?"

"She was a typical teenager," he muttered. "You know what they're like."

"No, I don't." Evan turned his attention to the husband. "Could you explain what you mean by that?"

"She was a bit up and down," interjected Mrs Macdonald, casting fearful glances at her husband. "We loved her dearly, but she could be difficult."

"Difficult? Could you give me some examples?"

He was good, Rob was impressed. He picked up on the vague answers and drilled down, looking for specifics. Trying to get them to reveal more than they intended.

"Oh, let me see . . ." She stared at her hands. "Giving us backchat, refusing to clean her room, going out with her friends and coming home late, normal teenage stuff. She could also be very rude to her father."

"How did that make you feel?" Evan asked him.

His lips stretched into a thin line. "We tried to discipline her, but she wouldn't listen."

"How did you discipline her?"

Rob held his breath.

"We grounded her," he said, evenly.

Evan nodded. "How did she take that?"

"Not very well," sighed her mother.

"And this was before she disappeared?" Evan clarified, leading them back to the point where their daughter was taken.

Mrs Macdonald nodded. "She was still grounded when she disappeared. That's why we didn't call the police straight away. We thought she might have gone to her best friend's house in an act of defiance. She and Daisy were inseparable."

"But she wasn't there?"

Evan had read the case file, as had he. Chrissy had gone to buy a drink after school with her friend and they'd parted ways at the bus stop. The friend had got home safely, but Chrissy was never seen again.

Mrs Macdonald stifled a sob. "No, she wasn't."

Evan paused for a moment. "Was there a reason why Chrissy might not want to come home, other than out of defiance?"

"What do you mean?" asked Mr Macdonald. He was a big guy, over six foot, with beefy arms and a barrel chest.

Where he once might have been firm, his belly was turning to fat.

"I mean, had you had an altercation with her the day before? Maybe been a bit heavy-handed?"

"I don't like what you're implying," he growled. His wife whimpered.

"Mrs Macdonald?" enquired Evan. "Is there something you want to tell me?"

She couldn't look at him. "No, nothing."

Her husband had her under his thumb. Probably under his fist, when they were at home. Something wasn't right there. If they wanted to get the truth out of Chrissy's mother, they'd have to interview her separately.

Evan obviously came to the same conclusion because he tied up the interview shortly after that and let them go.

"There's something they're not saying," he told Rob back in the incident room.

"Agreed," said Rob. "We need to get her alone."

"He's a building contractor," Evan said, "but he doesn't work every day. If I can find out when he's out, I'll pop round and speak to her privately. I'm worried questioning her alone now would only get her into trouble later."

He too had read the situation.

"Good idea," agreed Rob.

There was definitely something suspicious going on there.

* * *

The second interview went a lot easier. Angie Nolan's mother was a feisty woman in her mid-thirties, younger than Rob expected. But then Angie was only ten when she had been taken. She came in alone, clicking down the corridor in tight jeans and three-inch heels.

"I have two other children now," she told Evan.

They discussed the days leading up to Angie's disappearance, and whether anything had been bothering her daughter.

"Well, my first husband, Angie's father, wasn't a very nice man."

Rob glanced up at the screen.

"What do you mean?" asked Evan.

"He was a brute. He used to beat me, and I suspected he was doing the same to Angie, although I had no proof."

"What made you think that?"

"Angie had these odd bruises all over her body," she said. "Even the school noticed. They reported it to social services. We had to meet with a social worker."

"Do you remember his or her name?" asked Evan.

She shook her head. "It was a he, but no, sorry."

"How did Angie find it?" asked Evan.

Rob leaned forward, hanging on to every word.

"I'm not sure." She sighed. "Angie denied her father had hurt her. There was nothing they could do."

"But you could."

She nodded. "I'd had enough by that stage. I was looking for an excuse to kick the bastard out, so next time he went drinking I had all the locks changed. He was so angry when he got back, I had to call the police." She smirked. "He spent the night in a jail cell. Served him right."

No love lost there.

"I'm sorry you had to go through that," said Evan.

"I divorced him." Her voice cracked. The tough talk vanished and she shrivelled up. "I blamed him for Angie's disappearance. If he hadn't been so rough with her, she might still be alive."

CHAPTER 41

"Both Chrissy and Angie may have had abusive fathers," said Rob.

It was a new day, much like the others, except it was raining. Puddles formed on the pavements and rivers ran down the gutters. He and Jo had shared an umbrella on the way to work.

The whole task force was in, except Celeste, who'd gone to the mortuary.

"Angie Nolan saw a social worker. Let's find out who it was and bring them in. I want to hear his thoughts."

"Yes, guv." Will's hands flew across his keyboard.

"Also, do we have a statement from Chrissy Macdonald's friend Daisy?"

Jenny passed it to him. He scanned the page. Daisy had got on the 33 bus, while Chrissy had walked home. According to Daisy, her friend appeared normal, hadn't mentioned that anything was bothering her. He noted the address. Dorking.

Last night, after he and Jo had taken Trigger for a walk, Jenny had called to say Rosie Hutton had broken her arm falling off a climbing frame at the park. Hospital records, however, told a different story. She'd presented in A&E with multiple bruises that weren't synonymous with a fall.

A big question mark there.

"Sir, the social worker is here for questioning," said Mike.

"Which one?" Rob asked.

"Alan Simpson. The one questioned in relation to Anna Dewbury's disappearance. The girl from Hemel Hempstead."

"What was his relationship to the victim?"

"Apparently, he'd been assessing her after a report was made by her maths teacher."

"Do we have a copy of the report?" Rob felt his pulse tick up a notch.

"Yeah, here." Mike handed it over.

He scanned it. She'd been quiet and withdrawn at school. Her grades were dropping. She'd always been an excellent student, but it seemed like she'd lost interest in learning. Her teachers were concerned."

"Why did he fall under suspicion?"

"He saw her several times in the week before she disappeared, but when questioned, he provided an alibi for the day of her disappearance. He was visiting another client across town. They vouched for him."

"Okay, you interview him, Mike. We need to know if Anna confided in him. Do you think you can handle that?"

"Yes, guv." The Londoner puffed out his already impressive chest. "Thank you, guv."

"Okay, get to it."

* * *

Mallory updated the whiteboard. Rosie Hutton, Chrissy Macdonald, Angie Nolan and Anna Dewbury could have been victims of physical abuse, possibly more. Without proof it was hard to say. Angie had seen a social worker, as had the Hemel Hempstead girl. Unless they'd talked, it would be impossible to prove.

"What was Angie's social worker's name?" he asked.

Jenny retrieved a battered document from a pile on the table. "A man called Paul Daley."

"It's not the same person Mike's interviewing."

"No, sir."

Different men. Different counties.

He turned to Jo. "If you were a young girl with problems, who would you turn to?"

"A friend? I don't know. Maybe a priest if my family was religious, or a social worker, if one was appointed. I might have called Childline or something similar."

Rob knew a priest. Well, a vicar. And his church was close to the burial ground at Bisley Common. Within walking distance.

"Only Arina Parvin lived in Bisley." It was as though Mallory had read his mind.

"Still, it might be worth talking to him again."

Mallory nodded. "I'll give him a call."

* * *

Mike burst into the room. "The social worker suspected that Anna Dewbury was being sexually abused by her stepfather."

Rob stopped what he was doing.

"*Sexually* abused? Did he actually say that?"

"Yes, although there wasn't any proof. Whenever he spoke to Anna, she clammed up. It was more her reaction to her stepfather that convinced him. He recommended moving her to a place of safety, but it never happened. The mother insisted there was nothing going on and that Anna was just upset because they wouldn't buy her a mobile phone. This was eight years ago, remember. Every kid has one now."

"What did the post-mortem say?"

Mike sat down and opened his laptop. "Give me a moment."

He browsed through several documents. "Here it is. She *was* sexually active."

"At fourteen? She's a minor. Why wasn't that flagged?"

"I don't know, guv."

Rob frowned. "Was the stepfather ever a suspect?"

"No, it doesn't look like it. He was away on a business trip when Anna disappeared, and didn't get back until late the next day. It couldn't have been him."

Very convenient.

"He was guilty of having sex with a minor, though," hissed Jo. "He should be prosecuted for that."

"Now that she's dead, there's no evidence against him," Rob pointed out. "She can't testify, and if there was no DNA taken at the time of the abuse, it'll be very hard to prove he's guilty."

"It's not right."

"No," he agreed. "It isn't."

* * *

Tessa opened the door in a tracksuit. She was out on bail, awaiting trial. Her face appeared ghostly white against the dark interior of her house.

"I'm sorry to bother you," Rob began. "But I need to ask you some questions about Arina. We're still trying to find the person who killed her." If the other girls were victims of abuse, she might have been too.

She nodded. No fight left. "Come in."

They followed her into her dingy living room with piles of books and the armchair by the window. She switched on the overhead light, but it didn't do much to illuminate the room. Nothing shone here.

They sat down.

"This is a bit sensitive," he said. "But it's come to our attention that the other girls found in the woods may have been abused by a member of their family. Did Arina mention anything like that to you?"

To their surprise, she bent over, hid her face behind her hands and burst into tears. They were tears of a woman who'd reached the end of her tether.

Rob felt awful. "I'm sorry, Tessa. Would you like a minute? Can I get you something?"

She shook her head. Then, she looked up. "I suspected he was abusing her, but I didn't know for sure. I should have come out and asked her, but I was too scared."

"Of your husband?" Mallory asked.

"Yes, he had a terrible temper."

"Was he violent towards you?" Rob asked.

She nodded. "Sometimes, but it was Arina I was worried about."

"Tell us why," encouraged Rob.

She took a deep, wobbly breath. "She used to act strangely when I left them alone together. Wouldn't come out of her room. Wouldn't eat supper. At first, I thought it was just her being a teenager, but then I began to suspect Ramin might have something to do with it. They'd never had much of a relationship, but every now and then I'd catch him looking at her." She shuddered. "That's why I was so worried when Arina disappeared and he left the country. I thought he'd done something to her."

It was becoming clearer now. "Why didn't you tell us this before?"

She shrugged. "It's not something you tell, is it? It's shameful." Her voice dropped to a whisper. "And it wasn't him, anyway. It wasn't him who took my girl."

"No, it wasn't," said Rob. "But he should have still been reported for what he was doing to Arina."

"I tried to report him once," she said, her voice barely audible.

"What?" asked Rob.

"I saw a flyer for one of those children's charities at the library and brought it home. I put it on the kitchen counter. I was going to call them. Then Arina came home, so I hid it in a drawer and forgot about it. Later, when I went to look for it, it was gone. I thought Ramin had found it and got rid of it."

If only she'd made that call.

"Could Arina have taken it?" he asked.

She shrugged. "I don't know." Tears welled again. "It was all so long ago, and what does it matter now? She's not coming back."

"It matters," said Rob quietly. "It matters to you. I know it does because that's why you kidnapped Katie. You wanted Arina's case reopened, and now it is. We're going to find the person who did this."

But the light had gone out of her eyes. "I wanted to know if she was really dead. I hope you catch the man who did this, but it won't bring her back."

There was nothing he could say to that.

* * *

"I'll get on to Childline," said Mallory, once they got back to the station. "I didn't manage to get hold of Father Ed, by the way. His phone kept diverting to voicemail. Do you want to have him picked up?"

"No, don't worry. I'll take a drive out there. I want to have another look at the crime scene. Can you hold the fort here?"

"Sure." Mallory nodded.

"Want some company?" Jo asked, stretching her back. "I need some fresh air. I've been tied to this desk for too long."

Rob smiled. He hadn't done much of that lately. It felt weird, like his face might crack. "Actually, that would be great. There's something I want to run by you."

* * *

"Have you found anything interesting?" asked Rob as they turned onto the busy A316 and merged with the flow of traffic. The busy arterial road would take them onto the M3, the motorway that cut through the south-western part of Surrey.

"Nothing I haven't read before," she said. "I'm still familiarising myself with the details of the investigation. There weren't any CCTV cameras in the town back then, so the police relied on witness accounts. Rachel said goodbye to her friend in the street — a shopkeeper saw them go their separate ways. She had a five-minute walk until she got home. That's not a lot of time for someone to take her. Also, it was late afternoon, so not exactly dark. There would have been people milling about. It was a Saturday, as I recall."

How much of this sounded familiar. Same story. Different day. "Do you remember who this friend of hers was?"

She wrinkled her brow. "I don't, it's in the files back at the station. I'll look it up when we get back. Why do you ask?" She glanced across at him.

"It might be worth talking to him again."

She blinked. "What, now? After all these years? He probably doesn't even remember Rachel."

"I'm sure he'd remember a friend who went missing." Rob braked behind a large truck at a traffic light. He could smell the exhaust fumes seeping in through the air conditioning unit.

"Maybe," she mused. "Anyway, what was it you wanted to run by me?"

He hesitated. "Did you and your sister have a good relationship with your parents?"

"She did," Jo said straight away. "I didn't. My mother doted on Rachel."

"What about your father?" he asked.

"Dad was always away," she said. "He worked on projects all over the country. We often wouldn't see him for months at a time."

Rob decided to come clean. "You know there's a pattern of abuse with the other dead girls . . ."

He didn't have to continue. Jo leaped to the right conclusion easy enough.

"No," she gasped. "Nothing like that."

He nodded. "I didn't think so, but if it's the same killer . . ." He left it hanging.

Jo went very quiet. He left her to dwell on it. Sometimes it was only after the shock wore off that people saw things they should have seen all along, but didn't.

261

He approached a turn-off for a McDonald's drive-through. "Shall I stop?" he asked.

She nodded, distracted.

He pulled in. "A cheeseburger okay?"

When she didn't reply, he ordered two, and two cokes to go with it. They'd had enough coffee to last a lifetime.

They ate in silence in the car park. It was only after she'd finished that she spoke up. "I really don't think it's possible. My father wasn't there for long enough, and he wasn't the type." She shook her head.

"I'm sorry," he said. "I had to ask."

"There was an uncle though."

Rob looked at her. "Could he have been molesting your sister?"

She sighed. "Maybe. I don't know."

"Was he there often?"

"They lived a few doors down. We were always at each other's houses. They had two rowdy boys, my cousins. I lost touch with them after Rachel disappeared because I moved in with my grandparents, but I remember playing football in their garden." She smiled sadly. "Those were happy times. Imagine if he was . . . Oh, God. It doesn't bear thinking of." She squeezed her eyes shut.

Rob got out of the car and threw away the rubbish. When he climbed back in, Jo said, "You need to know, don't you?"

He bit his lip.

"*I* need to know. If my uncle was abusing my sister, that means she was just like the others."

"It's another link," he said. Although what it meant, he had no idea.

"I'm going to find out," she decided.

He frowned. "How?"

"I'm going to visit my mother. I'm going to force her to tell me. If anyone knows, it's her."

"I thought she was in a home." He started the engine.

"She is, but she's not that far gone that she won't remember something like that." Jo's cheeks were flushed. She was agitated. He was just grateful she hadn't taken offence, but then that wasn't her style. She was a detective, first and foremost. Her desire to know the truth would supersede any delicate sensibility she may have.

That was one of the many things he liked about her.

CHAPTER 42

Father Ed invited them for tea in the vestry.

Rob walked in warily, never having been this deep inside a church before. Was it unholy to drip on the floor?

"I'm glad you've come." He took their coats and hung them on a hook behind the door. "We're having a vigil tomorrow night for those girls. The whole village will be there. You will come, won't you?"

"Of course," Rob said.

"Wouldn't miss it." Jo gave him one of her heart-warming smiles.

He beamed, throwing his hands in the air like he was giving an enthusiastic sermon. "Wonderful. I'll just pop on the kettle and then you can ask me your questions."

"Is that a northern accent I detect?" asked Jo.

He grinned at her. "Aye. I was born in Ireland, but we moved around a lot when I was a lad. Liverpool, Birmingham. Goodness, I can't remember all the places we lived in."

"Manchester?" asked Jo. "That's where I'm from."

"Aye, Manchester too, but not for long. I think we were only there for a few weeks before we moved on."

"Do you remember when that was?" Jo asked. "We might have lived there at the same time."

He paused, kettle in hand. "I think I was about sixteen at the time, but I can't be sure. Like I said, we moved around a lot."

Rob met Jo's gaze.

"What brought you to Bisley?" Rob accepted a cup of tea.

"I was offered a position here at St John the Baptist. It looked like a cosy town with a small parish. Those are the best kind, you know. So I accepted. I'm not married, so it was easy enough to move."

"When was this?" Rob asked.

"Oh, twelve years ago now." He smiled. "Best decision I ever made."

* * *

"It *could* have been him," said Jo. They were walking up the footpath behind the church. It was still drizzling, but not hard enough to forgo a visit to the well.

"Sixteen is very young to kill someone," he said. "And we don't even know if he knew your sister."

"I didn't want to spook him by asking." She hesitated. "Do you think we should?"

"Let's leave it for now. We can ask him at the vigil tomorrow night. Maybe bring a photo with you to jog his memory."

"Good idea. This it?"

They stopped at the small rectangular stone block. "Yep, this is it."

The trickle was heavier now, as it flowed from the pipe onto the already-wet pebbles below.

Jo crouched. "I was expecting something a bit grander from a thousand-year-old well."

He chuckled. "That's what we thought. But the interesting thing is, that's Bisley Wood."

She stood up and peered over the graveyard, across the grey meadow, towards the dense grouping of trees in the near distance. "That's where the bodies were buried?"

"Yep. It's not a mile from here."

She cocked her head. "I'm up for a walk if you are?"

* * *

They set off along the footpath. It was patchy in parts, disappearing almost entirely in the overgrown areas.

"Careful you don't slip." Rob took her hand. They clambered over a rickety turnstile into the meadow where, unbelievably, two cows were grazing, oblivious to the rain.

The dark oaks and pines up ahead lured them in. As they got closer, the grass degraded to leaf-covered dirt.

"I see what you mean by creepy." Jo took his hand. He'd tried to describe the burial site to her before, but she'd wanted to see it for herself.

"Maybe it's the thought of so many lost souls buried here for years."

The path disappeared completely.

"Do you know where we're going?" Jo asked.

Rob tried to gauge where they were. He consulted the map in his head.

"I think it's that way." He pointed towards the tangled mesh of trees.

"Well, we can't get through that, we'll have to go around."

They veered to the right where it wasn't so overgrown and picked their way around the matted foliage until there was space to walk between the trees again.

"Here we go." They'd looped back on their previous bearing.

"It can't be much further." At least, he bloody hoped not. A large drip fell down the back of his neck. This was not the day to go rambling.

Ten minutes later, they emerged into the clearing.

"Well done!" She laughed, recognising the burial ground from the photographs.

"Thank God. I thought I'd got us totally lost."

Jo walked around, studying the five open graves, the mounds of dirt discarded beside them. The police cordon

266

had been taken down, but it was obvious something sinister had occurred here. It resembled a scene from a zombie movie.

"Where was Arina buried?" she asked.

"To the left, just beyond those trees."

"So not in the clearing?"

"No, she was under that huge oak."

"I wonder why he decided to bury her there, when he buried the others in the clearing." She glanced up at the sky. It was barely visible between the overhanging branches, slithers of grey beyond the pine.

"Maybe he ran out of space."

Jo peered back the way they'd come. "Do you think he came this way? From the church?"

"It's a long way to carry a body. It's more likely he pulled up in a vehicle of some sort. The road is less than a mile that way." He pointed in the opposite direction. "This clearing is actually fairly isolated. It's not even on a map of the common. You'd have to be a local to know it was here."

"Either way, he would have had to carry the bodies a fair distance," Jo said. "He'd have to be strong to do that. Unless they were alive when he brought them here."

Rob shook his head. "The way they were posed — the sheeting, the clips in their hair . . . I don't think he did that here."

"I agree. It's more likely he carried them, already prepared for burial."

"Tony said he was protecting them from something."

Jo studied him. "From what? Their parents? The sexual or physical abuse?"

He shrugged. "Maybe. What else could it be?" Thunder rumbled in the background. He raised his head. "It's going to bucket down."

Jo wrapped her arms around him and they hugged. In the middle of the clearing. It didn't seem nearly so creepy anymore.

"We'll find him," she said, breaking away. "We'll get the bastard who did this."

CHAPTER 43

"Haven't they been through enough?" growled Rob as they stared at the flat-screen television mounted on the squad room wall. It showed a live news broadcast of Chrissy Macdonald's parents being interviewed.

"Turn it up," someone called.

Jenny, who was closest to the remote, increased the volume.

"We're just glad to have some closure," Mrs Macdonald was saying. "Now we can grieve properly for poor Chrissy."

Her husband stood beside her staring at his feet.

Rob clenched his jaw.

"Makes you sick, doesn't it?" Jo came up beside him. "Knowing what he's done. Knowing what they all did."

Rob gestured to the TV. "What does this achieve? Nothing. It's only going to bring them more heartache. Now they're going to see their daughter's face every time they open a newspaper."

"Are there any leads in the case?" the reporter, a slick brunette was asking.

"Nothing we know of," she replied.

Rob rolled his eyes. Not an hour ago they'd issued a press release divulging the identities of the bodies found in Bisley Wood, and here they were hounding the parents. Typical.

Evan came up to him. "If it's okay with you, I'm going to drive to Dorking tomorrow morning and see if I can catch Mrs Macdonald while her husband's out."

"Absolutely, good idea."

* * *

Circumstantial evidence, hearsay, guesswork. They didn't have anything that actually proved the girls were abused. A fact that the chief superintendent pointed out to him in his office after the broadcast.

"Get some DNA, Rob, something definitive that we can act on. All this supposition is getting us nowhere. So what if they were all abused? Unless we can prove it, we can't use it."

"It docs show a connection between the victims, sir," he pointed out.

"We need to find the killer, not more dead girls. Jesus wept." He paced up and down his office. "I'm not even going to tell you what the commissioner said."

Rob sat down wearily.

"They want to send in someone from the NCA to take over the investigation. It's only your reputation that's holding this task force together, Rob. I can't keep the wolves at bay for much longer."

Shit. The last thing they needed was some bigwig waltzing in and taking over the case. It would be like starting from scratch.

"The case is too complex," he said. "It would take anyone days to catch up, I don't care how experienced they are."

Lawrence shrugged. "Then find something, Rob. And find it soon. To be honest, I'm tempted to hand this entire mess over to someone else."

"You don't mean that, sir?"

He grunted. "Just find me something concrete to tell the commissioner. That way we can all keep our jobs."

* * *

The Shepherd watched as Chrissy's parents were interviewed.

What hypocrites!

How could they stand there and talk about grieving their daughter when they were the ones who'd made her life a misery.

"*You're* the reason she had to die," he hissed at the screen. "*You*, with your filthy urges and animalistic desires."

She'd never have sought him out, otherwise.

He seethed as the journalist asked leading questions about the investigation, about the detective in charge. DI Rob Miller. Except he was never the one giving the press releases. It was always that other bloke, the good-looking, mixed-race one. The type of image the police force wanted to portray.

He'd glimpsed DCI Miller at the burial ground. Tall, purposeful, with a determined walk. He was a worthy adversary. But he wouldn't catch him, for he had the Lord on his side.

He was untouchable.

Guided by the path of the righteous, he led the little children to safety. He ended their pain and suffering. He was their salvation.

Switching off the television, he wondered if he had time to go to church and light a candle for the dead before his next appointment.

CHAPTER 44

Jo left for Manchester early the next morning.

As the train pulled out of Euston station, she leaned back in her chair and watched the tall concrete apartment and corporate buildings, mostly covered in scaffolding, whizz by.

London was constantly changing. More buildings going up where others had been torn down. Urban regeneration. Or perhaps they were just trying to hide the decay that was already there, patching it up so nobody noticed.

Was that what her mother had done? Put a bandage over Rachel's abuse, hidden it away from the world so no one would know?

She'd been ten at the time, too young to notice those things. The lustful glances, the fearful looks, the withdrawal and depression. Rachel had always been so vivacious, so popular. Was it possible she'd been harbouring a deep, dark secret?

She spent the two-and-a-half-hour journey reading through more of her sister's case files. The ones she could fit in her bag, anyway. Witness statements by her sister's friends.

I didn't see her that weekend. She said she had to study.

There was a party, but Rachel didn't come.

No, she didn't have a boyfriend, although there was this weird guy she used to hang out with. I don't know his name, he didn't go to our school.

Jo had a dim memory of a slim, geeky boy with glasses who lived in the neighbourhood. Who was that guy? Michael? Was that it? He used to walk Rachel home sometimes.

She fiddled through the file. Damn, she didn't have the right one.

Hauling out her phone, she rang Rob.

"Miss me already?"

She smiled. "Yes, but that's not why I rang."

He chuckled. "What's up?"

"I need a favour. Remember that kid my sister used to know, the last person to see her alive? Could you look up his name for me? I've left the folder in the incident room. It should be on the table, I was looking at it yesterday."

"Sure, hang on."

She listened to the sound of him rifling through the folders on the table where she sat. She'd left them in a neat pile in case anyone else needed access to them.

"Okay, got it. Michael Robertson's statement."

"Michael! I thought that was it. Thanks, Rob."

"Is that all you need? You don't want me to send you a photo of it?"

"No, it was just his name. Thanks, Rob. I'll call you later."

They signed off.

Michael Robertson.

She googled him using her phone, but several hundred hits came up. Facebook. LinkedIn. Twitter.

"Oh, God," she moaned. That wasn't going to work.

She tried "Michael Robertson Manchester", which narrowed it down, but still provided far too many results to read through. Why did he have to have such a common name? She didn't even know what he looked like. There was no picture of him in the file, and her memory was fuzzy at best.

The statements by Rachel's friends were telling in themselves. Why had Miss Popularity suddenly shunned all her friends?

Not going out. Studying. That didn't sound at all like the Rachel she knew.

And then there was this boy. This nerdy guy who nobody knew. Why was her sister hanging around with him?

She leaned back and closed her eyes.

Hopefully, her mother would have the answers.

* * *

Rob stared at the witness statement. Michael Robertson. The last person to see Rachel Maguire alive. He also googled him, but like Jo, realised his mistake when thousands of results returned in a nanosecond.

He typed Michael Robertson into the criminal database. It took longer than Google's giant search engine, but eventually returned two results. Neither were particularly enlightening.

The first entry was of an eighteen year old arrested for breaking and entering. He glanced at the date. Two weeks ago.

Moving on to the next one. Michael Robertson, sixteen, cautioned for getting into a fight at school. Let off with a warning.

He wrote the name on a Post-it note.

"Where are you now, Michael?" he murmured, as he stuck it to the table where DS Jenny Bird sat.

The neon blue digits on the squad room clock said it was nearly 7 a.m. He had another hour or so before people began arriving.

Nicking the flip chart from next door, he wrote all seven victims' names down the left side. Next to them he wrote what he knew about their injuries.

Rosie had a broken arm, Angie had been sexually abused, as had Anna Dewbury and Lucy Chang. All three were underage. Chrissy and Rosie's bodies were too badly degraded to be able to tell.

What about Rachel? Since her body had never been discovered, there was no way to know. He hoped Jo's mother could shed some light.

273

A burly shadow caught his eye. DCS Lawrence strode across the floor towards his office. The chief superintendent prided himself on being the first person in the office, and he wouldn't like that Rob had beaten him to it.

Sure enough, two minutes later his solid frame appeared in the doorway.

"Getting an early start, Rob?"

"Jo left for Manchester this morning, so I thought I'd come in while it's quiet and go over everything again."

"Good idea," he said. "Find a suspect yet?"

"Not yet, sir," he grimaced.

Lawrence gave him a hard look before turning away. "I'm counting on you, Rob." He marched back to his office.

What they needed was some DNA. The two victims most likely to yield any were Angie Nolan, who'd only been buried for ten months, and Anna Dewbury, whose body had been discovered within a day or two of her death.

Knowing he was in for a bollocking, he called Liz Kramer's direct line.

"Don't tell me you've found another dead teenager?" she barked into the phone.

"No, nothing like that," he said. "Just something I wanted to ask you."

"Anything that isn't a dead body can wait until I've got some clothes on."

She hung up.

Rob chuckled, despite himself.

"Right, what is it?" she said when she rang back twenty minutes later. Rob heard her indicator going and knew she was in her car on the way to the mortuary.

"The youngest victim, Angie Nolan," he began. "You mentioned she had some flesh under her fingernails. Did you ever find out who it belonged to?"

"I sent it to the lab," she said. "As far as I know, they haven't emailed through the results. I'll chase them up, but there's a backlog at the moment."

With six bodies to process, Rob wasn't surprised.

"Please. I'm desperate, Liz. We need a lead."

"I understand, Rob. I'll see what I can do."

* * *

He looked up the friend of Chrissy Macdonald. She'd be seventeen or eighteen now.

He dialled her home phone number, aware that it may have changed. He didn't need permission to speak to her, but he thought it best to go through her mother, if possible.

A woman answered the phone, her voice groggy. Most of the country hadn't woken up yet.

"This is DI Miller from the Putney Major Investigation Team. I'm sorry to bother you so early, but I was wondering if I could speak to your daughter, Daisy, in connection with a friend of hers, Chrissy Macdonald."

"Chrissy, goodness," murmured the woman. "There's a name I haven't heard for a while. Yes, I'll see if she's up."

Rob heard her climbing the stairs and pictured her going to wake her daughter. Low murmurings, an exclamation of some sort, and then a sleepy voice. "Hello?"

"Sorry to bother you, Daisy," he said. "I'm the detective looking into Chrissy's death and I needed to ask you some questions. Would that be okay?"

"Yeah."

"Could you tell me if Chrissy was acting like herself in the days or weeks leading up to her disappearance?"

She hesitated, then he heard her say, "It's all right, Mum. I got this."

The sound of a door closing.

"Hi." She sounded breathless.

"Do you need me to repeat the question?" he asked.

"No . . . Um . . . Chrissy was a bit sad before she disappeared. She wasn't herself. She hadn't been for a while."

"What do you mean?" His heart thumped in his chest.

"I don't know how to explain it. She was just down, you know? She didn't want to do anything or go anywhere.

There was this guy she was seeing, Raff, but she'd dumped him too."

"Did you talk to her about it? Did she say what was wrong?"

"No, not really. She said she had issues at home. Her father was a bully. I remember going over there once and he cornered me in the kitchen. He creeped me out."

There it was again. Suggestions, suppositions, but still no damn proof.

"Did Chrissy keep a diary?" he asked. Maybe there was some record of her father's abuse.

"No, she would have told me. I think she was afraid of him. She'd stay at my house until her mother rang, telling her to go home."

"Do you know if she told anyone else about her problems at home? A counsellor perhaps, or a teacher?"

"Oh, yeah. There was someone. I can't remember who. She said she'd told an adult about it and they were going to sort it. I think she trusted him."

"Him?"

"Yeah, it was a man. I don't know who."

"You didn't meet him?"

"God, no. It was private. Chrissy only told me 'cos I was her best friend."

"Daisy, do you know how she contacted this person? Was it through the school? Or a church group, something like that?"

Daisy laughed. "Church, no way. I think she called a number, like Childline or something."

Tessa Parvin's words echoed in his head.

I saw a flyer for one of those children's charities at the library . . .

They went over a few of the details again, then he told Daisy she'd been extremely helpful.

"I heard there's going to be a vigil tonight," she said shyly. "In Bisley, wherever that is."

"Yes, are you going?" he asked.

"Definitely. My boyfriend's going to take me. Will you be there?"

"Yeah, I'll be there."

"Okay," she said. "See you later, I guess."

"Bye, Daisy."

CHAPTER 45

Jo drove into the Lavender Hill Nursing Home car park and shivered. Seeing her mother always unsettled her, but this time it was different. This time they needed to have a talk. A proper talk. She only hoped her mother was with it enough to remember.

"She's through here, dear," said the nurse, opening the door to a bright common room.

Valerie, her mother, sat in an armchair by the window knitting. Jo watched for a moment as her forefinger twisted the wool around the protruding needle, before pulling it back. Then it thrust out a second time like a fencer lunging forward in a dual. A cup of tea sat untouched beside her.

"Hi, Mum." She moved into the woman's frame of vision.

The woman turned and smiled, but it didn't reach her eyes. It was the glazed look Jo remembered. There, but not fully present.

"Hello, Jo," she said. "Long time no see."

"Yes, I'm sorry I haven't been to see you for a while. I've been busy at work."

"A policewoman," Valerie murmured. "Who would have thought?"

Jo took a deep breath. Her mother always wound her up, even when she didn't intend to. "I'm looking into Rachel's death, Mum." She pulled a chair up beside her. There was no point in small talk. There was nothing to say. Her mother wasn't interested in her life, in who she was seeing, or her job. Because she wasn't Rachel.

That got her attention. Her face lit up and she leaned forward. "Have you found out who took my darling girl?"

Jo recognised the flicker of hope in her eyes. The need to know what had happened. She saw it in the mirror every time she thought about her sister.

"Nearly, Mum," she lied. "I just need to clarify a few things. Do you feel up to helping me?"

Valerie gave a tired nod. "Can't remember much, it was so long ago, but fire away. I'll do my best."

It was a start. "Okay, thanks." She composed her thoughts. Where to begin, though? She didn't want to send her mother into a catatonic state with the first question.

"Was Rachel upset about anything before she disappeared?"

"Upset? What did she have to be upset about? She was beautiful, clever and she had lots of friends."

A perfect life. Except it wasn't.

"I remember her staying at home more in the days before she disappeared." Jo watched her mother for a reaction to her words. "Her friends said she didn't want to go out, turned down invitations to parties and get-togethers. Doesn't that strike you as odd?"

"Nonsense," said Valerie, but something about her expression made Jo push on.

"Come on, Mum. I know there was something wrong. What was it?"

"Oh, dear. It was so long ago. Why is this important now?"

"Because it might have a bearing on the case." She only just kept the exasperation out of her voice.

"It doesn't. Rachel hadn't been feeling well, that's all. She'd been fighting off a virus. It was nothing serious."

Was that all it was? "What happened to Uncle Hubert?"

Her mother twitched and dropped a stitch. "Whatever made you think of him?" She fumbled with the needles.

"I don't know. I remembered he used to come over a lot when Dad was away. We were always going over to their house for barbecues, do you remember? Then Rachel disappeared and you stopped seeing him."

"I was too distraught to see anyone after she disappeared." Her voice was a whisper. Jo thought she'd pushed her too far, but she had to know. Although her hands were trembling, she remained *compos mentis*. "Were you and Uncle Hubert having an affair?"

Her mother didn't reply, just stared off into the past.

That's a yes, thought Jo. She took a deep breath. Her next question could push her mother over the edge.

"Was he abusing Rachel?"

Her mother blinked, but the tears welled up in her eyes.

"Is that what happened, Mum?" Jo asked gently. "You found out and broke up with him. But it was too late for Rachel, wasn't it? The damage had been done."

"She was pregnant," whispered Valerie. Tears overflowed and cascaded down her face.

Jo had never seen her mother cry before. She usually shut down in a sort of glazed numbness, cocooned from the world. This was better.

"Rachel told me one night when I tucked her up. She said it had been going on for months. I was furious. I wanted to kill him."

Jo felt the rage bubble up inside of her and she took her mother's hand. "Then what happened?"

"I went round there and screamed at him in front of Margaret and the children. I couldn't help myself, I was so angry."

"That's understandable," Jo said. "What did he do?"

"He denied everything. Told me it was all rubbish and that Rachel was lying."

Jo glimpsed a flicker of indignation, although it didn't burn long enough to ignite. "What happened?" she whispered.

Valerie shrugged. "Hubert stormed out. I ran home to make sure he hadn't gone there, but he was too much of a coward for that. I never saw him again."

"Dad must have been furious." Her father had been away at the time. Her recollection of what had happened after his return was sketchy at best. Jo had flimsy memories of him coming and going, and then he wasn't there anymore.

"I'd never seen him so angry. Of course, I didn't tell him who was responsible until he got home. That's when he confronted Hubert."

Jo's eyes widened. *Go Dad.*

"They had a massive fight. Margaret had to call the police. They both spent the night in jail."

There'd be a record of that somewhere.

"Why didn't you tell the police about her pregnancy?" asked Jo. "About Uncle Hubert?"

Valerie shook her head. "I didn't want everyone to know. I was so ashamed."

Jo put her head in her hands. "Mum, how do you know it wasn't Hubert who took her?" He'd had more than enough of a motive.

She shook her head. "Rachel disappeared the day of the fight. Both your father and Hubert were in police custody."

A nurse came to check on them and enquired if they'd like some fresh tea. After that discussion, Jo was tempted to ask her if they had anything stronger. "Tea would be lovely," she replied.

When she turned back to her mother, Valerie's face was wet with tears. Moved, Jo shook her hand. "I can't believe you never told me any of this."

"You were too young to understand."

"But what about when I was older? I had a right to know."

Valerie didn't respond. Had she pushed her too far? Caused all those painful memories to come flooding back? Hopefully, her mother wouldn't have a relapse.

"Hubert should have been prosecuted," Jo muttered. "Men like him are predators and need to be locked up."

Valerie nodded, but the glazed look was coming back. Jo saw her mother zone out and she knew that she'd lost her. Telling her youngest daughter the truth had taken it out of her. There was no point in continuing the conversation.

She got up to leave, kissing her mother on the forehead. "Bye, Mum, I'll come and see you again soon."

No response.

She sighed. Maybe it was better if she didn't. Her mother couldn't cope with remembering.

Then, she recalled Michael Robertson. "Mum, do you remember a boy who Rachel was friendly with? Tall, skinny, with glasses?"

No response.

"Okay, never mind. I'll see you soon."

She left her mother sitting there like a zombie, the knitting in her lap, and went to speak to the nurse.

CHAPTER 46

"I've got the DNA results back," said Liz.

Rob clutched the phone. "Yes?"

"Not your perp, I'm afraid. It belongs to her father, Cole Nolan."

Fuck.

"I'm sorry, Rob. I know you were hoping for a lead."

She didn't know how much. He sighed heavily. "Thanks, Liz."

He collapsed into his chair. *Fuck.* How was it the killer could murder and bury six girls and not leave a shred of evidence?

"She was ten years old," said Jenny, beside him. Most of the team were in now, only Evan was missing. "What kind of monster rapes his ten-year-old daughter?"

Rob shook his head. It was beyond comprehension.

"We've got him, though. Got his DNA under her fingernails. I'm going to have a word with the prosecutor." That he could act on, at least.

"I hope a jury convicts him and he spends a very long time behind bars."

"And is put on the sex offenders register," added Celeste, who'd been listening in.

"How are you getting on with Father Ed?" Rob asked her.

She rolled her eyes. "I keep wanting to call him Father Ted."

Rob managed a grin.

"The family moved around a lot, as you know. His father was a project manager for a supermarket company. Every time they built a new store, the family would move."

"Couldn't have been much fun for little Ed."

"No, eventually the father retired and started his own company in Liverpool."

"And Ed went off to become a vicar."

"That's right. He doesn't have a criminal record, he's DBS-checked and according to his Facebook profile, he's a pescatarian."

"Good to know." Rob glanced at the whiteboard. "Doesn't really fit the profile, does he?"

"Not really," said Mallory. "Any history of violence?"

Celeste shook her head. "No domestic abuse charges laid against his father, no social disturbances, no hospital visits. Apart from the constant moving, Ed appears to have had a happy childhood."

"Still, he could have been in Manchester when Jo's sister disappeared," said Rob. "He's the right age."

"The company doesn't have those records anymore," Celeste confirmed. "There's no way to tell exactly when he was there."

"Speaking of profiles," said Mallory. "Have you updated Tony on the sexual angle?"

Rob nodded. "I tried calling him last night, but he didn't pick up. I've left a message on his voicemail. Are you coming with me to the vigil tonight?"

Mallory grinned. "Do you want me to?"

"Yeah, Jo was going to come but she's away. I think the two of us should be there, just in case the killer returns to the burial site." It was a known fact that arsonists and serial offenders often went back to the scene of the crime.

"Do you think we should go too?" Jenny gestured to herself and Will.

"If you can spare the time. The more eyes we have on the ground the better."

* * *

In the end, the entire team went to the vigil.

They positioned themselves in a semicircle outside the church, but didn't speak to or acknowledge one another. The idea was to keep an eye out for anyone who looked suspicious. Particularly men in their mid to late forties, strong but socially awkward. Loners.

Father Ed stood on the doorstep under the porch light wearing a smart black suit with a clerical collar. The massive oak door to the church was open behind him, and inside Rob could see rows and rows of candles.

The vicar waited until just after eight, then held up his hands. A hush fell over the crowd.

"Welcome," he bellowed, his voice striking a rich timbre. "Thank you for taking time out of your busy lives to come and pay your respects to the six girls who were buried in Bisley Woods. Tonight, we are honouring and remembering our friends and loved ones with our candlelight of hope, unity and love."

Rob let his gaze roam over the participants. They stood together in groups, eyes on the vicar, candles at the ready. He couldn't spot anyone who didn't look like they belonged there. Every man was accompanied by a woman and/or a teenager. Husbands. Fathers. No loners.

"I don't see anyone suspicious, do you?" Rob whispered.

Mallory shook his head. "No, not from where I'm standing."

Before they'd left the station in their separate vehicles, Rob had told everyone that if they saw anything suspicious, to take a picture with their phone. It wouldn't be unusual in a crowd of teenagers, many of whom were filming the vicar's introductory speech and taking snaps for their Instagram Stories.

The vicar was finishing up now. "As Leonard Cohen, world-renowned poet and songwriter, said, 'There is a crack in everything, that's how the light gets in.' May the light of our candles, both here and online, bring comfort and solace to the friends and families of those who were found here."

"Bravo," said Mallory.

"I didn't know this was being broadcast online?" Rob turned around, looking for a cameraman or a film crew.

"There, to the left of the church." Mallory pointed.

A shadowy figure was aiming a camera mounted on a tripod at Father Ed.

"The killer could be watching this from his living room," hissed Rob.

"And give up the thrill of being here in person?"

Yeah, Mallory was right. It would be so much more of an adrenalin rush to be here.

"Let's split up. I'll meet you back at the car in half an hour."

Rob strolled to the left, trying to blend in. He realised, ironically, that he was exactly the type of person he was looking for. Male. Alone. Reasonably fit and strong.

He surveyed the crowd but saw mostly families and groups of teens. Could the killer be with someone? Did he have a partner? A family? He wondered what Tony would say about that.

Now the speech was finished, the youngsters lit their candles and held them up, talking among themselves. Organ music emanated from the church and some people went inside, probably more out of curiosity than for any spiritual reason.

Seeing the vicar approaching him, Rob moved away from the group of teenagers he was standing beside.

"DI Miller, so glad you could join us."

He nodded. "Great speech."

"I try to pander to my audience." He grinned. "The youth of today aren't interested in the old ways. We have to jazz things up if we want to keep their attention."

"It's a good turnout," Rob remarked.

He beamed. "Yes, we paid for a social media marketing campaign to target friends of the deceased. Worked like a charm."

Rob was impressed. "Do you know much about how the victims died?" he asked.

The vicar leaned forward. "Only what I read in the papers."

"They went peacefully. There were no signs of violence or a struggle."

"Praise the Lord."

Indeed. Could he know more than he was letting on?

The vicar remained impassive and engaged. "I'm glad they are at peace now."

"Well, they will be once their bodies are returned to their families."

Father Ed nodded. "I'm glad to hear it. Now, if you'll excuse me, I must go and make sure no one's burning down my church. All those candles are a health-and-safety nightmare." He strode back into the candlelit interior.

If he was their killer, he was damn good at hiding it.

CHAPTER 47

Jo caught the 20.55 train back to London. Staying in Manchester overnight wasn't appealing, not after the conversation with her mother. The train was preferable to an empty hotel room. Alone with her thoughts. Besides, she had everything she'd come for.

After she'd left the home, she'd gone to the storage unit where her mother's belongings were kept and had a good root around. Eventually, she'd found what she was looking for — a taped-up cardboard box with "Rachel" written in black marker pen across the top. It was all she had left of her sister.

She remembered packing the box with her grandmother in her sister's room with the pink chandelier and matching curtains. Her mother had been "resting", which Jo had later learned was the code word for sedated.

"Is there anything here you'd like to keep?" her grandmother had asked her.

The ten-year-old Jo wasn't into girly things, so her grandmother had packed what she'd thought Jo might appreciate one day. Books, drawings, magazines, some items of clothing, a fluffy pillow, a favourite teddy bear her sister had been loath to part with.

Jo knew, because she'd unpacked the box when she'd first looked into her sister's disappearance. Back then, she'd been a newly qualified DC, passionate and idealistic. She'd opened the box hoping to find a journal or a diary, some clue as to where her sister had gone or who she'd met the evening she'd vanished. There had been nothing, so Jo had taped the box back up again and left it in the storage unit.

Now, she was looking for a reference to Michael, the mysterious boy who'd befriended her sister in her time of need. The boy who'd been by her side when she'd turned her back on her friends. Who the hell was he?

Instead of lugging the box with her, she'd bought a cheap suitcase at the station and transferred all the books, papers and magazines into it. She'd left the clothes, fluffy pillow and teddy bear in a charity recycling bin. Maybe they'd bring comfort to some other lost soul.

As the train raced through the night, Jo went through the contents of the box. She took each piece of paper, smoothed it out and studied it. Rachel had talent. Most of her drawings were of pastel wildflowers, fantastically green trees or picturesque landscapes, but they were good. She might even frame one.

One in particular caught her eye. It had religious overtones, which was surprising. Rachel had never been spiritual. An angel with large fluffy wings rose above a field of flowers. Spring flowers. The sun shone around her — or maybe it was a halo, she couldn't tell. The expression on the angel's face was one of blissful serenity.

She continued browsing. It was weird looking at the world through her sister's eyes. Everything was perfect. The books were teenage romances with happy endings, the magazines were old favourites like *Just Seventeen* and *Smash Hits*, and the photographs were family snaps. She peered closer at the characters, hardly recognising them.

Her father stood tall and proud at the back, his hand resting on Jo's shoulder. Next to him posed her mother, resplendent in a white bathing suit with a sarong wrapped around her waist and a wide-brimmed hat. She was dressed for the South of France, not Brighton. And between them was Rachel. Tall, leggy, beautiful, her long brown hair catching the breeze, a serene smile on her face.

Looking at these, Jo couldn't believe what had become of them. Rachel was dead. Her father was too. And her mother was in a home, pumped full of tranquilisers, too afraid to feel. She was the only real one left.

Jo shook her head. She bought a small bottle of wine from the drinks trolley. As she watched the dark countryside flash by, she made two decisions. One, she was going to find out who killed her sister, and two, when all this was over, she was going to track down her Uncle Hubert and make him pay for destroying her family.

* * *

Rob jumped at the sound of Trigger's high-pitched bark. He'd just dozed off in his favourite chair and was floating somewhere between reality and dreamland. The voice of the television presenter. Studio laughter. Shadowy faces. A girl screaming.

He sat up, his pulse racing. Trigger darted to the door, then back again.

"What's up, boy?" That was his excited bark.

A moment later, the doorbell rang.

Rob saw Jo's blurry outline through the frosted glass panels. He eased himself off the chair and went to get the door.

"This is a nice surprise." He stood aside to let her enter. "What are you doing back so soon?"

She moved silently into his arms and he held her for a long moment savouring her warmth, the feel of her. "Is everything all right?" he murmured into her hair.

"It is now," she breathed. Slowly, she detangled herself. "I didn't feel like staying in Manchester overnight."

He grinned. "Well, you're always welcome here."

She followed him into the living room. "Still working, I see?"

A pile of case files lay on the floor.

"Until I dozed off."

She laughed.

"How was your trip?"

"Awful. Mum was like a zombie, but she did tell me the truth about Rachel."

He studied her. "And?"

She sighed. "It's a long story."

"Would a glass of wine help?" Rob asked. "I've got a bottle of red on the go."

"Sure."

He poured her a glass while she started her story.

"Poor kid," he said when she'd finished. "It's a pity she didn't report him. She could have got him locked away."

"At fourteen you don't think about that." Rob had moved to the couch and she sat beside him, cradling her wine glass, her legs curled up beneath her. "At that age, you're just terrified someone's going to find out."

"These are people in a position of trust," Rob muttered. "Fathers, uncles, stepfathers. It's shocking how they abuse it."

"And how their partners are oblivious or turn a blind eye."

Rob shook his head.

"The worst part is, my Uncle Hubert's still out there. God only knows what he's been up to since, how many young lives he's ruined."

Rob told her that Angie Nolan's father's DNA was found under her fingernails. "At least we can prosecute him," he said. "That's one more predator off the street."

"That's good." She gazed at him. "When this case is over, I might just look up my uncle and make sure he's behaving himself."

Her mouth was set in a grim line. He knew that look. Uncle Hubert better watch out.

"I need to trace this Michael Robertson," she told him. "He might be able to tell us something."

"I've got Celeste working on it. But twenty years is a long time. He could be anywhere by now. He could have left the country, be living in America. He could be dead for all we know."

"I know it's a long shot," she said. "But it's the only lead I have."

"Not the only one . . ."

She raised an eyebrow. "Have you been keeping something from me, DI Miller?"

He grinned. "No, but I was mulling over it before you arrived."

"Do tell."

"Well, Anna Dewbury had a social worker — so did Angie Nolan. Tessa told me she brought home a flyer for a children's charity, but it went missing. She thought her husband had destroyed it. I was wondering if Arina hadn't found it and decided to contact a helpline to tell them what was happening."

Jo studied him intently. "Go on . . ."

"Arina didn't have a mobile phone, she was only twelve, but she could have used the landline in the house."

"And—?" She raised her eyebrows.

"I went through their phone records in the weeks before Arina disappeared and there is one call to a free number. I googled it and it belongs to The Homestead, a registered children's charity."

Jo crinkled her forehead. "So, she called a helpline. Do you think that's how he's targeting them?"

"I'm not sure yet, but I do think it could be via the social care system. Chrissy Macdonald had called a helpline too. That's four out of the seven victims who reached out to a social worker or a helpline. More than just a coincidence, don't you think?"

"Is it the same charity?" she asked.

"I don't know. Haven't got much farther than that."

"It's definitely worth exploring," she acknowledged. "Have you checked the other girls' phone records for the same number?"

"No, I haven't had time. We'll get on it first thing."

Jo stifled a yawn. It was past midnight.

"Come on, let's go to bed." Rob took her hand and pulled her to her feet. "You look done in."

"I feel it." She followed him out.

They switched off the lights and traipsed upstairs, Trigger at their heels.

CHAPTER 48

Loose and casual, that's the way she wanted it. He'd thought that's the way he wanted it too, but something had changed since she'd got back from Manchester. This morning, she'd held him a little tighter, kissed him a little longer and made love to him more tenderly than ever before. Now, as they walked to work together, their fingers loosely entwined, Rob had never felt so content.

As soon as they reached the austere brick building, Jo released his hand. He winked at her and let her go up the stairs ahead of him. They walked in one at a time, mentally switching into work mode.

* * *

"Today, I want us to focus on finding out as much information as we can about the social workers that Anna Dewbury and Angie Nolan spoke to. Find out which agency they're from, how they got in touch with the girls and where they've worked before."

Jenny and Will nodded.

Rob told the team what he'd discovered. "It's just a theory at this point, but I want us all to focus on it. Celeste, I know you're off to the mortuary again today. Please keep me updated."

"Will do, guv."

"Evan, Harry, go through the phone records and look for any calls to children's helplines. If we don't have the relevant call logs, get them. I'm happy to sign off on any warrants needed. That means landlines and mobile phones for all members of the family, including siblings, if there are any."

"Yes, boss," they said in unison. Now Harry was calling him boss too.

"Should we carry on looking for other victims?" Mike motioned to himself and Jeff.

"Please. We still have an unidentified girl in the morgue. She must have come from somewhere. Let's find out who she is so her mother can rest easy. Also, it's possible our killer's been active for nearly twenty years, so look into unsolved cold cases as well as those where a conviction was secured."

He'd had a situation before where a man had been wrongfully imprisoned for the murder of his girlfriend. Ben Studley, his name was. Rob would never forget it. The false conviction had led them to believe the murdered girl wasn't a victim of their serial killer when, in fact, she was his first. The poor guy had served six years of a life sentence before the outcome of their investigation had given him grounds for an appeal. Now he was a free man. Rob wouldn't make the same mistake again.

"I'm going to try to find this boy my sister knew, Michael Robertson." Jo glanced around the room. "If anyone comes across that name, or any variation of it, let me know."

They nodded. Everybody liked Jo. Her management style was relaxed and efficient, kind of like she was. Even the chief superintendent didn't mind her bouncing back and forth between the National Crime Agency and here. She'd proved her worth.

He smiled at her now, then checked his phone as it began vibrating in his hand. He stepped outside. "Tony, about time."

"Sorry, mate," the profiler said. "I've been at a symposium for two days. How are you getting on with your serial offender?"

"There've been some developments," Rob explained. "I wouldn't mind running them by you — off the books, of course."

"Sure thing." Tony never minded helping out when he could. "You free for lunch? I'm going to be in your neck of the woods. It's our ten-year anniversary tomorrow and I've got to get Kim something special."

"Hey, congrats! That's amazing."

Rob had met Kim several times and both liked and admired her. A paediatric nurse, she was perfect for Tony. Although, how they found time for each other with their busy schedules, he didn't know. But it worked. Maybe that's why it worked.

"What's amazing is that she's stuck with me all this time." He laughed. "How does one o'clock at the Argentinian sound?"

"Perfect. See you then."

* * *

"Angie Nolan's social worker was employed by a company called The Homestead," said Jenny. "It's a children's charity based out of Woking."

A slither of ice slid down his back. "That was the name on the flyer Tessa Parvin brought home."

Heads bobbed up.

"It's the same one Chrissy Macdonald called," said Evan quietly.

"Holy crap, Rob." Jo stopped typing. "What was his name again?"

"Paul Daley," supplied Jenny, wide-eyed.

Jo typed his name into Google. "According to his LinkedIn profile, he's worked for various charities over the last few years as a social worker and a volunteer counsellor."

"The Homestead?" asked Rob.

Jo looked up and nodded. She turned the laptop around so they could see his profile picture. A man about Rob's age, with wispy brown hair and a kind, open face with dark eyes stared back at them.

"He could be our man," whispered Jenny.

"He wasn't Anna Dewbury's social worker," pointed out Mike. "That was a guy called Alan Simpson."

"That was eight years ago," pointed out Jo.

"Mike, call Alan Simpson and ask him if he knows Paul Daley."

Mike nodded and pulled out his phone.

Adrenalin shot through him. They had a lead. A real one. Something he could take to the chief superintendent. But would it be enough to keep the National Crime Agency off their back?

* * *

The 300-gram rib-eye steak sizzled on the board as it was placed in front of him. Rob's stomach growled. "This looks great. I'm ravenous."

His friend laughed. "That's when you know you're working too hard, when you forget to eat."

He wasn't wrong there.

"So, tell me what you've got."

Rob took a bite and savoured the taste for a moment. It was fantastic. Succulent and cooked to perfection. "It seems several of the victims, if not all of them, were sexually assaulted," he said, once he'd finished chewing.

Tony started. "By the killer? That doesn't sound likely."

"No, by a person they trusted. Either their father, step-father or, in one case, an uncle. We've also discovered three of the girls sought help via a children's charity or helpline. That's the only link we can find between them."

Tony paused for a moment as he ate his steak. Rob could see his brain ticking over. He let him think while he dived in to his own meal.

Finally, Tony said, "It makes perfect sense."

"It does?"

"Absolutely. We already know your killer must have had a violent childhood or witnessed extreme violence at some point in his formative years. What if that was sexual abuse? Maybe he suffered at the hands of an abuser, or he watched someone close to him suffer. A sibling or a parent. Think about it. He *knows* what it's like. He empathises to the point where he wants to save these girls, protect them."

"By killing them?" Rob stared at his friend, his fork poised in the air.

"In his mind, yes. If he can't stop the abuse, he might view death as the preferable option."

"Jesus."

Rob put his knife and fork down. In a weird, fucked-up way, what Tony said made sense.

"Especially if there's a religious angle," continued the profiler. "He might even see the killings as merciful, a mission from God."

Rob felt his stomach churn. "That's messed up."

"Indeed, but then so many of these people are. Most serial offenders feel their actions are justified in some way or another. Ridding the world of sex workers, hatred towards women, homosexuals or other marginalised groups, revenge . . ."

Rob knew all about that last one.

"It's misplaced rage, fuelled by a dysfunctional upbringing. Sometimes there are mental health issues too, which don't help. Paranoid schizophrenia, PTSD. But in this case, I'd say your killer is in complete control of his emotions. He strikes me as a thorough, meticulous man, possibly with an obsessive–compulsive disorder."

"Why OCD?" Rob wanted to know.

"The way the bodies were posed. All exactly the same. Precise. Blue hair clips."

"What do you think the hair clips mean?"

Tony smiled. "I'm glad you asked that. I think the person he watched suffer wore them. With every girl he 'saves', he's recreating that first kill."

Rob shuddered.

"They like to relive the experience," Tony told him. "I'll bet he goes back to the burial site often. He probably keeps souvenirs or trinkets from his victims too. Things to remind him of their final moments."

"That's sick." Rob knew serial offenders often took mementos of their crimes, but to hear it put like that made his skin crawl.

Tony met his gaze across the table. "That's the mind of a serial killer."

CHAPTER 49

"Thank God! Now that's what I want to hear."

DCS Lawrence beamed at him from across the desk. "Great work, Rob, and to your team too. We finally have a suspect."

"We're still trying to tie him to the murders," Rob pointed out. He didn't want to give the chief superintendent false hope, but at the same time, he needed to give him something to feed to the NCA. "But as soon as we do, we'll bring him in for questioning."

"Excellent. Now, I know it's premature, but the public wants to hear we're making progress. There's been so much in the media lately about these girls, including the one we've yet to identify. Did you see that spread in *The Times* yesterday?"

Rob shook his head.

"I need you to give them an update. Make a splash. Tell them you're following up on a promising line of enquiry and expect to have a suspect in custody in a few days."

Rob opened his mouth.

The DCS held up a finger. "I know what you're going to say, that it's too soon, but we're not actually admitting we've got the guy. And it'll keep the commissioner happy."

Rob hated the politics in policing.

"I'll get DS—"

"I want *you* to do it, Rob. The public has faith in you. You're a hero in their eyes. Take Jo with you. She looks great on camera and it'll be good to have a woman up there."

Rob barely resisted rolling his eyes.

"I know, I know," he said. "I hate it too, but it's just the hoops we have to jump through."

"I'll let Vicky know." Rob got to his feet.

* * *

The press accumulated on the pavement outside the Putney offices, cameras poised, microphones buzzing. The air crackled with anticipation. The SIO was making an announcement, which meant a major development in the investigation.

Rob, prepped by Vicky and sporting a tie for the first time since his wedding, walked purposely out of the front door and came to a halt in front of a podium, behind which stood an enormous array of bristling microphones.

Jo, immaculate in one of Vicky's "you never know when you're going to need them" white silk blouses, stood a few yards back.

Lenses snapped and video cameras began rolling.

"Ladies and gentlemen, good afternoon," Rob began. "I'm Detective Chief Inspector Rob Miller from the Major Investigation Team. I would like to take this opportunity to give you an update on the ongoing investigation into the deaths of Arina Parvin, Rosie Hutton, Elise Mitcham, Chrissy Macdonald, Angie Nolan, Lucy Chang and Anna Dewbury." He looked around at the blur of expectant faces. "I am pleased to inform you that following a recent breakthrough in the case, we are now looking at one individual in connection with these murders."

A murmur spread through the group. Frantic clicking. Then an impatient silence.

"We can't divulge the individual's name, for obvious reasons, but we would like to reassure you that we expect to have this person in custody soon. Thank you." What a crock of shit. He only hoped the commissioner bought it.

Placing his folder under his arm, he walked back into the police station, Jo at his side.

"That was a waste of a perfectly good silk blouse," she murmured, as they pushed their way through the revolving doors. "And I take offence at being the token female."

"Bloody politics." He headed straight for the stairs. "But if it gets the press, the commissioner and the NCA off our back, it'll be worth it."

She sighed. "I suppose you have a point. Let's just hope we haven't raised expectations unrealistically. We don't know anything about this guy, yet."

"Well, we've given him fair warning we're coming for him."

* * *

The Shepherd stared at the television. Where had he seen that woman before? There was something about her confident glare, her cocky walk. Usually he was good with faces, but he couldn't place her. It wasn't recent, he knew that much. She was a figure from his past. From long ago.

He wasn't bothered by what Miller had said. The man was an idiot. He might look like he knew what he was doing, but they were way off the mark on this one. There was nothing linking the girls back to him. No DNA. No witnesses. No trail. He'd made sure of that. They hadn't even questioned him.

In custody soon. What a joke.

"I hope they catch him," commented his partner. "A man like that should be locked up."

He turned around, pasting a smile on his face. "Couldn't agree more. The police seem to have it in hand. Shall we go out for dinner this evening or would you rather order a takeaway?"

"Do you mind terribly if we order in? I'm knackered."

She was a primary school teacher in Hammersmith, West London. Before he met her, he had no idea teachers worked so hard. Six weeks off in the summer. How bad could it be? But the stories she'd told about difficult children, staffing shortages, inadequate facilities. The endless preparation, marking and grading . . . And for what? Most of her class couldn't speak English anyway.

They only saw each other a few nights a week. Neither of them had the time for anything more.

"No worries, love. Indian okay?"

"Lovely."

She leaned over and kissed him on the cheek.

That's it!

She was Rachel's sister. The tomboy. Wow, she'd certainly blossomed. A late bloomer. Back in the day she'd been a grubby little thing with messy hair and scrapes on her knees. What was her name again? Something boyish. Jack? Jules? Jo! That was it.

So, little Jo had become a copper. Given what had happened to her sister, perhaps it wasn't all that surprising. People needed answers. It was a pity she'd never find them.

"I'll give the Curry Garden a ring," he said, getting out his phone.

He put Jo out of his mind. He wasn't interested in her. She was one of the lucky ones.

CHAPTER 50

"Paul Daley is a licensed independent social worker," said Jenny. "He works for the charity on a part-time basis."

"In what capacity?" asked Rob.

Jenny swallowed. "His job is to listen and respond to young people who have got in touch via phone, online chat or email. He then offers support for whatever is bothering them, whether it's bullying, abuse, self-harm or family relationships."

"Jesus," hissed Rob.

The rest of them stared at her, horrified. A child-killer in *that* job. It was unthinkable.

"According to the charity spokesperson, he's really good with the kids. He's one of their best counsellors."

"I'll bet he is," muttered Mike, his hands curling into fists on the table.

"That's not all," said Jenny.

Could it get any worse?

"He also works as an assessor for child protective services."

"You've got to be kidding?" Rob ran a hand through his hair.

"Nope. He's the one who decides if the child is at risk, and whether measures need to be put in place to protect them. Often, it involves moving the child to a safe place, like a relative's, and if no one's available, into care."

"What do they say about him?" Rob was almost afraid to ask.

"Glowing references," she said.

"If you think about it, it's the perfect job for someone like him," said Jo. "He kills these girls because he thinks he's saving them from a fate worse than death, quite literally. This way he gets to do it legally too."

"But why kill them if he has the power to stop it happening anyway?" asked Jenny.

"Maybe those are the ones he can't save," said Rob. "We know Angie Nolan denied everything. Said her father hadn't touched her."

Evan frowned. "I thought her parents were divorced."

"What about visitation rights? Or even worse, what if she was at her father's mercy every second weekend?"

"I can't bear to think about it." Jenny squeezed her eyes shut.

Even Jo was looking rather pale. "So he takes the fear away," she whispered.

"Did you get a number for him?" asked Rob.

"Yes, and a home address."

"Great. Let's get a warrant for his phone records and tomorrow we'll pay him a little visit."

"You're not going to bring him in?" asked Jo.

"No, not yet. I don't want to spook him. He'll just lawyer up, and right now we don't have anything to charge him with. Even if we connect him to all the girls, there's no evidence he did anything to them."

"Then, let's get that evidence," Jo said, an edge to her voice.

"How are we going to do that?" asked Jenny.

"Firstly, we need to find a link between Daley and Rosie Hutton, Elise Mitcham, Lucy Chang and Anna Dewbury."

"I can help with that last one," Evan said. "Alan Simpson *does* know Paul Daley. Daley used to cover for him."

"Yes!" Rob punched the air.

"Did he cover for him when he was seeing Anna Dewbury?" asked Jo.

"Simpson can't say for sure, but he might have done. He can't remember that far back. But they definitely know each other."

Rob exhaled. "I think we can assume that's how he made contact with Anna. He either covered for Simpson or vice versa. He must have been working for child protective services then, since her case was referred to them by the school."

"Yeah, CPS confirmed that much, but that's all they would tell me."

"Okay, good work. Thanks, Evan. That leaves Rosie, Elise and Lucy. But that can wait until tomorrow. Let's go home and get some rest."

* * *

"I want to question Daley," Jo said when everyone had gone.

There was a long pause.

"Are you sure?"

"Rob, this could be the man who killed my sister. I've been waiting my whole life for this moment. Of course I'm sure." There was a determined glint in her eye.

"Can you be impartial?"

"I'm a professional. I know what I have to do."

"It'll be different when you're sitting there facing him. Trust me, I know." He'd been investigated the year before last for losing control when apprehending a suspect. Luckily, the review had found in his favour, but he knew first-hand what happened when a case got personal.

"I can control myself."

"I thought I could too."

She sighed. "I'll be fine, Rob. Please. I have to do this. For my sister. I have to know."

He was silent. Sure, she was a professional, but who wouldn't be affected when facing their sister's killer?

"Besides, I might recognise him. He could be Michael Robertson."

"You think he changed his name?"

"I don't know. He could have. There were too many Michael Robertsons to go through. Bloody thousands. So, I tried Paul Daley, but I couldn't find any records for him going back further than fifteen years."

"That is odd," agreed Rob.

"According to his LinkedIn profile, he studied social work at the University of Hertfordshire and then got a job at a children's charity based in Watford. He was with them for three years before moving to CPS, also based in North West London."

"That's when he met Anna Dewbury," Rob said.

"Right. There's no mention of which school he went to, he doesn't appear to be on social media and he's not on any sixth form register."

"Have you checked with the Deed Poll Office?"

"Yeah, nothing. If he did change his name, he didn't do it legally."

It did sound very much like this could be Michael Robertson.

"Okay, fine," he said. "You can lead the interview. Let's catch him early. Say, seven o'clock?"

"Yes! Thank you." She leaned forward and gave him an unexpected kiss.

He slipped an arm around her waist. "Are you coming back to mine tonight?"

She shook her head. "I'd love to, but I haven't been home yet and I'm desperate for a long hot bath and a change of clothes. Meet you here at six tomorrow? We can drive together."

"Sure, sounds great."

CHAPTER 51

The red-brick townhouse where Paul Daley lived was just like any other in the street. Ex-council, functional, uninspiring.

As Rob pulled up outside, Jo tried to still her frantic heart. In a few moments she could be face to face with her sister's killer.

"You okay?" he asked.

She exhaled slowly, pushing the fear aside. It was the moment of truth. "I'm good. Let's do this."

They walked up the short path to the front door. It fed four apartments, two on each side. Rob rang the doorbell. It sounded like a death knell.

Footsteps, then a feminine voice called out, "I'll get it."

Jo glanced at Rob. Had they got the right apartment?

It was too late to do anything but say hello, as a woman with a round face and tired eyes opened the door. She was dressed for work in smart, practical clothes and flat shoes. Waitress? Teacher?

"Can I help you?"

Jo took a small step forward. "I'm DCI Maguire and this is DI Miller from the Putney Major Investigation Team. Is Paul Daley in?"

She nodded. "Just a minute, he's upstairs." She looked over her shoulder. "Paul! There are two policemen here to see you." She smiled at Jo. "Sorry, policewoman."

"And you are?" asked Jo.

"Dessie, Dessie Barton." She gave an apologetic grimace. "I'm sorry, I don't mean to be rude, but I have to dash. I'll be late for school."

They watched as she picked up her bag and an armful of files and carried them out to a car parked further up the road.

"Teacher," muttered Rob, as the battered blue Ford chugged off.

"I'm Paul Daley," said a voice from within.

They both turned as an older version of the man in the LinkedIn profile picture came down the stairs.

Jo's heart sank. He didn't look like the Michael Robertson she remembered. That boy had been skinny, nerdy, with big glasses. This guy had a stocky build, a little soft around the edges, with understanding eyes and a full, non-judgemental mouth.

"What can I do for you?" he said.

Jo cleared her voice. "I'm DCI Maguire and this is DI Miller. We understand Angie Nolan was one of your clients?"

He didn't pretend not to know who she was. "Yes, I read her body had been found on the heath in Bisley. So tragic."

Jo narrowed her eyes. "Yes, it was. Do you mind if we come in and ask you a few questions? It shouldn't take long."

He gestured for them to enter. They followed him into a sparse but clean living room and took a seat on the couch. It creaked under their dual weight. Daley sat down opposite them.

"When did you last see Angie Nolan?" Jo opened her notepad. It was more for show than because she needed it. She had the questions memorised in her head. She'd been through this interview a thousand times.

Now she was here, in his house, it *was* different. Had this man really killed Rachel and all those other girls? It was so . . . normal. But then what did a serial killer's house look like?

She pushed the self-doubt aside and waited for an answer.

"Gosh, it was some time ago now." He scratched his head. "I think my last session with her was October last year."

"So, just before she disappeared," said Jo.

"I wouldn't know."

Jo looked into his dark, empty eyes and she knew. *It was him.* She didn't know how she knew. She just did.

She supressed a shiver. "Could you tell us what your sessions were about?"

"That is confidential information. I'm not sure I'm allowed to talk about it."

"It would be confidential if she were still alive," Jo pointed out. "But since Angie is deceased, there's no reason not to tell us."

His dark gaze flickered. "Still, I should probably check with my employer."

"We can wait," she said evenly.

There was a pause.

"You know what, I'm sure you're right. The poor thing has been dead nearly a year, what difference does it make now?"

Jo smiled benignly.

"She was referred to me by social services. Her teacher had reported she'd become withdrawn of late, wouldn't engage with others, and there were odd markings on her skin."

Jo nodded for him to go on, grateful for Rob's solid, reassuring presence beside her.

"At first, she was reluctant to talk, but her mother encouraged it. I think she was worried her husband was physically abusing her daughter."

"What then?"

"It turned out that Angie's father had a filthy temper, and when he mixed that with alcohol, he ended up taking it out on his family."

Jo shook her head. Empathising. She had to act normally or else he'd know. That she knew. Then he'd clam up.

He leaned forward. "But that wasn't the worst of it. He'd been forcing himself on Angie too." His voice hardened. "She was ten years old."

His anger surprised her. But she couldn't fault him for that. She wanted to throttle the man herself. "Did you report him to the authorities?"

"I tried to persuade Angie to talk to the police, but she wouldn't. She said if she was questioned, she'd lie. She was terrified of her father."

"I'm not surprised."

"I only saw her a couple of times, and then I filed my assessment. I recommended removing Angie to a place of safety, but then her mother got divorced."

"That's a good thing, right?"

He settled back in his chair. "You'd think so, but her father was appointed joint custody."

Rob stiffened beside her.

"She was trapped." Jo studied him, looking for a spark of malice, a twist of the lips, anything that would indicate the monster he was inside.

He nodded sadly. "There was nothing I could do. The case was closed. In order to reopen it, we'd need another referral, which wasn't forthcoming."

"Did you see Angie after that?"

"No, but I spoke to her on the phone. I called the house to see how she was getting on, and her mother let me speak to her. She answered in monosyllables. I could tell she'd given up. She knew help wasn't coming."

"And you just left it at that?" Jo asked. "When you knew she was still being abused?"

He met her gaze. "I did my best. As I'm sure you know, Detective, we can't save them all."

His words turned her cold. Was that a reference to Rachel? Was she imagining things now?

She took a deep, steadying breath, surveying the room as she did so. The shiny coffee table, the out-of-date television, the even older computer standing on a worn desk in the corner. Paul Daley wasn't materialistic.

"Was that your wife we saw leaving when we arrived?" she asked, conversationally.

He laughed. "No, that was my partner, Dessie. We don't live together."

Jo nodded. She opened the file on her lap.

"Do you know any of these girls?" She showed him a photograph of Elise Mitcham.

He shook his head.

She held up Lucy Chang.

Another shake.

Finally, Arina Parvin.

"*Should* I know them?" he asked.

"They were all found buried in the woods with Angie Nolan. I thought they might have been clients of yours?"

"I can't say I recall those girls, but I have seen a large number of teenagers over the years. It's possible I did see them, or spoke to them over the phone, and don't remember."

"Do you speak to a lot of the children on the phone?" she asked.

"Oh, yes. I volunteer for several child hotlines."

Jo looked at the desk again and saw a modern, cordless landline resting in its cradle. "You work from home?"

"When I'm not doing house calls or centre visits."

"Centre visits?"

He smiled patiently. A smile reserved for those who were a bit slow or didn't understand things the first time round. "Sometimes teenagers prefer to meet in a neutral space rather than at their home. That's what the centres are for."

"Where is it?" asked Jo.

"Woking."

"Mr Daley, can I ask you where you were on the fifteenth of November 2018?"

His eyes widened. "I'm afraid I don't have that good a memory. Do you mind if I consult my diary?"

"Go ahead."

They watched as he got up and walked over to the desk. He opened the top right-hand drawer and pulled out a leather-bound Filofax.

"Luckily, I write down all my appointments," he said.

Jo glanced at Rob.

He thumbed back through the crowded pages. "Ah, here it is. Thursday. I was at the centre that morning and I had a home visit in the afternoon."

"Do you know what time that home visit was?" Jo enquired. Tension twisted in her belly.

He looked down again. "Three o'clock. In Bracknell."

Damn.

"Do you mind giving us your client's details? I'm sorry, but we have to check ourselves."

"Sure, but you've already met her. I was seeing Dessie's daughter, Gail."

Jo blinked. "You were her daughter's social worker? Is that allowed?"

He chuckled like she was so silly. "We weren't seeing each other then. Gail was having problems at school. Bullying, that sort of thing. She walked into the centre and asked for advice. I was there and we had a chat. That's how I met Dessie."

"Do you always follow up walk-ins with a home visit?" Jo asked.

He shrugged. "Sometimes, if the parents are open to it. In this case, Dessie was all for it. She was a single mother, overworked, and she was worried about her daughter. I went round there once or twice to see how Gail was getting on, and to our mutual surprise, we hit it off. After Gail finished school, we started dating. It's all completely above board."

His open, sincere face gave nothing away. This guy had an answer for everything. She couldn't make him slip up.

"How old was Dessie's daughter when you saw her?"

"She was sixteen. She's at a drama school in London now. Doing quite well for herself." He smiled fondly.

Jo closed her file. "Well, thank you for talking to us, Mr Daley."

He got up. "Let me show you out."

At the door, Rob turned to him. "Just one last thing, Mr Daley. Where did you go to school?"

Jo watched his expression carefully. It didn't change. "Gosh, that's going back a while. Why do you ask?"

"For our records," Rob said.

"St Thomas's. I've got them to thank for my ingrained Catholic guilt."

Rob nodded. "Thank you. We'll leave you in peace now."

Daley saw them out, then watched from the doorway as they walked down the path to their vehicle.

CHAPTER 52

"I know it's him," said Jo the moment they got into the car.

Rob pulled away. "Did you recognise him? Was it Michael?"

"I didn't think so at first, but the way he looked at me — I'm sure he recognised me." She shivered. Those empty eyes. "And I don't believe for a second he didn't know those girls."

"We can get a warrant for the charity's phone line," said Rob.

"Let's do it."

"Tony said he'd be a loner," said Rob. "Daley has a girlfriend. And he didn't look socially inept to me."

"Tony could be wrong." She frowned. "Did you notice there was nothing personal in his living room? No photographs, no meaningful items, no paintings on the wall. Nothing."

"I don't have any paintings on my wall either. It doesn't mean anything."

She sighed, exasperated. "Your ex-wife took yours."

He broke into a lopsided grin.

"The partner, the schoolteacher, could be a disguise — to throw us off."

"Could be."

She could tell he wasn't convinced.

"Did you see how angry he got when I mentioned Angie Nolan? He couldn't stand that he hadn't helped her."

Rob nodded. "I saw, but I was angry too. So were you."

"I know, but that's not the point. He was really angry — I could see it in his eyes." She shook her head.

"We need to check out his alibi. Speak to Dessie," said Rob.

"Of course, she's going to vouch for him," muttered Jo. "She's his lover."

Rob sighed. "He just didn't strike me as a cold-blooded killer."

"Maybe he's not," said Jo. "Maybe he's a hot-blooded one. He kills them because he can't protect them any other way. That's what Tony said, right?"

Rob was silent.

"I know it, Rob. Trust me on this one. He's our killer."

"If you're right," said Rob, as he picked up speed on the motorway, "the evidence will lead us back to him."

* * *

It didn't.

Mallory and Jenny interviewed Daley's partner, Dessie, who partially confirmed his alibi. "He was here for at least an hour, holed up with Gail in the study. I didn't want to interrupt them."

"Are you sure of the date?"

"As sure as I can be. Paul keeps meticulous notes, so if he said it was the fifteenth, then it was the fifteenth."

When Jenny checked with The Homestead, however, they confirmed the appointment. Daley was in Woking that afternoon and nowhere near Bagshot, where Angie was taken.

"What about the other disappearances?" asked Jo.

"We'll have to bring him in if we're going to go through all of them." Rob glanced at the list of names on the white-board. "Question him under caution."

"Let's do it," said Jo. She was out for blood. "If we rattle him enough, he might crack and confess."

"He's not going to confess," said Rob. "He knows we've got nothing that'll stick."

* * *

Will made a whooping noise. "Yes! There's a call from Elise Mitcham's home phone to The Homestead helpline on the second of March 2016." He grinned like a madman. "Another link!"

Jo raced around to his side of the desk. "Show me."

"Here it is. The call is highlighted in yellow." He handed her the printout.

"Is there a record of this call?" she asked Will. "Do they record them?"

"Not all organisations do. I'll find out."

He got on the phone.

"Yes, they do monitor the calls, but they can't share them without a warrant," he confirmed once he'd hung up.

"Get one," snapped Rob.

An hour later, Will was faxing the warrant through to the charity. An hour after that, the call log landed in Will's inbox.

The entire team listened to the conversation.

Hello?

Hello, you've reached The Homestead helpline. What is your name, please?

"Is that him?" asked Jenny. "Is that Daley's voice?"

"It's him," said Jo.

Elise.

She was too young to think about using a false name.

Hello, Elise. Is there something you'd like to discuss?

Um . . . I don't know.

It's okay to feel nervous. Take your time.

A long pause.

My daddy hurts me.

Jenny's eyes filled with tears. "Oh, God."

The rest listened, tight-lipped.

How does he hurt you, Elise?

Daley was good, Rob gave him that much. He was a seasoned counsellor. His tone was warm and friendly, he reassured her, used her first name.

He makes me do things that I don't want to do.

"I can't listen to any more," said Jenny.

Will looked at Rob, who nodded. He turned it off.

"We've heard enough," Rob said coarsely. "It's him all right."

* * *

"Boss," Evan piped up, breaking the heavy silence that had descended over the incident room. "Paul Daley drives a white Vauxhall Combo Cargo. It's similar to the one we picked up on camera the evening Arina Parvin disappeared."

"Have you got a shot of it?" Rob looked over at Jo. Her cheeks were flushed, her eyes bright. They were closing in.

"Not the real thing, but this is what it looks like." He turned his screen around and zoomed in on the bottom panel. Beside it, he'd placed the image taken from the CCTV camera. "They're identical."

Rob took a deep breath. "Okay, let's bring him in. I want that vehicle searched as well as every room in his house. If there's a shred of DNA in that place that belongs to any of the girls, we've got him."

CHAPTER 53

The Shepherd got home and hung his jacket on the coat hook by the door. God, he was tired. There was nothing nice about a police cell. It stank of sweat and disinfectant and fear.

He shuddered when he thought about all the miscreants who'd slept there before him.

He couldn't get upstairs fast enough before he stripped off his clothes. Naked, he stood in the bath and let the hot water run over him, purifying him. Then, he lathered himself from head to foot and scrubbed his skin until it was raw.

When he got out, he could still smell the stench of unwashed bodies on him.

He threw his soiled clothes into the rubbish bin. There was no way he was wearing those again.

He made himself a cup of tea and put some bread in the toaster. The smell made his stomach rumble. He couldn't remember the last time he'd eaten. They'd kept him there for hours, asking the same questions over and over again.

Did he know the dead girls?

Were they clients of his?

Was that his voice on the phone call?

He'd deflected them with ease. How was he supposed to have remembered every single call from years ago?

He was disappointed not to have seen Jo again, though. Two other detectives had interviewed him. Maybe she'd been watching from afar. He'd thought he could feel her eyes on him.

He admired her. She was feisty. But then she always had been.

Or maybe he'd spooked her after this morning's chat.

It was then that the phone rang.

"Hello?"

Dessie was the only person who called him on his landline.

"Oh, my gosh," she gushed. "I've been so worried."

"It's okay." He watched the steam from his cup of tea curl up towards the ceiling making his mouth water. "I'm fine, they released me. It was all a big misunderstanding."

"Are you sure, Paul? Because they questioned me too. I was terrified, I've never been questioned by the police before."

"What kind of questions?"

"About the afternoon you came round to talk to Gail." He relaxed. They'd said they'd check out his alibi.

"So, what's the problem? I was with you guys all afternoon. You did the right thing by telling them that."

He heard her sniffling and softened his tone. It was an automatic response. He used it on the kids he counselled every day. "Calm down, Dessie. There's nothing to worry about. I'm fine. It's over now."

"Paul, I'm scared for you."

"You've got nothing to be scared of. Everything is going to be all right."

"No, it's not." She was crying now.

He sighed and leaned over to reach for his tea.

"You see, I remembered something that doesn't make sense."

He bristled, tea poised halfway to his lips. "What's that?"

"You *weren't* here on the fifteenth, when you said you were. You came on the fourteenth. I remembered because the fourteenth is the annual flower show at Garson's Farm, and I went that morning to stock up on geraniums for my hanging baskets. They have those lovely ones that flop over the side of the pot."

He clenched his jaw. "I think you're mistaken, dear. I never get my days muddled. It *was* the fifteenth I was there."

She sniffed. "It wasn't, Paul. I'm absolutely certain of it. Why did you tell the police you were here on the fifteenth, the day that girl went missing, if you weren't?"

Cold fury clutched at his heart. Stupid woman. She was going to ruin everything.

He put the tea back down on the table.

Think!

"You didn't have anything to do with her disappearance, did you?" Her voice trembled.

"Of course not, don't be daft. I'll have another look at my diary. It's possible I made a mistake."

He turned the pages of his Filofax loudly.

It had been almost a year ago. He'd spoken to Angie Nolan on the phone. One last follow-up call after her mother's divorce. He'd told her he was going to make everything better, that she just had to meet him that night in the alleyway behind her house. He'd take care of everything.

She'd been so desperate, she agreed.

He'd promised her he'd take away the pain and the fear. That if she went with him, she'd be safe. No one would ever hurt her again.

"Oh, bugger. I'm so sorry, it's my mistake. I've got your appointment written in on both days. I must have changed it and forgotten to take the other one out. That's why I got confused."

"So, it's a mistake?"

"Yes, a stupid mistake. I'll call the police and rectify it. I was at the centre that day, I'm sure of it. There'll be a record somewhere."

She let out a shaky breath. "Oh, thank goodness, Paul. I was really worried there for a moment. You know, with everything they were saying . . ."

"What *did* they say?"

She hesitated. "You know what, it's not important. The main thing is we got to the bottom of it. Listen, I have to go, my bath is getting cold. I'll talk to you tomorrow, okay?"

"Okay. Night, Dessie."

"Night, Paul."

After she hung up, he stood staring at the phone until his tea went cold.

* * *

The lights were off, so he knew she'd gone to bed. It was midnight, but she didn't stay up late, she was always too exhausted. Her job took it out of her.

He went around the back and stopped in front of the faulty window. She'd once told him it was her backup plan if she ever got locked out. He even knew how to wiggle it so that it gave just a little and the inside hook jumped off the knob. It barely creaked as he eased it open.

It was a quiet night, only a sliver of moon. A tiny crescent frowning down at him. Was that the Lord's way of telling him he was committing a sin?

He pulled the window wide open and climbed inside, using the pot plant below as a ledge. Bloody geraniums.

He'd killed before, but never like this. This was different. It *felt* different. Adrenalin pumped through his veins. Tonight, he wasn't killing to save an abused child. He was killing to save himself.

Didn't he count too? Weren't they all God's children at the end of the day?

He padded through the room, his trainers silent on the thick carpeting. He knew the layout of her house by heart, could have done it blindfolded.

He placed his hand on the railing and made his way silently up the stairs to the master bedroom. Dessie had converted Gail's room into a makeshift office while she was away in London. At the moment it was filled with test papers she had to mark, and flip charts she had to finish.

The landing was in darkness, as was the crack beneath the bedroom door. Dessie couldn't sleep if there was a glimmer of light.

He placed his hand on the door handle and turned it slowly, hoping it wouldn't creak. It emitted a soft groan but not loud enough to wake her. She was a deep sleeper.

He clenched the coil of rope in his gloved hand. It would be over quickly. He didn't want her to suffer. She was a good woman, just a little dim-witted. Especially for a teacher.

He'd been able to tell by her voice she was spooked, that she didn't believe him. He couldn't risk her telling the police what she knew.

Once he'd done the deed, he'd trash the place. It would look like a break-in gone wrong. He might even take a trinket, something to remember her by. Nothing too garish, though. She didn't have very good taste.

He pushed the door open and slunk towards the bed. He could see her sleeping shape. She was on her side facing away from him. Closer he crept, until he stood right beside her. Still she didn't move.

He raised the rope and twisted it around his hands, then he bent down to wrap it around her neck.

Suddenly the light flicked on.

A thunderous voice yelled, "This is the police. Stop and put your hands in the air!"

He froze. What the—?

As his eyes adjusted to the light, he saw the detective, Miller, and his sidekick from the Common both pointing guns at him, along with four other armed officers.

He dropped the rope and stuck his hands in the air.

The woman in the bed sat up.

He gasped. "You!"

"Paul Daley," Jo said, getting out from under the covers, "you're under arrest for the attempted murder of Dessie Barton."

CHAPTER 54

Jo entered the interrogation room. "Hello, Paul," she said. "Or should I call you Michael?"

The dark eyes followed her as she walked.

"Which do you prefer?"

"Paul."

She sat down. "So, Paul. Why didn't you tell us you were also Michael Robertson, the boy who lived up the street from me and my sister in Manchester?"

"You didn't ask."

"So, you don't deny that was you?"

He scoffed. "Why would I deny it? It's not a crime to change your name."

"No, it's not."

She studied him from across the cold interview table. Gone was the congenial open-faced smile. Now he regarded her with suspicion.

"I remember you, though."

"Oh, yes?"

"Yes. You were a scrawny little thing, always following Rachel around like a lapdog."

It was true, she'd worshipped her big sister. "What happened to her, Paul? What did you do to her?"

"I didn't do anything to her. I was as upset as anyone else when she went missing."

"You were the last person to see her alive," Jo pointed out.

"We sat in the park and talked, then we went to the shop and she went home. I said goodbye to her and watched her walk up the street."

"You didn't see her again after that?" she asked.

"No."

Jo paused for a moment. Then she opened the file she'd brought with her and took out a drawing. She placed it on the table in front of Paul. "Do you recognise this?"

He stared at it for a moment, then shook his head. "Should I?"

"It's one of Rachel's pictures. Good, isn't it?"

He tilted his head to the side.

"I think she had a certain flair."

He didn't respond.

"Do you know what it's of?" Jo asked.

"An angel?" He shrugged.

"It's an angel, yes. With wings and a halo. She's floating above a forest, on her way to heaven."

Paul's dark eyes flickered.

"You see, I think it's a self-portrait. She's the angel going up to heaven. I think she wanted to die, Paul."

Pain flashed across his face, but he didn't speak.

"I'm right, aren't I?" she whispered. "Rachel asked you to help her kill herself."

His eyes glistened, and his lower lip started to tremble.

"It's okay, I know what happened. I didn't at the time, but I do now. She was pregnant and couldn't see any other way out. She didn't want to have her uncle's baby, but she didn't believe in abortion ether. And then there was the fact she'd been raped."

Paul's hands balled into fists and he pounded the table. "He used to tie her up, did you know that?"

Jo stared at him. It took a moment for her brain to compute the horror of what he was saying.

"He'd tie her to the bedstead so she couldn't get away while he raped her, repeatedly. It had been going on for months. She couldn't tell your mother because *she* was sleeping with him too, fucking whore."

Jo was finding it hard to breathe.

"That's why she wore all those bracelets. They covered the bruises on her wrists."

"Oh my God." Her hand flew to her mouth. She remembered Rachel's bracelets. Coils of silver around her wrists, jingling as she walked.

He sneered at her. "You were oblivious. You had no idea what was going on. Your father was useless, he was away more than he was home. There was nobody she could turn to. Nobody."

"Except you?" whispered Jo.

He nodded, his eyes filled with tears. "When she told me what was happening, I was furious. I tried to help her. I told her to go to the police, to report him, but she wouldn't. She was too frightened of what he'd do to her when he found out."

Oh, Rachel. Poor, poor Rachel.

"The longer it went on, the more desperate she became. Then she found out she was pregnant."

Jo nodded. "My mother told me."

He struck the table again, making his solicitor jump.

"Stupid *bitch*. She went straight to him and told him that she knew, that she was going to report him. How do you think that made Rachel feel? The world would know her shame."

Jo shook her head. She couldn't even comprehend what her fourteen-year-old sister must have gone through.

"She wanted to die. She couldn't live with the shame of other people knowing what he'd done to her."

"So she asked you to help her commit suicide," Jo whispered.

He nodded. "After we said goodbye on the street in front of the shop, we met around the block and sneaked off into the woods. I had a plastic bag with me and she had a packet of her mother's sleeping tablets."

Jo didn't want to hear any more, but she had to. She had to know how her sister had died.

"She swallowed the tablets and we lay together until she fell asleep. I held her hand until I felt her grip loosen. Then I placed the bag over her head and held it tight until she stopped breathing. It only took a few minutes."

It was only when a tear rolled down her face and hit the table that Jo realised she was crying.

"She looked so peaceful lying there, surrounded by wildflowers, those sparkly blue clips in her hair. Like an angel." His gaze drifted to the drawing. "Just like that."

There was a pause.

"Where is she?" whispered Jo.

"In the woods," he told her. "I buried her in the woods at our secret spot. There's a clearing where we'd go and watch the squirrels frolic and imagine we were someplace else. Anywhere but there."

Jo wiped her eyes. "Will you show me?"

He nodded sadly. "I loved her, you know. She was everything to me."

She understood that now. "Thank you for telling me."

He raised his gaze to hers. "Are you going to dig her up like the others?"

Jo froze.

"Erm, I don't know. Probably, yes. I'd like to see she has a proper burial."

"She had a proper burial. I made sure of that. She was happy there. She loved that spot."

Jo chose her next words carefully. "Is it as beautiful as the clearing in Bisley Woods?"

He smiled. The smile of a man who answered to a higher power.

"Prettier, if that's possible. Although Bisley has the healing fountain. They used to baptise children with the water from that fountain. It felt like a sacred place."

"It is." Jo gaze fell on the camera behind his head. "The vicar said as much at the vigil. Were you there?"

He nodded. "Of course. I had to pay my respects to my little angels. Such tortured souls, just like Rachel."

"Is that why you killed them, Paul? Because you couldn't save them?"

He nodded. "I tried, but there was nothing else I could do. I couldn't let them suffer anymore."

"Did they fall asleep? Just like Rachel?"

"Yes," he whispered. "They didn't suffer."

"Do you remember their names?" she said. "So we can pay our full respects?"

He nodded.

Jo glanced at Jenny, who slid a blank piece of paper and a pen across the table. "Would you write them down for us? I don't want to get them wrong."

Her heart beat frantically in her chest as she watched him write down the names of the seven murdered girls, including the unidentified one. Stacy Bancroft, her name was.

CHAPTER 55

Rob stood beside Jo at the grave. It was cold up here in Manchester, but that didn't matter. Nobody was focusing on the weather.

The pastor said a few words, and they watched as Rachel's body was laid to rest.

Jo held his hand, while her mother stood wide-eyed and silent next to them.

Paul Daley had been charged with eight counts of murder. There were probably more, but they'd never know for sure. The case was now closed.

DCS Lawrence had retired. He'd walked out to raucous applause. The squad room had been packed with well-wishers. During his speech, there hadn't been a dry eye in the house.

Before he'd left, Lawrence had recommended Mallory for the Woking post. Last order of business. It had turned out they needed a DI. Rob would miss him, but it was well deserved.

They threw flowers onto the coffin. Wildflowers, her favourite. Then she was covered up, to rest in peace. Finally.

They'd chosen a pretty spot for the burial. It was close to the woods that she'd loved. Where she'd chosen to die. Jo had seen to that.

Jo was currently on suspension. Pearson hadn't given her leave, as it happened. A small point she'd neglected to tell him. Jo had walked out after a row.

Pearson would take her back, of course. There were extenuating circumstances. He hadn't realised her sister was a victim of the notorious child-killer.

She'd forfeited her promotion, though.

"It doesn't matter," Jo had told Rob, smiling. "I'm not sure I want it anyway."

"Why not?"

"I think I need a bit of a break. I thought I might take some time off."

He'd left it at that.

* * *

The burial was over. The few friends and family members who'd come to pay their respects were going back to the hotel for canapés.

"Ready?" he asked her.

She smiled. "Yes, let's go."

Together they walked towards the hire car. It was parked beside a thick lavender bush, enveloping them in its sweet fragrance.

Jo turned to him. "Rob, there's something I've been meaning to say, and now seems like the right time."

He met her clear, uncomplicated gaze. "What is it?"

A smile played on her lips. A gust of wind lifted her hair off her forehead. He felt his chest swell. He loved her too. He knew it now, but he couldn't say it. Not first.

She looked into his eyes. "I'm pregnant."

THE END

ACKNOWLEDGEMENTS

Many people helped make this book possible. Firstly, thank you to Emma Grundy Haigh and Jasper Joffe for their ongoing support. This is the third book in the Detective Rob Miller series, and I've loved working with Team Joffe on every single one of them.

I'd like to thank my copy editor, Cat Phipps, who painstakingly checked every detail of the manuscript for errors and inconsistencies and my proofreader, Matthew Grundy Haigh, whose eye for detail is unmatched. A huge thanks goes to Nebojsa Zorić, the amazing designer who is responsible for making the cover so eye-catching; the marketing team, particularly Annie Rose and Nina Kicul; and everybody else who worked on the book.

A special thanks goes to Graham Bartlett, who advised me on police procedure and made sure everything involving the Major Investigation Team was plausible and authentic. His advice has been invaluable.

I'd like to pay tribute to my beta readers whose loyalty and feedback is so much appreciated. And finally, I want to thank my family for their support, especially my son, whose faith in me has never wavered.

Thank you for reading this book.

If you enjoyed it please leave feedback on Amazon or Goodreads, and if there is anything we missed or you have a question about, then please get in touch. We appreciate you choosing our book.

Founded in 2014 in Shoreditch, London, we at Joffe Books pride ourselves on our history of innovative publishing. We were thrilled to be shortlisted for Independent Publisher of the Year at the British Book Awards two years in a row.

www.joffebooks.com

We're very grateful to eagle-eyed readers who take the time to contact us. Please send any errors you find to corrections@joffebooks.com. We'll get them fixed ASAP.

Made in United States
Troutdale, OR
03/29/2024

18806073R00206